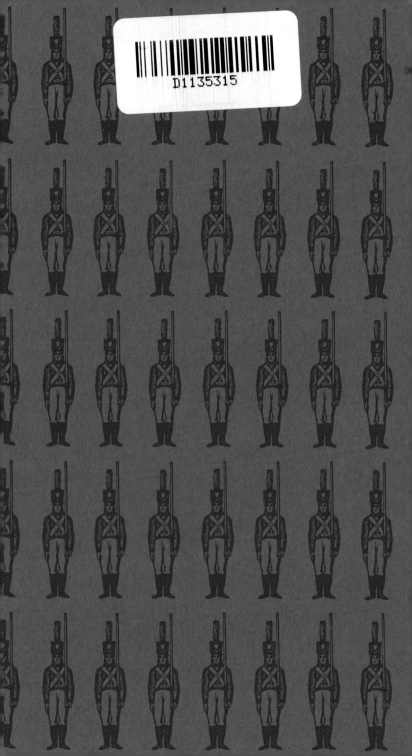

A Publication distributed by Heron Books

WAR AND PEACE

TOLSTOY

WAR AND PEACE

In Three Volumes
Volume II

Illustrations by
Christian Wilhelm von Faber du Faur

DISTRIBUTED BY
HERON BOOKS

The illustrations by Christian Wilhelm
von Faber du Faur were taken from the
collection of lithographies entitled
"Sheets from my portfolio sketched on
the spot during the campaign in Russia
of 1812", published at Stuttgart in 1845.

Published by arrangement with
J. M. Dent & Sons Ltd.

THE INVASION

1807–1812

BOOK SIX

CHAPTER I

In 1808 the Czar Alexander repaired to Erfurth, to hold another interview with Napoleon; the magnificence of this imperial ceremony was for a long time the chief subject of conversation in the aristocratic circles of St. Petersburg.

In 1809 the "arbitrators of the world's fate," as the two sovereigns were then called, were so closely allied that, when Napoleon declared war with Austria, the Emperor Alexander commanded a division of the Russian army to march across the frontier to support his former foe against his former ally the Emperor of Austria, and a report got about that a marriage was on the *tapis* between Napoleon and one of the Russian monarch's sisters.

Besides the agitations and speculations resulting from her foreign policy, Russia was deeply interested at this period in the reforms decreed to be carried out in every department of the administration. Still, notwithstanding all these important subjects of discussion, everyday life—the practical life of each individual, with its home questions of health and sickness, of toil and rest, with its intellectual aspirations and tastes for science, poetry, music, what not, with its passions, loves and friendships—ran its regular course, without troubling itself to any serious extent about an alliance or breach with Napoleon, or about the great reforms in progress.

Peter's philanthropic schemes, which in his hands had for the most part come to nothing for lack of perseverance, had, on the contrary, all been carried into execution by Prince Andrew, who had not quitted his country home, and who brought them to bear without any great display, or any serious impediment. Gifted as he was with the quality his friend most lacked, practical tenacity of purpose, he knew exactly how to give impetus to an enterprise without effort or shock; the

1

three hundred serfs who were attached to the soil on one of his estates were registered as free labourers—one of the earliest instances of such emancipation in Russia; on his other lands, the *corvée*, or tale of gratuitous labour, was commuted; and at Bogoutcharovo he had settled a midwife and nurse at his own cost, and paid the priest an additional stipend to teach the children of the peasants and servants to read. He divided his time between Lissy-Gory, where his little boy was still under petticoat rule, and what his father called his hermitage at Bogoutcharovo.

In spite of the indifference which Prince Andrew had chosen to assume before Peter, he watched the course of events from day to day with keen interest, and read a great quantity of books; and he noted, with surprise, that his father's visitors fresh from St. Petersburg, from the very headquarters of action, who might therefore be supposed to know what was doing in domestic and foreign politics, were often far less well informed than he was, living secluded in the country.

Although the management of his estates, and his various reading, took up a great deal of his time, Prince Andrew found time to write a critical history of the last two campaigns and their disasters, and to work out a scheme of reform in the codes and rules of the military establishment.

At the end of the winter of 1808–9, he made a tour of inspection to some property in Riazan, belonging to his little son, of which he was the administrator. Sitting at his ease in his travelling-chariot, under the glorious spring sunshine, he gave himself up to vague dreaming, gazing to right and left, and feeling his whole being expand under the charm of the first verdure budding on the birches, and of the light clouds that fled across the deep blue sky. After passing the ferry, where, the year before, he had crossed the river with Peter, then a poverty-stricken village with its granaries and cattle-pens, down a slope where some snow still lay thawing slowly, and along a clay dyke that crossed the cornfields, he got into a little wood which fringed the road closely on each side. There was no wind, so that it was almost warm; not a breath stirred the birch-trees covered with sprouting leaves of tender green, all glutinous with sap. In many places, between the trees, the first blades of grass and tufts of tiny purple flowers were pushing their way through the carpet of dead leaves that strewed the ground; while a dark pine-tree here and there was still an unpleasant reminder of winter, in its mournful and monotonous

Prince Andrew had not quitted his country home for over two years

hues. The horses tossed their heads and snorted; the air was so mild that they were streaming with sweat. Peter, the man-servant, made some remark to the coachman, who assented; but his sympathy did not satisfy the man, who looked back at his master and said: "How good it smells, excellency!"

"What—what did you say?"

"How sweet everything is."

"Yes, indeed!" said Prince Andrew, and he went on to himself: "The spring-time, he means no doubt. Very true. How green it is already, and so early! The birch, the wild-cherry, the elm—all are quite green; but the oaks—I do not see any . . . Yes, there is one."

Just at hand, by the side of the road, ten times as tall and as stalwart as its brothers the birches, stood a gigantic oak, spreading its gnarled branches over a wide space, its limbs and trunk deeply scarred where the bark had been ripped away. Its lean, knotted, straggling arms made it look like some savage and haughty monster scorning, in his hoary age, the youth that clustered round him, and who could smile at the spring and the sunshine which he, as yet, had failed to feel.

"Spring—love—happiness! Can you still cherish such vain illusions?" the old oak seemed to say. "Is it always to be the same false tale? There is no such thing as spring-tide—as love and joy! . . . Look at the storm-beaten firs; they are always the same. Look at the haggard limbs that I throw out from my scraggy body. I am what they have made me, and I have no faith in your hopes and delusions."

Prince Andrew turned to look at it more than once as he drove past, as if he expected it to confess some mysterious secret; but the oak stood sullen and gloomy in the midst of the flowers and turf that were springing at its feet. "Aye, the old oak is right—quite right. We must leave youth in the enjoyment of its illusions. But we—we know what life is worth; it has nothing more in store for us. . . ." And a whole swarm of sad and sweet thoughts rose up in his soul. He glanced back at his past life and came to the disheartening, but yet soothing, conclusion that henceforth there was nothing for him but to vegetate aimless and hopeless, to avoid doing evil and keep himself from worry.

CHAPTER II

PRINCE ANDREW was obliged by his duties as his boy's guardian, to pay a visit to the *Maréchal de Noblesse* of the district, Count Ilia Andréïévitch Rostow; and he set out early in May. By this time the woods were in full leaf, and the heat and dust were so intolerable that the sight of the merest thread of water made the traveller long to bathe in it. His mind was occupied with the business on which he was visiting the count, and before he was aware of it, he was driving up the avenue that led to the house at Otradnoë. Presently he heard gay young voices in one of the clumps of trees, and saw a party of girls running forward to look at the travelling-chariot. The foremost, a very slight young creature, with black eyes, in a nankeen frock with a pocket-handkerchief thrown over her tossed and tumbled hair, came eagerly towards him, saying something as she ran; but at the sight of a stranger she turned, and without stopping to look at him, fled with shouts of laughter.

Prince Andrew was painfully impressed. The day was so fine, the sun so bright, the air seemed full of happiness; and everything, including this frail-looking girl, was so full of joy —and the girl herself, in her giddy, happy heedlessness, troubled her head so little about him—that he asked himself, sadly enough—"What on earth has she to be so glad about? What does she think about? Not the military code, nor the organisation of peasants' dues, that is very certain."

Count Ilia lived at Otradnoë just as he always had done, keeping open house and arranging hunting-parties, entertainments, and dinners with music to amuse his guests. Every visitor was hailed and welcomed; thus Prince Andrew was forced to yield to his pressing invitation to sleep there.

He found the day intolerably dull; his host and hostess and the more important guests, of whom, owing to the old count's approaching name-day, the house was full, took possession of him entirely. However, he often found himself looking at Natacha, who was amusing herself with the young people of the party, and every time he asked himself again: "What does she find to think about?"

At night it was long before he could get to sleep; he read for some time, then he put his light out, then he light ed it again. The heat in his room was suffocating, for the shutters were closed, and he fumed at "the old idiot"—Rostow—for having detained him by assuring him that he had not the required papers; he was even more annoyed with himself for having yielded to his invitation.

He got up to open the window; as he pushed out the shutters, the moon, which seemed to have been on the watch, flooded the room with light. The night was clear and calm, the air transparent; in front of the window was a tall clipped hedge, on one side black, on the other silvered, at the bottom a rank growth of grass and leaves glittered with diamond drops. Farther off, beyond the hedge, a roof shone with dew; to the right spread the boughs of a large tree with satiny white bark that reflected the full moon riding high in the clear and almost starless spring sky. Prince Andrew leaned his elbow on the window-sill and gazed out at the scene. Then he heard from a window overhead the chatter of women's voices. So they were not asleep either.

"Once more—do, please," said one voice, which Prince Andrew at once recognised.

"But when will you go to sleep?" remonstrated another.

"It is not my fault if I cannot sleep. Just once more. . . ." And the two voices softly hummed a tune.

"Heavens! how lovely it is! Well, now let us go to sleep."

"You may go to sleep if you like. I cannot—it is impossible."

He could hear the light rustle of the speaker's dress, and even her breathing; she must be leaning out of the window. Then all was still, motionless; the lights and shadows cast by the moon might have been petrified. Prince Andrew was afraid of making some movement that might betray his involuntary presence.

"Sonia, Sonia," said the first voice again, "how can you sleep? Do come and see how lovely it is. Good heavens! how lovely!—wake up." And she went on with eager feeling: "There never was such a lovely night, never, never! . . ." Sonia murmured some reply.

"Do come—look at that moon, my darling, my little soul; . . . if one were to sit down like that on one's heels, grasp one's knees—tight, tight as possible, and fly away. That's what I should like to do!"

"Take care, you will fall out."

There was a little scuffle; then Sonia said rather crossly: "Do you know it is nearly two o'clock?"

"Oh, you spoil all my enjoyment! There, go away."

Then all was silent once more; but Prince Andrew could hear, by her sighs and little stir, that she still was there.

5

"Oh, dear! oh, dear!" she said suddenly. "Well, to bed then, since I must!" and she shut the window with a slam.

"Now what does my existence even matter to her?" said Prince Andrew to himself. Without knowing why, he had half hoped, half feared, to hear her speak his name. "But it is she again; it is as if it were on purpose. . . ." And a confused medley of sensations and hopes surged up in his heart—thoughts so youthful, so far removed from his usual habits of mind, that he forbore to analyse them. He threw himself on his bed and fell asleep at once.

CHAPTER III

NEXT morning, having taken leave of the old count, he left without seeing any of the ladies. In the month of June, as he was returning to his "hermitage," Prince Andrew again found himself in the birch-wood. The bells on the harness echoed through it less crisply now; everything was leafy, thick, and shady. The scattered firs did not mar the beauty of the scene; nay, the yellow tips of their dark boughs showed plainly that even they had yielded to the bland influences of the spring.

The day was hot and thunderous. A light shower had laid the dust and refreshed the earth; the forest on his left lay in shadow; on his right, the trees, softly swayed by the breeze, sparkled with moisture in the sunshine; everything was green or blooming, and far and near the nightingales gurgled their song.

"I fancy there was an old oak here that understood me well," thought Prince Andrew, looking to his left, and unconsciously attracted by the beauty of the very tree he was seeking. The oak was transfigured. It spread a dense and luxuriant dome of verdure, its boughs rocking gently in the full light of the setting sun. Its knotted and scarred limbs were no longer visible; its aspect had ceased to be bitterly defiant or morosely sad; nothing was to be seen but the vigorous young leaves that had forced their way through the time-hardened bark, and it was difficult to believe that they derived their life from the gnarled patriarch.

"To be sure, that is the tree!" exclaimed Prince Andrew, with a sudden rush to his heart of the ecstasy of the spring

Having taken leave of the old count he left without seing any of the ladies

revealed in this resurrection. The dearest and most solemn memories of his life rose before him: the blue sky—the sky of Austerlitz; the mute reproach on his wife's face; his conversation with Peter by the ferry; the young girl enraptured with the loveliness of the night; that night—that moon—all distinctly remembered.

"No, my life cannot be closed and sealed at one-and-thirty! It is not enough for me to be conscious of what is in me; others must know it, too! Peter must learn to know me, and that child who was ready to fly away skywards! My life must find a reflection in theirs; theirs must mingle with mine!"

On his return from this tour, he made up his mind that in the autumn he would go to St. Petersburg, and he racked his brain to find some legitimate excuse for the journey. A whole series of reasons, each more cogent than the last, proved it to be absolutely necessary. . . . That had changed his whole life. He could not understand how he had ever doubted that there must still be work for him in the future. And whereas, not more than a month ago, he had believed it impossible that he could quit the country, he now told himself that his past experience would all be wasted, and his life a pure *non sequitur*, if he turned it to no practical account. He could not understand how, on the strength of such poor and illogical reasoning, he could ever have believed that it would be beneath him, after all he had seen and learnt, to look forward to the possibility of being useful, of being happy, and of loving once more. His reason now told him just the contrary. He was weary and bored; his ordinary occupations had lost their interest, and often, when alone, he would go up to the mirror and look at himself steadily; then he would gaze at Lisa's portrait, with her hair turned off her face, and little curls falling over her forehead; he could almost fancy that she leaned out of the gilt frame, and forgetting her last words, watched him with affectionate curiosity and a bright smile. Sometimes he would pace up and down the room, his hands crossed behind his back and his brows knit; or else smiling at his fantastic and incoherent visions—Peter, the young girl at the window, the oak-tree, the beauty of womanhood, the soldier's glory. When anyone interrupted him in these moods, he answered shortly, dryly and sternly, but with logical accuracy. "My dear," Princess Maria would say at such moments, "little Nicholas must not go out to-day. It's too cold." "If it were warm" he would answer his sister, looking particularly evil, "he could go out only in his shirt, but as it is cold he must put on warm things, which is what they are intended for. That is what should be the result of cold, not that a child who should have air, is kept indoors," saying this with emphasis of its reasonableness, as if punishing somebody for the illogical working of their brain . . . ; and this made Princess Maria say that "intellectual occupations dried up the hearts of men."

CHAPTER IV

PRINCE ANDREW arrived at St. Petersburg in the month of August 1809. At this time, young Spéransky was at the zenith of his glory and of his energetic zeal for reform. Just at this time, too, the czar had sprained his foot by falling out of his carriage; and being obliged, in consequence, to spend three weeks on the sofa, he had Spéransky every day to work with him. Then and there were elaborated the two famous ukases which were intended to revolutionise society. One decreed the abolition of court rank, and the other regulated certain examinations which were henceforth to be passed before taking office as *assesseur de collège*[1] and councillor of state; it also gave rise to a complete scheme of government offices by which the administration of finance, law, etc., was radically altered, from the imperial cabinet down to the least town council board. The dreams of liberal reform which the Emperor Alexander had cherished ever since his accession were gradually taking shape and reality with the aid of his councillors, Czartorisky, Novosiltzow, Kotchoubey, and Strogonow, whom he called in jest the Committee of Public Safety.

At this immediate juncture, Spéransky represented them all for civil questions, and Araktchéïew for military affairs. Prince Andrew, in virtue of his appointment as one of his majesty's chamberlains, went to make his bow at court; but, though he twice placed himself in the emperor's way, Alexander did not speak a word to him. He had always fancied that his majesty had some dislike to him or to his appearance, and this suspicion was confirmed by the cold eye that met his; indeed, he soon ascertained that the czar had been annoyed by his retirement from active service in 1805.

[1] An officer in the civil service of a grade corresponding to that of major in the army.

THE INVASION

"Well, we cannot control our liking," said Prince Andrew to himself. "I shall do better not to present my report on the military code in person, but to have it laid before him to take its chance on its own merits!" He placed it in the hands of an old marshal, a friend of his father, who took charge of it very kindly, and promised to mention it to the sovereign.

In the course of the week, Prince Andrew was bidden to attend on the minister of war, Count Araktchéïew. At nine in the morning on the appointed day, Prince Andrew made his appearance in the count's ante-room; he did not know him personally, and what he had heard of him did not command either respect or esteem.

"But he is minister of war, and he is in the emperor's confidence; what can his personal qualities matter to me? It is part of his business to examine my report, and he is the only person who can forward my interests," said Prince Andrew to himself. At the time when he had held an appointment as aide-de-camp, he had been present at the audiences granted by various dignitaries, and had noted that each man had his own peculiarities. This reception, however, struck him as exceptional. The faces of all those who were waiting for admission bore a half-disguised stamp of anxious embarrassment, with a look of affected submissiveness. The highest in military rank tried to dissemble their ill-concealed uneasiness under a free-and-easy demeanour, jesting about themselves and the minister; others sat in gloomy silence, while some giggled and whispered, speaking of the great man as Sila [1] Andréïévitch. One general, evidently much offended at having to wait so long, crossed his legs, and looked about him with a smile of contempt.

But no sooner was the door opened, than every face fell to the same expression of fear. Prince Andrew had asked the officer in waiting to be good enough to announce him, and had been told ironically that his turn would come. A military man, whose scared and miserable face had particularly struck Prince Andrew, was admitted to the minister's *sanctum* when some who had had a previous audience had been shown out by the officer in attendance. This interview was a long one; an unpleasant voice was heard in violent outbursts, and presently the officer came out and hurried through the ante-room, pale, with quivering lips, and his hands clasped to his head.

[1] *Sila* means strength: in the original Russian a play on the words is conveyed.

9

It was now Prince Andrew's turn.

"To the right, next the window," someone muttered in his ear.

He was admitted to a private office, neatly but not luxuriously furnished, and saw before him a man of about forty, with a singularly long body, and a no less oddly long head. His hair was closely cropped, his face deeply wrinkled, and his thick brows met over dull greenish eyes and a drooping red nose. This dignitary turned his head towards the new-comer, and said, without looking at him:

"What do you want?"

"I want nothing, your excellency," said Prince Andrew, quietly.

Araktchéïew looked up. "Take a seat," he said. "You are Prince Bolkonsky?"

"I want nothing. His majesty the emperor has condescended to send my *mémoire* to your excellency. . . ."

"Allow me to tell you, my dear fellow, that I have read your *mémoire*," interrupted Araktchéïew, beginning with some suavity, but, after a word or two, returning to his tone of angry contempt. "You propose some new regulations for the army? There are plenty of old ones and no one enforces them. . . . People only write them nowadays; it is the easier thing to do."

"It was his majesty's wish that I should wait upon your excellency, to ask you what you propose to do with my paper."

"I sent it to the committee, endorsed with my opinion. I do not approve of it," he added, rising. He took a document off the table and handed it to Bolkonsky. "There!"

Across the back was written in pencil, ill-spelt, and without any stops: "No logical basis copied from the French code differs from ours on no reasonable grounds."

"What committee is to inquire into it?"

"The committee of revision of the military code; and I have placed your highness's name on the list—without honorarium."

Prince Andrew smiled. "I should not have joined it otherwise."

"Honorary member; you quite understand. Good morning.—Well, who next out there?" he shouted, as he showed Bolkonsky out.

CHAPTER V

IN anticipation of an official intimation of his appointment as a member of the committee, Prince Andrew called on such of his acquaintances as were in power and might prove useful. A restless and irresistible wonderment, something like what he had felt on the eve of a battle, attracted him to those higher spheres where measures were being concerted that must influence the lives of millions of human beings. He could make a guess by observing the irritability of the seniors—by the eager inquisitiveness of those who were dying to know, and the reserve of those who did know—by the anxious excitement of all—by the endless committee meetings and sittings, that a tremendous civil battle was brewing at St. Petersburg in this year 1809, of which Spéransky was to be the general in command; and Spéransky had for Bolkonsky all the attraction of an unknown genius. In short, the great reform and the reformer so wholly occupied his thoughts that the fate of his own report became a secondary consideration.

His own rank and position gave him access to the opposing parties among the aristocratic circles. The party of reform hailed him sympathetically; in the first place by reason of his remarkable intelligence and knowledge; and in the second, on account of the reputation as a liberal which he had won by the emancipation of his serfs. At the same time the conservative party, who set their face against the new movement, hoped to find an ally in him, as sharing his father's opinions. The women regarded him as a wealthy and brilliant marriageable man— nay, as moving in a halo of romance derived from his own supposed death in battle and his wife's melancholy end. Those who had known him in former days thought him singularly altered for the better: Time had softened him, he had lost a great deal of his pride and his airs; he had gained the self-possession that years alone can give.

The day after his visit to Araktchéïew he went to an evening party at Count Kotchoubey's, and told him of his interview with "Sila Andréïévitch," of whom Kotchoubey spoke in the same tone of doubtful irony that had struck Bolkonsky among those who were waiting in the great man's ante-room:

"My dear fellow," added Kotchoubey, "even when you are one of the committee you will not get on without Michael

Mikaïlovitch Spéransky; he is the great factotum. I will speak to him this evening—he promised to look in . . ."

"But what can Spéransky care about the military code?" asked Prince Andrew. Kotchoubey smiled and shook his head in astonishment at his simplicity.

"We have spoken of you—of your free labourers. . . ."

"Oh! It is you, then, prince, who have liberated your serfs?" exclaimed rather sharply an elderly man who remembered the good old days of Catherine.

"It was a very small estate which brought in very little," said Bolkonsky, trying to palliate the truth so as not to annoy the old man.

"You were in a devil of a hurry!" the older man went on, and, looking at Kotchoubey, he added: "What I want to know is who is to till the ground if the peasants are emancipated?—Take my word for it, it is easier to make laws than to govern by them; and allow me to ask you, count, who is to be appointed judge when all are to go through examinations?"

"Well, those who can pass them, I suppose," said Kotchoubey.

"For instance, there is Prianichnikow—a capital man, but he is sixty. How is he to pass an examination?"

"Of course that is a difficulty—all the more so as very few people know anything; but . . ." Kotchoubey did not finish his sentence; he put his hand through Prince Andrew's arm and led him forward to meet a tall man who had just come into the room. The new-comer did not look more than forty, though his vast bald forehead had only a few remaining hairs; his long face and plump hands were remarkable for the dull whiteness of the skin, which was like the sickly pallor of a soldier who has been a long time in hospital. He had on a blue coat. Andrew at once knew who it was and was somewhat startled at the sight. Was his feeling respect, envy, or merely curiosity? He could not decide. Spéransky was beyond a doubt strikingly original. Andrew had never seen any man so perfectly calm and self-assured, or, at the same time, so clumsy and so impassible—a glance at once so soft and so keen as that in those half-closed, half-sleepy eyes—or so much determination betrayed by a smile of general affability. This was Spéransky, the secretary of state—Spéransky, the czar's right hand, his companion at Erfurth where he had several times had the honour of speech with the emperor of the French.

The great man looked round at the company but was in

12

no haste to speak. Being quite sure of being listened to, he never raised his voice above a certain pitch; its calm and measured cadence struck Prince Andrew very agreeably. He never looked at anyone but the person he was talking to. Bolkonsky watched his every gesture, and listened to every word. Knowing him well by reputation, he was prepared to find him a sum of human perfections—a delusion to which those in the habit of forming foregone conclusions are very liable.

Spéransky apologised to Kotchoubey for not having come earlier; he had been detained at the palace. He avoided saying, "detained by the emperor," and Prince Andrew noted this affectation of modesty. When Kotchoubey introduced him, Spéransky slowly turned his eyes upon him, and looked at him with a fixed smile for a moment or two in silence, then he said:

"I am happy to make your acquaintance; I have heard much about you."

Kotchoubey, in a few words, sketched Araktchéïew's reception of Bolkonsky. Spéransky smiled a little more defiantly and replied:

"Mr. Magnitsky, the president of the commission, is a friend of mine, and if you like I can promise you a personal interview with him." He articulated very distinctly every word, every syllable, and after a full stop at the end of this sentence, he added: "I hope you will find him cordial, and anxious to promote everything that can be useful."

A little circle had now gathered round them. Prince Andrew was surprised at the calmness, not unmixed with contempt, with which this man—not long since an obscure priestling— answered the old man who had bewailed the new reforms, seeming to condescend in explaining them; but when his antagonist raised his voice he said no more, but merely smiled, observing that he did not think himself competent to judge of the utility or the uselessness of any decision of the czar.

After a few minutes of this general conversation he rose and led Prince Andrew aside to the other end of the room: it suited his views to converse with him.

"I was so overridden by that worthy old gentleman's excitement that I have not had time to exchange two words with you, prince," he said, with that slightly scornful smile, as if he wished to convey that he was well aware of the futility of the society he had been mixing with. Prince Andrew felt flattered.

13

"I have known you a long time by reputation," Spéransky went on. "First by the liberation of your peasantry—an example I could wish to see followed; and next as being the only one of the court chamberlains who has not taken offence at the recent ukase as to order of rank at court, which has given rise to so much dissatisfaction and recrimination."

"Very true; my father did not wish me to take advantage of my privileges and I began service at the bottom."

"Your father, though a man of a past generation, is very superior to those of our own contemporaries who criticise the measure; it only aims, after all, at re-establishing justice on a sound basis."

"Nevertheless, I am inclined to think that there is some ground for criticism," said Prince Andrew, making an effort to shake himself free of this man's influence; it vexed him to give in on every point—nay, he longed to contradict him; but his mind was so much engaged in observing him that he could not express himself with his usual readiness.

"That is to say criticism based on personal vanity," said Spéransky, quietly.

"Partly, no doubt; but in my opinion on the interests of the government itself."

"How is that?"

"I am a disciple of Montesquieu," said Prince Andrew; "his maxim: 'that a monarchy is based on honour,' seems to me incontrovertible; and there are certain prerogatives and privileges of nobility which I believe to be the best safeguards of this feeling."

The smile faded from Spéransky's face, which gained enormously by the change. Prince Andrew's remark had interested him:

"Oh! if you look at the matter from that point of view!" he said as quietly as ever, but speaking French with some little difficulty, and so even more slowly than when he expressed himself in Russian. "He said that honour cannot be sustained by privileges when they are injurious to the service; hence honour must consist either in abstention from blameworthy actions or in the feeling which stimulates us to win the approbation and rewards that bear witness to it. Consequently," he went on to clinch the argument, "any institution which gives rise to such emulation of honour is precisely, and in every respect, such an institution as the great French Emperor's Legion of Honour. It would be impossible, as it seems to me, to say that that is mischievous, since it promotes the good of the service and is not a court or caste distinction."

"That I willingly admit; but I also think that court distinctions tend to the same end, since those who hold them feel it incumbent on them to fulfil their functions worthily."

"And yet you have not chosen to avail yourself of them, prince," said Spéransky, thus giving an amiable turn to a discussion which must inevitably have ended in the discomfiture of the younger man.—"Well, if you will do me the honour to call on me on Wednesday, as I shall by that time have seen Magnitsky, I may be able to give you some interesting information; and at any rate I shall have the pleasure of talking with you at greater length. . . ." Then, bowing farewell, he slipped away—in the French fashion—without taking leave or being observed.

CHAPTER VI

DURING the early part of his residence in St. Petersburg Prince Andrew could not fail to feel that the ideas which had grown up within him during his solitude had been thrown into the background by the trivial cares which now crowded upon him. Every evening, on his return home, he wrote down in his note-book four or five visits that must be paid and as many appointments to be kept the next day. The arrangement of his day, so as to enable him to be perfectly punctual for every engagement, took up all his endeavour; he could do nothing, think of nothing; and the opinions he occasionally expressed, with great success, were nothing more than the outcome of his meditations in the country. At first he was annoyed with himself for repeating the same things, in the course of the same day, in different houses: but he was soon swept into the eddy, and had not time to detect that he had forgotten how to think.

He went to Spéransky on the following Wednesday, and a long and intimate conversation left him deeply impressed.

In his anxiety to find in another the ideal at which he himself was aiming, he easily believed that Spéransky was in fact the type of virtue and intelligence that he had fancied him. If the minister had been a man of the same social "set" as himself, if their education, their habits of life and their ways of

15

judging had been the same, he would no doubt have been quick to perceive the weak and prosaically human side of his character; as it was, that well-balanced and amazingly logical intellect commanded his respect—all the more because he did not altogether understand it. The great man, on the other hand, made the best of himself to Prince Andrew: was this because he really appreciated his fine capacity, or because he was desirous of gaining his adhesion? Be this as it may, he never missed an opportunity of flattering him with delicate skill, of giving him to understand that his superior intelligence made him worthy to be the peer of the highest, and that he alone could really enter into the depth of his schemes, and understand the absurdity of other people. More than once he said such things as these to his new ally:

"To *us* everything which is outside routine, which is above the common level . . ." or: "*We*, you know, want to protect and feed the wolves as well as the sheep . . ." or: "*they* do not understand us . . ." with a tone and a look that implied: "You and I know what *they* are worth, and what *we* are."

This second, and more familiar, interview only confirmed the first impression produced on him by Spéransky, in whom he saw a man of superior intellect and a deep thinker, who had risen to power by the strength of an irresistible will, and who made use of it for the good of his country. He was, in fact, the philosopher whom Bolkonsky was seeking—the philosopher he himself would fain have been—accounting by logic for the mysteries of existence, admitting nothing as true that was opposed to common sense, and examining everything by the light of reason. His ideas took form with such admirable lucidity that Prince Andrew, in spite of himself, yielded to his opinion on all points, and only raised a feeble objection now and then as a protest of independence. Everything in Spéransky was perfect and right excepting his cold gaze—icy, keen, and inscrutable—and his delicate white hands. Those hands riveted Prince Andrew's attention, he could not look away from them; the hands of a man in power sometimes have that attraction—and they roused him to a dumb irritation which he could not account for. The scorn and contempt which he affected for the world at large was also unpleasing to Bolkonsky; and the constant shifting of his methods of argument. He used every figure of logic and rhetoric, except comparisons; but Prince Andrew objected to his abrupt transitions from one form to another. He would set up for a practical reformer and fling

16

at visionary dreamers; now heaping bitter irony on his opponents, and now working out a close line of argument, and rising to metaphysical abstractions—of this, indeed, he was particularly fond. Taking his stand on ineffable heights he would wander into definitions of space, time, and mind; would twist them into ingenious refutations, and then return to the subject under discussion.

One characteristic feature of his powerful intellect was an immutable belief in the force and rights of intellect. It was at once evident that doubt, which was a habit of mind with Bolkonsky, was unknown to Spéransky; and that the fear of failing to express his thoughts, or a suspicion of the infallibility of his own beliefs had never for an instant troubled him. And it was this particular trait of Spéransky's mind that Andrew so admired.

In short, Prince Andrew conceived for the minister the same enthusiastic admiration as he had felt for Napoleon. Spéransky was the son of a priest, and this to vulgar minds was a reason for despising him; hence Prince Andrew, by the unconscious reaction against his own enthusiasm, only added to its intensity.

In speaking of the commission charged to revise and co-ordinate the laws Spéransky told him, laughing at it, that it had been sitting for the last hundred and fifty years; that it had cost millions of roubles, and had resulted in nothing; that Rosenkampf had stuck labels on all the articles of comparative legislation, and that this was all that had come of the millions that had been spent: "And now we want to give new judicial powers to the senate, and we have no laws! So you see, prince, it is a positive crime in men like yourself, to withdraw into private life."

Prince Andrew remarked that this class of functions required men who had had a special education.

"Show me such men! It is a vicious circle; there is no way out but by breaking it."

A week later Prince Andrew was appointed member of the committee in charge of the revision of the military code, and moreover—when he least expected it—president of one of the sections of the legislative commission. He accepted this post by Spéransky's particular desire, and undertook to study civil law; to this end he had recourse to the codes of Justinian and Napoleon, and set to work on the section entitled: "Of the rights of individuals."

CHAPTER VII

ABOUT two years before this, in 1808, Peter, on his return from his tour in the provinces, found himself quite unexpectedly the leader of the freemasons of St. Petersburg. He organised irregular lodges and established regular or "tiled" lodges, for which he obtained charters and title-deeds; he undertook propaganda, gave money for the building of the temple, and made up, out of his own pocket, the alms not procured by collection —for the members were apt to be niggardly and unpunctual in their payments. He also defrayed the expenses of the almshouse founded by the brethren; but as for himself, he succumbed to the same temptations and led the same life as of old. He liked good living and good drinking, and could never resist the pleasures of a bachelor life, while acknowledging that they were immoral and degrading. In spite of the enthusiasm with which he had started on his various enterprises, he knew, at the end of a year, that the promised land of freemasonry was unstable under his feet. He felt like a man who steps out boldly on level ground, and is aware that he is sinking in a quaking bog; then, trying with the other foot to steady himself, he sinks in up to the knees and must now struggle onward as best he may.

Bazdéïew, who had nothing to do with the St. Petersburg lodges, now never left Moscow. Peter's brethren were men whom he met every day of his life; and he found it almost impossible to recognise as his brothers men such as Prince B. or Mr. D., whom he knew to be utterly weak and commonplace. Under their aprons and insignia he could not help seeing their uniforms and orders—the true end and object of their existence. Often when he was collecting alms, and put down twenty or thirty roubles in gold, or even only in promises, against the names of half a score of members, as rich as himself, Peter could not help remembering their vow to give their goods to their neighbour; and doubts, which he vainly tried to silence, would rise up in his mind.

He divided the brethren into four classes: the first consisted of those who took no active part in the concerns either of their lodge or of mankind, who devoted themselves exclusively to meditating on the mysteries of the order, and on the meaning of the Trinity; to studying the three elements of sulphur, mercury, and salt, or the significance of the square and the other

18

Peter, on his return from his tour in the provinces

symbols of Solomon's Temple. These Peter could look up to; they were the elders, including Bazdéïew himself; still, he could not understand what pleasure they found in their studies, and did not feel in the least drawn towards the mystical side of freemasonry.

The second category, in which he ranked himself, was composed of adepts who, though waverers like himself, sought the right path; and who, though they had not yet found it, did not despair of discovering it some day.

The third class, the majority, were those who saw nothing in the order beyond its external forms and ceremonies, and were satisfied with a strict observance of them without troubling themselves about their hidden meaning. Among these were Villarsky and the Worshipful Master himself.

The fourth and last were the men, at that time also very numerous, who, believing in nothing, and hoping for nothing, clung to the brotherhood simply for the sake of being intimate with rich people and getting some benefit out of the intimacy.

Peter's various forms of activity failed to satisfy him: he blamed the order, as it then existed at St. Petersburg, for its unqualified formalism, and without attacking its foundations he told himself that the freemasons of Russia were on a wrong track in departing so widely from the principles on which it was based. He therefore decided on travelling abroad to gain initiation into the highest mysteries.

He came home again in the course of the summer of 1809. The masons of Russia had been apprised by their correspondents that Bésoukhow, having gained the confidence of the grand dignitaries of the order, had been initiated into the highest mysteries, and subsequently exalted to the highest grade; also that he was returning with various schemes in prospect; and when they visited him immediately after his return, they suspected that he had some surprise in store. It was resolved that a general meeting should be held including even the lowest apprentices, in order that Peter might deliver to all the message with which he had been charged. The lodge being complete and all the formalities accomplished, Peter spoke as follows:

"My dear brethren," he said with much hesitation, and holding his speech, ready written out, awkwardly in his hand. "My dear brethren, it is not enough that we should accomplish the mysteries of our order in the privacy of the lodge; we must do, we must act. We are torpid and we must set to work . . ."

but after these few introductory words he resigned himself to reading his address.

"In order to diffuse truth, and bring about the triumph of virtue, we must uproot prejudice, establish rules consonant to the spirit of the time, devote ourselves to the task of educating youth, and bind ourselves by the closest bonds to all enlightened men, so as to fight boldly and conquer superstition, faithlessness, and human folly, by our union; we must form a band of labourers among those who are devoted to the cause, united by community of purpose, and with strength and power in their hands. To achieve this the scale must be weighted on the side of virtue, and men must be rewarded, even in this world, for their good actions. But, it will be objected, our existing political institutions are antagonistic to the accomplishment of these noble aims. What then is to be done? Are we to foment revolt? To overturn society, and by force, resist force? No. We are far from advocating violent and arbitrary reforms; they are indeed mischievous, for they can never remedy evil so long as man remains unchanged. Wisdom has no need of violence.

"When our brotherhood shall have succeeded in drawing the virtuous out of the obscurity in which they dwell, and not till then, will it have any right to agitate, and work gradually up to the end we have in view—in a word, to the establishment of a universal scheme of government, without seeking to break social bonds or to disturb those conditions of administration by which, at the present time, we are enabled to carry out our object; that is to say, the triumph of virtue over vice. Christianity tended to the same end when it preached that men should be good and wise, and follow the example of virtuous souls, to the attainment of goodness.

"When the world was still sunk in darkness, preaching was sufficient; the novelty of the truths taught gave them a force which is now much diminished; we must have recourse to more decisive means. What is indispensable is that man, guided by his senses, should find in virtue an actual and captivating charm. The passions cannot be uprooted; they must therefore be directed and trained; they must find satisfaction within the limits of virtue, and we must supply the means.

"When a knot of men of mark shall have banded themselves together in each country, each member will, in his turn, form the nucleus of another group; thus closely allied they will meet with no obstacles, and an order which has already done humanity so much secret good will find nothing impossible."

THE INVASION

This address produced a deep impression and revolutionised the lodge. The majority, regarding it as dangerous and tending to mystical illuminism, received it with a coldness that surprised Peter. The Worshipful Master took him to task, and led him to enlarge with growing enthusiasm on the opinions he had just stated. The meeting was a stormy one, and divided into parties; some accused Peter of illuminism; others upheld him; and, for the first time, he was struck by the infinite and inherent variety in human beings, which results in no two regarding any truth from quite the same point of view. Even among those of the brethren who seemed to agree with him, each one suggested some alteration or limitation which he could not accept from a conviction that his scheme ought to be adopted as a whole.

The Worshipful Master observed, somewhat ironically, that in the excitement of the discussion Peter seemed to have been carried away by anger rather than by charity. Peter made no reply; he briefly inquired whether his proposition would be accepted, and when the president plainly answered: "No," Peter left without going through the customary formalities, and went home.

CHAPTER VIII

PETER spent the three next days on the sofa; he did not stir out; he was a victim to disappointment and chagrin.

He received a letter from his wife, who besought him to grant her a meeting, described her grief at their separation, expressed her wish to devote her life to him, and announced her intention of returning in a short time from abroad to St. Petersburg.

Not long after this, one of the freemasons who was not particularly respected, insisted on being shown up to him, and leading the conversation to the subject of conjugal happiness, reproached him bitterly for his injustice and severity to his wife—a severity adverse to the masonic rule of life, which enjoins forgiveness to the penitent.

Then his mother-in-law sent for him, if only for a few minutes, on pressing and serious business. Peter now suspected a conspiracy; but in his present state of moral feeling, and a victim to his immediate annoyance, he felt perfectly indifferent about the reconciliation which he saw was impending; nothing in life seemed of much importance, and he no longer cared particularly to retain his own liberty or to inflict any further punishment on his wife.

"No one is right, and no one is wrong; so she, too, is innocent!" thought he. Was it not a matter of complete indifference to him, with interests so remote to occupy him, whether she lived with him or no? However, shaking off his apathy, which was all that prevented his consenting, he determined, nevertheless, to go to Moscow and consult Bazdéïew before giving his answer.

PASSAGES FROM PETER'S DIARY

"Moscow, Nov. 17.—I have just hurried home from seeing the Benefactor, and must make a hasty note of all I have gone through. He lives penuriously, and for three years has been suffering from a painful malady—never a complaint, never a murmur. From morning till late at night, excepting the few minutes he gives up to his very frugal meals, he devotes himself exclusively to scientific studies. He welcomed me affectionately, and made me sit down on his bed. I greeted him with masonic signs of the East and of Jerusalem, to which he responded, and asked me, with a sweet smile, what I had learnt in the Scotch and Prussian lodges. I told him; and at the same time reported the proposals I had made to the brethren at St. Petersburg, the bad reception I had met with, and my differences with them. He lay silent for a long time, and then gave me his opinion, which at once threw a light on my past and my future life; I was struck by his asking me, 'Do you remember the three objects of the order: 1st, The preservation and study of the mysteries; 2nd, Self-purification and discipline, in order to partake of those mysteries; 3rd, The perfecting of humanity by a craving after purity? Which is the most important of these three? Self-improvement beyond a doubt, for this we can always promote, under any and all circumstances; at the same time it is what needs the greatest efforts, and we run the risk of sinning by pride, by directing our introspection to the mysteries while our impurities make us unworthy to comprehend them, or by undertaking to reform the human race while we ourselves remain perverse and unworthy. Illuminism has lost much of its purity; it is marred by pride, having allowed itself to be turned aside into the channel of public beneficence.'

22

From this point of view he could but blame my own discourse and all I had done. I admitted that he was right. In speaking of my domestic affairs, he went on to say that, as the first duty of a true mason was self-discipline, we are tempted to think we shall attain perfection quicker by ridding ourselves of all impediments at one stroke; whereas the contrary is the truth: we can only progress by fighting the battles of life, and by knowing ourselves, to which we can only attain by comparison. Nor must we forget the crowning grace, the love of death. Vicissitude alone can teach us the vanity of life, and nourish that love in us; that is to say, the belief in another life. His words struck me all the more forcibly, because notwithstanding his terrible state of illness, Bazdéïew is not weary of life. Still, he loves death, though with all his purity and elevation of mind, he does not think himself fitly prepared for it. In explaining to me the grand square of creation, he told me that the numbers 3 and 7 lie at the root of everything. He advised me to avoid a rupture with the St. Petersburg brethren, to be content with the second grade, and to use my influence to wean them from the sin of pride, and forward them in the path of truth and progress. He warned me to keep a strict watch over myself, and gave me this book to keep a record of all my actions.

"St. Petersburg, November 23rd.—I am living again with my wife. My mother-in-law came to me in tears to assure me that Helen entreated me to hear her, that she was innocent, and miserable at my desertion, etc. I knew that if I allowed her to come I should not have the courage to resist her entreaties; I did not know what to do, or to whom to turn for advice. If Bazdéïew had been here he would have helped me. I read over his letters, I recalled his conversation, and I came to the conclusion that I ought not to refuse any who sue, but must hold out a hand to all—and much more to her who is one with me; in short, that I must bear my cross. Still, since my only motive for forgiveness is right-doing, at any rate our reunion could be in spirit only. This is what I have decided and written to Bazdéïew accordingly. So I told my wife that I could only beg her to forget the past, and to forgive me wherein I had wronged her; that, for my part, I had nothing to forgive. I was happy to say this. I only hope she may never know how painful it was to see her again! I have established myself in the top story of the house, and I am happy in the sense of a regenerate spirit."

23

WAR AND PEACE

CHAPTER IX

THE "upper ten thousand" of St. Petersburg society, which met at court or at fashionable balls, was divided—as it always is—into sets, each stamped with its own peculiarities. The largest of these circles was the so-called French set—a Franco-Russian mixture—that of Roumiantzow and Caulaincourt. Immediately on her reconciliation with her husband, Helen took a leading position in this circle. The French embassy and several persons well known for wit and amiability frequented her drawing-room.

She had been at Erfurth at the time of the memorable meeting of the emperors, and had there made acquaintance with all the most remarkable people in Europe, and with Napoleon's immediate suite. Her success had been splendid. Napoleon himself, struck by her beauty at the theatre, had remarked, "What a splendid animal!" Her triumph as a young and lovely woman had not surprised her husband, for she was more beautiful than ever; but he was surprised at the reputation she had won during the last two years as a charming woman, as clever as she was handsome. The celebrated Prince de Ligne corresponded with her, writing her eight pages at a time. Bilibine treasured up his best witticisms to fire them off in the Countess Bésoukhow's presence; admission to her drawing-room was equivalent to a certificate of wit and talent. Young men would read up a subject before going to her parties, to have something to say; ambassadors and secretaries trusted her with their secrets; in short, Helen had become a real power in her degree. Peter, who knew how ignorant she really was, was sometimes present at her dinners and parties, where politics, philosophy, and poetry were discussed, and he listened with a mixture of amazement and anxiety. He felt as a conjuror must feel expecting to have his tricks detected every time he plays them; but no one ever found her out. Was such a *salon* as this a fool's paradise for human obtuseness, or did the dupes take pleasure in being duped? The truth was that Countess Bésoukhow, having established a reputation as a clever woman, was licensed to talk the greatest nonsense; her every word was listened to with admiration, and discovered to have some profound meaning which she herself had never suspected.

This eccentric and absent-mannered man—this lordly, mute

24

husband, who was in nobody's way and did not detract from the very select tone which reigned of course in such a circle— Peter, in short, was the very husband for this brilliant beauty born to shine, and an admirable foil for his wife's elegance and perfect demeanour. The abstract ideas that had occupied his time and thoughts for the last two years had inspired him with a certain contempt for everything outside their circle and given him an absent demeanour, tinged with a kind of benevolent indifference, which by its evident sincerity commanded involuntary deference. He walked into his wife's drawing-room as he would have entered a theatre. He knew everyone and was equally polite—and equally distant—to all. If the conversation happened to interest him he would join in it, frankly expressing his views, which were not always those in vogue at the moment, with perfect indifference to the presence of the gentlemen of the embassy. But everyone had a cut-and-dried opinion of this "oddity," married to the most elegant woman in St. Petersburg, and no one ever thought of taking his sallies seriously.

Among the younger men who frequented the house most constantly was Boris Droubetzkoï, whose career was a very brilliant one. Helen affected to call him her "page," treated him as a boy, and smiled on him as on everyone else; and yet this smile hurt Peter. Boris, on his part, treated the master of the house with a sort of dignified and compassionate respect that irritated Peter still more. Having gone through so much three years ago, he made an effort to avoid another equally humiliating experience, first by tacitly resigning his own claims on his wife, and next by resolving that he would not allow himself to be suspicious.

"Now that she has set up for a blue-stocking, she has no doubt got over her more youthful impulses. No one ever heard of a blue-stocking who carried on a love-intrigue," so he told himself, repeating this axiom, though Heaven knows where he had found it, as though it were a mathematical certainty. And yet, strangely enough, the mere presence of Boris had a physical effect upon him; he seemed to lose his arms and legs, to be too paralysed to move freely. "Antipathy!" he said to himself.

So Peter, in the eyes of the world, was a fine gentleman, the blind and rather ridiculous husband of a very charming wife; eccentric but intelligent, doing nothing, interfering with nobody; a thorough good boy, in every sense of the word—while in the depths of his soul the arduous and difficult travail of moral

25

development was going on; a process that brought him many discoveries, and some great joys, but weighted with some terrible doubts.

CHAPTER X

PASSAGES FROM PETER'S DIARY

"November 24th.—Rose at eight. Read the gospel, went to the meeting [Peter, by Bazdéïew's advice, had consented to be a member of a committee]; came home and dined alone. The countess has company I do not like. Ate and drank moderately; after dinner copied some papers required by the brethren.—In the evening joined the countess; told a story about B., and only discovered too late, by the shouts of laughter that greeted it, that I should not have repeated it.—To bed early and well content. Almighty Lord, help me to walk in Thy steps. (1) To conquer anger by quietness and not over-hastiness; (2) to conquer desires by temperance and disgust; (3) to get away far from all vanities but not from (a) attending to my duties in the Government service; (b) my duties to family life; (c) my friendships, and (d) my economic duties.

"November 27th.—Rose late and lay idly on my bed for a long time—Lord help me and preserve me!—Read the gospel, but not with due concentration. Brother Ouroussow came to talk over the vanities of this world, and the emperor's schemes of reform. I was on the point of criticising them, but I remembered our rules and the Benefactor's exhortations: a true mason, as an active unit in the state, when he is called upon to lend his support must be a passive spectator of all that does not immediately concern him. My tongue is my enemy.—Brothers V., G., and O. came to speak with me as to the initiation of a new apprentice. They want me to undertake the duties of initiator. I do not feel myself worthy. . . . Then he went on to discuss the meaning of the seven pillars and the seven steps of the Temple, the seven sciences, the seven virtues, and the seven gifts of the Holy Ghost. Brother O. is very eloquent. The apprentice was received this evening and the new arrangement of the lodge added greatly to the impressiveness of the ceremony. Boris Droubetzkoï was admitted; I was his sponsor. A strange feeling disturbed me during our private interview. I felt a hatred for him which I am vainly

26

trying to conquer. And because of it, I sincerely wish to save him from all that is evil and to lead him to the path of righteousness, but my evil thoughts would not leave me. It seemed to me that he had no other object in joining the order than to curry favour with such of the brethren as are powerful in the eyes of the world. He asked me several times whether N. and S. were attached to our lodge, which I could not tell him. I watched him, and do not think him capable of genuine respect for our holy order; he is too full of business, too well satisfied with the superficial man to desire moral perfection. I believe him to be deficient in sincerity, and noticed that he smiled disdainfully at what I said to him. As we stood alone in the darkness of the temple I could gladly have thrust him through the heart with the sword I held to his breast. But I was not eloquent, and I could not make the Worshipful Master share my doubts.—May the Great Architect of the Universe guide me in the way of truth and lead me far from the labyrinth of falsehood!

[Three sheets of the book were blank here, and then it went on as follows:]

"Had a long and edifying conversation with Brother B., who advised me to hold by Brother A. Much was shown to me, though I am unworthy. Adonais is the name of Him who created the Universe. Eloim is the name of Him who rules it. The third—the name that must not be pronounced—has the meaning of the 'All.' These discussions with Brother B. strengthen, freshen, and confirm in me the resolve to follow the path of virtue. In his presence there seems no room for doubts. I see clearly the difference between the poor lessons of science and our holy all-comprising views. Human science divides everything in order to understand it, kills everything in order to examine it. In the holy science of our order all is one, all is known in its entirety and its life. The Trinity is the three beginnings of all things—sulphur, mercury and salt. Sulphur is a fiery element, and in its combination with salt, magnetises it by its fieriness, to attract mercury, seize it, hold it, and thus combination produces all things.—Christ, the Holy Ghost, He.

"December 3rd.—Woke late; read the gospel but coldly. Left my room and walked up and down the study; . . . wanted to meditate, but instead the imagination called up an event that took place four years previously. I met Mr. Dologhow

27

after the duel, in Moscow, and he said to me that he hoped I was quite quiet now, although my wife was abroad. At the time I found no answer for him, but now, remembering all the details of this meeting, I said many fierce and cutting words to him in my imagination. I only remembered myself and put aside these thoughts, when I saw myself flushed with anger: but I fear I have not repented sincerely enough. . . . Boris Droubetzkoï called and told me a heap of stories; his presence worried me and I contradicted him. He retorted, and I grew angry and answered him disagreeably and rudely. Then he said no more, and, too late, I realised what my conduct had been. I can never control myself with him; the fault lies in my self-conceit; I fancy myself his superior and that is not right; he makes every allowance for my weaknesses, while I look down on him. O Lord! enable me, when in his presence, to know my own shortcomings and may he, too, benefit by my knowledge. After dinner I slept and as I was dropping off, I heard very plainly a voice saying into my left ear 'Your day.' I dreamt that I was walking along in the dark, and was suddenly surrounded by dogs. But I felt no fear. Then one of them, not a very big one, seized me by the left trouser-leg with its teeth and would not let go. I began to throttle it with my hands. But as soon as I tore it off, another, a bigger one, began to bite me. I lifted it, and as I lifted it it grew heavier and heavier. Suddenly I saw Brother A. who took me by the arm and led me to a building, which could only be entered by crossing a narrow plank. I stepped on to it and it gave way and fell, while I began to climb over a fence, the top of which I could barely reach with my hands. After many struggles, I dragged my body over so that the upper part of me was on one side, and my legs on the other. On looking round I saw Brother A. standing on the fence and pointing out a big garden and avenue, and in the garden a beautiful building. Then I awoke. O Lord, the Great Architect of the Universe! Help me to rid myself of the dogs—my passions, and the greatest of them that combines in it the strength of all the others, and help me to reach the Temple of Righteousness, which appeared to me in my dream!

"December 7th.—I had a dream that I. A. Bazdéïew is in my house and I want to entertain him. And it appeared to me that I keep on chattering with outsiders, and suddenly remember that this cannot please him, and want to approach him in order to fold him in my embrace. But as I approach him his face seems suddenly transfigured, grown very young,

28

and he whispers something to me of the teaching of our order, but so low that I cannot hear him. Then it was as if we all left the room. And here something extraordinary happens. We are all sitting or lying on the floor and he is saying something to me. And wanting to show him my feelings, I don't listen to what he says but imagine my inner being, and the mercy of God which has illuminated me. Tears come to my eyes and I am happy that he has noticed them. But he glances at me with irritation, jumps to his feet and cuts short what he was saying. I get frightened and ask him whether what he said was meant for me, but he does not reply and only looks at me gently. Then we are suddenly in my bedroom, where there is a double bed. He lies down on the edge of it and I feel a wish to caress him and lie down too. And he appears to ask me: 'Tell me, what have you the greatest passion for? Have you recognised it?—I think that you have.' Confused by this question I answer that idleness is my chief sin, to which he doubtfully shakes his head. And then more confused than ever, I answer that though I have taken back my wife as he advised, I live with her not as a husband with his wife. To this he replies that I have no right to deprive my wife of my caresses, and makes me feel that therein lies my duty. But I answer that I am ashamed, and suddenly everything disappears. And I wake with this text of the Holy Gospel in my mind: 'Life is a light to man, and light burns in the darkness, and darkness cannot swallow it.' Bazdéïew's face was young and radiant. This day I have had a letter from him in which he writes of my duties as a husband.—Come, Saviour, and succour me! I shall perish in corruption if Thou dost not rescue me.

"December 9th.—I had a dream from which I woke with a trembling heart. I saw, as if in my house in Moscow, Bazdéïew enter the big reception-room from the small drawing-room next door. And as if I immediately knew that some process of regeneration had taken place in him I ran to meet him. And I embrace him and kiss his hands, while he says: 'Have you noticed that my face is different?' I look at him, continuing to hold him in my arms, and see that his face is youthful, although there is no hair on his head, and that his features are quite different. And I say: 'But I would have recognised you wherever we had met,' thinking meanwhile 'Am I telling the truth?' And then suddenly I see him lying like a corpse, but gradually reviving, . . . he goes into my study with me, holding a big folio book. And I say: 'I have written that,' to which he replies by bending his head. I open the book and on every page there is a beautiful drawing. And I seem to know that these drawings represent the amorous adventures of the soul and its lover. And it seems to me that I see on these pages the picture of a maiden in transparent robes and with a transparent body floating up to the skies. And it seems as if I know this maiden to be a representation of the 'Song of Songs.' And it is as if I, gazing at these pictures, am doing something wrong, and yet I cannot tear my eyes from them. O Lord, help me! If this abandonment of me is your will, then be it so; but if I am myself the cause of it, teach me what I should do: I shall perish in corruption if Thou leavest me."

CHAPTER XI

IN spite of two years spent entirely in the country, Count Rostow's affairs had not recovered their balance.

Nicholas, faithful to his promise, was still serving without demur in the same regiment, though this was not likely to offer him any brilliant opening. He spent but little; but the style of living at Otradnoë, and above all Mitenka's mismanagement of the estates and income, made debt grow like a snowball. The old count saw but one way out of the difficulty, namely to seek some government appointment. The whole family accordingly moved to St. Petersburg, that he might look for employment, and, as he said, to give the girls a last season's amusement. Soon after their arrival there, Berg proposed to Vera and was accepted.

At Moscow the Rostows were as a matter of course received in the highest society; but at St. Petersburg their acquaintances were rather mixed, and they were treated as provincials by many who, after taking full advantage of their hospitality at Moscow, hardly condescended to know them at St. Petersburg. However, they kept open house and the strangest mixture of guests assembled at their suppers: a few old neighbours, not rich ones, from Otradnoë, their daughters, a maid of honour named Péronnsky, Peter Bésoukhow, and a son of a district postmaster who had a place at St. Petersburg. The intimates in the house were Boris Droubetzkoï, Peter, whom the old count had met in the street and brought home with him, and Berg, who spent whole days in paying to Countess Vera the attentions expected of a young man about to propose. He proudly displayed the hand that had been hurt at Austerlitz, and elaborately held his sword in his left. His persevering repetition of the story and the importance he lent it had at last won credence in its authenticity, and he had been rewarded twice.

When the war was carried into Finland he distinguished himself no less: he picked up a fragment of shell, which had just killed an aide-de-camp by the general's side, and carried it to his colonel. This achievement, which he related till everyone was sick of hearing it, also gained acceptance, and he was again rewarded. Thus in 1809 he was captain in the guard, and wore a medal, and from the point of view of pay held a very enviable position. Some envious tongues, to be sure, would still run down his merits; yet there could be no denying that he was a brave soldier, punctual on duty, in favour with his superiors, irreproachable as to moral conduct, on the high road to a brilliant future, and secure already in a very good position.

Four years previously, one evening at the theatre at Moscow, Berg had seen Vera Rostow, and pointing her out to a fellow-officer, a German like himself, he said: "There is the girl I will marry." Now, after having fairly weighed his chances and compared his own position with that of the Rostows, he had made up his mind to the decisive step.

At first his proposal was received with a degree of astonishment which was anything but flattering: "How could the son of a nobody, a gentleman of no rank, from Lithuania, dare to aspire to the hand of a Countess Rostow?" But his most characteristic trait was a naïve egotism that smoothed every difficulty; he was so convinced of his own merits that, by degrees, the conviction infected the family, and at last the union was all that could be wished. The Rostows' fortune was sadly dilapidated: the aspirant must be well aware of that. Vera had seen four-and-twenty springs, and in spite of her good looks and extreme propriety no husband had yet presented himself. The parents therefore consented.

"You see," said Berg to his comrade, whom he called his friend because it was "the thing" to have a friend, "I have arranged and settled everything, and I would not marry if any hitch interfered with my plans. My papa and mamma want for nothing since I have succeeded in getting them a pension, and I can manage to live very well at St. Petersburg on my

31

pay with my knowledge of the world and my fiancée's little fortune. I am not marrying her for money—that would be shabby; but after all, the wife as well as the husband must contribute her share to the housekeeping. My rank in the service counts for something on my side, and on hers I reckon her birth and connections, and her little settlement, small as it may be; and with all this to back us I shall get on very well. Then she is handsome and a woman of character; she loves me, and," he added with a blush, "I love her, for she has plenty of good sense—she is the very opposite of her sister, whose temper is odious, and whose mind is shallow—she really seems hardly to belong to the family;—but my Vera is a pearl! You will see her, I hope you will often come . . ." he was about to say "to dinner," but thought better of it, and said, "to take tea with us," as he blew off a neatly curled ring of smoke from his cigar—the emblem of the happiness of which he dreamed.

As soon as they had got over the first spasm of indecision the family put on the festive air which is proper on such occasions; but it was perceptibly factitious and mingled with some embarrassment caused by the satisfaction they felt at getting Vera off their hands, and which they feared was but ill-concealed. The old count, greatly straitened as he was for money, was indeed too much in debt to fix the amount of his daughter's settlement. When the girls were born he had intended to give them each an estate of three hundred serfs on their marriage, but now one of these villages was sold, and the other mortgaged and the interest on it so overdue that it also would have to be sold; therefore it was impossible to give them estates. Money there was also none. They were now within a week of the wedding, and he had said nothing about a settlement to Berg, though the young people had been engaged a month. Should he give Vera the Riazan estate? Should he sell a forest, or borrow money on a bill? He was trying to make up his mind when Berg came into his room one morning, and with a polite smile on his lips, asked him in so many words to tell him what he proposed to settle on Countess Vera. The count, greatly disturbed by the question which he had known must come, and had dreaded painfully, answered by generalities:

"My dear fellow, you will be quite satisfied with my arrangements—however, I am glad to see you careful of your interests —that is right, very right"—and patting his future son-in-law on the shoulder he rose as if to put an end to the matter. Berg, however, still smiling, explained with perfect coolness that unless he knew exactly what to count upon as his wife's fortune, and unless indeed part of it came into his hands on the day of his marriage, he should feel under the necessity of withdrawing his pretensions.

"You will agree with me, count, that it would be too atrocious to marry without knowing on what I had to depend for my wife's maintenance."

The count, carried away by a liberal impulse, and anxious to avoid future discussion, closed the conversation by formally undertaking to sign a bill for 80,000 roubles. Berg kissed his future father-in-law on the shoulder in token of gratitude, saying that he should require 30,000, or at least 20,000 down, to furnish his house, and that in that case the bill would of course be only for 60,000.

"To be sure, to be sure—very right," said the old man, eagerly. "But you will allow me, my dear fellow, to give you the 20,000 in addition to the 80,000. . . . Rely on me, I will have it so—say no more about it."

CHAPTER XII

NATACHA was now sixteen. This year of grace, 1809, was the date she had fixed in her own mind as the limit of her waiting for Boris after that kiss given four years since; from that time to this she had never seen him. When his name was mentioned Natacha felt no embarrassment, to her that love-making had been a childish flirtation, and nothing more; nevertheless, at the bottom of her soul, she would secretly wonder whether her promise as a child were not a real pledge that bound her to him.

Boris had never come to see the Rostows since his first departure for the army, though he had several times been at Moscow, and even within a short distance of Otradnoë. Natacha concluded that he wished to avoid her, and her parents' reflections confirmed her in this idea:

"Nowadays," the countess would say, "it is the fashion to forget old friends."

His mother, too, was more rarely their visitor; she had assumed a certain air of dignity, tempered by exuberant enthusiasm for her son's merits and brilliant success. Now, when the Rostows came to St. Petersburg, Boris went to call in the most matter-of-course fashion. His romance with Natacha survived in his mind only as a poetical reminiscence, and he wished to make them clearly understand that their juvenile intimacy entailed no responsibility either on himself or on her. He had a brilliant position in society, thanks to his close friendship with Countess Bésoukhow. His rapid promotion, which he owed to the protection and confidential regard of a man in a highly influential position, required him to crown his fortune by marrying some rich heiress—a dream that might easily be realised.

Natacha was not in the drawing-room when he arrived, but as soon as she was informed that he had called she ran in with a bright blush, and a smile of frank affection lighted up her face. Boris, who remembered her as a little girl in short skirts, with bright black eyes, tumbled curls, and a gay pealing laugh, was astounded at seeing a young lady, and could not conceal the impulse of admiration that came over him. Natacha perceived it, and was glad.

"Would you have recognised your heedless little play-fellow?" said the countess. Boris kissed Natacha's hand, exclaiming involuntarily:

"How handsome you have grown!"

"Of course I have!" answered those saucy black eyes.

Natacha did not join in the conversation; she sat studying the betrothed of her childhood, down to the minutest details. Boris was fully conscious of this friendly but scrutinising gaze, and stole a glance now and then at her, in return. She noticed at once that his uniform, from his spurs to his stock, and the way his hair was cut, were all in the latest and most approved fashion. He sat upright in his easy-chair and employed his right hand in smoothing the well-fitting white doeskin glove that he wore on his left. He gave a sketch of the pleasures of the capital in a tone of airy contempt, and glanced with a spice of irony at the society they had known at Moscow, and their acquaintances there. Natacha was not to be taken in, however, by the incidental way in which he mentioned a ball at one of the embassies, and his invitations to two other grand parties. At length her silence and her quiet observation of him quite disconcerted him; he kept turning to her, and interrupting himself in the middle of his sentences. After staying about ten minutes he took leave, Natacha's keen and mocking eyes watching his every movement. Boris was forced to confess to himself that she was quite as bewitching as ever—perhaps even more so; but he must not dream of marrying her, for her lack of fortune would be a serious obstacle in his future career. It was impossible to think of renewing their old intimacy, so he determined to avoid her for the future;—nevertheless, a very few days after forming this wise resolution, he reappeared at the Rostows', and took to spending the chief part of his time there.

He told himself more than once that he must come to an explanation; that he must make her understand that they must both of them forget the past, and that in spite of everything—well, that he could not marry her; but he never succeeded in attacking this difficult subject, and allowed himself to float down the stream without pausing to think. Natacha, on her part, seemed to think constantly of Boris, or so Sonia and her mother thought. She sang his favourite songs, showed him her albums, and made him write verses in them; never allowed him to refer to the past, but made him understand how blissful the present was; so that he left her every evening in a state of indecision, not having said a word to her of what he wanted to say, and not foreseeing how it could all end. He even neglected the fair Helen, who wrote him daily notes full of reproaches—but they did not prevent his returning to Natacha on the morrow.

CHAPTER XIII

ONE night, when the countess-mother, divested of her additional curls, wrapped in her dressing-gown, and her head tied into a night-cap which only half covered her white hair, was sighing and bewailing herself with much signing of the cross and murmuring of *mea culpa* before the Holy Images, the door was suddenly opened and Natacha, barefoot, also in dressing-gown and curl-papers, rushed in like a whirlwind. Her mother, who was muttering her last prayer: "And if this bed to-night should be my tomb, etc.," frowned as she turned round and paused in her devotions. Natacha, eager and blushing, seeing her at her prayers, stopped short and put out her tongue, like a boy caught in the act, and then stood waiting. Seeing that her mother's exercises did not come to an end, she danced up to the

35

bed and slid in between the sheets of the couch which, as it would seem, had such terrors for the countess. It was a very high bed, piled up with eiderdown quilts and five storys of pillows of different sizes. Natacha was completely swallowed up in it; she pulled up the feather counterpane, crept under it, rolled it round her and covered her head with the sheet, peeping out from time to time to see what her mother was about. The countess, having performed the final genuflexions, came towards the bed with an air of severity which at once gave way to a loving smile.

"Well. . . ." she said: "Have you hidden yourself?"

"Mamma, can we have a good talk—can we?" said Natacha. "One kiss—a little one just there, under the chin." She threw her arms round her mother with her usual vehemence, but she was tender and careful, too, and never hurt her.

"Well, what have you got to say to me to-night?" said her mother, burying herself on her side in her pillows, while Natacha rolling over and over like a ball, came close up to her and stretched herself out with an air of business. These nightly visits, before the count came home from his club, were one of her mother's sweetest pleasures.

"Come, what is it? I want to speak to you, too, about . . ." Natacha laid her hand on her mother's lips:

"About Boris?" she said. "I know. That is what I came about. I say, mamma—he is very nice—very nice, is not he?"

"Natacha, you are sixteen: at your age I was married! He is nice, you ask? Certainly he is, and I love him as a son. But what do you want? What are you thinking about? I can see but one thing: you have turned his head, and what is to come of it?" The countess glanced at her daughter, who lay perfectly still, her eyes fixed on one of the mahogany sphinxes which guarded the corners of the huge bed; the child's grave and thoughtful expression struck the countess: Natacha was listening and considering. "What is to come of it?" repeated the countess. "Why have you set to work to turn his head? What do you want of him? You cannot marry him, you know that."

"Why not?" asked Natacha without moving.

"Because he is very young, because he has no money, because he is nearly related to you, and because you do not love him."

"Who told you so?"

"I know it—and that is not right, my darling."

"But if I choose to do it?"

"Don't talk nonsense."

"But if I choose to?"

"Listen to me—I am quite serious . . ."

But without giving her time to finish her sentence Natacha seized her mother's fat hand and kissed first the back and then the palm, and then each finger as she folded it down, saying: "January, February, March, April, May.—Well, mamma, what have you to say?"

Her mother had remained silent, feasting her eyes on her favourite child. "You are wrong," she said. "No one remembers anything about your familiarity as children, and his intimacy with you now might do you mischief in the eyes of other young men.—Besides, what is the use of tormenting him? He might have found a rich wife, which is what he wants, and as it is he has quite lost his head."

"Has he lost it?" asked Natacha.

"I will tell you of a similar instance: a case which concerned myself. I had a cousin . . ."

"Yes, I know, Cyril Matvéévitch.—But he is an old fellow!"

"He was not always old. . . . Well, I will speak to Boris; he must not come here so often."

"Why not, if he likes it?"

"Because it can come to no good."

"How can you be sure of that?—Do not say anything to him, mamma—I beg you not," cried Natacha, in the tone of a person who is wrongfully deprived of a possession; "I will not marry him if you do not like it, but why prevent his coming here since he likes it, and I like it, too? Why not go on as we are?"

"How, as we are, my pet?"

"Why, as we are, of course. It is quite understood that I am not to marry him . . . very well, then we go on as we are!"

Her mother went into a fit of laughter: "As we are, as we are!" she repeated.

"Come, mamma, do not laugh so; the bed shakes! You are just like me; you laugh as easily as I do. Wait a minute," and taking her mother's hand again she went on with her fortune-telling: "June, July and August—mamma, he is desperately in love; do not you think so?—Was anyone ever so much in love with you? And he is nice—very nice! Only not quite to my taste; straight and narrow like the tall clock in the dining-room. Do not you understand? quite narrow and pale grey . . ."

"What nonsense!"

"Why do not you understand? Nicholas would understand exactly. Now Bésoukhow is blue, dark blue and red; and he makes me think of a square thing . . ."

"I believe you are flirting with him too . . ." and again the countess could not help laughing.

"No, indeed! Besides, he is a freemason. I found that out. He is as good as gold, thoroughly good; but I see him blue and red—how can I make you understand?"

"Little countess, are you not asleep?" said the count at this moment, outside the door. Natacha bounded out of bed, seized her slippers, and vanished into her own room through the opposite door.

It was long before she went to sleep; she was thinking of a hundred things at once, and always came to the conclusion that no one knew how much she understood, nor half her value. "Sonia even! does she understand me?" And she looked at her cousin who lay sleeping, curled up in a pretty little ball, with her thick plaits of hair bound round her head.

"Not in the least! She is so virtuous! She loves Nicholas and cares for nothing else in the world.—Nor yet mamma! It is really very strange—I am very intelligent . . . How pretty she is!" she added, mentally, ascribing this last remark to a third person, a creature of her imagination, a phœnix among men—a superior being. "She has everything, everything in her favour," said this delightful unknown paragon. "She is pretty, fascinating, as neat-handed as a fairy; she swims, she rides to perfection, and what a voice! a marvellous voice! . . ." And Natacha hummed a few bars of her favourite air in Cherubini's mass; then flinging herself on her bed with a happy smile, she called her maid Douniacha and bid her put the light out. Before Douniacha had fairly left the room Natacha was in the land of dreams, where everything was as lovely and was smooth as in real life, but even more charming, for it was altogether different.

The next day the countess had a long talk with Boris, who thenceforth ceased to frequent the house.

THE INVASION

CHAPTER XIV

On the 31st of December, 1809, a grand ball was to be given by a dignitary, who, in the time of Catherine, had been a personage of the highest importance. The *corps diplomatique* were all invited, and the czar himself had promised to be present. The house, which was situated on the English quay, was blazing with lamps; the entrance was hung with red cloth; and all the town functionaries, from the constables to the sergeants and chief of the police, were collected on the pavement. Carriages drew up and drove away, and chasseurs, in full livery and plumed hats, seemed endless. The carriage doors were flung open, the heavy steps turned down with a clatter; civil and military officials in splendid uniforms, glittering with gold lace and orders, dashed out, or ladies, in satin dresses wrapped in ermine cloaks, swiftly and noiselessly passed up the red cloth corridor.

As each carriage drove up, the crowd snatched off their hats asking: "Is it the czar? . . . No, only a minister—a foreign prince—an ambassador—you see his feather?" said one to another; while one man, rather better dressed than the others, could name everyone, and seemed to know all the fresh arrivals.

A third of the guests had already arrived, while at the Rostows' they were still in the bustle of dressing and putting the finishing touches to their toilets. What preparations and what heart-burnings had there not been in view of this ball! Would they be invited? Would their dresses be ready in time? Would everything turn out as they hoped and wished?

An old maid of honour, Maria Ignatievna Péronnsky, a lean and sallow personage, but, as an old friend and relation of Countess Rostow, the chaperon by right of her country cousins, was to accompany them; and it was agreed that they were to call for her at ten o'clock at the Tauride Palace—but at five minutes to ten the young ladies were not yet ready.

It was Natacha's first grand ball, and she had been up ever since eight in the morning in a state of feverish bustle all day; she had but one present aim in life: that her mother, Sonia, and herself should be dressed to perfection—a serious matter which had been left to her sole responsibility. The countess had a velvet dress, while the two young girls, with their hair dressed alike *à la Grecque*, were to wear light skirts of tulle, with moss roses, over pink silk.

39

All the most important part of their toilet was accomplished; they had perfumed and powdered their faces, throats, and hands, not omitting the ears; silk-lace stockings were tightly drawn over their little feet and covered with white satin slippers; the maid was putting the finishing touch to their heads. Sonia, indeed, had her dress on, and was standing in the middle of the room, fastening the last bow to her bodice, and hurting her fingers by trying to push in a perverse pin that creaked as it pierced the ribbon. Natacha, keeping an eye on everything, was seated in front of the long glass, a dressing-cape thrown over her slim shoulders, very much behindhand.

"Not so, Sonia, not like that!" she exclaimed, turning her head suddenly, and putting her hand up to her hair which the maid had not had time to release. "Come here!"

Sonia did as she was bid, and knelt down in front of Natacha, who put the bow on to her fancy.

"But, miss, it is impossible . . ." the maid began.

"There, that is right so . . . look, Sonia, like that!"

"Are you nearly ready?" cried the countess from her room. "It is just ten o'clock."

"In a minute, mamma, directly! Are you ready?"

"I have only my turban to put on."

"Not without me; you will not do it right!"

"But it is ten o'clock!"

At half-past ten they were to be at the ball, and they were to fetch the old maid of honour—and Natacha was not yet ready. Natacha's hair being finished, she jumped up, her little feet, in their satin slippers, showing below her short petticoat, and flew to examine Sonia; then she rushed into the next room, seized her mother's *toque*, fastened it on to her head, and hastily kissed her grey hair. This done, she danced back to hurry the two maids, who, biting their threads off, were hastily shortening her silk slip which had been made too long; a third, with her mouth full of pins, was going backwards and forwards between the countess and Sonia, and a fourth held up Natacha's airy tulle skirts.

"Quick, Mavroucha, please make haste."

"Give me the thimble, then, miss."

"Have you nearly done?" asked the count, looking in at the door; "old Péronnsky will be in quite a stew. Here is some scent for you."

"It is done," said the maid, tossing up the tulle dress which she held high above Natacha's head, and giving it a shake and a puff as if to testify to its lightness and immaculate freshness.

"Papa, don't come in!" cried Natacha, eclipsing her head under the cloud of tulle. "Sonia, shut the door!"

But a minute after the count was admitted; he, too, had beautified himself; he was scented and oiled like a young dandy, in his dark-blue coat, knee-breeches, and buckled shoes.

"Papa, you are lovely to behold!" exclaimed Natacha, inspecting him on all sides.

"One moment, miss, allow me," said the maid, who was kneeling at her feet and devoting all her attention to making the skirts hang of equal lengths, while, by a wonderful manœuvre of her tongue, she passed a whole packet of pins, one by one, from one corner of her mouth to the other.

"It is heart-breaking!" cried Sonia, who was watching all her proceedings. "The slip is too long—much too long!"

Natacha, stepping away from the glass to see better, agreed that it was too long.

"No, I assure you, miss," said Mavroucha, crawling after her on hands and knees, "I assure you it is not too long."

"Yes," said Douniacha, decidedly, "it is too long. But we will tack a hem," and, taking a needle out of the handkerchief she wore crossed over her bosom, she set to work again.

At this instant the countess came shyly into the room.

"Oh! how nicely she looks!—She beats you all to nothing!" exclaimed the count, gallantly advancing to kiss her; but, for fear of being tumbled, she gently put him aside, colouring like a girl.

"Mamma, your *toque* must go more on one side—I will pin it for you. . . ." And Natacha sprang towards her mother so suddenly as to tear the frail tissue of her dress, to the despair of the two maids who could not follow her quick movements.

"Oh dear!" cried Mavroucha. "But it really was not my fault."

"It does not matter," replied Douniacha. "It will not be seen!"

"Oh! my beauties—my queens!" exclaimed the old nurse, who had stolen in to admire them. "Sonia, too — what beauties!"

At last, by a quarter-past ten, they were off and driving towards the Tauride Palace.

In spite of being old and ugly, Miss Péronnsky had gone through the same elaborate processes, but less hurriedly, as she was more used to them; and her ancient person, laced up, scented, and invested with a yellow satin gown decorated with the monogram of a maid of honour, had excited no less enthusiasm in her lady's-maid. She was, of course, waiting, but lavished her praises on the mother and daughters. Finally, after many compliments on all sides, the ladies carefully bestowed their dresses and themselves in their respective carriages.

CHAPTER XV

NATACHA had not had a moment's rest the whole day, not a second, even, to think of what she was going to see; but she had ample leisure during the long drive through the cold and damp, in the gloom of the ponderous vehicle in which she was packed, and jolted or rocked as it might happen. Her fancy painted the scene in vivid colours; the room bright with candles, the orchestra, the flowers, the dancing, the czar and all the brilliant youth of St. Petersburg. The bright vision seemed so remote from the cold and darkness she was experiencing, that she could not believe in its imminent realisation; and she hardly knew where she was, when, after hurrying along the strip of red carpet at the entrance, and taking off her wraps in the hall, she found herself walking arm in arm with Sonia, and in front of her mother, up a brilliantly lighted staircase. Then, for the first time, it occurred to her to think how she was to behave, and to try to put on that calm and demure demeanour which she thought indispensable in a young lady at a ball; but, at the same time, she was aware, happily for her, that her eyes were not doing her bidding, that they were wandering in every direction, that excitement was making her heart beat at a hundred a minute, and prevented her seeing clearly what was going on round her. Hence she found it impossible to preserve the dignity she wished, which would have been awkward and ridiculous; it was all she could do to control her excitement and hide her agitation, and this, in fact, was the behaviour which best became her. The Rostows went upstairs in the midst of a crowd of guests, splendidly dressed and chatting together. Immense mirrors lined the walls and reflected the figures of the ladies in white, rose-colour, or blue;

their shoulders and arms blazing with diamonds or the softer gleam of pearls.

Natacha glanced into the mirrors with some curiosity, but could not succeed in distinguishing herself, everything was so mixed and confused in this dazzling procession. On entering the first room she felt quite dazed and bewildered by the hum of voices, the bustle of the crowd, and the brisk fire of greetings and compliments, besides being blinded by the blaze of light. The host and hostess stood by the door, where they had been for the last hour, welcoming their guests with the eternal repetition of: "So happy to see you!" which the Rostows heard in their turn, like everyone else.

The two girls, dressed alike, with roses in their black hair, curtsied alike and at the same moment; but the mistress of the house involuntarily gazed at Natacha's easy grace; she smiled at her with a different smile from the stereotyped grimace with which she welcomed the rest of her company. Perhaps some distant memory of her own first ball and early girlhood flashed into her mind. The host looked after Natacha as they moved on, and asked the count which of the two was his daughter. "She is charming!" he said, kissing his finger-tips.

There was a crowd round this door, for the czar was now expected, and the countess's party stopped too, just in front of a group. Natacha felt that she was attracting attention; she guessed that her appearance had pleased those who inquired who she was, and this soothed her excitement to some extent. "There are some as nice as we are, and some not so nice!" she thought to herself.

Old Miss Péronnsky told them the names of some of the more interesting people.

"That grey-headed man—do you see?—with curly hair. That is the Dutch minister," she said, pointing to an old man surrounded by ladies, whom he was sending into fits of laughter. "Ah! and here is the queen of St. Petersburg, Countess Bésoukhow," she added, as Helen made her appearance. "How handsome she is! She really holds her own by the side of Maria Antonovna. Look how old and young men rush to pay their court to her. She is handsome and clever; the prince, they say, is madly in love with her . . . and those two women—they are plain enough, as you see, but they are more courted, if possible, than the fair Helen; they are the wife and daughter of a great millionaire! Over there is Anatole Kouraguine," she went on, pointing out a tall and very handsome horse guardsman who had just passed them, holding his head very high, and without seeing them. "Is not he handsome? He is going to be married to the millionaire heiress. Your cousin, Droubetzkoï, is paying her attentions, too. To be sure, that is the French ambassador, Caulaincourt himself," she went on, in answer to a question from the countess. "He might be a king! But all these Frenchmen are most agreeable; no one can be more charming in society. Ah! here she is at last! the fairest of the fair, our lovely Maria Antonovna;—and how simply she is dressed; quite exquisite! That big man, in spectacles, is the magnanimous freemason Bésoukhow. Mercy, what a guy by the side of his wife!"

Peter was making his way through the crowd, rolling his big person, bowing and nodding right and left with his usual easy good-humour, and as much at his ease as if he were crossing a market-place; he seemed to be looking for someone. Natacha was glad to see a face she knew—this "guy" as Miss Péronnsky called him—for he had promised her he would come to the ball and find her partners. He was close to her, when he paused to speak to an officer in a white uniform, a man of middle height with a pleasant face who was talking to a very tall personage covered with stars: the smaller man was Bolkonsky, and Natacha recognised him at once. She thought he looked brighter, younger, and handsomer.

"Mamma, there is someone else we know," she said. "He slept one night at our house at Otradnoë. Do you see him?"

"Oh! do you know him?" said old Miss Péronnsky. "I cannot endure him. He is quite in the ascendant just now, and as full of pride as his father was before him. He and Spéransky are great allies, and he is concocting all sorts of schemes for reforming the laws. Just look at his way of behaving to those ladies. One of them is speaking to him and he turns his back upon her. I would give him my mind if he treated me so!"

THE INVASION

CHAPTER XVI

SUDDENLY a thrill ran through every group; there was pushing forward, shrinking back, parting to make room—the orchestra struck up a triumphant flourish, and the emperor made his appearance, followed by the host and hostess. He passed quickly, bowing to the right and left, and evidently anxious to get through these inevitable demonstrations as soon as possible. He went on into the next drawing-room; the crowd closed up and followed him, till those in front threw them back again, and the doorway was left free; within, the czar was talking to the mistress of the house, while the music played a fashionable polonaise tune adapted to the words: "Alexander and Elizabeth stir us to enthusiasm." An agitated gentleman begged the ladies to stand back; but several of them, ignoring all polite manners, and even forgetting the risk to their clothes, elbowed and struggled into front places, for the couples were beginning to stand up to dance.

Space was cleared. The emperor, with a smile, gave his hand to the lady of the house, and stepping all out of time, led the polonaise. The host came next, leading the beautiful Maria Antonovna Naryschkine; then came ambassadors, ministers, and generals. Most of the ladies had partners and were in the line of dancers; Natacha, with her mother and Sonia, sat out with the minority. Her arms hung idly by her side; her bosom, with its childlike swell, rose and fell gently as she looked about her with bright, anxious eyes; the expression of her face varied as if undecided between great delight and keen disappointment. Neither the czar nor the big-wigs interested her at all now; she had but one thought: "Will no one come and ask me to dance?" she said to herself. "Am I to have no dancing all the evening? All these men do not seem to see me, or, if they see me, they think no doubt that it would be waste of time to trouble themselves about me. To be sure, they cannot know that I am dying to dance, that I dance beautifully, and that I would amuse them too if they would dance with me." The music, which went on playing, added to her melancholy, and she was ready to cry.

Miss Péronnsky had left them to their fate, and the count was at the other end of the room; isolated and lost among this rabble of strangers, no one cared a straw about them or took the smallest trouble to please them. Bolkonsky, leading a lady, passed quite close without recognising them. Anatole, smiling and talking to his partner, glanced at Natacha as he went by with as much indifference as though she had been actually part and parcel of the wall. Boris passed them twice, and each time looked another way. Berg and his wife, who were not dancing, joined the forlorn trio.

Natacha's pride was deeply piqued by this family party in the midst of a splendid ball-room. Had they not time and to spare at home for discussing private affairs? So she paid no attention to what Vera was saying about her dress.

At last the czar had finished his third round—he had taken a fresh partner for each—and the music stopped. An over-zealous aide-de-camp rushed up to the Rostows and besought them to stand farther back, though they were already leaning against the wall, and the first bars of a smooth and inviting waltz struck up. The emperor, still smiling, glanced round at the ladies; no one had yet ventured into the middle of the room. The aide-de-camp who acted as master of ceremonies went up to Countess Bésoukhow and invited her to dance; she responded by lightly laying her hand on his shoulder; the officer putting his arm round her waist led her out into the vacant space; they glided across to the farther end of the room, and then taking his lady's right hand, he set off spinning her round and round, and flying faster and faster as the music accelerated the time to the clatter of spurs, while the fair Helen's velvet skirt floated out like a sail in rhythm to the flowing waltz tune. Natacha watched them with envious eyes, and could have cried with disappointment at not being asked for this first waltz.

Prince Andrew, in his white cavalry uniform and colonel's epaulettes, with silk stockings and buckled shoes, in the best possible spirits, was standing a few yards off talking to Baron Firhow about the first sitting of the imperial council, which had just been fixed for the morrow. The baron, who knew of Bolkonsky's intimacy with Spéransky and of his legislative labours, was gaining from him some accurate information on a subject which had given rise to much commentary and discussion. The prince, however, was not listening very attentively to his remarks; he looked first at the czar, and then at the groups of gentlemen making their engagements for dancing without being able to decide on following their example; and he watched, with amazed curiosity, the men who were bashful in the presence of the sovereign, and the women who were dying to be asked to dance.

At this moment Peter came up to him. "You who still dance—will you ask my little friend, Countess Natacha Rostow?"

"Where is she? . . . Excuse me, baron, we will return to the subject and finish our conversation another time; here our duty is to dance," he added, and he followed Bésoukhow. Natacha's melancholy little face struck him at once; he recognised her and easily guessed what her feelings were; remembering her tones that moonlight night, he went up to the countess willingly enough.

"Allow me to introduce my daughter," she said, colouring.

"I have the honour of knowing her already, but I do not know whether she remembers me," replied Prince Andrew, bowing with a deferential politeness which contradicted Miss Péronnsky's severe opinion of him. He asked Natacha to dance this waltz, and put his arm round her waist. Her face suddenly lighted up, and a radiant smile full of gratitude and delight parted her lips, speaking in her eyes, and chasing away the tears that had been almost ready to flow. "I have been waiting an eternity for you," they seemed to say. They were the second pair to dance; he was justly regarded as one of the best dancers of his day; she, too, danced beautifully, and her little feet flew over the polished floor with no thought of shyness. Her lean shoulders, thin, angular arms, and childish figure could not of course compare with Helen's shoulders and arms, that shone, as it were, with the polish left upon them by a thousand admiring eyes. Natacha was no more than a little girl, wearing a low frock for the first time in her life, and who would certainly have felt ashamed of being seen in it if she had not been told that it was a matter of course.

Prince Andrew was fond of dancing; he had, to be sure, chosen Natacha simply to oblige his friend, to put an end to a tiresome political discussion which bored him, and because hers was the first pretty face his eyes happened to light on. But he had no sooner put his hand round her slender flexible figure, and felt her leaning and floating in his embrace, had no sooner smiled a response to that smile on lips so near his own, than the fascination of her innocent beauty mounted to his brain like new and generous wine. When they had made the round of the room, and paused for breath, he released her as they stood for a few minutes' rest, looking on at the other dancers; and he was gladly conscious of his return to youth and life.

CHAPTER XVII

BORIS, the aide-de-camp who had started the dancing, and several other partners, soon engaged Natacha, who was indeed unable to accept them all, and handed some on to Sonia. She danced the whole evening, her colour rose, she gave herself up heart and soul to enjoyment, and noticed nothing of what was going on around her: not the emperor's long conversation with the French ambassador, nor his attentions to Miss C——, nor the presence of a foreign prince of the blood, nor Helen's wonderful success, nor even his majesty's withdrawal. This she only guessed by the increased energy of the dancers. Prince Andrew danced with her again, the cotillion before supper; he reminded her of their first meeting at Otradnoë, of her wakeful night under the moon, and told her how he had heard all she had said. Natacha blushed at these reminiscences and tried to excuse herself, as if she was somewhat ashamed of having been thus overheard.

Prince Andrew, like all men who have lived much in society, was delighted to come across a being distinct from the herd, and not stamped with the universal monotony. Such a one was Natacha with her childlike astonishments, her unbounded enjoyment, her shyness, and even her mistakes in French. Seated by his side she talked of this and that, the simplest and most unimportant things; he spoke to her with gentle and affectionate delicacy, and was charmed by the radiance of her eyes and smile, which had nothing whatever to do with what she was saying but was the expression of her overflowing contentment. He admired her ingenuous grace while she danced the figure for which a partner came to lead her out; as soon as she came back breathless to sit down, another dancer wanted her to start again—tired and panting she was on the point of refusing, but she could not resist; she flew off, with a smile for Prince Andrew on her lips. "I would rather stay with you," that smile said, "for I am quite tired, but I cannot help it—I am carried off, and I am so glad, so glad!—Oh! I love everyone this evening—and you understand me, don't you?"

How much that smile said!

Natacha crossed the room to ask two ladies to join in the figure with her.

"If she speaks to her cousin first she will be my wife," said Prince Andrew to himself, almost against his will.—She stopped

48

in front of Sonia. . . . "What follies come into my head sometimes!" he went on. "But one thing is quite certain, and that is that so sweet and original as she is she will be married within a month. There is nothing here to compare with her!" and he looked round at Natacha, who, as she took her seat beside him, pinched out the rose in her bodice which had got a little crushed.

When the cotillion was ended, the old count came towards them and invited Prince Andrew to call on them; he asked his daughter if she was enjoying herself. She answered with a brilliant smile. How could he ask?

"I am so happy! I never was so happy in my life!" she said, and Prince Andrew saw her slender arms rise with an involuntary impulse to hug her father, but she dropped them again at once. In point of fact her happiness was complete; it had reached that climax when happiness alone is enough to make us kind and perfect; when we cease to believe in evil, or in sorrow, or in misfortune.

Peter, on the contrary, was suffering for the first time acute humiliation; his wife's position in these higher circles stung him to the quick. He stood, gloomy and absent-minded, his brow deeply knit, in a window bay: his fixed gaze saw nothing. Natacha, as she went to supper, passed close by him; his sad and heart-broken expression struck her; she longed to comfort him—to give some of her superfluous gladness: "How delightful it is, count,—do not you think so?"

"Yes? I am so glad," said Peter at random, with a mechanical smile.

"Can any one be sad this evening?" thought Natacha. "Above all such a good fellow as Bésoukhow!" For it seemed to her that all there must be kind and good, and love each other like brothers, and consequently must be happy.

CHAPTER XVIII

Next morning a recollection of the ball for a moment flashed across Prince Andrew's mind.

"It was a very handsome affair," said he to himself, "and that little Rostow girl, what a sweet creature! There is something so fresh about her; she is so different from the St. Petersburg girls. . . ." And that was all; his tea drunk, he went back to his work again. But somehow, whether it was fatigue or late hours, he did no good; he found endless fault with his work, and could not get on with it; he was quite glad at last of the interruption of a visit from a man named Bitsky. This Bitsky, who was engaged on many committees, received in all the "sets" of St. Petersburg society, and a fervent admirer of Spéransky, was the recognised hawker of all the gossip and rumours of the day—one of those men who always follow the fashion in their opinions as in the cut of their clothes, and who, in consequence, come to be regarded as earnest supporters of every new social doctrine. He snatched off his hat as he rushed into Prince Andrew's room, and gave him at once the fullest details of the sitting of the imperial council which had met that very morning, and which he had just heard all about. He dilated with enthusiasm on the address spoken on the occasion by the emperor—an address in every way worthy of a constitutional monarch: "His majesty said openly that the council and the senate formed the body of the state; that a government must be based on solid principles, and not on arbitrary rules; that finance was to be reorganised and the budgets laid before the public. Yes," he added emphatically, rolling his eyes, "it is an event that marks a new era, a magnificent era, in our history!"

Prince Andrew, who had looked forward to the opening of the council with eager impatience, and had regarded it as a step of the highest importance, was surprised to find that he felt perfectly indifferent to the accomplished fact. He answered Bitsky's rhapsody with a coldly ironical smile, wondering what it could matter to Bitsky or to him, how the emperor had expressed himself to the meeting and how either of them could be the better or the happier for what he had said.

This reflection suddenly chilled the interest he had, till this moment, felt in the new reforms. Spéransky was expecting him to dinner that day—a confidential party, "*en petit comité*," as he himself described it; and this intimate assembly of the closest friends of the man he so greatly admired ought to have had a special attraction for him, as he had never yet seen Spéransky at home and surrounded by his family. But he felt only that it was a bore to have to go at the appointed hour to Spéransky's unpretending residence, not far from the Tauride Gardens. Prince Andrew was a little late; when he arrived at five o'clock, he found all the guests assembled in the dining-room; the house struck him at once by its extreme neatness

50

and somewhat monastic aspect. Spéransky's daughter, still a child, and her governess, composed his family. The guests were Gervais, Magnitsky, and Stolipine, whose voices and loud laughter fell on his ear as soon as he entered the ante-room. One voice in particular, no doubt that of the great reformer himself, shouted, "ha, ha, ha!" in a sharp, piercing laugh, which Prince Andrew now heard for the first time.

The gentlemen were grouped in front of a window round a table spread with *zakouska*.[1] Spéransky had on a grey coat with the star of some order, white waistcoat, and a high stock; the very dress in which he had lately sat at the famous imperial council. He seemed in the best spirits, and was listening with an anticipatory laugh to a story Magnitsky was telling; but the speaker's words, as Bolkonsky came in, were drowned by a roar of merriment from the rest. Stolipine laughed heartily with his big bass tones, munching a piece of cheese the while; Gervais bubbled up gently, like frothing wine; the master of the house seemed to eject his mirth in his shrill, sharp, thin voice.

"So glad to see you, my dear prince," he said, holding out a fine white hand—"one moment. . . ." and he turned to Magnitsky—"remember our agreement. Dinner is a truce—not a word on business. . . ." And he laughed again. Prince Andrew was cheated of his expectations; this mirth jarred on his nerves. Could this be the true Spéransky? The mysterious charm that had won him had vanished; now that he saw him his real self he was no longer to be fascinated.

The conversation went on as before, one long string of anecdotes. Hardly had Magnitsky finished a story when another guest capped it. These narratives referred to officials of every rank and grade, and their intrinsic triviality was so self-evident to the listeners that the ridiculous light they threw on the personages named seemed the only point of the stories. Spéransky himself related how, at that morning's council, one of the members who was deaf, being invited to express his opinion, replied to his interrogator that he "entirely agreed with him." Gervais told a long story of an inspection which had been remarkable for the stupidity displayed on the occasion. Stolipine, who stammered, fell hammer and tongs on the past administration and its abuses; but Magnitsky, fearing lest this should give a too serious turn

[1] A preliminary "snack" served in Russia before the company sit down to dinner.

to the conversation, hastened to laugh at him for his vehemence, and Gervais having perpetrated a joke, they all followed his lead back to a lighter vein.

It was quite evident that Spéransky enjoyed such relaxation after work, and that his friends, lending themselves to his bent, amused themselves while they thoroughly amused him. But this kind of gaiety disgusted Prince Andrew; he felt it heavy and factitious. Spéransky's harsh, sharp tones displeased him, and his perpetual laugh had a false ring that hurt his ear. He did not feel inclined to join heartily in the amusement, but he was afraid of betraying his feelings, and tried again and again to take part in the conversation; but it was in vain. He soon felt that in spite of every effort he could not hit the right note; every word he spoke seemed to rebound, as a cork is flung back by water. It was not that anything that was said at table was wrong or in bad taste; but the wit and pleasantry had not the faintest flavour of the subtlety and finish which are the true salt of such gaiety.

When dinner was ended Spéransky's little daughter and her governess rose; the father drew the child to him and caressed her fondly, but even these caresses seemed affected in Bolkonsky's prejudiced eyes.

The gentlemen remained at table in the English fashion, drinking port, and discussing the war in Spain; they all approved of Napoleon's conduct in the matter. Prince Andrew could not resist the impulse to deliver himself of a diametrically opposite opinion. Spéransky smiled and immediately told a story which had no connection with the matter, with the obvious intention of changing the subject; then, for a few seconds, everyone was silent.

The master of the house took advantage of this pause to recork a bottle of wine, which he handed to the servant, observing: "Good wine is not to be got every day. . . ." And then the whole party, beginning again where they had left off, followed their host into the drawing-room. As soon as he got there two huge letters, brought by a special messenger, were put into his hands, and he withdrew to his own study. He had hardly disappeared before the spirits of the party fell utterly flat, and they began talking seriously in subdued tones; but Spéransky presently returned:

"Recite something for us," he said, addressing Magnitsky. "He has quite a talent for it," he added, turning to Prince Andrew. Magnitsky acceded, stood up in an attitude, and recited some verses of his own in French, full of allusions to persons of distinction in St. Petersburg; he was eagerly and vehemently applauded at various passages. As soon as he had finished Prince Andrew rose to take leave of his host.

"Already! Where can you be going so early?"

"I have an engagement for this evening," replied Bolkonsky. Then they were both silent, and Prince Andrew had the opportunity of studying those glassy and impenetrable eyes.

"How could he have looked for such great things from this man and his labours, or have held him in such high estimation? It was simply ridiculous!" This was his thought; and all the evening Spéransky's affected laugh seemed to be ringing in his ears.

When he got home he fell into a meditative mood, and glancing back at the last four months was startled to see his stay in St. Petersburg in a new light. He recalled his anxieties and efforts, and all the long-drawn red-tapism which had attended his scheme of military reform—admitted for reading by the committee and then set aside because another project of the same kind, very inferior to his own, had been already laid before the emperor! He thought of the meetings of that committee—Berg was one of the members; their discussion had never gone beneath the surface or touched on the root of the matter; he remembered, too, his report on the law, and his laborious translation of the code—and he felt quite ashamed of it all. Then, allowing himself to return in thought to Bogoutcharovo, and his interests there, and picturing himself as applying "the rights of individuals" to the amelioration of his peasants' condition instead of classifying their rights elaborately under heads, he was horrified at having devoted so many months of labour to such a barren task.

CHAPTER XIX

In the course of the next day Prince Andrew paid some visits; among others one to the Rostows, with whom he had renewed his acquaintance at the ball; but this act of simple civility covered a desire to see the bright and charming girl who had impressed him so agreeably in her own home.

She happened to be the first to receive him, and he thought her dark-blue morning dress set off her beauty even better than her ball-dress. She and all the family treated him as an old friend; they welcomed him with simple cordiality, and the whole party, whom he had formerly criticised severely, now struck him as consisting exclusively of worthy good souls, full of kindliness and warmth. The count's pressing hospitality, even more conspicuous here than at Moscow, gave him no chance of refusing his invitation to dinner. "Yes," thought he, "they are excellent people, but it is easy to see that they are incapable of appreciating the treasure they possess in Natacha —a young creature overflowing with life, and whose brilliant originality shines forth so poetically against the background of her family."

He felt ready to discover unknown delights in a hitherto unrevealed world—a world whose joys had dawned on him for the first time on the road leading to Otradnoë, and afterwards, that night at the open window under the silvery moonlight. He was angry with himself for having kept so long aloof from it, and now that he had come near it—had entered in—he recognised it and found it full of fresh joys.

After dinner Natacha, at his request, went to the piano and sang. He sat by a window and listened while talking to some ladies; suddenly he was silent—the sentence he was uttering remained unfinished; something rose in his throat; he felt his eyes fill with tears—honest and tender tears such as he had never believed he could live to shed again. He looked at Natacha, and a sudden flash of joy and happiness seemed to burst into being within him. Sad and happy, both at once, he wondered what could have made him weep; was it the past, his wife's death, his faded illusions, his hopes for the future, or was it the sudden revelation of a sentiment which formed so strange a contrast to the craving for the infinite of which his heart was overfull, and to the narrow, material world where their two natures had met and mingled in a common emotion? This crushing contrast oppressed him while it made him happy.

As soon as her song was over, Natacha came to ask him if he had liked it; but even as she spoke she became uneasy lest her question should be inopportune; he smiled, and told her that her singing had charmed him, like everything she did.

Prince Andrew did not leave the house till very late. He went to bed as a matter of routine; but failing to go to sleep, he got up again, lighted a candle, and walked up and down his room for a time; then he went back to bed. Still, his want of sleep did not wear him out. Nay, to see him you might have supposed that he had lately been released from an atmosphere loaded with heavy vapours, and that he now found himself once more free and relieved of a burden, on God's fair earth, breathing the fresh air in eager draughts! He was not thinking of Natacha; he never dreamed that he was in love with her; but her image was constantly before his eyes, and it lent new zest and energy to life. "What am I doing here? Of what use are all my attempts? Why should I bruise myself in this narrow sphere when all existence lies before me with its many joys?" he asked himself; and for the first time for years he began making plans of life, and came to the conclusion that he must attend to his son's education; find him a tutor; quit the service and travel in England, Switzerland, Italy. "I must take advantage of my liberty and my youth. Peter was right: 'To be happy,' said he, 'we must believe in happiness,' and I believe in it now! Let the dead bury their dead; while we are alive, let us live and be happy."

CHAPTER XX

COLONEL ADOLPHE BERG, with whom Peter was acquainted, as he was with everyone i Moscow and in St. Petersburg, elaborately got up in a spotless uniform, and with his whiskers closely trimmed like the czar's, called on Bésoukhow one morning.

"I have just left your wife, the countess," he said with a smile. "She would not condescend to grant my petition; I hope to have better luck with you, count."

"What is it, colonel? I am quite at your service."

"We are quite settled now in our new rooms," Berg went on, as if he were fully convinced of the pleasure this interesting communication must afford every hearer; "I should like to give a little party and invite our friends—my wife's and mine. I came to request the countess and you to do us the honour of taking a cup of tea—and supper . . ." And he closed the sentence with an effusive smile.

Countess Helen, considering the Bergs quite beneath her, had, however, unluckily refused point-blank to conform to this attractive programme. But Berg made it so clear to Peter

why he particularly wished to collect a select circle round him,
w.ay it would oblige him, and why he, who never gambled and
never wasted his money, was quite ready to be prodigal when
a reception of grand company was in hand, that Peter had no
loophole for escape.

"And not too late, count, I beg; at ten minutes to eight,
if I might ask it. Our general will be with us . . . he is very
good to me; there will be cards, count, and supper—so I rely
on you."

And Peter, who was always too late, was five minutes earlier
than the appointed hour.

Berg and his wife, having completed all their preparations,
were awaiting their guests in the drawing-room, brilliantly
lighted up and decorated with pictures and statuettes. He
was sitting by Vera, buttoned tightly into a uniform as new
as the furniture, and explaining to her how indispensable it
was to have acquaintance among people of a higher rank
than themselves; how, indeed, none others could be of the
smallest use and advantage: "In that way we can always
find something to imitate or to ask for; it is the plan I have
pursued ever since I was first promoted." (Berg never counted
by years, but by promotions.) "Look at my contemporaries
—mere nobodies; while I am within a little of commanding
a regiment, and have the honour of calling you my wife." He
rose and kissed Vera's hand, and then replaced the corner of
the carpet, which had been turned up. "And how did I
achieve it? Above all by my tact in choosing my acquaintance . . . of course by behaving myself and doing my duty
as well!"

Berg smiled, proudly conscious of his superiority over a poor
weak woman, for his wife, charming as she was, no doubt, was
after all as weak as the rest of her sex, and as incapable of
understanding the true worth of a man—the whole meaning of
being a man. She, too, smiled, and from precisely the same
impulse; for she was profoundly conscious of her undoubted
superiority over this worthy and estimable husband, who, like
all men, took an utterly wrong-headed view of life, and calmly
believed himself a person of exceptional intelligence, while
he was, in fact, nothing but a simpleton and conceited
egotist. Berg, putting his arm round his wife, but very carefully, for fear of tearing a certain lace kerchief for which he
had paid a large sum, pressed a kiss exactly in the middle of
her lips.

"And we do not at all want a tribe of children, do we?" he said, leading up, as his way was, to a practical conclusion.

"Oh, dear no!" said Vera. "Above all things, we must live for society!"

"Prince Youssoupow had just such another," said Berg, touching his wife's kerchief with a satisfied air.

Count Bésoukhow was now announced; the husband and wife exchanged glances of intense delight, each taking the credit of having attracted their visitor.

"*That's* what comes of knowing the right people! *That's* what it is when you know how to behave properly!" thought Berg.

"Now, I do beg of you," said Vera, "do not come and interrupt me every minute when I am talking. I know very well what is likely to interest people and what is best to say to the person to whom I may happen to be speaking."   -

"But," said Berg, "men sometimes like to talk to each other about graver matters, and . . ."

Peter came in, and looking round the little drawing-room, saw no place where he could sit without destroying the perfect symmetry of its arrangement. Berg was, in fact, obliged to disturb it; but after magnanimously pushing an arm-chair forward and a sofa back to accommodate his honoured guest, left Peter a choice of the easier seats. Berg and his wife, enchanted at this promising beginning of their party, vied with each other in trying to entertain him, each constantly interrupting the other. Vera, in her supreme wisdom, had made up her mind that the French embassy was a proper subject of conversation, and started it forthwith. Berg, convinced that a graver theme was more suitable, cut in with some remarks on the war with Austria, and after speaking of war in its more general aspects, judiciously diverged into his own views of tactics, spoke of the offer that had been made to him to take a command in this campaign, and explained his reasons for refusing. In spite of the disjointed effect of their antagonistic efforts at conversation, and Vera's indignation at being interrupted, the host and hostess beamed with joy at seeing their soirée so well launched, and as like every other party of the same kind as one drop of water to another—with wax-candles, tea-table laid out, and fragmentary talk.

Boris was the next arrival; his manner to the Bergs betrayed a shade of loftiness and patronage. Soon after came a colonel and his wife, a general, and the Rostows; the party was really quite a soirée! The little bustle occasioned by the entrance of so many guests, by greetings, broken phrases, and the rustle of dresses, filled the master and mistress with ecstasy. Everything was exactly as it was everywhere else! The general, who was exactly like all other generals, admired the rooms immensely, patted Berg familiarly on the shoulder, and then proceeded with quite paternal intimacy to organise a party to play boston, seating himself by Count Rostow, the most distinguished member of the company. The old people gathered into a group; the young men and girls formed another. Vera took her place at the tea-table, which was covered with silver baskets full of cakes identically similar to those that had been served at the Panines; in short, their party was in every detail like any other party.

CHAPTER XXI

PETER was so lucky as to be called upon to play boston with the old count, the colonel, and the general. He sat, by chance, just opposite Natacha, and was struck by the change in her appearance since the night of the ball; she did not speak a word, and would almost have looked ugly but for her expression of sweet and calm indifference. "What is the matter with her?" he asked himself. She sat by her sister and answered Boris, who was talking to her, with absent inattention, not even looking at him. Peter had just turned five tricks when he heard steps and an exchange of civilities, and his eyes involuntarily resting on Natacha he gazed in astonishment: "What is the meaning of this?" thought he. Her face was raised and blushing, and she could scarcely control her breathing as she spoke to Prince Andrew, who was standing in front of her, looking down on her with gentle tenderness. The flame she cherished in her heart had again transfigured her; she had recovered all the beauty which, a minute since, she seemed to have lost. . . . This was the Natacha of the ball!

Bolkonsky went up to Peter who, noticing a look of gladness and youth in his face that was new to it, spent the rest of the time during which he had to sit at the card-table in watching them both. "Something serious is going on between those two," thought he, and a mixed feeling of joy and regret moved him to forgetfulness of his own griefs. The six rubbers ended, he was set at liberty, the general declaring that such bad play as his was beyond endurance! Natacha was now talking to Sonia and Boris, and Vera to Prince Andrew. She had noticed his attentions to Natacha, and thought proper to take the first opportunity of throwing out hints for his benefit on the subject of love affairs in general and her sister in particular. Knowing him to be very swift of apprehension she tried her subtlest diplomacy on him, and she was quite delighted with herself and dilating into eloquence when Peter asked permission to join in their conversation—unless indeed some great secret were under discussion—and then he noticed with some surprise that his friend seemed uncomfortable.

"What is your opinion?" Vera was saying. "You, whose keen insight detects shades of character at a glance; what do you think of Natacha? Do you think that, like some other women,"—and she thought of herself—"she is likely to remain eternally faithful to a man once she loves?—for that is the only true love. What do you think, prince?"

"I know her too little," said Prince Andrew, hiding his confusion under an ironical smile, "to form an opinion on so delicate a matter; though indeed I may frankly confess that the less attractive a woman is the more likely she is to be constant."

"Very true; but in our time . . ." Vera liked to talk of "her time" as people do whose scope is so limited as to lead them to believe that natures change with years, and to fancy that they see more clearly than anyone else into the peculiarities of the times. "Nowadays, young girls have so much freedom that a love of attentions smothers the truer feeling. And, I must say, Natacha is very open to such excitements." This re-introduction of Natacha's name annoyed Prince Andrew, and he was about to rise, but Vera detained him with a more gracious smile than ever. "She has been more courted than most girls, but till quite lately no one ever succeeded in winning her good graces. You, count," she added, turning to Peter, "know that; and between ourselves, Boris—handsome cousin Boris—was very much in love with her. . . . You know him very well, prince, I think?"

"Yes, we are acquainted."

"He has told you, no doubt, of his devotion as a boy to Natacha?"

"As a boy—oh yes," said Prince Andrew, who had coloured scarlet.

59

"And you know between cousins such an intimacy often leads to love; cousins are dangerous friends."

"Oh, certainly!" said Prince Andrew; and he went on to warn Peter with forced merriment against running any risks in his intimacy with his cousins of fifty, at Moscow; then he rose and led him aside.

"What is it?" asked Peter, startled by his excitement and the look he threw at Natacha.

"I want to speak to you.—Our gloves, you know," he meant the gloves which a freemason presents to the lady he deems worthy of his love.—"I . . . no . . . by and by." There was a strange light in his eyes, he turned away, and with an agitation that at once betrayed him, crossed over to sit by Natacha.

Peter asked her something and saw how she flushed as she answered him. But at this moment Berg approached him and insistently invited him to take part in a discussion between the general and the colonel on Spanish affairs.

Berg, perfectly happy, never lost his smile. His party, exactly repeating every other party, was quite a success; the ladies talked the same trivial nothings; the general raised his voice over his game; the samovar and the cakes were for all the world like other people's. One thing only had been wanting for absolute similarity with other gatherings of the same kind; this was something like an animated discussion among the men on a serious and interesting topic. But now the general had crowned his happiness by starting one, and he appealed to Peter to support it.

CHAPTER XXII

NEXT day, by the count's invitation, Prince Andrew went to the Rostows'; he dined and spent the evening with them. No one had the smallest doubt as to why or for whom he stayed, for he made no attempt to disguise it. Natacha, in the seventh heaven of happiness, understood that a solemn crisis was impending; and the impression spread to the rest of the family. The countess gazed at Bolkonsky with grave and melancholy meaning as he sat talking to her daughter, and whenever their eyes met began to expatiate on some indifferent subject. Sonia was equally afraid of leaving Natacha to her fate and of being in the way if she sat by; while Natacha turned pale with agitation when she was left for a second alone with Prince Andrew. His embarrassment puzzled her; she guessed that he had something to say to her, and could not make up his mind to speak.

When Bolkonsky had said good night her mother went up to her. "Well?" she said, in a low voice.

"Mamma, for pity's sake—not now; ask me nothing. I have nothing to tell you! . . ." But that night, in bed, excited and tremulous, her eyes fixed on vacancy, she told her mother all he had said that was kind and flattering, his plans for travelling, his questions concerning Boris, and as to where she and the family meant to spend the summer. "Never, never have I felt like this before . . . only, with him I am afraid! What does it all mean? This time, perhaps—perhaps it really is—really and truly! Mamma, you are asleep?"

"No, my darling. Only I am afraid, too. . . . But go to bed and to sleep."

"To sleep? — How absurd! Mamma, I never felt like this . . ." she went on; the unknown feeling shocked and frightened her. "Could we possibly have foreseen this?"

Natacha, though she was fully convinced that she had fallen in love with Prince Andrew at first sight when he had come to Otradnoë, could not help trembling at the advent of this wonderful and quite undreamed-of happiness.

"It was fated—he was to come to St. Petersburg and to find us here, and to meet us at that ball where he admired and liked me.—Yes, it was Fate! It was to be, that is quite clear.— Even when I had scarcely seen him I felt quite strange, quite different."

"What did he say to you? What were those lines? Repeat them to me," said her mother, trying to recall a verse of poetry that Prince Andrew had written in her daughter's album.

"Mamma, is it not wrong to marry a widower?"

"What nonsense! Oh, Natacha, pray to God. Marriages are made in Heaven."

"Mamma, darling little mother, how much I love you! How happy I am!" cried the girl, hugging her mother, and crying with joy and excitement.

That same evening Prince Andrew confided to Peter his love for Natacha, and his determination to marry her.

There had been a large party in Countess Helen's rooms, the French ambassador was there; and the foreign prince, who had lately been an unfailing attendant on the mistress of the house, had shed his radiance amid a large assembly of men and women of distinction. Peter had gone round the rooms, but everyone had noticed his absent and gloomy looks. Since the ball, and yet more since he had been appointed one of the emperor's chamberlains—in return, no doubt, for the long visits the foreign prince paid to the countess—he was liable to prolonged fits of depression. From that date he never felt free from an incubus of distress and humiliation, his old reflections as to the misery of human life had returned, more black than ever, and were now revived by the sight of the growing love between his favourite Natacha and his friend Bolkonsky, and the cruel contrast between their situation and his own. He strove not to think of them, or of his wife; and constantly, in spite of himself, worked back to the doubts that had tortured him of old. As of old, everything appeared trivial as measured by eternity, and again and again he asked himself: "What does it all lead to?" Night and day he toiled at his freemason's craft, hoping to exorcise the demon that possessed him.

That evening, after withdrawing from his wife's reception between eleven and twelve, he had just retired to his own room, which reeked of tobacco; he sat wrapped in a dirty, shabby dressing-gown, and was writing out the regulations of the Scotch lodges, when Prince Andrew unexpectedly walked in.

"Ah! it is you!" said Peter vaguely. "I am at work, you see . . ." he added, in the tone of a miserable man, who tries to find some remedy for the woes of life in any kind of occupation.

Prince Andrew, radiant and transfigured with happiness, did not observe his friend's gloom; he stood in front of him with a bright smile.

"Listen to me, my dear fellow; I was on the point of speaking to you yesterday. To-day I have made up my mind, and that is why I am here. I am in love, my good friend!"

Peter sighed deeply and dropped, with all the weight of his ponderous person, on the sofa where Prince Andrew had seated himself.

"With Natacha Rostow? Is that it?"

"Certainly; who else should it be? I could never have believed it, but this passion is too much for me. Yesterday I was miserable, I was in torment, and yet I found pleasure in it. Till now I have never lived—I live now, but I want her; and can she ever love me? I am too old! . . . Speak to me; you say nothing!"

"I . . . what would you have me say?" exclaimed Peter,

starting up, and walking up and down the room. "That girl is a perfect treasure—a treasure! A pearl. My dear friend, I entreat you, do not stop to consider; marry her as soon as you can, and there will be no happier man on earth, of that I am certain."

"But she?"

"She loves you."

"No jesting," said Prince Andrew, smiling as he looked straight into his eyes.

"She does; I know it," said Peter, in a tone of annoyance.

"Listen—you must listen to me!" cried his friend, holding him by the arm. "You cannot imagine what my feelings are. I must pour out my heart to you; it is too full!"

"Talk away. Really and truly I am heartily glad." Peter's expression had indeed wholly changed; his gloomy manner gave way to frank satisfaction at seeing Prince Andrew another man than his old self. Where were his depression, his contempt of life, his spoilt illusions? Peter was the only man to whom Prince Andrew could utter all his mind, and his confidence was complete; he told him everything: his plans for the future to which he could now look forward without a qualm, the impossibility of sacrificing his whole existence to his father's caprice, his hope of persuading him to approve of his marriage and be fond of Natacha, and, in case of his father's refusal, his firm determination to marry without his consent. He could not stop talking of this irresistible storm of feeling, to him so new and strange, which had rushed down upon him, and which he could not resist.

"I should have laughed at any man who told me a few days ago that I could love as I do. It is not like anything I ever felt before. The world to me consists of two halves: one is entirely filled by her—there are happiness, light, and hope; the other is where she is not—there desolation and darkness reign. . . ."

"Darkness and night! Yes, I understand that," said Peter.

"I cannot help loving the light, it is beyond my control; and I am happy. Do you understand? Yes, I believe you are glad."

"Yes, indeed, indeed I am!" and Peter looked into his face with his sad kind eyes. As his friend's future grew brighter, his own rose before him darker and more desolate than ever.

CHAPTER XXIII

As Prince Andrew could not marry without his father's sanction, he started for the country the very next day. The old prince listened with apparent calmness to his son's communication, but it was only a cloak for violent wrath. He could not bring himself to understand how his son could want to make any change in his life by introducing a fresh element, when his own was so near its close. "He might have left me to live it out in my own way. When I am gone they can do as they please," was his thought. But he nevertheless used all the tact he usually displayed on important occasions, in discussing the matter with his son; he examined it from all sides, and tried to prove to him, first, that his choice was by no means a brilliant one as to birth or fortune; secondly, that being past his first youth his health required care—and on this he particularly insisted—hence this girl was too young; thirdly, that he had a son, and what would become of him in the hands of the new wife; and fourthly, "I entreat you," he added, looking at him with an edged smile, "put it off for a year. Go abroad, recover your health, find a German tutor for Prince Nicholas; and when a year is past, if your love, your passion, your obstinacy survive, well, marry her. This is my last word—you understand, my last word." And he spoke in a peremptory tone to convey his inflexible determination. He hoped that the test might prove too severe, and that neither his son's love nor the young girl's would outlive a year's waiting . . . or that perhaps he himself would die by then. Prince Andrew quite understood, and made up his mind to submit. He would propose and put the wedding off for a year.

About three weeks after that evening at the Rostows' he returned to St. Petersburg. Natacha, after her conversation with her mother, had spent the whole of the next day in expecting Prince Andrew, but he did not come; and many days passed without his giving any sign. Not knowing that he had been away from St. Petersburg, she did not know what to think of it. Peter, too, had ceased to call.

Three weeks passed in this way, she refused to go anywhere, but wandered from room to room like a languid and forsaken ghost. She had nothing more to say to her mother, she coloured up and turned fractious at a word; it seemed to her that every-one must know what her disappointment was, and that she was an object of general ridicule or pity. Ere long genuine grief was added to her sense of outraged feeling, and increased the misery of her mortification.

One day, when she was about to say something, she suddenly burst into tears, and cried like a child who is beaten and does not know for what. The countess tried to soothe her, but Natacha fired up: "Do not say another word, mamma! I have ceased to think of him—I will never think of him again! He came because he found it amusing, and now he is tired of it and he comes no more . . . that is the whole story! I will never marry," she went on, trying to control her voice. "I was frightened at it before, and now I have quite got over it and am easy in my mind again."

Next day Natacha came down in an old gown she was particularly fond of, as she said it brought her good luck whenever she wore it, and she at once resumed her usual occupations, which had been quite neglected since the night of the ball. After taking her morning tea she went into the great drawing-room, which was particularly good for music, and set to work to sing her scales and exercises. Presently she stood up in the middle of the room and went through all her favourite songs, listening to herself, and finding keen pleasure in her own rich tones and pearly runs which seemed to fill the room, and harmonise with the echo that sent them back to die on her lips.

"Why do I think so much about all that?" she said gaily to herself. "Life is so good, even as it is!" and she walked all round the room, setting her heels down first and then her little toes, with a tap on the polished floor. This noise and the creaking of her shoes seemed to delight her as much as her singing. As she went by a mirror she looked at her own image. "Yes, that is just myself," thought she. "And it is well; I want nobody!" A servant came in to dust the room, but she sent him away and resumed her walk, indulging her admiration for her little self, a not uncommon frame of mind with her, and which she found a very pleasant one. "Natacha is a delightful creature," said she to herself, giving the words to the purely fictitious hero of her dreams. "Her voice is lovely, she is young and pretty, and does no one any harm—cannot you leave her in peace?" But she confessed in a lower depth of her soul that even if she were left in peace, the peace she craved would never again be hers; and she presently proved it by experience.

65

The outer door opened and a voice said: "Are they at home?" This voice snatched her from the contemplation of her person; she was all ears, and though she stood still, gazing at the mirror, she saw nothing there. It was he! She was sure of it, though the doors were all shut, and she heard steps approaching.

Pale and scared she rushed into the sitting-room. "Mamma, Bolkonsky is come; oh, mamma, I cannot bear it! I will not be so cruelly hurt! What am I to do?"

Her mother had not time to reply before Prince Andrew was shown in; he was grave but visibly excited. As his eyes lit on Natacha, his face grew radiant. He kissed the countess's hand and her daughter's, then he sat down.

"We have not had the pleasure of seeing you for a long time," the countess began, but she was interrupted by Prince Andrew with eager apologies and explanations.

"I have been to see my father; I wanted to speak to him on a very serious matter, and I only returned last night. I should be glad," he added, after a short pause and glancing at Natacha, "if I might have a few words with you, countess."

She looked down and sighed. "I am quite at your service," she said.

Natacha understood that she was expected to leave them, but she had not strength enough to move; something was choking her, and her wide-open eyes were fixed on Prince Andrew. "What! Now—at once? Impossible!" she was thinking. He looked round at her again, she understood that so it was, that her fate was about to be decided.

"Go, Natacha, I will send for you," said her mother, in a low voice.

Natacha cast an imploring glance, first at her and then at Bolkonsky—and left the room.

"I have come," said Prince Andrew, "to ask your daughter's hand."

The countess coloured and did not immediately answer.

"Your proposal," she began, with grave embarrassment. . . . "Your proposal . . . is very flattering, and for my part I accept it. I am most happy—and my husband will be too, I hope; but she, she alone, must decide."

"I will speak to her when I have your definite answer—I may rely on you, then?"

"Yes,"—and the countess held out her hand. He bent to kiss it, and she pressed her lips to his brow with a mixed feeling of anxiety and affection; though she was quite ready to love him as a son, this stranger on her hearth gave her a certain sense of alarm.

"My husband will say as I do," she said, "but your father?"

"My father, to whom I have communicated my intentions, has made his sanction conditional on our waiting a twelve-month: this was what I wanted particularly to tell you."

"Natacha is very young, to be sure; but a year—that is a long time to wait."

"There is no alternative," said Prince Andrew, with a sigh.

"I will send her to you," and the countess left the room. "Lord, have mercy upon us!" she murmured, again and again, as she went to find her daughter. Sonia told her that Natacha had gone to her room. She was sitting on her bed with a white face and dry eyes fixed on the Holy Images, crossing herself and muttering a prayer. As her mother came in she threw her arms round her neck.

"Well, mamma, what is it?"

"Go—he is waiting for you; he asks you to marry him," replied the countess, in a tone her daughter thought stern. "Go." And her eyes, full of melancholy and mute reproach, followed the girl, who flew off.

Natacha never could remember how she got into the room; she stopped short in Prince Andrew's presence. "Can this stranger have come here only for me?" she asked herself; and the answer was in her heart:

"Yes, only for me. And he is dearer to me, he alone, than all the rest of the world put together."

Prince Andrew came forward to meet her, but he did not look up as he spoke:

"I have loved you from the first day I saw you. Is there any hope? . . ."

Then he raised his eyes, and the intense gravity and passion of her expression startled him. "Why," her look seemed to say, "why doubt what no one can help knowing? Why use words when they can never utter half of what we feel?"

She took a step forward and stopped again; he took her hand and kissed it.

"Can you love me?" he asked.

"Yes, yes," she said, almost violently; and gasping for breath, as if she were suffocating, she melted into tears.

"Oh! what is the matter? Why are you crying?"

"For happiness!" she said, smiling through her tears.

She leaned forward, hesitated a second, wondering if she might kiss him—and she kissed him.

Prince Andrew held her two hands in his, and looked straight into her eyes: but in this instant the character of his love was changed: the poetical and mysterious longing to call her his own had given way in his heart to tender pity for her weakness as a woman and a child; to dread lest he should fail to respond to her sweet self-abandonment; to a sense, at once glad and distressful, of the obligations that bound him to her under the conditions of this new form of love, which, though perhaps less effulgent and less rapturous than his previous passion, was stronger and deeper.

"Did your mother tell you that we cannot be married for a year?" he asked her, still gazing into her face.

"Am I the same Natacha, who was but a little girl such a short time since?" thought she. "I who have suddenly grown up to be the equal and the wife of this stranger, so clever, so good, a man whom even my father looks up to? Can it be true? Can it be that henceforth I must take life seriously; that I am grown up now; that I must now be responsible for every word and every action? . . . What was it he asked me?"

"No," she replied, not half understanding his question.

"You are so young," Prince Andrew went on, "and I have gone through so much. I am afraid for you; you do not know yourself."

Natacha listened attentively, but she did not take in his meaning.

"This year of patience will be hard to bear," he went on. "But it will give you time to study your own heart. In a year I shall come and entreat you to make me happy; till then you are free, our arrangement will be kept secret. Perhaps you may come to see that you do not love me—that you love someone else . . ." and he tried to smile.

Natacha broke in: "Why do you say such things? You know very well that I have loved you ever since that day when I first saw you at Otradnoë. I love you," she repeated, with the truth of conviction.

"A year's delay . . ." he began again.

"A year! a whole year!" cried Natacha, who had just understood the postponement of her marriage. "Why, oh why?"

He explained the reasons, but she scarcely heeded them. "And nothing can be done?" she cried. He did not answer, but his face plainly showed how impossible it was to fulfil their desires.

"It is dreadful, dreadful!" exclaimed Natacha, bursting into tears. "I shall die of it! A whole year! It is impossible, it is frightful!" She looked up in his face and saw his expression of pity and surprise. "No, no; I agree to everything!" she said, and checked her sobs: "I am so happy!"

Her father and mother now came into the room, and gave them their blessing. From that day Andrew came to the Rostows' as a future husband.

CHAPTER XXIV

THERE was no ceremonial of betrothal, and their engagement was not made public by the special desire of Prince Andrew. As he alone was responsible for the delay, he ought, he said, to bear all the burden of it; and he constantly insisted that Natacha was perfectly free; but that he considered himself irrevocably bound by his word; that if, six months hence, she should have changed her mind, she had an entire right to say so. He repeated this at frequent intervals; but neither Natacha nor her parents would admit that such a thing was possible. Prince Andrew, however, assumed none of the rights of a fiancé; he addressed Natacha with a certain formality, and never did more than kiss her hand. Their simple, natural, trustful manner made it seem as though they had only really known each other since the day when Prince Andrew had made his proposal; and they often recalled what they thought of each other at a time when they were still hardly more than strangers. "We were a little on our guard then," they confessed, "but now we are sincere and frank."

The constant presence of the future son-in-law was at first a little check on the freedom of the family, who were all disposed to think of him as a man in another sphere of society, and Natacha had much to do to reconcile them to his frequent visits. She would declare proudly that she was not in the least shy of him, and that they ought not to be afraid of him either; that he was just like other people, and that it was only his appearance that made him seem different. They presently got accustomed to him; at the end of a few days their life fell into the old quiet groove, and he found his place in it quite naturally, talking of agriculture with the old count, of dress with Natacha and her mother, and of worsted work and albums with Sonia. Many times, in his absence, or, indeed, in his presence, they would expatiate and marvel over the various incidents which had brought them together, and the forecasts that had warned them of the event: Prince Andrew's visit to Otradnoë, that of the Rostows to the capital, the singular likeness between Natacha and her lover—which the old nurse had remarked the first time he had called—the difference between Nicholas and Bolkonsky so long ago as 1805, and various other phenomena not less interesting and significant.

The sort of poetical and silent dullness that always seems to hang round an engaged couple had fallen upon this home; sometimes for long hours not a word would be spoken, even when they were left to themselves. They said very little about the future; Prince Andrew dreaded the topic, and was scrupulous, too, about mentioning it to Natacha; and she shared his feeling, instinctively guessing all that passed through his mind. One day she asked him about his little son; he coloured—as he often did, and Natacha thought it a bewitching weakness—and said his boy would not live with them.

"Why not?" she asked, in alarm.

"I could not take him away from his grandfather; and besides . . ."

"I should have been so fond of him," she said. "But I understand. Your first point is to avoid anything that can entail blame."

The old count would constantly go up to his future son-in-law, embrace him, and ask his advice about Nicholas or Pétia; the countess was apt to sigh as she looked at the lovers. Sonia was always afraid of being in the way, and puzzled herself to find excuses for leaving them to themselves, though they showed no particular desire for it. When Prince Andrew related some incident—and he talked well—Natacha listened with pride, and noticed in her turn, with a mixed feeling of joy and anxiety, how he followed all she said with marked attention, and watched her with a scrutinising eye. "What does he hope to find in me?" she asked herself, uneasily. "What does he expect to discover? Suppose he were to fail in finding what he seeks?" Sometimes he would give way to a fit of careless mirth, and she loved to hear him laugh, because he gave himself up to his merriment all the more freely since these outbursts of light-

70

heartedness were rare, and they brought him down for the time to her own level. Her happiness would have been perfect if the prospect of their parting had not filled her soul with terrors. And he, when he thought of his departure, grew pale and cold.

The day before he left, Prince Andrew brought Peter to call on the Rostows; it was some time since he had been to see them. He looked scared and bewildered. While he sat talking to the countess, Natacha was playing chess with Sonia.

"Have you known Bésoukhow long?" Prince Andrew suddenly asked her. "Do you like him?"

"Yes; he is a dear good fellow—but so queer!" said Natacha, going on to prove her criticism by a number of instances of Peter's extraordinary absence of mind.

"I have told him our secret, for he is one of my oldest friends. He has a heart of gold!—I entreat you, Natacha," Prince Andrew went on, very earnestly—"you must promise me—I am leaving you, and God knows what may happen. You may cease to love me. . . . I ought not to say so, I know. Still, promise me, that whatever may happen in my absence . . ."

"What can happen?"

"In case of any disaster, go to him and to no one else, I beseech you, for help or advice. He is absent, I know, and odd, but such a good soul!"

No one, not Prince Andrew himself, could have foreseen the result that this parting had on Natacha. With flushed cheeks and dry sparkling eyes she wandered about the house that day in painful excitement, attending to all sorts of trifling matters, and not seeming to understand what was happening. When he kissed her hand in farewell, she did not shed a tear. Only she murmured: "Do not go—" in a tone of such anguish, that for an instant he hesitated; and he recalled the sound of her voice at that moment, long, long after. When he was gone, still she did not weep; but she sat day after day in her own room, taking no interest in anything, only saying now and then: "Why did he leave me?"

At the end of a fortnight, however, she came out of this torpid state as abruptly as she had fallen into it, to the great surprise of her family. She took up her usual occupations, and was as bright as ever; but she was changed, as a child's face changes in a long illness: the terrible shock had altered her moral physiognomy.

CHAPTER XXV

OLD Prince Bolkonsky's temper and health grew worse and worse in his son's absence; he became daily more irritable, and his explosions of rage, without rhyme or reason, commonly spent themselves on his hapless daughter. It really seemed as though he took pleasure in discovering the tenderest spots in her nature to inflict the utmost torture. Two passions, and thus two forms of happiness, filled up Princess Maria's whole existence—religion and her little nephew. These, in consequence, were the two favourite subjects of mockery for her father, who was always sneering at old maids and their superstitions, or at spoiling children by over-indulgence: "If you go on like this you will make him"—little Nicholas—"an old maid like yourself. A pretty piece of work, on my word! Prince Andrew wants a son, not a girl!" And he would appeal to Mademoiselle Bourrienne, and ask her what she thought of "our priests," "our images," etc., with a fresh outbreak of bitter irony.

He took every opportunity of wounding poor Princess Maria in the most cruel way, while she never even dreamed of owing any grudge in return. How was it possible that he should be to blame? How could he be unjust to her—for, in spite of everything, he certainly loved her? Besides, what was injustice, after all? She had never thought about this proud word "justice." All human law and duty was summed up for her in one simple and compendious formula: Charity and self-sacrifice, as they were taught by Him, who being God, suffered for love of man. Outside of this, what could the justice and injustice of others matter to her? She recognised no duty but that of loving and enduring; and she fulfilled it without a murmur.

In the course of the winter Prince Andrew spent a few days at Lissy-Gory; his good spirits and gentle tenderness led his sister to suspect some cause for such a transformation; but, excepting that she knew that the father and son had a long *tête-à-tête* just before Prince Andrew left, she gained no further information; but they both seemed dissatisfied.

A short time after she wrote a long letter to her friend Julia Karaguine, just now in mourning for her brother, who had been killed in Turkey. Like all young girls, Maria had cherished a daydream; it was that Julia should marry Prince Andrew. The letter was as follows:

"Dearest and kindest friend, grief is the lot of all in this world. Your loss is so terrible that I can only regard it as a special mercy sent to you by a loving Saviour to purify you and your dear mother. Ah! my dear friend, religion alone can avail, not indeed to comfort us, but to save us from despair; that alone can account for a mystery which, without it, is inscrutable to man: Why God should recall to Himself just those who are good, noble, and happy, while those who are vicious and mischievous are left to be a burden to us. The first death I ever knew was that of my dear little sister-in-law; it made a deep impression on me, and I shall never forget it. I asked Providence why Lisa, that poor little angel whose soul was purity itself, should be snatched away, as you now wonder why your charming brother is taken from you. And shall I tell you, my dear? Five years have passed since then, and my dull mind is only just beginning to guess at the secret of death: I regard it as a visible manifestation of God's infinite mercy— whose acts are too often misunderstood, though they are, in fact, constant proofs of His unfailing love to His creatures. I cannot but think that, with all her angelic purity, she would have lacked the needful strength to fulfil her duties as a mother, while as a wife she was irreproachable. In heaven no doubt she has won a place which I dare not hope for, and has left in our hearts—especially in my brother's—a deep and lasting regret. Not to speak of her gain, her early and terrible death, in spite of the bitterness of grief, has had a most softening influence on Prince Andrew and on me. These thoughts, which at that fatal time would have shocked and horrified me, have only grown up slowly in my mind, but their light has now dispelled all doubt in my soul. I write all this to you, dearest friend, to the end that you, too, may open your eyes and your soul to the gospel-truth which I have made the rule of my life. Not a hair falls from our head without the will of God, and His will is governed by infinite love, which desires nothing but our good in all the chances and changes of life.

"You ask me whether we spend next winter at Moscow. I think not; and notwithstanding the joy I should feel in seeing you, I cannot wish it; and Napoleon is the cause! You are astonished — but the explanation is this: my father's health is perceptibly failing; he cannot bear the slightest contradiction, and his natural irritability is always especially provoked by political discussion. He cannot bring himself to allow that Bonaparte has risen to be the equal of all the sovereigns of Europe, much less of the grandson of the great Catherine. I am as indifferent as ever to all that goes on in the world; but my father's conversations with Michael Ivanovitch keep me informed as to political matters, and the honours paid to Napoleon, whose title and position as a great man and the Emperor of the French are, it seems to me, denied nowhere but at Lissy-Gory. Thus my father foresees that his opinions, and his frankness, which spares no one, and the vehement discussions which must necessarily be the result, would give rise to unpleasantness, and make it difficult for him to live at Moscow. Indeed, the good effect of the medical régime he follows would, I believe, be counteracted by his hatred of Bonaparte. However, all this must be settled before long.

"Here nothing is changed, excepting that we miss my brother terribly. I told you in my last letter how much he has altered. He has only lately come to life again, so to speak, since his wife's death: he is kind, gentle, affectionate, as good as gold—I know no one to compare with him. He has learnt to see that his life could not be at an end; but, on the other hand, his health has deteriorated as his mind has mended; he is thin and nervous, and I am not easy about him. So I strongly approved of his travelling, and hope he may get quite well again. You tell me that he was a great success at St. Petersburg, and is quoted as one of your most distinguished young men, intelligent and hard-working; I never had a doubt about it; and you will excuse my sisterly pride, which is justified by the good he has done on all sides among the peasantry and the nobility of our district. Such praise was only his due.

"I confess I am surprised at the wonderful stories which are current among you, and which have travelled from St. Petersburg to Moscow, as to his marrying again, and to that little Rostow girl of all others!

"I do not think Andrew will ever be able to make up his mind to marry again; at any rate little Natacha Rostow would not be his choice. Though he never speaks of it, I know that the memory of his wife is deeply rooted in his heart, and he will never let her place be filled, or give our little darling a stepmother; and that young girl is certainly not suited to please him as a wife. In fact, to tell you the truth, I have no wish for such a thing.

"But I am ashamed of all this gossip; I have filled two

sheets already. Farewell, my dearest friend: God have you in His holy and Almighty keeping. My amiable companion, Mademoiselle Bourrienne, sends affectionate remembrance.

"MARIA."

CHAPTER XXVI

IN the course of the summer Princess Maria received a letter from her brother, dated from Switzerland; in this Andrew gave her the wonderful and unexpected news of his engagement to Countess Natacha Rostow. His letter was full of the most rapturous love, and of affectionate and tender confidence in his sister. He confessed to Maria that he had never loved as he loved now; that, till now, he had never understood the whole meaning of life; and he ended by craving her forgiveness for having kept his intentions a secret from her when he was at Lissy-Gory, though he had discussed them with his father; he had been afraid, he said, of her exerting her influence over the old prince to win his consent; since, if she had failed, the irritation her attempts would have produced would have fallen on her devoted head.

"At that time," he wrote, "matters were not so ripe or so certain as they now are, for my father had fixed a year for probation; six months have gone by, and my determination is unchanged. If the doctors and their treatment did not detain me at the baths I should have been at home by this time; but my return must be postponed for three months. You know the terms on which my father and I live. I have and ask nothing from him; I always have been, and always mean to be, independent; but half my happiness would be lost to me if I snatched it in opposition to his will, and incurred his anger when he has perhaps so short a time to live. But I am writing to him once more; try to find a propitious moment for giving him my letter and let me know how he receives it, what he thinks of it, and whether there is any hope of his abridging the time by three months."

After much hesitation and many prayers, Princess Maria obeyed his request.

"Write to your brother," replied her father, after reading the letter without any display of wrath, "that he has only to wait for my death—it will not be long, and that will set him free."

Princess Maria timidly tried to argue the point, but her father interrupted her, raising his voice: "Oh, yes! get married, by all means, get married, my dear boy. . . . A pretty family to marry into, on my word! Are they clever—eh?—or rich, eh?—A pretty stepmother indeed you are giving Nicolouchka! And I will marry Bourrienne . . . ha, ha! Then he will have a stepmother, too.—Only, as there are women enough in the house, he will have the kindness to live somewhere else. . . And perhaps you, you also, will join him? Well, go! Welcome! . . . welcome! . . . And the Lord be with you! . . ."

After this violent scene the subject was never again mentioned between them, but the Prince's simmering wrath at his son's weakness constantly betrayed itself in his treatment of his daughter; and a fresh and inexhaustible theme for cruel jesting was added to the old ones: that of a possible stepmother and his admiration for the young French woman.

"Why should not I marry her?" he would say. "She would make a charming princess!'

In fact, Maria observed with dismay that her father's attentions to Mademoiselle Bourrienne had altered in character, and that he liked to spend hours together in her society. She wrote her brother a full account of the disastrous results of his letter, though she still led him to hope that she might succeed in gaining her father's consent.

Little Nicholas, Andrew, and her religion were her only joys and comfort; but as, like every human soul, she could not live without some personal aspirations, she cherished at the bottom of her heart a dream, a mysterious hope which kept her spirit alive, and which the pilgrims she continued to receive without her father's knowledge helped to encourage. The longer she lived and the more she studied life, the more she wondered at the blindness of those who seek satisfaction for their desires here on earth, who suffer, and struggle, and toil, and injure each other, in their pursuit of an unattainable and intangible mirage—the source of endless temptations to sin—which they call happiness. Had she not seen her brother, who had loved his wife, aim at achieving happiness by loving another woman, while her father had yielded to wrath in opposing him because he thought the choice beneath him? . . . They were all suffering for each other's wrongdoing, and risking their immortal souls to win joys that were as transient as a flash of

76

lightning. "Not only do we know it by our own experience, but Jesus Christ, the Son of God, came down from Heaven and taught us that life is but a passage, a time of probation—and yet we will not cease to seek for happiness! No one has really grasped this truth," said Princess Maria to herself, "except those poor pilgrims who come to me, with their wallets over their shoulders, up the back stairs for fear of meeting my father —not to escape ill-usage, but to spare him a temptation to evil. To give up home and family, to renounce all worldly possessions, to wander from place to place under an assumed name in pilgrim's sack-cloth, never to do any harm, but to pray—to pray—for those who despitefully use you as for those who feed and shelter you—that is the true life; life in the highest sense of the word!"

Among the women who had devoted themselves to this wandering existence, one had won Princess Maria's most particular interest. This was a little, frail body of about fifty, by name Fédociouchka, who for the last thirty years had walked the world barefoot and worn a hair shirt. One evening, when she was listening, by the dim religious light of the lamp burning before the images, to the history of her pilgrim friend's peregrinations, the feeling that this poor creature had found the only true way took such possession of Princess Maria that she resolved to follow her example. For a long time after Fédociouchka had departed, she sat lost in meditation, and quite made up her mind that, however strange it might seem, she, too, ought to lead the same life. She confessed her desire to her spiritual director Father Hyacinthe, a monk; having his approbation, she pretended that she wanted to make a present to one of the pilgrim women, and purchased for herself a complete outfit: hair shirt, hemp sandals, a gown and kerchief of coarse black wool. Standing in front of the wardrobe which contained these treasures, she asked herself many a time, with some trepidation, whether the hour were not come when she should carry her scheme into effect.

How often had she been tempted to flee from everything and set off with these women, whose tales, repeated with mechanical monotony till she knew them by heart, had some strange power of exciting her enthusiasm by suggesting a mystical and hidden meaning. She could picture herself tramping by Fédociouchka's side along a dusty road, staff in hand, dressed, like her, in shabby rags, with her bag on her shoulder, and dragging out a wandering life from place to place, with no earthly tie, free from envy, human love, and vain desires, until she eventually reached the place where there was neither grief nor desire, but eternal happiness and bliss.

"I shall stop at a place," thought she, "and pray there; and then, without allowing myself to grow used or attached to it, I shall go on—on and on, till my feet will carry me no farther; then I will lie down and die, no matter where, and find at last that haven of peace where there is neither sorrow nor regret.

But when she next saw her father and the child, her resolve died out, though she wept bitter tears in secret, accusing herself of being a miserable sinner, and of loving men better than God.

BOOK SEVEN

CHAPTER XXVII

THE Bible tells us that a man's happiness before the Fall consisted in the absence of toil. Fallen man, however, has a taste for the same beatitude; but he cannot indulge in it, not merely by reason of the curse that lies upon him and compels him to earn his bread in the sweat of his brow, but by the very essence of his moral nature. A secret voice warns him that idleness is sin—and yet, if only he could be of use and fulfil his duty by remaining quiescent he would no doubt enjoy one of the privileges of primeval bliss. As a matter of fact, a whole class of society —that of the military—lives in comparative idleness which is not only permitted to them but a condition of their life, and which has no doubt always proved one of the great attractions of the service.

Nicholas Rostow had enjoyed all its advantages, since 1807, in the same regiment, and was now in command of the squadron formerly led by Denissow.

He was now very steady—a thorough good boy, rather rough in his manners, which his Moscow acquaintances might have thought not quite the thing; but he was looked up to and loved by his comrades, his inferiors and his chiefs, and perfectly content with his lot. Nothing disturbed his habitual peace of mind but his mother's letters, which had lately been frequent and full of lamentations over the precarious condition of the family finances, and in which she implored him to come home and be the comfort of his aged parents.

He thought with horror of their wishing to tear him from his profession which gave him the means of living calmly and happily, and free from all anxiety; he foresaw that, sooner or later, he would be obliged to plunge into that labyrinth of mismanagement, of accounts to rectify, of squabbles, intrigues and social intercourse—and, added to all else, Sonia's devotion to him and his own promise to her. The prospect scared him; it was all a confused tangle of difficulties, and his answers to

79

his mother, beginning and ending with the regulation formula: "My dear mamma."—"Your dutiful son"—were cold, and threw no light on his intentions.

In 1810, he was duly informed of Natacha's engagement to Bolkonsky, and that the marriage, not being approved of by the old prince, was postponed for a year. The news distressed Nicholas; he could not bear to think of Natacha as leaving the home nest; she was his favourite companion. On the other hand, with his hussar's truculence, he regretted not having had the opportunity of explaining to Bolkonsky that the connection was not such a very distinguished honour, and that if he were really so much in love he might dispense with his lunatic father's consent. Now, should he ask leave of absence to go to see Natacha? He hesitated: it was the season for manœuvring the troops, and besides this the prospect of possible complications at home turned the scale at the time; however, in the course of the spring, another letter from his mother, written without her husband's knowledge, implored him to return. The state of their affairs absolutely required his presence; otherwise everything would be sold by auction and they would be left destitute. The count in his weak good nature had perfect confidence in Mitenka who, like everyone else, took him in, and everything was going to rack and ruin: "In Heaven's name, come to the rescue without a moment's delay if you hope to extricate us from our miserable predicament!"

This letter had the desired effect. Nicholas, who had the sound sense of mediocre minds, saw that there was no alternative and that he must go.

After his midday nap he ordered out his old charger, Mars —he had not ridden him for some time—mounted, and when he brought him back lathered with sweat, some hours later, he announced to Lavrouchka—who was now his servant—and to a party of his comrades, that he was about to ask leave of absence to go to see his family. It seemed strange to be forced to go before he knew whether he had got his promotion, or the Cross of St. Anne, for the manœuvres that were just over; strange to set out without having sold to Count Goloukhovsky the three roans which he had been bargaining over for weeks, and which Rostow had bet he could sell for two thousand roubles. And he would not be present at the ball to be given by the hussars to Pani Pchasdetzka, and to turn the tables on the Uhlans who had just entertained Pani Borjozovska. And what a dismal bore to have to leave this peaceful existence, to plunge into confusion and difficulties of all kinds!—Leave was granted. His fellow-officers gave him a dinner at fifteen roubles a head, with music and a chorus; Rostow danced the *trépak* with Major Bassow; the officers, one more tipsy than another, made fun of him, hugged him, and let him fall; the men of his squadron did the same and cheered him; then they carried him to his sledge and escorted him as far as the first stage.

Throughout the first half of his journey, from Krementchoug to Kiew, Rostow's heart was with his regiment, but as he went on the images of the three roans and of the quart :rmaster faded from his mind, and gave way to anxious curiosity. What should he find at Otradnoë, which he pictured more vividly as he drew nearer to the end of his journey? It was as though this feeling, like a physical gravitation, increased in compound proportion: when he reached the last post-house he tossed three roubles to the postilion, and as he at last drew up at the front steps, he sprang out of the sledge in the greatest excitement.

When the first agitation of his return home was over, he was conscious of the uneasy chill of bare reality which always falls a little below our anticipation; he even repented of the fevered zeal which had brought him home so rapidly, since he found no increase of gladness there. By degrees, however, he got accustomed to the home life, which had not undergone any marked change. His father and mother were older, and an indefinite misunderstanding, a certain remoteness, which had never before existed and which had its rise in their money difficulties, was now very perceptible in their manner to each other.

Sonia was now twenty, in the full bloom of her beauty; she could not be expected to improve any more; but, as she was, she charmed all who saw her. Since Nicholas's return she was radiant with happiness and love, and that faithful and devoted love was a real joy to the young hussar. He was astonished at the improvement in Pétia and Natacha; the little boy, now thirteen, was a handsome lad, tall, intelligent and bright, and his voice was beginning to break already. The transformation in Natacha struck him still more; he watched her with amazement, and could not help exclaiming with a laugh:

"But do you know, you are not yourself one bit?"

"Am I altered for the worse?"

"Quite the contrary; and what dignity, princess!" he added in a low voice.

81

"Oh, yes!" she exclaimed joyfully—and she told him the whole history of her little romance, from Prince Andrew's visit to Otradnoë. As she showed Nicholas his last letter she said: "Are you not glad? I am so happy and so calm."

"Nothing can be better," said Nicholas. "He is a delightful man—but are you really in love with him?"

"What can I say? I was in love with Boris, with my singing-master, with Denissow; but this is not in the least the same thing. I am calmly happy; I stand on solid ground. I see that he is as good as man can be, and I am happy. . . . It is not in the least like anything else."

Nicholas spoke of his annoyance at the delay in the marriage; but Natacha said it was unavoidable, that she herself had insisted on it, as her first wish was not to enter her husband's family against his father's wish. "You know nothing about it," she added, and Nicholas gave way and said no more.

Afterwards, watching her when she did not suspect it, he could not detect the smallest trace of the devoted fiancée who mourns her lover's absence. Her temper was even and bright, she had altered in no essential point of character; in fact, he doubted at last whether her betrothal were so certain a thing as she said it was—all the more since he had never seen her and Prince Andrew together; and he began to fancy that there must be some hitch in the scheme. Why this delay; why had there been no formal betrothal? One day, when he was opening his heart in the matter to his mother, he was surprised, but, in a way, glad to find that, at the bottom of her soul, she felt as he did, and that she had no confidence in the future.

"Just fancy," she said, in the aggrieved tone which most mothers involuntarily assume when they speak of their daughter's future happiness: "Just fancy, he says he cannot return before December. What can detain him so long? He must be ill, for his health is far from good. But say nothing about it to Natacha; if she can be happy so much the better; these are the last days of her happy girlhood, and when she gets letters from him I can see what is going on in her mind. However, who knows? He is a noble and gallant gentleman, and by God's help she may be happy. . . ." And this was always the end of the countess's jeremiads.

THE INVASION

CHAPTER XXVIII

BUT Nicholas was anxious and absent-minded for several days. The imperative necessity for acceding to his mother's wishes, and going into every tiresome detail of the management of their affairs, worried him quite beyond words; the very day but one after his arrival he made up his mind to get through it as quickly as possible and swallow the bitter dose at one gulp. With brows knit and a set face he went straight off, without answering any preliminary questions, to the wing of the house in which Mitenka had his rooms, and desired him to show him "the whole of his accounts." What the whole of the accounts might be, Nicholas had no notion; and Mitenka, startled and confused, knew no better; consequently his explanations were to the last degree muddled. The starosta, the clerk of the village mayor, and the starosta of the district, who were waiting in the ante-room, to their horror— but also somewhat to their satisfaction—heard the young count's voice pitched in a high key, and storming forth a volley of abuse that fell sharp and hard as hail.

"Wretch, rascal, dog, I will be the death of you. . . ." Till at length, to the growing delight and alarm of the audience, they saw Nicholas come out, his eyes bloodshot and his face purple with rage, dragging Mitenka by the collar and pushing him on with powerful kicks and shoves from the knee, while he yelled at him all the time: "Get out, wretch! Get out! Never let me see you again!"

Mitenka, thus shot forward, slipped down the six steps outside the house and rolled into a large clump of shrubs—a frequent shelter and sanctuary for the Otradnoë folks when they were guilty of any misdemeanour; the steward himself, when he came home drunk from the town, had sometimes availed himself of its protecting shade, and others, like him, had found it an invaluable refuge. Mitenka's wife and her sister peeped, with terrified faces, out of their half-opened door, whence issued the fumes of a samovar, and through which a bed was visible covered with a quilt of many-coloured patchwork. Rostow passed them as he came out breathless, and made his way back to his own quarters with an air of determination.

The countess was soon informed by the maids of what had taken place, and came to the comforting conclusion that now everything would be settled without difficulty; still, being

83

uneasy as to the effect this scene might have produced on her son, she went again and again to listen and peep at his study door; she found him quietly smoking his pipe.

"Do you know, my dear fellow," said his father, next morning, "you got into a rage with Mitenka on no ground at all; he has told me all about it."

"Oh, of course!" thought Nicholas. "I knew I should not be able to pull things straight in this mad world."

"You were angry with him for having failed to put down seven hundred roubles; but they are included in the sum total. . . . You did not turn over-leaf."

"I tell you, father, he is a thief, and a rascal; I know it and only did what was right. . . . Still, if you wish it, I will say no more about it."

"No, my dear boy, no, I beg of you look into the thing; I am an old man and . . ." The count broke off; he knew better than anyone what a bad manager he was, and how far responsible to his children for the mistakes he had made and could not rectify.

"I know even less about it than you do, father; so forgive me if I have vexed you. Devil take all the serfs and the money and the sum total over-leaf! I used to know pretty well what was meant by doubling on six tricks, but as to sums brought over! I am quite at sea." And he vowed to himself that he would let things alone for the future.

One day his mother wanted his advice about a "promise to pay" that she held from Anna Mikhaïlovna, for two thousand roubles that she had lent her some time since. What would he do under the circumstances?

"Nothing can be plainer," said Nicholas, "since you allow me to give you my advice. I do not like either Anna Mikhaïlovna or Boris, but we have treated them as friends and they are poor. This is the only thing to do. . . ." And he tore the bill across while his mother cried with joy. Henceforth Nicholas, to fill up his leisure, addicted himself to hunting on horseback, a sport for which they had a splendid establishment.

THE INVASION

CHAPTER XXIX

THE first white frosts had laid their thin film of ice over the earth which was soaked with autumn rains. Where the grass had been trodden, or grew thickly, it stood out in patches of bright green, in the fields where the cattle had been feeding, and the withered haulms of the summer's wheat streaked the pale tints of the spring crops chequered by russet plots of buckwheat. The woods, still densely clothed with verdure till the end of August, like islands surrounded by stubbly fields and black earth ploughed for sowing, were now crimson and gold, and showed in vivid contrast against the tender green of sprouting corn. The hare was changing his fur, young foxes were quitting the nest, and the wolf-cubs were by this time as big as large dogs. It was the height of the hunting season.

Our young Nimrod's pack of hounds, though well trained, had already been rather hard worked, so by common consent it was agreed that they should have three days' rest and that on the 16th of September they would have a day out, beginning at Doubrava, where they were certain to find a litter of wolf-cubs.

In the course of the 14th the cold rapidly increased, and during the day there was a sharp frost, but towards evening the air grew softer and a thaw set in, so that on the morning of the 15th, when Nicholas, wrapped in his dressing-gown, looked out at a very early hour, the weather was all he could wish, perfect hunting weather: the grey sky seemed to melt, to flow, to be softly falling; there was not a breath of air; the beads of dropping mist, so fine as to be almost invisible, rested for an instant on the leafless twigs with a transient sparkle and then trickled down till they were caught on the leaves that slowly fluttered off one by one. The garden soil was as black and shining as jet in the foreground, and at a short distance disappeared under the grey, damp shroud of mist. Nicholas stepped on to the balcony, where everything was dripping with moisture; on the air came the smell of the kennel, and the peculiar fragrance of forests in autumn when everything is fading and dying. Milka, the great black-and-tan bitch, with heavy hind-quarters and large prominent eyes, got up when she saw her master, stretched herself and crouched; then, with one leap she bounded up and licked his face, while another borzoi, with his stern in the air, came galloping up from the garden at a top pace to rub against Nicholas.

85

At the same moment a loud "Ohoï!" rang through the air —the peculiar halloo of the hunter, a mixture of bass notes and a shrill crow, and round the corner of the house came Danilo the huntsman, a man of wrinkled aspect, with hair cropped close after the fashion of Little Russia. He carried a long whip; his expression was that of thorough contempt for things in general—a look rarely seen in any but huntsmen. He took off his cap in his master's presence, but his expression did not alter—indeed, it had no trace of insolence. Nicholas knew very well that this stalwart fellow with his scornful mien was his man, a hunter after his own heart.

"Hey there, Danilo!" he shouted, at once carried away by the irresistible passion for the chase, the day made on purpose, the sight of the dogs and the huntsman, and forgetting all his good resolutions as a lover forgets everything in his mistress's presence.

"What are your orders, excellency?" replied a deep bass voice, hoarse with shouting to the dogs, and two bright black eyes were fixed on the face of the young count who remained silent: "Will he resist the temptation?" those eyes seemed to say.

"Well,—a good day for a hunt?" said Nicholas, pulling Milka's ears.

"Ouvarka was out at daybreak," said the bass voice, after a moment's pause. "He says she went off into the plantation at Otradnoë. He heard them howling."

This meant that a she-wolf he had tracked had gone into the wood with her cubs; the plantation was detached from the rest of the property, and lay about two versts off.

"We must go after her. What do you think?—Bring up Ouvarka."

"Very good."

"Stop—give them nothing to eat."

"All right."

Five minutes later Danilo and Ouvarka came into the sitting-room. Danilo was not remarkably tall, and yet, strange to say, he looked in a room very much as a horse or a bear might look in the midst of domestic furniture. He himself was conscious of it; he kept as close as possible to the door, spoke as low as he could, tried to keep still for fear of breaking something, and made haste to say all he had to say that he might get into the open air again and under the wide sky, instead of standing under the ceiling which seemed to crush him.

Nicholas having questioned the men, and being told again and again that the pack would be better for a run—Danilo himself was dying to be off—ordered the horses to be brought round. Just as the huntsman was quitting the room Natacha rushed in. She was not brushed nor dressed; she had thrown her old nurse's great shawl round her.

"You are starting! I said so. Sonia said no. I was sure you would be off to take advantage of such a perfect day!"

"Yes," said Nicholas reluctantly; for he meant work and did not want to take either Pétia or Natacha. "We are going after a wolf—it will not amuse you."

"On the contrary—you know it will. It is very mean of you to have the horses saddled and never say a word to us."

"The Russian ignores all obstacles—hurrah! On we go!" shouted Pétia, who had followed his sister.

"But you know mamma will not let you go."

"I shall go—I will go, whatever she says," replied Natacha, resolutely. "Danilo, order out my horse, and tell Mikaïlo to bring round my leash of hounds."

Danilo, very uncomfortable at finding himself under a roof, was completely abashed at receiving an order from the young lady: he cast down his eyes and tried to make his escape without seeming to hear, taking great care, however, not to run against her or hit her by some clumsy movement.

CHAPTER XXX

The old count, though he had always kept up a hunting establishment on a grand footing, had ceased to hunt since he had placed it in his son's hands; however, on this 15th of September, feeling well and in good spirits, he decided on joining the party.

The hunters and horses were soon assembled in front of the house. Nicholas as he passed Natacha and Pétia was too much absorbed in his arrangements to heed what they said to him. How could a man be expected to think of trifles at such a serious moment? He saw to everything himself, sent forward the huntsmen with the hounds, mounted his chestnut horse Donetz, and whistling to his own dogs, rode off across country towards the plantation. A groom followed leading a dark bay

87

mare which the old count was to ride, after driving to a certain rendezvous in his drosky.

Fifty-four hounds with forty greyhounds and several dogs in leash, six huntsmen and a whole troop of keepers—in all a hundred and thirty dogs and twenty horsemen, set forth at once. Each dog knew whom he was to obey, and answered to his name; each man knew what he was to do and where he was to stand. When they had quitted the park they silently turned down the high road, but soon left it for the fields, where the horses' hoofs sank noiselessly into the deep turf or splashed up the water in the puddles in the lanes. The dull mist was still softly falling; the whistle of a huntsman rang now and then through the still air—a horse whinnied, a long whip cracked sharply and the truant dog thus recalled to duty whined plaintively. The cavalcade had gone about half-way when suddenly a party of five or more horsemen emerged from the fog, followed by their dogs, and joined the Rostows; at their head rode a handsome old man of dignified mien, with a long, thick grey moustache.

"Good morning, little uncle!" said Nicholas.

"A sure find! . . . Forward, quick march!" said the new-comer, a small proprietor of the neighbourhood and distantly related to the Rostows. "I was quite certain—I said you would be sure to come out; and you were in the right. It is a sure find. . . . Forward, quick march!" he repeated—his favourite watchword. "Close round the wood as soon as possible, for my man tells me that the Ilaguines are out near Korniki and they might carry off the whole litter under your nose. . . . But it is a sure find. Forward, quick march!"

"I am going straight there. Shall we get our packs to-gether?" The order was given, and the two horsemen rode on, side by side.

Natacha, with a shawl wrapped round her so that nothing was to be seen of her eager face but the sparkling eyes, soon came up with them, followed by Pétia, Mikaïlo the huntsman, and a stable lad, who served her as body-guard. Pétia laughed without rhyme or reason and teased his pony with his whip. Natacha, graceful and firm in her saddle, checked her steed's ardour with a practised hand; a handsome Arab, with a lustrous black coat.

The "little uncle" cast a disapproving side-glance at the youngsters, for wolf-hunting is a serious business and allows of no frivolities.

The hunters and horses were soon assembled in front of the house

"Good morning, little uncle; we are of the party you see!" cried Pétia.

"Good morning, good morning.—Don't ride the dogs down," said the old man sternly.

"Nicholas, what a dear beast Trounila is! He knew me at once," said Natacha, whistling to her favourite dog.

"In the first place, Trounila is not a beast, but a wolf-hound," said Nicholas, with a glance which was intended to convey to his sister a due sense of his own superiority, and the gulf between him and her. She understood.

"We shall not be in your way, little uncle," she went on. "We will get in no one's way; we will stay where we are posted without stirring."

"Nothing can be wiser, little countess. Only mind you do not fall off your horse, for if you do, it will be a sure find— no picking you up again! Forward, quick march!"

By this time they were within two hundred yards [1] of the plantation. Rostow and the little uncle having decided from which side the pack should be started, Nicholas pointed out a place where Natacha might stand—and whence, in all probability, she would see nothing—and pushed on beyond a little ravine.

"Steady, little nephew; the old one is the mother! Do not let her slip!"

"You will see," replied Rostow.—"Hi, Karaë!" he called to a dog, hideous from old age but safe to fly at a she-wolf, even when alone.

The old count knew by experience what an eager hunter his son was, and he made haste to join the party; hardly had each man taken his place when the drosky came rolling easily across the level ground, and set down Count Ilia Andréïévitch on the spot he had chosen for himself beforehand. His face was ruddy and his spirits high; he tucked up his fur cloak, and heavily mounted his steady old mare, desiring the coachman to take the carriage home again. He was not a very keen sportsman, but he adhered to all the rules of the hunt; he took up his position on the skirts of the wood, gathered up the reins in his left hand, settled himself in the saddle, and, his arrangements being complete, looked about him with a smile. . . . He was ready.

By his side was his body-servant Sémione Tchekmar, a good horseman but heavy with years, holding in leash three long-

---

[1] Or rather more: the *sajene* is about 6 feet 10 inches.

haired, grey Russian wolf-hounds—a peculiar breed—keen dogs, though like their master, aged, and lying at his feet. About a hundred paces off was the count's groom, Mitka, a bold rider and a reckless sportsman. The count, faithful to an old habit, swallowed a dram of capital hunter's brandy, ate a little slice of meat, and washed it down with half a bottle of his favourite Bordeaux. The liquor and the fresh air gave him a colour, his eyes brightened, and as he sat in his short fur jacket, he looked like a child brought out for a treat.

Tchekmar, a lean, hollow-cheeked fellow, having likewise made himself comfortable, looked at his master—for the last thirty years they had been inseparable companions—and seeing him in such a pleasant temper, proceeded to open a conversation as pleasant as his mood. A third person, also on horseback, an old white-bearded man in a woman's pelisse and wearing a preposterously high cap, now came noiselessly to the spot, and drew up a little way behind the count.

"Well, Nastacia Ivanovna,"—Nastacia was the buffoon of the neighbourhood—"mind what you are about. If you frighten the brute you know what Danilo will have to say to you." The count spoke in a whisper and winked at the fellow.

"Oh, I have teeth and nails, too," replied Nastacia Ivanovna.

"Hush—hush!" whispered the count, then turning to Sémione he asked: "Have you seen Natacha Ilinischna? Where is she?"

"With her brother, near the thicket by Yarow: what a treat for her, and she is quite a young lady, too!"

"But is it not wonderful to see her on horseback, Sémione? How she rides! She might be a man!"

"It is really wonderful! She is afraid of nothing, and so firm in her saddle!"

"And where is Nicholas?"

"Out by Liadow. . . . Never fear, he knows the best places—and what a rider! Danilo and I wonder to see him sometimes!" said Sémione, who was very ready to flatter his master.

"Aye, aye, sits a horse well, doesn't he?"

"Quite a picture! The other day, for instance, in the plain by Zavarzine, when he was riding down the fox on that horse of his. It cost a thousand roubles—but the rider is beyond price! And such a handsome fellow! You would have to look a long time to find a match for him!"

"Aye, aye," said the count again. "Yes, indeed. . . ."

And he picked up the skirt of his fur cloak and felt in his pocket for his snuff-box.

"Then the other day," Sémione went on, seeing how much pleasure he was giving his master, "coming out of church, when Michael Sidorovitch met him .. .." but Sémione broke off short; the rush of the pack in hot pursuit, and the barking of some of the dogs struck his ear through the still air; he put down his head and made a sign to the count to keep silence: "They have found the scent," he whispered, "they are going off towards Liadow."

The count, still smiling over Sémione's last speech, sat gazing into the distance with his snuff-box in his hand, without thinking of taking a pinch. Danilo's horn warned them that the wolf had been seen; the packs followed close to the three leading hounds, and all gave tongue in the peculiar note that meant they were on the scent of a wolf. The whips now only shouted encouragement. Above all other voices and cries Danilo's was distinctly heard, passing from the deepest bass to the shrillest yell, and loud enough by itself to ring through the wood and far across the country with its cheering call.

The count and his squire soon perceived that the pack had been divided; one half, barking vociferously, was becoming more distant and the others, driven by Danilo, were breaking through the wood at a few paces from where they were posted; presently the direction of the noise told them that the hunt was moving farther afield. Sémione sighed and freed one of the hounds that was entangled in the leash; the count, too, sighed, and his attention reverting to his snuff-box, he opened it and took a pinch.

"Back!" cried Sémione at this instant to one of the dogs that was struggling to make for the open. The count was startled and let his snuff-box fall. Nastacia dismounted and picked it up.

Suddenly—as will happen occasionally—the hunt was coming their way; all those yelping, baying throats seemed to be close in front of them—upon them!

The count looked to the right and caught sight of Mitka, who, with his eyes starting out of his head, was signalling to him with his cap to look at something in the opposite direction. "Look out!" he shouted in a voice that was all the louder for long suppression; and slipping the dogs, he rode up at full gallop.

The count and Sémione rushed out of the wood, and, on their left, saw the wolf coming towards them at a swinging trot, with easy bounds and no appearance of hurry. The excited dogs tore themselves free, and flung themselves on his track.

The brute paused, turned his heavy head to look at them, with the deliberate awkwardness of a man suffering from angina, then, cocking his tail, went on his way and in two leaps vanished in the thicket. At the same moment, from the opposite skirt of the plantation, out came a dog, then another; then the whole pack, astray and puzzled, crossed the clearing in pursuit of the game, and Danilo's chestnut, covered with foam, came pushing his way between the nut-trees. The rider, bending as low as he could, and bareheaded, his grey hair all on end, his face red and streaming, was shouting till his voice cracked to rally the dogs. But when he saw the count his eyes flashed fire. He threatened him with his whip, roaring out a thundering oath: "Devil take such hunters! . . . To have let the game slip! . . ."

Judging, no doubt, that his master, who looked quite scared, was unworthy of further comment, he let the blow that had been meant for the count fall on the quivering and steaming flank of his innocent steed, and disappeared among the trees after the hounds. The count, taken aback by this audacious scolding, tried to smile and turned to Sémione with a look of pathetic appeal; but Sémione was gone too. Riding in and out of the brushwood he was trying to start the wolf again, and the hounds, were working right and left; but the beast sneaked off through the cover and was soon lost to their ken.

CHAPTER XXXI

NICHOLAS, expecting every minute to see the wolf pass, had not left his post; and as he heard the cry—sometimes near and sometimes far—and the different bark of the hounds under various circumstances, when the shouts and yelping were at their height, he could form a good idea of what was happening. He understood that there must be two old wolves in the plantation with their cubs; that the pack had divided after finding the two tracks; and he instinctively felt that some bad luck had come in the way. Then he invented a thousand theories, and tried to calculate which side the game would come from, and how he would finish it—but nothing came. His hopes turned to despair; he even found himself praying—entreating Providence—as we do under the stress of some feeling, even while owning to ourselves the triviality of the object prayed for.

"Why not grant me this?" he muttered. "Thou, O Lord, art great, and perhaps it is a sin to long for it, but I implore Thee, O God! Let one of the two old wolves come my way, so that Karaë may fly at the beast's throat and bring him down— here, where little uncle can see him! . . ." And during this half-hour his restless, eager eye had examined again and again every furrow of the clearing that lay before him—every inch of the plantation close by, where two gnarled oaks stretched their boughs over a clump of young aspens, and the ravine with its water-worn banks; while the "uncle's" cap towered above the scrub on his left.

"No; it is just my luck—everywhere the same," he said to himself. "In war, at play—always the same thing; at Auster- litz, and that evening at Dologhow's! Only this once! Only just once grant me the joy of seeing a big wolf killed!" . . . he prayed. . . .

He strained his eyes to mark the slightest movement, and his ear to catch the faintest change of tone in the cry of the hounds. Presently, as he glanced again to the right, he saw something come leaping towards him, across the open ground. "Is it possible!"—he could scarcely breathe in the agitation of seeing his hopes on the eve of fulfilment; and this piece of good fortune, so hoped for and despaired of, was coming straight down upon him, noiselessly, with no preliminary fuss or warn- ing. He could hardly believe his eyes, but soon it was beyond a doubt. It was the wolf, and no mistake—an old wolf, with a grey coat and russet belly, trotting at his ease, safe from pursuit, striding heavily across ridge and furrow.

Rostow, holding his breath, looked at his dogs: some were lying down, others standing by, but none had seen the game— not even old Karaë, who, with his head thrown back and his muzzle half-open, showing his yellow teeth, clattered his jaws while he hunted the fleas on his hind leg. "Up, dogs! Wolf!" said Rostow in a low voice. The dogs pricked up their ears, and Karaë, ceasing his search, started up as if he moved by a spring, wagging his tail, and shedding a few tufts of hair.

"Shall I slip the leash?" said Nicholas to himself.

The wolf, quitting the cover, was coming on in a direct line, suspecting nothing. Suddenly he checked himself: he had just seen a man's eyes fixed on him, no doubt—a sight hitherto unknown to his experience. He stood hesitating and seeming to reflect: Should he turn back, or go on? "Beware," he seemed to think. He started again with apparent indifference, but at a round pace, and went off with long leaps, and without looking behind him.

"At him! Wolf!" shouted Nicholas. His clever bay went off like an arrow over hedge and rut, to reach the open after the wolf. The hounds, swift as lightning, soon outstripped him. Nicholas, perfectly unconscious of all minor details—of his own shout, of the terrific pace at which he was riding, and of the ground he was riding over—saw nothing but the wolf. The brute, without turning to the right or left, went faster and faster, straight for the hollow. Milka, the large brindled hound, was the first to overtake him; nearer and nearer—she was on the point of gripping him when he just cast a side glance at the foe, and Milka, instead of setting her teeth in him, as usual, cocked her stern.

"At him! Wolf!" yelled Nicholas. Liubime, a large red-haired dog, close on Milka's heels, flew at the brute and gripped his haunch, but shrunk off again in alarm. The wolf crouched for an instant, and showed his teeth, then he galloped on again, followed, within a couple of feet,[1] by the dogs who dared not attack him.

"He will escape to a certainty!" thought Nicholas, and he tried to incite the dogs, but his voice was husky; he looked round for his staunch old hound, his only hope, and shouted to him with a vigorous call: "Karaë—Wolf! At him!"

Karaë, with every muscle strained to the utmost his age allowed, was keeping pace side by side with the terrible brute, evidently intending to outrun him, and attack him in front; but Nicholas could see from the swift wiry action of the wild beast, and the heavier pace of the dog, that this manœuvre would be frustrated. He saw with horror that the space between the animals and the copse, which would be the salvation of the wolf, was diminishing rapidly; but in a moment his hopes revived, for, beyond the wolf and coming towards him, a huntsman and several dogs were now approaching. One, a dark-coloured hound, unknown to Nicholas, and belonging, no doubt, to a strange pack, flew at the brute, and nearly overthrew him; but he recovered his balance, and attacked the dog with amazing nimbleness, setting his teeth in his flesh; and the

[1] An *archine*, about 28 inches.

hapless aggressor, with a gash in his loins, beat his head on the earth with howls of anguish.

"Karaë! oh, merciful Heaven!" cried Nicholas, in despair.

The wolf, scenting fresh danger from old Karaë—who, now that his foe was checked, barred his way—tucked his tail between his legs and went off with a bound at a tremendous pace; but, wonder of wonders! Nicholas saw Karaë suddenly leap on the brute's back and set his teeth in his throat, and then wolf and dog rolled over together, and down into the dell beyond.

The whole pack rushed after them. The sight of the struggling wolf down in the hollow, in the midst of that chaos of heads, where all that appeared of the prey was now and then his dull fur or a kicking hind leg, or his panting muzzle with ears laid back—for Karaë still gripped him by the throat—was one of the keenest delights Rostow had ever known. He laid his hand on his saddle, and was about to dismount and go down to dispatch the foe, when the brute, shaking his great head free above the dogs, sat upon his haunches; then, showing his teeth, with a whisk of his tail, he leaped up and was out of reach in an instant. Karaë, either wounded or bruised, and with his hair on end, dragged himself with difficulty out of the ravine into which he had fallen with the wolf.

"Oh! what a grievous pity!" cried Nicholas, in despair.

Fortunately the little uncle's huntsman, followed by his dogs, was ready to fly off at a gallop after the fugitive and intercept him in time. He was again surrounded; Nicholas, his groom, and the little uncle with his huntsman, all pranced round him, shouting: "At him! Wolf!" prepared, whenever he crouched, to jump off their horses, and riding forward to circumvent him each time he pulled himself together to make a rush for the thicket, which was his last and only chance for life.

At the very beginning Danilo had come tearing out of the plantation, and, looking on at the struggle, had taken the victory for granted; but seeing the brute make good his escape, he rode off in a straight line to the copse to cut off his retreat, and, thanks to this manœuvre, came up with him just as the little uncle's pack once more held him at bay. Danilo rode up without a word, his bare knife in his left hand, while he flogged his bay with his huntsman's whip as if it had been a flail, till the foam lay in streaks on his reeking flanks. He flew past Nicholas, and the next instant Rostow heard a heavy fall; it was Danilo, who had thrown himself on the wolf's haunches and seized him by the ears. They all—even the wolf—knew that this was the finish. The foe made a final effort to free himself, but the dogs held him fast. Danilo rose and then again dropped with all his weight on the brute, still gripping him by the ears. Nicholas went forward to stab the panting beast.

"No need for that," said Danilo. "We will put a bit between his teeth!" He set foot on the wolf's throat, and forced a short thick stake between his tightly-set jaws; then the men tied his legs, and Danilo took the brute on his broad shoulders.

Tired, but triumphant, all helped to tie the wolf on the back of Danilo's horse which stood quivering with alarm, and he was carried off to the rendezvous of the hunt, followed by all the dogs in full cry. Everyone came up to examine the victim, whose great, square head hung down from the weight of the stake in his jaws, while his glassy eyes glared at the crowd of dogs and men. His limbs trembled at every touch. Count Ilia Andréïévitch came up with the rest: "Ah! an old one! It is an old one, is not it?" he said to Danilo.

"Certainly, an old one," said Danilo, taking his cap off respectfully.

"Do you know you were in a terrible rage just now?"

Danilo did not reply, but he smiled with the embarrassed shy look of a spoilt child.

CHAPTER XXXII

THE old count rode home; Natacha and Pétia promising to follow him soon. The day was still young, and they took advantage of it to ride a little farther. Two dogs were sent into a thick cover at the bottom of the dell, and Nicholas took up a position whence he could see all the men. His beater, placed just opposite to him, stood hidden in a ditch and screened by a clump of nut-trees. The dogs were hardly out of sight when they gave tongue, and in a few minutes the view halloo rang out; the pack rushed off towards the open, and Nicholas, waiting to catch sight of the fox on the level, saw the huntsmen in their red caps ride on to the front. His man had only just time to slip the dogs, when he spied a red fox of peculiar colour and shape scurrying across country; the pack had surrounded it in a moment. Sweeping the ground with his brush, the fox ran round and round in decreasing circles, till one dog—a white

The day was still young

one—gripped him; then a black one; the mêlée was general; the dogs' heads, all turned on the prey, formed an irregular circle, but he could scarcely distinguish their movements. Two huntsmen, one in a red cap and one wearing a green overcoat, went up together.

"What is the meaning of that? Where does that strange huntsman come from? It is not the little uncle's man!" thought Nicholas.

The huntsmen dispatched the fox, but it seemed to him, from a distance, that they still stood in a knot, close to their horses, without tying the beast up; some of the dogs had lain down, while the men were gesticulating fiercely and pointing to the carcass; presently a bugle call was sounded, announcing that a dispute had arisen.

"It is one of Ilaguine's men quarrelling with Ivan," said the groom. Nicholas sent the man back to fetch Natacha and Pétia, and slowly rode forward to the spot where the keepers were collecting the pack; there he dismounted and waited, with Natacha and Pétia who had just ridden up, for the issue of the squabble. The huntsman who had been taken to task by the other came towards his young master, with the fox hung up to his saddle. He took off his hat, and made evident efforts to be respectful though he was choking with rage; he had a black eye, too, but of this he did not seem to be aware.

"What is going on here?" said Nicholas.

"Are they to be allowed to hunt with our dogs? And it was my mouse-coloured dog, too, that nipped him. . . . He would not listen to reason, and had got hold of the fox when I came up—and I rolled them over together. Here is the fox, properly tied up. . . . Perhaps you would like a taste of this!" he went on fiercely, and he drew his knife—he fancied, no doubt, that he was still haranguing his adversary.

Nicholas turned to Pétia and Natacha, and begged them to wait while he went to try to settle the matter. The victorious huntsman was telling all the details of his achievement to his comrades, who were full of sympathetic curiosity.

It happened that Ilaguine, who was on bad terms with the Rostows, and, indeed, carrying on a law-suit against the count, was hunting that very day over ground which, by custom and tradition, had long been regarded as theirs; and, as if he had done it on purpose, he had chosen to go to the wood where they were stationed, and had even allowed his man to follow the fox that the Rostows had put up.

Nicholas, who knew no moderation in his feelings and opinions, was not personally acquainted with Ilaguine; but he accepted for truth certain reports of arbitrary and violent behaviour on his part and hated him cordially; so he went straight up to him, gripping his whip, and quite prepared to come to blows without a moment's reflection. As soon as he got out of the wood his eyes fell on a big horseman, wearing a cap bordered with beaver, riding a fine black horse, and followed by two grooms; this was Ilaguine himself.

But instead of a foe to be summarily dealt with, Nicholas found himself face to face with an amiable gentleman, well-bred, and anxious to make his acquaintance; who lifted his cap, expressed the greatest regret at the quarrel between their followers; assured him that his huntsman should be severely punished for hunting with any pack but his own, and finally invited Rostow to hunt on his, Ilaguine's, land.

Natacha, who had felt very uneasy lest the interview should take a serious turn, had followed her brother at a distance; now, seeing the adversary bowing and amiable, she joined the group. Ilaguine immediately took off his hat and expressed his admiration of the young huntress, declaring that she was like Diana, no less by her love of sport than by her beauty. To win forgiveness for his man's misdemeanour, he entreated Rostow to come with him at once and start a hare at a spot about a verst farther on, which, as he said, swarmed with hares. Nicholas was quite willing, and the army of hunters, thus considerably increased, was once more put in motion.

They had to ride across country; the gentlemen rode together, each of them furtively examining his neighbour's pack, and quaking at the possibility of finding him possessed of a dog superior to any of his own in form or scent.

Rostow was particularly struck by the beauty of one pure-bred hound, long in the body, with muscles like cast steel, a fine sharp nose, prominent black eyes, and spotted with tan; it belonged to Ilaguine. He had heard much of the swiftness of some of Ilaguine's coursing dogs, and saw that this perfect little dog was a match for his own Milka. In the midst of a dull conversation on the crops, he suddenly said, turning to Ilaguine: "You have a nice dog there, it strikes me. Full of go?"

"That one? Yes, she is a good dog, does her work well," said Ilaguine, affecting indifference, though, in fact, Erza had cost him three families of house-servants.

"Then you, too, had a bad harvest this summer," he went

on, taking up the thread of the conversation. Then, feeling that he ought to return the compliment, he added: "But you, count, have a splendid dog, too—that one with black spots."

"Milka? Yes, she is not a bad dog—a good one to go. . . . You will soon see," added Nicholas to himself, "what sort of a dog Milka is, if only we can put up an old hare," and he turned to his groom and told the man he would give anyone a rouble who would find a hare on her form.

"I cannot understand," Ilaguine went on, "how sportsmen can be so jealous about each other's packs, and the game they kill. For my part I enjoy the whole thing—the ride, and pleasant company—such as I have lighted on to-day, for instance"—and he lifted his hat to Natacha. "But as to counting skins or heads, that is not in my line; indeed, to tell you the truth, I really do not care about it."

"And you are quite right."

"What do I care if my dog is out of luck; I can watch the run with just as much interest. Besides . . ."

A shrill halloo from one of the beaters interrupted him; the man was standing on a hillock holding up his whip, and now repeated his call; that was the signal that a hare was squatting a few feet in front of him.

"I believe he has found her," said Ilaguine with affected indifference. "Well, let us give her a run."

"Come on—let us all go," said Nicholas, with a glance of defiance at Erza and uncle's Rougaï, his Milka's two rivals, though they had never been pitted against each other before. "And if she were to be ignominiously beaten?" thought he, as he went forward.

"Is it an old hare?" asked Ilaguine, and he whistled to Erza, not without anxiety. "And you, Michael Niknoro-vitch?" he added, turning to the little uncle, who looked extremely sullen.

"I will have nothing to do with it. Your dogs!—a sure find; forward, quick march!—Why, they cost a village each and are worth thousands of roubles!—I will look on while your dogs settle it between them!—Rougaï, good dog," he added, with all the affection and confidence he felt as he called his favourite.

Natacha understood and shared her brother's excitement, and the anxiety which he and the two elder men vainly tried to conceal.

The pack and the rest of the hunting party followed more

slowly; the beater who had found the hare still stood on his little knoll without moving, waiting for the gentlemen.

"Which way is her head?" asked Nicholas; but the hare did not give time for the answer. With one bound she was off; the dogs rushed down the slope after her, and the horsemen started at a gallop; some to help the dogs to turn her, and some to keep their heads in the right direction. Ilaguine, Natacha, and the little uncle flew on, without heeding where they were going—now following the dogs, and now pursuing the game, dying with terror lest they should lose their match. The hare was old and strong; laying back her ears to listen to the shouts and the tramp of horses and dogs that had so suddenly closed her in on all sides, she took a few long leaps, and then, as the dogs came nearer, understanding her danger, she chose her course, cocked first one ear and then the other, put forth her utmost speed and made towards the stubble. A few yards ahead lay a marshy meadow. The two dogs belonging to the beater who had put her up were the first to get the scent, but they had not come up with her when Erza, Ilaguine's dog, outstripped them. Within a short distance of the game she made a leap to stop it; but she missed her spring, fell, and rolled over. Then Milka tore down upon the hare and gained upon her.

"Miloucha, good dog! My little Miloucha!" cried Nicholas, his triumphant shout ringing through the air. Milka seemed to be on the point of seizing the hare, but her impetus carried her too far, the hare having stopped short. Erza now came to the front again; she leaped forward: to see her fly through the air it might have been thought that she had measured, this time with careful accuracy, the distance she must take to fall exactly on her prey.

"Erza, well done, Erza!" cried Ilaguine, with a pathetic intonation that Erza did not stay to listen to, for at the moment when she was about to nip the game it was off again, along the ridge between the field and the meadow beyond. Erza and Milka, running side by side like a well-matched pair, had gained on the hare, but she found the going on the ridge easier, and the hounds could not overtake her quite so quickly.

"Rougaï. Have her, Rougaï!—a sure find, forward, quick march!" shouted a third voice, and Rougaï, the little uncle's round-shouldered dog, bending his back and stretching his legs, came up with the others, passed them, and by a supernatural effort seized the hare, which with one nip he flung back into

100

the field; he caught it with another spring, and then rolled over with it into the mud, which stuck to his skin in large patches.

The men and dogs gathered round them. The little uncle, triumphantly happy, dismounted, picked up the game and cutting off the pads shook them in the air for the blood to drop off. His excitement sparkled in his eyes which wandered in every direction with a scared look; he moved with rough jerks and his words were incoherent: "A sure find . . . forward!—There is a dog for you! He is worth all the others put together, dear or cheap! . . . A sure find—forward, quick march!" He was hoarse and breathless, and to see the furious glances he cast on the others it might have been supposed that he thought them all his enemies, and that after being insulted and ill-used, he had just achieved some brilliant reprisals:

"Look at your thousand-rouble dogs! Here, Rougaï, old boy, you may have that; you have earned it well!" and he threw him one of the hare's muddy pads.

"She is quite done up—she ran the game down three times by herself," said Nicholas, not addressing anyone in particular, and paying no heed to what was going on around him.

"He took her sideways; a pretty way of doing it!" said Ilaguine's groom.

"Of course when Erza had run her out, any dog could grip her—a farmyard cur even!" added Ilaguine, whose face was crimson and his breath short after his mad ride.

Natacha, no less excited, was shouting too, with wild cries of delight of which perhaps she would have been ashamed anywhere else, but which were only the utterance of her own excitement and of that of the others. The little uncle tied the hare's legs and hitched it across the horse's crupper, and still preserving his sullen, domineering expression, he moved on without another word. Nicholas and Ilaguine were too much piqued in their pride as sportsmen to recover their assumed indifference, and they watched Rougaï for a long time yet. The old round-shouldered hound, muddy up to his ears, trotted at his master's heels with the lordly philosophy of success. "As you see, I am just like any other dog!" he seemed to be saying, "but when it comes to work, that is quite another thing.—Mark me well!"

When, after this incident, the little uncle addressed Nicholas, the young man felt such a mark of condescension an honour, in spite of all that had passed.

WAR AND PEACE

CHAPTER XXXIII

IT was getting late when Ilaguine took leave of Rostow; and it was only then that Nicholas suddenly became aware of the immense distance they had come from home. He gladly accepted the little uncle's invitation, when Michael Niknorovitch proposed that the hunting party from Otradnoë should spend the night at his house. "And suppose you were to come on there, too? What do you say to that? A sure find—quick march!—It is a damp evening, you will get a rest, and the young countess shall be driven home by and by."

The suggestion was gladly acceded to; one of the keepers was sent to Otradnoë to fetch a carriage, while the whole party were conducted by the little uncle to his domain and house. They were met at the front door by four or five men-servants who attended on their master, and a dozen or so of women, old and young, appeared at a back door, their curiosity much excited by the advent of the cavalcade. When Natacha rode up, a woman on horseback, this was the climax; excitement was too much for them; they pressed forward to examine her, and the boldest even stared her in the face, making their remarks with perfect frankness, as though she were some supernatural being and would neither hear nor understand them.

"Only look, Arina, she sits on one side, and her skirt hangs down—and look, she has got a horn!"

"Merciful Heaven! and a knife!"

"How do you keep on?" asked one more forward than her companions and addressing Natacha.

The little uncle dismounted on the steps of his timber-built house, which was buried in the depths of an uncultivated garden. With a glance at his people he bid them stand back; and each of them having received the necessary orders for the entertainment and comfort of the guests, they all instantly vanished. Then returning to Natacha, he helped her to dismount, and gave her his hand up the worm-eaten steps.

Inside the house, which was far from being dazzlingly clean, the beams were not even whitewashed, and it was easy to perceive that the last thing that ever would occur to the inhabitants was to remove the stains and dirt that were everywhere conspicuous. A smell of fresh-gathered apples pervaded the narrow hall, which was hung with the skins of wolves and foxes. They were led to a small room containing a folding-table of mahogany and a few chairs, then into the drawing-room, where the principal object again was a round, birch-wood table in front of a sofa. Beyond this was the master's private room which reeked of tobacco and dogs. The upholstery, like the carpet, was ragged and squalid; on the wall hung a portrait of Souvorow with those of the little uncle's father and mother, and his own, in military uniform.

He begged his guests to be seated, and then left them for a few minutes; Rougaï meanwhile, unwashed, came into the room, took his usual place on a settee, and proceeded to make his toilet by licking and nibbling himself. The room opened by another door on a passage, part of which was divided off by a ragged screen, and they could hear laughter and women's voices beyond. Natacha, Nicholas, and Pétia threw off their outer garments and stretched themselves on the deep sofa. Pétia indeed, supporting his head on his arms, was, in a few minutes, sound asleep. Though their faces were scorched and tingling from the cold air, Nicholas and Natacha were in high spirits, and above all desperately hungry. Nicholas, being no longer on his dignity as a man and a sportsman, answered his sister's twinkle of amusement with a hearty laugh, in which she joined without caring why.

The little uncle soon reappeared in a short jacket, blue trousers, and evening boots; this costume, which once before at Otradnoë had been the subject of much amusement and mockery to Natacha, did not strike her here as being more absurd than other folks' frock-coats. The little uncle, in a radiant mood, laughed in chorus:

"That is all right, little countess! Ah ha! Youth is a good find—forward! . . . I never saw her like before," he added as he handed a long Turkish pipe to Nicholas, he himself filling a short one that he handled lovingly with three fingers. "In the saddle all day like a man, just as if it were nothing at all!"

At this instant a girl—who was, no doubt, barefoot, to judge from the noiselessness of her tread—opened a door to admit a woman of about forty, rather stout and fresh-coloured, with a double chin and coral lips; she was carrying a huge tray. Her kindly look and cordial smile as she came in with a respectful curtsy to her master's guests, bespoke genial hospitality. Though the bulkiness of her figure obliged her to hold her head thrown back, she was not the less extremely nimble in all her movements. When she had set down the tray, with plump

103

white hands she quickly set out the bottles, glasses and little dishes of *zakouska* (savoury snacks) with which it was loaded. Then retiring to the door, she paused a moment, still smiling.

"Look at me," she seemed to say before she vanished. "Now do you understand the little uncle?" It was impossible not to understand. It was so self-evident that not only Nicholas but even Natacha could guess the full significance of Anicia Fédorovna's anxious and proud expression each time she came into the room.

And what had she not piled on to that tray? A bottle of herb-liqueur and one of fruit syrup, pickled mushrooms, wheat and buckwheat cakes, butter, fresh honey, prepared honey, mead, apples, fresh nuts, baked nuts, nuts preserved in honey, fruit jams of sugar and of molasses, and above all a fine ham and a fowl roasted to a turn. And all cooked and arranged by herself, and exhaling a savoury fragrance, with the exquisite and appetising cleanliness that characterised her own person.

"Taste this—take a little of that, countess," she kept saying, offering her one thing and another, and Natacha ate with a famous appetite. She thought she had never eaten, never seen such light pastry, such delicious preserves, such capital nuts, nay, even so tempting a fowl. Nicholas and the little uncle, washing down their supper with fruit liqueur, discussed sport past and to come, Rougaï's merits and Ilaguine's pack. Natacha, perched on the settee, listened to all they said with sparkling eyes, trying now and again to rouse Pétia to take his share of all the good things; but his vague replies showed that he was too sound asleep. She was beside herself with delight in this domestic scene, so new to her; and her only fear was lest the drosky should come which must carry her home again.

It was after a brief silence, such as must sometimes occur when the master of a house is entertaining strangers for the first time, that the little uncle, talking to himself in response to some undercurrent of thought, exclaimed:

"Yes, this is the way I would end my life! When once I am dead—a sure find! forward! . . . There is no one to come after me."

He looked almost handsome as he spoke, and Nicholas remembered how highly his father always spoke of him. He was known through all the country-side to be as disinterested and noble as he was eccentric, and he was constantly chosen to be arbitrator in family differences, executor and confidant. He was almost always unanimously re-elected judge, and he had filled a great variety of offices by election; but nothing could overcome his objection to active service. His time was regularly divided; in autumn and spring he rode all over the country on his old stallion, in winter he stopped at home in his squalid mansion, and he spent the summer lying in the shade of the copse he called his garden.

"Why don't you make up your mind to go on active service again, little uncle?"

"I have served and had enough of it . . . no good . . . It is all very well for you, but for my part, I never could see the good of it. But hunting—ah! that is quite another thing . . . A sure find—forward!—I say, open the door there; who shut it?"

The door at the farther end of the corridor led into a room where the beaters and huntsmen generally took their meals. The girl's bare feet were heard outside, an invisible hand opened the door, and the sounds of a *balalaïka*—a kind of guitar— struck by the fingers of a skilled musician, fell on their ears.

"It is Mitka, my coachman, who is playing; I bought him a first-rate instrument, I am fond of this kind of music." In fact it had become a custom that when they came in from hunting Mitka should indulge his musical inventiveness, while his master listened with keen enjoyment.

"It is really very pretty," said Nicholas with affected indifference, as if he was ashamed to confess that he admired the music.

"Very pretty!" exclaimed Natacha indignantly. "Why it is charming, beautiful!" Indeed the song to which she was listening struck her as an ideal melody, just as the mushrooms, the honey, and Anicia's preserves seemed to her the best she had ever eaten.

"Again—more, please," said Natacha when the music ceased. Mitka tuned the instrument and began the *Barina*, with variations, in a different key. The master of the house, with his head on one side and a smile on his lips, listened devoutly. The air was returned again and again to the musician's ready fingers, and the strings rang again and again to the same tune, but the audience were not tired of it. Anicia Fédorovna stood leaning against the door-post.

"Listen to him, countess," she said, with a smile like her master's. "He plays very well."

"That was not right!" the little uncle suddenly exclaimed with an energetic gesture. "Those notes should go faster, shorter.—Take them off!—Quick march!"

105

"Do you play the *balalaïka*?" asked Natacha, in some surprise.

"Aniciouchka!" and the good man smiled knowingly, "just see whether my guitar has no strings broken; it is a long time since I last touched it."

Anicia obeyed him with evident satisfaction, and brought the instrument. He took it with care, blew away a little dust that had settled upon it, and screwed up the strings with his lean fingers; then, settling himself comfortably, he curved his left elbow with a somewhat theatrical air, gripped the frets, and with a side glance at Anicia, struck a full ringing chord and began to improvise variations on a well-known popular tune. The rhythm was slow, but the burthen of it was softly and tenderly cheerful—with the cheerfulness of Anicia—it went to the heart of Nicholas and Natacha, and their spirits sang in unison. Anicia blushed and looked radiant, still smiling she hid her face in her handkerchief and left the room. The little uncle went on with the utmost steadiness and precision, and his gaze was fixed with vague inspiration on the spot where she had been standing. A subtle smile played under his grey moustache, and grew broader whenever he emphasised the tune or accelerated the measure to mark the rhythm, or when a string creaked on a difficult passage.

"Delightful, delightful! . . ." Natacha sprang up, threw her arms round the little uncle and kissed him, exclaiming, "Nicholas, Nicholas!" appealing to her brother to share her surprise.

The little uncle had begun again. Anicia and several others of the house-servants stood looking in at the door while he struck up the tune of, "There—out there, where the fountain flows, the maiden bids me wait," finishing off with a chord and a slight shrug of the shoulders.

"Well—well—and what next?" said Natacha, in a tone of such entreaty that her life might have depended on what should follow. The little uncle rose; it was as though there were in him two different men, and that one responded by a grave smile to the other, the musician who was earnestly pressing him to dance.

"Forward then, little niece!" he suddenly exclaimed, and Natacha, flinging off her shawl, sprang into the middle of the room, put her hands on her hips and waited, slightly swinging from her waist.

How, and by what mysterious intuition had this little countess,

106

taught by a French emigrant, so completely absorbed with her native air all the inimitable and indescribable actions of the children of the soil, motions so genuine, so typical—in short so Russian—and which Ioghel's famous shawl dance might long ago have effaced from her nature? As she stood waiting for the signal to begin, her eyes sparkling with fun and a confident smile on her lips, Nicholas and the rest of the bystanders ceased to feel a doubt as to her performance. It was like magic—of course she could do it: they had only to gaze and admire.

Her every movement was so absolutely perfect that Anicia, after giving her the little handkerchief which was indispensable to the performance, stood laughing and crying both at once with all her heart, as she watched the steps and attitudes of this slender and gracious creature. In fact Natacha—a being very superior to the young countess brought up in velvets and silks —knew exactly how to feel and express, not only all that Anicia could feel and understand, but every sentiment that throbbed in the heart of her father, her mother—in every Russian heart.

"Bravo, little countess! A sure find! forward!" cried the little uncle, as she ended. "Now all we want is to find a handsome young husband for you!"

"Not at all, he is found already," said Nicholas.

"Oh, bless me!" said the old man, taken aback. Natacha nodded with a glad smile, "And he is so handsome!" she added.

But hardly had she uttered the words when a new set of ideas flashed through her mind. What is the meaning of Nicholas's smile as he said "He's chosen already"? Is he pleased about it or not? "Nicholas seems to think," thought she, "that my Andrew would not share or even approve of our jollity this evening, but I am sure he is wrong.—Where is he now, I wonder?" And for an instant her sweet face was clouded. "But what is the use of thinking of that!" And flashing into gaiety again she sat down by the little uncle and entreated him to sing a song. He readily agreed.

He sang as the peasant sings who thinks only of the words of the song, and to whom the tune is merely an accessory which comes as a matter of course and is of no use but to emphasise the rhythm. This way of singing as the birds sing, was singularly charming and attractive in the worthy little uncle. Natacha in her enthusiasm declared she would never touch the harp again, but would learn to play the guitar; and she succeeded in striking a few chords.

At near ten o'clock a *lineïka* [1] arrived, with a drosky and three men on horseback, all sent in search of the young people. The count and countess had been very much alarmed, the servant said, not knowing what could have happened to them. Pétia was lifted without waking him into the *lineïka*. Nicholas and Natacha got into the drosky, the little uncle covered and packed them warmly with paternal care, and he escorted them as far as the bridge, which they had to leave behind them, and to ford the river lower down where he had sent his men to wait with lanterns.

"Good night, dear little niece!" was the last thing Natacha heard through the darkness, in the voice whose singing still rang in her ears.

Ruddy fires gleamed in the huts of the village as they drove through it, and the wind blew the smoke about in sport.

"The little uncle is a perfect jewel!" said Natacha, as they were rolling along the high road.

"Yes," said Nicholas. "Are you cold?"

"No, I am very comfortable,—so comfortable!" she repeated, puzzled herself at her own gladness.

Then for a long time they were silent. The night was very dark and the fog dense, they could scarcely see the horses, though they heard them splashing through the mud.

What was going on in this child's impressionable soul—always open to the most dissimilar influences and transient emotions? How was it that she could feel them all at once, and harmonise them to a whole! She was glad, as she had said, and within a short distance of home she suddenly lifted up her voice in jubilant tones, and sang the burden of the song she had been vainly trying to remember and had only just hit upon.

"That is right, sure enough," said her brother.

"Nicholas, what were you thinking of just now?" she said; it was a question they often asked each other.

"I—I was thinking of Rougaï—he is rather like the little uncle, I think. If he had only been a man I fancy he would always have kept the uncle with him to hunt with him and make music. And you, what were you thinking of?"

"I—wait a minute—I was thinking of our ride; I was fancying that instead of finding ourselves at Otradnoë in a few minutes we might have to spend this dark night in some fairy castle, and then—no, that was all."

[1] A low, roomy carriage.

"But I can guess—you thought of him?"

"No," said Natacha.—But she had thought of "him," and of what he would have thought of the little uncle; "And then I kept repeating to myself all the time, how well Aniciouchka came in." And Nicholas heard her happy, careless ringing laugh. "Do you know," she said, "I do not think I shall ever be as happy and as glad as I am at this moment."

"What nonsense! That is sheer extravagance," said Nicholas; but he was thinking to himself: "Natacha is a perfect jewel, she is the dearest friend I ever had. . . . Oh! why need she marry when we might have spent all our lives together, running about the world?"

"What a dear fellow Nicholas is!" said Natacha, on her part. "Look, there are lights in the drawing-room still!" she exclaimed, pointing to the windows which shone out through the velvety gloom of the mist and darkness.

CHAPTER XXXIV

COUNT ROSTOW had given up his appointment as *Maréchal de Noblesse* of the district because it entailed too many expenses, and yet there was no improvement in the state of his affairs. Nicholas and Natacha often found their father and mother in anxious consultation, talking in low tones of the sale of their Moscow house or of their property in the neighbourhood. Having thus retired into private life, the count now gave neither fêtes nor entertainments. Life at Otradnoë was much less gay than in past years; still, the house and domain were as full of servants as ever, and twenty persons or more sat down to dinner daily. These were dependants, friends and intimates, who were regarded almost as part of the family, or at any rate seemed unable to tear themselves away from it; among them a musician named Dimmler and his wife, Vogel the dancing-master and his family, an old Miss Bélow, Pétia's tutor, and the girls' former governess; besides others who found it simpler to live at the count's expense than at their own. Thus, though there were no more festivities, life was carried on almost as expensively as of old, and neither the master nor the mistress ever imagined any change possible. Nicholas, again, had added to the hunting establishment; there were still fifty horses in the stable, still fifteen drivers; handsome presents were given on all birthdays and fête-days, which invariably wound up as of old with a grand dinner to all the neighbourhood; the count still played whist or boston, invariably letting his cards be seen by his friends, who were always ready to make up his table and relieve him without hesitation of the few hundred roubles which constituted their principal income. The old man marched on blindfold through the tangle of his pecuniary difficulties, trying to conceal them, and only succeeded in augmenting them, having neither the courage nor the patience to untie the knots one by one.

The loving heart by his side foresaw their children's ruin; but she could not accuse her husband, who was, alas! too old for amendment; she could only seek some remedy for the disaster. From her woman's point of view there was but one, Nicholas's marriage with some rich heiress. She clung desperately to this last chance of salvation; but if her son should refuse the wife she proposed to him, every hope of reinstating their fortune would vanish. The young lady she had in view, the daughter of people of the highest respectability, the Rostows had known from her infancy,—Julia Karaguine, who by the death of her second brother had suddenly come into great wealth.

The countess herself wrote to Mrs. Karaguine to ask her whether she could regard the match with favour, and received a most flattering answer; indeed, Mrs. Karaguine invited Nicholas to her house at Moscow, to give her daughter an opportunity of deciding for herself.

Nicholas had often heard his mother say, with tears in her eyes, that her dearest wish was to see him married; her daughters being now provided for, the fulfilment of this wish would sweeten her remaining days, she would say, adding covert hints as to a charming girl who would exactly suit him. One day she took the opportunity of speaking plainly to him of Julia's charms and merits, and urged him to spend a short time in Moscow before Christmas. Nicholas, who had no difficulty in guessing what she was aiming at, persuaded her to be explicit on the matter, and she owned frankly that her hope was to see their sinking fortunes restored by his marriage with Julia!

"Then, mother, if I loved a penniless girl, you would desire me to sacrifice my feelings and my honour to marry solely for money?"

"Nay, nay, you have misunderstood me," she said, not

knowing how to excuse her mercenary hopes. "I wish only for your happiness!" And then, conscious that this was not her sole aim, and that she was not perfectly honest, she burst into tears.

"Do not cry, mamma; you have only to say that you really and truly desire it, and you know I would give my life to see you happy—that I would sacrifice everything, even my feelings."

But this was not his mother's notion; she asked no sacrifice, she would have none; she would sooner have sacrificed herself if it had been possible.

"Say no more about it, you do not understand," she said, drying away her tears.

"How could she think of such a marriage?" thought Nicholas. "Does she think that because Sonia is poor I do not love her? And yet I should be a thousand times happier with her than with a doll like Julia."

He stayed in the country, and his mother did not revert to the subject. Still, as she saw the growing intimacy between Nicholas and Sonia, she could not help worrying Sonia about every little thing, and speaking to her with colder formality. Sometimes she reproached herself for these continual pin-pricks of annoyance, and was quite vexed with the poor girl for submitting to them with such wonderful humility and sweetness, for taking every opportunity of showing her devoted gratitude, and for loving Nicholas with a faithful and disinterested affection which commanded her admiration.

Just about this time a letter came from Prince Andrew, dated from Rome; it was the fourth he had written since his departure. He ought long since to have been on his way home, he said, but the heat of the summer had caused his wound to re-open, and this compelled him to postpone his return till early in January.

Natacha, though she was so much in love that her very passion for Prince Andrew had made her day-dreams happy, had hitherto been open to all the bright influences of her young life; but now, after nearly four months of parting, she fell into a state of extreme melancholy, and gave way to it completely. She bewailed her hard fate, she bewailed the time that was slipping away and lost to her, while her heart ached with the dull craving to love and be loved. Nicholas, too, had nearly spent his leave. The Rostows' was not a gay household.

CHAPTER XXXV

CHRISTMAS came; but, excepting the pompous high mass and the other religious ceremonies, the endless strings of neighbours and servants with the regular compliments of the season, and the new gowns which made their first appearance on the occasion, nothing unusual happened on that day, except that a twenty degrees frost with brilliant sunshine, a still atmosphere, and a glorious starry sky at night, demanded something more to make this season memorable.

After dinner on the third day of Christmastide, when everyone had settled into his own corner once more, ennui reigned supreme throughout the house. Nicholas, who had been paying a round of visits in the neighbourhood, was fast asleep in the drawing-room. The old count had followed his example in his own room. Sonia, seated at a table in the sitting-room, was copying a drawing. The countess was playing out a "patience," and Nastacia Ivanovna, the old buffoon, with his peevish face, sitting in a window with two old women, did not say a word.

Natacha came into the room, and after leaning over Sonia for a minute or two to examine her work, went over to her mother and stood still in front of her.

The countess looked up. "Why are you wandering about like a soul in torment? What do you want?" she said.

"Want!—I want him!" replied Natacha shortly, and her eyes glowed. "Now, here—at once!"

Her mother gazed at her anxiously.

"Do not look at me like that, you will make me cry."

"Sit down here."

"Mamma, I want him, I want him! Why must I die of weariness? . . ." Her voice broke and tears started from her eyes. She hastily quitted the drawing-room and went to the housekeeper's room, where an old servant was scolding one of the girls who had just come in breathless from out of doors.

"There is a time for all things," growled the old woman. "You have had time enough for play . . ."

"Oh! leave her in peace, Kondratievna," said Natacha. "Run away, Mavroucha—go."

Pursuing her wandering, Natacha went into the hall; an old man-servant was playing cards with two of the boys. Her entrance stopped their game and they rose. "And what am I to say to these?" thought she.

"Nikita, would you please go . . . What on earth can I ask for? . . . Go and find me a cock, and you, Micha, a handful of corn."

"A handful of corn?" said Micha, laughing.

"Go, go at once," said the old man.

"And you, Fédor, can you give me a piece of chalk?" ·

Then she went on to the servants' hall and ordered the samovar to be got ready, though it was not yet tea-time; she wanted to try her power over Foka, the old butler, the most morose and disobliging of all the servants. He could not believe his ears, and asked her if she really meant it. "What next will our young lady want?" muttered Foka, affecting to be very cross.

No one gave so many orders as Natacha, no one sent them on so many errands at once. As soon as a servant came in sight, she seemed to invent some want or message; she could not help it. It seemed as though she wanted to try her power over them, to see whether, some fine day, one or another would not rebel against her tyranny; but on the contrary, they always flew to obey her more readily than anyone else.

"And now what shall I do, where can I go?" thought she, as she slowly went along the corridor, where she presently met the buffoon.

"Nastacia Ivanovna," said she, "if I ever have children what will they be?"

"You! Fleas and grasshoppers, you may depend upon it."

Natacha went on. "Good God! Have mercy, have mercy!" she said to herself. "Wherever I go it is always, always the same. I am so weary, what shall I do?"

Skipping lightly from step to step, she went to the upper story and dropped in on the Vogels. Two governesses were sitting chatting with Mr. and Mrs. Vogel, dessert—consisting of dried fruit—was on the table, and they were eagerly discussing the cost of living at Moscow and Odessa. Natacha took a seat for a moment, listened with pensive attention, and then jumped up again. "The island of Madagascar!" she murmured, "Ma-da-gas-car!" and she separated the syllables. Then she left the room without answering Mrs. Schoss, who was utterly mystified by her strange exclamation.

She next met Pétia and a companion, both very full of some fireworks which were to be let off that evening. "Pétia!" she exclaimed, "carry me downstairs!" And she sprang on to his back, throwing her arms round his neck, and laughing and galloping they thus scrambled along to the head of the stairs.

"Thank you—that will do! . . . Madagascar!" she repeated, and jumping down she ran down the flight.

After thus inspecting her dominions, testing her power, and convincing herself that her subjects were docile, and that there was no novelty to be got out of them, Natacha settled herself in the darkest corner of the music-room with her guitar, striking the bass strings, and trying to make an accompaniment to an air from an opera that she and Prince Andrew had once heard together at St. Petersburg. The uncertain chords which her unpractised fingers sketched out would have struck the least experienced ear as wanting in harmony and musical accuracy, while to her excited imagination they brought a whole train of memories. Leaning against the wall and half hidden by a cabinet, with her eyes fixed on a thread of light that came under the door from the rooms beyond, she listened in ecstasy and dreamed of the past.

Sonia crossed the room with a glass in her hand. Natacha glanced round at her, and again fixed her eyes on the streak of light; she had the strange feeling of having once before gone through the same experience, sat in the same place, surrounded by the same details, and watching Sonia pass carrying a tumbler. "Yes, it was exactly the same," she thought.

"Sonia, what is this tune?" she said, playing a few notes.

"What, are you there?" said Sonia, startled. "I do not know," she said, coming closer to listen, "unless it is from *La Tempête?*" but she spoke doubtfully.

"It was exactly so," thought Natacha. "She started as she came forward, smiling so gently; and I thought then, as I think now, that there is something lacking in her. . . . No," she said aloud, "you are quite out; it is the chorus from the *Porteur d'eau* [1]—listen," and she hummed the air. "Where are you going?"

"For some fresh water to finish my drawing."

"You are always busy, and I never . . . Where is Nicholas?"

"Asleep, I think."

"Go and wake him, Sonia. Tell him to come and sing."

Sonia went; and Natacha relapsed into dreaming and wondering how it had all happened. Not being able to solve the puzzle, she drifted into reminiscence once more. She could

[1] More commonly known as *Les Deux Journées* by Cherubini.

see him—*him*, and feel his impassioned eyes fixed on her face: "Oh! make haste back!—I am so afraid he will not come yet! . . . Besides, it is all very well, but I am growing old; I shall be quite different from what I am now!—Who knows? Perhaps he will come to-day? Perhaps he is here already! Here, in the drawing-room. Perhaps he came yesterday, and I have forgotten. . . ."

She rose, laid down the guitar, and went into the next room. All the household party were seated round the tea-table—the professors, the governesses, the guests; the servants were in waiting—but there was no Prince Andrew.

"Ah! here she is," said her father—"come and sit down here." But Natacha stopped by her mother, without heeding his bidding.

"Oh! mamma—bring him to me, give him to me soon— very soon," she murmured, swallowing down a sob. Then she sat down and listened to the others. "Good God! always the same people! always the same thing! . . . Papa holds his cup as he always does, and blows his tea to cool it as he did yesterday, and as he will to-morrow. . . ."

She felt a sort of dull rebellion against them all; she hated them for always being the same.

After tea Sonia, Natacha, and Nicholas sat huddled together in their favourite snug corner of the drawing-room; that was where they talked freely to each other.

CHAPTER XXXVI

"Do you ever feel," Natacha asked her brother, "as if there was nothing left to look forward to—as if you had had all your share of happiness, and were not so much weary as utterly sad?"

"Of course I have. Very often I have seen my friends in the highest spirits, and been just as jolly myself, and suddenly have been struck so dull and dismal, have so hated life that I have wondered whether we were not all about to die at once. I remember one day, for instance, when I was with the regiment; the band was playing, and I had such a fit of melancholy, that I never even thought of going to the promenade."

"How well I understand that! I recollect once," Natacha went on, "once when I was a little girl I was punished, for having eaten some plums, I think. I had not done it, and

you were all dancing, and I was left alone in the schoolroom.
. . . How I cried—cried because I was so sorry for myself,
and so vexed with you all for making me so unhappy."

"I remember; and I went to comfort you, and did not know
how . . . we were funny children then; I had a toy with bells
that jingled, and I made you a present of it."

"Do you remember," said Natacha, "long before that, when
we were no bigger than my hand, my uncle called us into his
room, where it was quite dark, and suddenly we saw . . ."

"A negro!" interrupted Nicholas, smiling at the recollection.
"To be sure; I can see him now; and to this day I wonder
whether it was a dream or a reality, or mere fancy, invented
afterwards."

"He had white teeth, and stared at us with his black eyes."

"Do you remember him, Sonia?"

"Yes, yes—but very dimly."

"But papa and mamma have always declared that no negro
ever came to the house.—And the eggs; do you remember the
eggs we used to roll up at Easter, and one day how two little
grinning old women came and began to spin round the table?"

"Of course.—And how papa used to put on his fur coat, and
fire off his gun from the balcony.—And don't you remember
. . .?" And so they went on, recalling one after the other, not
the bitter memories of old age, but the bright pictures of early
childhood, which float and fade on a distant horizon of poetic
vagueness, midway between reality and dreams. And as usual
Sonia was left far behind though their recollections should have
been identical. She did not remember much of what they
remembered, and what she did did not give rise to the same
poetic feeling that they were experiencing. She was only
happy in their happiness and did her best to get into harmony
with them. She only took part in the memories of her first
arrival at the house. Sonia remembered being frightened at
the sight of Nicholas in his braided jacket, and her nurse saying
that she would be tied up in it.

"And they told me you had been found in the garden under
a cabbage," said Natacha. "I dared not say it was not true,
but it puzzled me tremendously."

A door opened, and a woman put in her head, exclaiming:
"Miss, miss, they have fetched the cock!"

"I do not want it now; send it away again, Polia," said
Natacha.

Dimmler, who had meanwhile come into the room, went up

116

to the harp, which stood in a corner, and, in taking off the cover, made the strings ring discordantly.

"Edward Karlovitch, play my favourite nocturne,—Fields," cried the countess, from the adjoining room.

Dimmler struck a chord: "How quiet you young people are!" he said addressing them.

"Yes, we are studying philosophy," said Natacha, and they went on talking of their dreams.

Dimmler had no sooner begun his nocturne than Natacha, crossing the room on tiptoe, seized the waxlight that was burning on the table and carried it into the next room; then she stole back to her seat. It was now quite dark in the larger room, especially in their corner, but the silvery moonbeams came in at the wide windows and lay in broad sheets on the floor.

"Do you know," whispered Natacha, while Dimmler, after playing the nocturne, let his fingers wander over the strings, uncertain what to play next, "when I go on remembering one thing beyond another I go back so far, so far, that at last I remember things that happened before I was born, and . . ."

"That is metempsychosis," interrupted Sonia, with a reminiscence of her early lessons. "The Egyptians believed that our souls had once inhabited the bodies of animals, and would return to animals again after our death."

"I do not believe that!" said Natacha, still in a low voice, though the music had ceased. "But I am quite sure that we were angels once, somewhere there beyond, or perhaps even here; and that is the reason we remember a previous existence."

"May I join the party?" asked Dimmler, coming towards them.

"If we were once angels, how is it that we have fallen lower?"

"Lower! Who says that it is lower? Who knows what I was?" Natacha retorted with full conviction. "Since the soul is immortal, and I am to live for ever in the future, I must have existed in the past, so I have eternity behind me, too."

"Yes, but it is very difficult to conceive of that eternity," said Dimmler whose ironical smile had died away.

"Why?" asked Natacha. "After to-day comes to-morrow, and then the day after, and so on for ever; yesterday has been, to-morrow will be. . . ."

"Natacha, now it is your turn; sing me something," said her mother. "What are you doing in that corner like a party of conspirators?"

117

"I am not at all in the humour, mamma," said she; nevertheless she rose. Nicholas sat down to the piano, and standing, as usual, in the middle of the room where the voice sounded best, she sang her mother's favourite ballad.

Though she had said she was not in the humour, it was long since Natacha had sung so well as she did that evening, and long before she sang so well again. Her father, who was talking over business with Mitenka in his room, hurriedly gave him some final instructions as soon as he heard the first note, as a schoolboy scrambles through his tasks to get to his play; but he sat in silence listening, while Mitenka, too, standing in his presence, listened with evident satisfaction. Nicholas did not take his eyes off his sister's face and only breathed when she took breath. Sonia was thinking of the gulf of difference that lay between her and her friend, fully conscious that she should never exercise such fascination. The old countess had paused in her "patience"—a sad, fond smile played on her lips, her eyes were full of tears, and she shook her head, remembering her own youth, looking forward to her daughter's future and reflecting on her strange prospect of marriage.

Dimmler, sitting by her side, listened with rapture, his eyes half closed:

"She really has a marvellous gift!" he exclaimed. "She has nothing to learn—such power, such sweetness, such roundness! . . ."

"And how much I fear for her happiness!" replied the countess, who in her mother's heart could feel the flame that must some day be fatal to her child's peace.

Natacha was still singing when Pétia dashed noisily into the room to announce in triumphant tones that a party of mummers had come.

"Idiot!" exclaimed Natacha, stopping short; and dropping into a chair she began to sob so violently that it was some time before she could recover herself. "It is nothing, mamma, really nothing at all," she declared, trying to smile. "Only Pétia frightened me; nothing more." And her tears flowed afresh.

All the servants had dressed up, some as bears, Turks, tavern-keepers, or fine ladies; others as clowns. Bringing with them the chill of the night outside, they did not at first venture any farther than the hall; by degrees, however, they took courage; pushing each other forward for self-protection, they all soon came into the music-room. Once there, their shyness thawed; they became expansively merry, and singing, dancing, and sports were soon the order of the day. The countess, after looking at them and identifying them all, went back into the sitting-room, leaving her husband whose jovial face encouraged them to enjoy themselves.

The young people had all vanished; but half an hour later an old marchioness with patches appeared on the scene; none other than Nicholas; Pétia as a Turk; a clown—Dimmler; an hussar—Natacha; and a Circassian—Sonia. Both the girls had blackened their eyebrows and given themselves moustaches with burnt cork.

After being received with well-feigned surprise, and recognised more or less quickly, the children, who were very proud of their costumes, unanimously declared that they must go and display them elsewhere. Nicholas, who was dying to take them all for a long drive *en troïka*,[1] proposed that, as the roads were in splendid order, they should go, a party of ten, to the little uncle's.

"You will disturb the old man, and that will be all," said the countess. "Why, he has not even room for you all to get into the house! If you must go out, you had better go to the Mélukows'."

Mrs. Mélukow was a widow living in the neighbourhood; her house, full of children of all ages, with tutors and governesses, was distant only four versts from Otradnoë.

"A capital idea, my dear," cried the count, enchanted. "I will dress up in costume and go too. I will wake them up, I warrant you!"

But this did not at all meet his wife's views. For him to go out with his gouty feet in such cold weather was sheer folly! The count gave way, and Mrs. Schoss volunteered to chaperon the girls. Sonia's was by far the most successful disguise; her fierce eyebrows and moustache were wonderfully becoming, her pretty features gained expression, and she wore the dress of a man with unexpected swagger and smartness. Something in her inmost soul told her that this evening would seal her fate.

In a few minutes four sleighs with three horses abreast to each, their harness jingling with bells, drew up in a line before the steps, the runners creaking and crunching over the frozen snow. Natacha was the foremost, and the first to tune her spirits to the pitch of this carnival freak. This mirth, in fact, proved highly infectious, and reached its height of tumult and excitement when

[1] A team of three horses harnessed abreast.

119

the party went down the steps and packed themselves in the sleighs, laughing and shouting to each other at the top of their voices. Two of the sleighs were drawn by light cart-horses; to the third the count's carriage-horses were harnessed, and one of these was reputed a famous Orlow's trotter; the fourth sleigh, with its rough-coated black shaft-horse, was Nicholas's private property. In his marquise costume, over which he had thrown his hussar's cloak, fastened with a belt round the waist, he stood gathering up the reins. The moon was shining brightly, reflected in the plating of the harness and in the horses' anxious eyes as they turned their heads in uneasy amazement at the noisy group that clustered under the dark porch. Natacha, Sonia, and Mrs. Schoss, with two women servants, got into Nicholas's sleigh; Dimmler and his wife, with Pétia, into the count's; the rest of the mummers packed into the other sleighs.

"Lead the way, Zakhare!" cried Nicholas to his father's coachman, promising himself the pleasure of outstripping him presently. The count's sleigh swayed and strained, the runners, which the frost had already glued to the ground, creaked, the bells rang out, the horses closed up for a pull, and off they went over the glittering hard snow, flinging it up right and left like spray of powdered sugar. Nicholas started next and the others followed along the narrow way, with no less jingling and creaking. While they drove past the garden the shadows of the tall skeleton trees lay on the road, chequering the broad moon-light; but as soon as they had left it behind them, the wide and spotless plain spread on all sides, its whiteness broken by myriads of flashing sparks and spangles of reflected light. Suddenly a rut caused the foremost sleigh to jolt violently, and then the others in succession; they fell away a little, their intrusive clatter breaking the supreme and solemn silence of the night.

"A hare's tracks!" exclaimed Natacha, and her voice pierced the frozen air.

"How light it is, Nicholas!" said Sonia. Nicholas turned round to look at the pretty face with its black moustache under the sable hood, looking at once so far away and so close in the moonshine: "It is not Sonia at all," he said, smiling.

"Why, what is the matter?"

"Nothing," said he, returning to his former position.

When they got out on the high road, beaten and ploughed by horses' hoofs, and polished with the tracks of sleighs, his steeds began to pull and go at a great pace. The near horse, turning away his head, was galloping rather wildly, while the horse in the shafts pricked his ears, and seemed to doubt whether the moment for a dash had come. Zakhare's sleigh, lost in the distance, was no more than a black spot on the white snow, and as he drew farther away the ringing of the bells was fainter and fainter; only the shouts and songs of the maskers rang through the calm clear night.

"On you go, my beauties!" cried Nicholas, shaking the reins and raising his whip. The sleigh seemed to leap forward, but the sharp air that cut their faces, and the flying gallop of the two outer horses, alone gave them any idea of the speed they were making. Nicholas glanced back at the other two drivers; they were shouting and urging their shaft-horses with cries and cracking of whips, so as not to be left quite behind; Nicholas's middle horse, swinging steadily along under the shaft-bow, kept up a regular pace, quite ready to go twice as fast the moment he should be called upon.

They soon overtook the first troïka, and after going down a slope they came upon a wide cross-road running by the side of a meadow.

"Where are we, I wonder," thought Nicholas; "this must be the field and slope by the river. No . . . I do not know where we are! This is all new and unfamiliar to me! God only knows where we are! But no matter," and smacking his whip with a will, he went straight ahead. Zakhare held in his beasts for an instant, and turned his face, all fringed with frost, to look at Nicholas, who came flying onward.

"Steady there, sir," cried the coachman, and leaning forward, with a click of his tongue he urged his horses in their turn to their utmost speed. For a few minutes the sleighs ran equal, but before long, in spite of all Zakhare could do, Nicholas gained on him, and at last passed him like a lightning flash. A cloud of fine snow, kicked up by the horses, came showering down on the rival sleigh; the women squeaked, and the two teams had a struggle for the precedence, their shadows crossing and mingling on the snow.

Then Nicholas, moderating his speed, looked about him; before, behind, and on each side of him, stretched the fairy scene: a plain strewn with stars and flooded with light.

"To the left, Zakhare says. . . . Why to the left?" thought he. "We are going to the Mélukows. . . . But we are going where fate directs, or as Heaven may guide us. It is all very strange and most delightful, is it not?" he said, turning to the others.

"Oh! look at his eyelashes and moustache—they are quite white!" exclaimed one of the sweet young men with pencilled moustaches and arched eyebrows.

"That, I believe, is Natacha," said Nicholas to himself. "And that little Circassian—who is he? I do not know him, but I love him! Are you not frozen?" Their answer was a shout of laughter.

Dimmler was talking himself hoarse, and he must have been saying very funny things, for the party in his sleigh were in fits of laughing.

"Better and better," said Nicholas to himself, "now we are in an enchanted forest—the black shadows lie across a flooring of diamonds, and mix with the sparkling of gems. That might be a fairy palace, out there, built of large blocks of marble and jewelled tiles! Did I not hear the howl of wild beasts in the distance? . . . Supposing it were only Mélukovka that I am coming to after all! On my word, it would be no less miraculous to have reached port after steering so completely at random!"

It was, in fact, Mélukovka, for he could see the house servants coming out on the balcony with lights, and then down to meet them, only too glad of this unexpected diversion.

"Who is there?" a voice asked within.

"The mummers from Count Rostow's—they are his teams," replied the servants.

CHAPTER XXXVII

Pélaguéïa Danilovna Mélukow, a stout and commanding personality in spectacles and a flowing dressing-gown, was sitting in her drawing-room surrounded by her children, whom she was doing her best to amuse by melting wax[1] and tracing the shadows the children cast on the wall, when steps and voices were heard in the ante-room. Hussars, witches, clowns, and bears were rubbing their faces, which were scorched by the cold and covered with rime, or shaking the snow off their clothes. As soon as they had cast off their furs they rushed into the large drawing-room, which was hastily lighted up. Dimmler, the

---

[1] A form of fortune-telling at Christmas.

clown, and Nicholas, the marchioness, performed a dance, while the others stood close along the wall, the children shouting and jumping about them with glee.

"It is impossible to know who is who—can that really be Natacha? Look at her; does she not remind you of some one? . . . Edward Karlovitch, how fine you are! and how beautifully you dance! Oh! and that splendid Circassian— why, it is Sonia! What a kind and delightful surprise; we were so desperately dull. Ha, ha! what a beautiful hussar! A real hussar, or a real monkey of a boy—which is he, I wonder? I cannot look at you without laughing. . . ." They all shouted and laughed and talked at once, at the top of their voices.

Natacha, to whom the Mélukows were devoted, soon vanished with them to their own room, where corks and various articles of men's clothing were brought to them, and clutched by bare arms through a half-open door. Ten minutes later all the young people of the house rejoined the company, equally un-recognisable. Pélaguéïa Danilovna, going and coming among them all, with her spectacles on her nose and a quiet smile, had seats arranged, and a supper laid out for the visitors, masters and servants alike. She looked straight in the face of each in turn, recognising no one of the motley crew—neither the Rostows, nor Dimmler, nor even her own children, nor any of the clothes they figured in.

"That one—who is she?" she asked the governess, stopping a Kazan Tartar, who was, in fact, her own daughter. "One of the Rostows, is it not? And you, gallant hussar—what regiment do you belong to?" she went on, addressing Natacha. "Give some *pastila* to this Turkish lady," she cried to the butler; "it is not forbidden by her religion, I believe."

At the sight of some of the reckless dancing which the mummers performed under the shelter of their disguise, Péla-guéïa Danilovna could not help hiding her face in her handker-chief, while her huge person shook with uncontrollable laughter —the laugh of a kindly matron, frankly jovial and gay.

When they had danced all the national dances, ending with the *Horovody*, she placed everyone, both masters and servants, in a large circle, holding a cord with a ring and a rouble, and for a while they played games. An hour after, when the finery was the worse for wear and heat, and laughter had removed much of the charcoal, Pélaguéïa Danilovna could recognise them, compliment the girls on the success of their disguise, and thank the whole party for the amusement they had given her.

123

Supper was served for the company in the drawing-room, and for the servants in the large dining-room.

"No. Fortune-telling in the bath-house . . . that is enough to frighten you!" said an old maid who lived with the Mélukows.

"Why?" asked the eldest girl.

"Oh, you would never dare to do it—you must be very brave."

"Well, I will go," said Sonia.

"Tell us what happened to that girl—you know," said the youngest Mélukow.

"Once a young girl went to the bath, taking with her a cock and two plates, with knives and forks, which is what you must do; and she waited. Suddenly she heard horses' bells—some-one was coming; he stopped, came upstairs, and she saw an officer walk into the room; a real live officer—at least, so he seemed—who sat down opposite to her where the second cover was laid. . . ."

"Oh, how horrible!" exclaimed Natacha, wide-eyed. "And he spoke to her—really spoke?"

"Yes, just as if he had really been a man. He begged and prayed her to listen to him, and all she had to do was to refuse him, and hold out till the cock crowed—but she was too much frightened. She covered her face with her hands, and he clasped her in his arms . . . luckily some girls who were on the watch rushed in when she screamed."

"Why do you terrify them with such nonsense?" said Péla-guéïa Danilovna.

"But, mamma, you know you wanted to try your fortune, too."

"And if you try your fortune in a barn, what do you do?" asked Sonia.

"That is quite simple. You must go to the barn—now, for instance—and listen. If you hear thrashing, it is for ill-luck; if you hear grain dropping, that is good."

"Tell us, mother, what happened to you in the barn."

"It is so long ago," said the mother, with a smile, "that I have quite forgotten; besides, not one of you is brave enough to try it."

"Yes, I will go," repeated Sonia. "Let me go."

"Go by all means, if you are not afraid."

"May I, Mrs. Schoss?" said Sonia to the governess.

Now, whether playing games or sitting quietly and chatting, Nicholas had not left Sonia's side the whole evening; he felt as if he had seen her for the first time, and only just now appreciated all her merits. Bright, bewitchingly pretty in her quaint costume, and excited as she very rarely was, she had completely fascinated him.

"What a simpleton I must have been!" thought he, responding in thought to those sparkling eyes and that triumphant smile, which had revealed to him a little dimple at the tip of her moustache that he had never observed before.

"1 am afraid of nothing!" she declared. She rose, asked her way precisely to the barn, and every detail as to what she was to expect waiting there in total silence; then she threw a fur cloak over her shoulders, glanced at Nicholas, and went out.

She went along the corridor and down the back stairs; while Nicholas, saying that the heat of the room was too much for him, slipped out by the front entrance. It was as cold as ever, and the moon seemed to be shining even more brightly than before. The snow at her feet was strewn with stars, while their sisters overhead twinkled in the deep gloom of the sky, and she soon looked away from them back to the gleaming earth in its radiant mantle of ermine.

Nicholas hurried across the hall, turned the corner of the house, and went past the side door where Sonia was to come out. Half-way to the barn, stacks of wood in the full moonlight threw their shadows on the path, and beyond an alley of lime-trees traced a tangled pattern on the snow with the fine-crossed lines of their leafless twigs. The beams of the house and its snow-laden roof looked as if they had been hewn out of a block of opal, with iridescent lights where the facets caught the silvery moonlight. Suddenly a tree in the garden gave a loud crack; then all was still again. Sonia's heart beat high with gladness, as if she were drinking in, not common air, but some life-giving elixir of eternal youth and joy.

"Straight on if you please, miss, and on no account look behind you."

"I am not afraid," said Sonia, her little shoes crunching the carpet of snow as she ran to meet Nicholas who was within a couple of yards of her. And yet, not the Nicholas of everyday life! What had transfigured him so completely? Was it his woman's costume with frizzed-out hair, or was it that radiant smile which he so rarely wore, and which at this moment illuminated his face?

"But Sonia is quite unlike herself, and yet she is herself," thought Nicholas on his side, looking down at the sweet little face in the moonlight. He slipped his arms under the fur cloak that wrapped her, and drew her to him, and he kissed her lips, which still tasted of the burnt cork that had blackened her moustache.

"Nicholas—Sonia," they whispered; and Sonia put her little hands round his face. Then hand in hand they ran to the barn and back, and each went in by the different doors they had come out of.

CHAPTER XXXVIII

NATACHA, who had noted everything, managed so that she, Mrs. Schoss and Dimmler should return in one sleigh, while the maids went with Nicholas and Sonia in another. Nicholas was in no hurry to get home; he could not help looking at Sonia and trying to find under her disguise the true Sonia—his Sonia, from whom nothing now could ever part him. The magical effects of moonlight, the remembrance of that kiss on her sweet lips, tinged with the smell of burnt cork, the dizzy flight of the snow-clad ground under the horses' hoofs, the black sky, studded with diamonds, that bent over their heads, the icy air that seemed to give vigour to his lungs—all was enough to make him fancy that they were transported to a land of magic.

"Sonia, do you feel happy?"

"Yes—and you?"

Nicholas pulled up, and giving the reins to a man to drive, he ran back to the sleigh in which Natacha was sitting.

"Listen," he said in a whisper and in French. "I have made up my mind about Sonia."

"And you have spoken to her?" exclaimed Natacha, radiant with joy.

"Oh! Natacha, how queer that moustache makes you look! Are you glad?"

"Glad! I am delighted. I did not say anything, you know, but I have been so vexed with you. She is a jewel, a heart of gold. I . . . I am often naughty, and I have no right to have all the happiness to myself now. Go, go back to her."

"No. Wait one minute! Mercy, how funny you look!" he repeated, examining her closely and discovering in her face, too, an unwonted tenderness and emotion that struck him deeply.

126

"Natacha, is there not some magic at the bottom of it all, eh!"

"You have acted very wisely—go."

"If I had ever seen Natacha look as she does at this moment I should have asked her advice and have obeyed her, whatever she had bid me do . . . and all would have gone well." . . . "So you are glad?" he said aloud. "I have done right?"

"Yes, yes, of course you have! I was quite angry with mamma the other day about you two. Mamma would have it that Sonia was running after you. . . . I will not allow anyone to say—no, nor even to think any evil of her, for she is sweetness and truth itself."

"So much the better!" Nicholas jumped down and in a few long strides overtook his own sleigh, where the little Circassian received him with a smile from under the fur hood . . . and the Circassian was Sonia, and Sonia beyond a doubt would be his beloved little wife!

When they got home the two girls went into the countess's room and gave her an account of their expedition; then they went to bed. Without stopping to wipe off their moustaches they stood chattering as they undressed; they had so much to say of their happiness, their future prospects, the friendship between their husbands.

"But oh! when will it all be? I am so afraid it will never come to pass," said Natacha, as she went towards a table on which two looking-glasses stood.

"Sit down," said Sonia, "and look in the glass; perhaps you will see something about it." Natacha lighted two pairs of candles and seated herself. "I certainly see a pair of moustaches," she said, laughing.

"You should not laugh," said the maid very gravely.

Natacha settled herself to gaze without blinking into the mirror; she put on a solemn face and sat in silence for some time, wondering what she should see. Would a coffin rise before her, or would Prince Andrew presently stand revealed against the confused background in the shining glass?—her eyes were weary and could hardly distinguish even the flickering light of the candles. But with the best will in the world she could see nothing; not a spot to suggest the image either of a coffin or of a human form. She rose.

"Why do other people see things and I never see anything at all? Take my place, Sonia; you must look for yourself and for me, too . . . I am so frightened; if you could but know! . . ."

Sonia sat down and fixed her eyes on the mirror.

"Sonia Alexandrovna will be sure to see something," whispered Douniacha, "but you always are laughing at such things." Sonia heard the remark and Natacha's whispered reply: "Yes, she is sure to see something; she did last year."

Three minutes they waited in total silence.

"She is sure to see something," Natacha repeated, trembling.

Sonia started back, covered her face with one hand and cried out:

"Natacha!"

"You saw something? What did you see?" And Natacha rushed forward to hold up the glass.

But Sonia had seen nothing; her eyes were getting dim and she was on the point of giving it up when Natacha's exclamation had stopped her; she did not want to disappoint them; but there is nothing so tiring as sitting motionless. She did not know why she had called out and hidden her face.

"Did you see him?" asked Natacha.

"Yes; stop a minute—I saw him," said Sonia, not quite sure whether "him" was to mean Nicholas or Prince Andrew. "Why not make them believe that I saw something?" she thought. "A great many people have done so before, and no one can prove the contrary. Yes, I saw him," she repeated.

"How? Standing up or lying down?"

"I saw him—at first there was nothing; then suddenly I saw him lying down."

"Andrew lying down? Then he is ill?" And Natacha gazed horror-stricken at her companion.

"Not at all; he seemed quite cheerful, on the contrary," said she, beginning to believe in her own inventions.

"And then, Sonia, what then?"

"Then I saw only confusion—red and blue. . . ."

"And when will he come back, Sonia? When shall I see him again? Oh God! I am afraid for him—afraid of everything. . . ."

And without listening to Sonia's attempts at comfort, Natacha slipped into bed, and long after the lights were out she lay motionless but awake, her eyes fixed on the moonshine that came dimly through the frost-embroidered windows.

THE INVASION

CHAPTER XXXIX

It was not till some days after this that Nicholas confessed to his mother his love for Sonia, and his determination to marry her. The countess, who had long had an eye on them, expected this avowal. She listened in silence, and then, on her part, declared that, though of course he was free to marry whom he pleased, neither she nor his father would ever give their consent to this union. Nicholas, utterly astounded, felt for the first time that his mother, notwithstanding the affection she had always shown him, was now seriously angry with him and would never change her decision. She sent for her husband and tried to speak calmly as she told him what her son proposed; but anger had the upper hand, and she left the room sobbing with vexation. The old count, with some hesitation, urged Nicholas to give up his intention; but Nicholas told him that his word was pledged, and his father, much disconcerted by this formal declaration, only sighed deeply, changed the subject, and presently went after his wife. He felt that he alone was answerable for the dilapidated state of his son's fortune, so how could he blame him for declining to make a wealthy marriage and preferring Sonia, though penniless—Sonia, who would have been the ideal wife for him if Mitenka and his own lavish habits had not dissipated a splendid estate.

After this storm came a few days of calm; till one morning the countess sent for Sonia, rated her for ingratitude and accused her with a sternness she had never before shown, of trying to entrap her son's affections. Sonia stood with downcast eyes, answering not a word to this unjust attack; she did not know what was expected of her—she was ready to make any sacrifice for those whom she regarded as her benefactors; nothing was more obvious than that she should devote herself for them—only in the present instance she did not see what she was to do. She loved them all, she could not do otherwise; she loved Nicholas, who could not be happy without her. What, then, was to be done?

After this painful scene, Nicholas tried to frighten his mother by threatening to marry Sonia privately, and he ended by entreating her once more to sanction his happiness. She replied with icy indifference, strangely unlike her usual self, that he was of age, and that as Prince Andrew was about to marry without his father's consent, he, of course, could do the same; but that she could never regard that scheming and ungrateful girl as her daughter-in-law.

Nicholas, roused to anger by his mother's language, changed his tone. She wanted him, he said, to sell his affections; and he declared that unless she reconsidered her decision, this was the last time he ever . . . but before he could speak the fatal word, which his mother could anticipate only too surely, and which might perhaps have raised an insuperable barrier between them, the door opened, and Natacha came in, pale and very earnest: she had overheard the discussion.

"Nicholas, you do not know what you are saying. Be silent—say no more!" she exclaimed vehemently, to prevent his finishing his sentence. "And you, mamma, poor dear mamma—he does not mean that—you do not understand."

The countess, on the point of a final rupture with her darling son, looked at him in terror; but still she could not and would not give in; she was piqued and urged on by the very obstinacy of his resistance.

"Nicholas, I will explain presently—and you, little mother, listen to me. . . ." Her words were quite incoherent, but they achieved their purpose. The countess melted into tears, and hid her face on her daughter's shoulder, while Nicholas, desperately clasping his head in both hands, ran out of the room.

Natacha persisted in her efforts at reconciliation, and persuaded her mother to promise that she would no longer torment Sonia. Nicholas, on his side, pledged himself to take no steps without his parents' knowledge; and a few days later, depressed and unhappy at finding himself in opposition to them, he started to join his regiment, quite resolved to quit the service and soon return to marry Sonia, with whom he believed himself to be desperately in love.

Then the Rostows' home was melancholy indeed. The countess fell ill; Sonia, miserable in her lover's absence, could hardly endure the persecutions of her benefactress, who betrayed her hostile feeling in every word she spoke. The count, more taken up than ever with the precarious state of his affairs, found himself driven to extreme measures: to sell one of his properties and his house at Moscow; he ought to have gone himself to attend to these transactions, but the feeble state of his wife's health delayed their departure from day to day.

Natacha, who had borne the first months of separation from her lover with patience and almost cheerfully, grew sadder and more nervous every hour as she reflected that these long weeks, which she might have spent so happily in loving him, were being lost to her longing heart. She was quite vexed to think of Prince Andrew as living that life—visiting foreign lands, and making new acquaintances—while she could only think of him and dream. The more entertaining his letters were the more they provoked her, for she found no consolation in writing to him. Her letters, which her mother always looked through to correct the spelling, were dry and formal compositions; for she found it impossible to express on a sheet of paper lying before her what she could have said in one word—in a look or a smile. Hence she wrote simply as a matter of wearisome duty, and attached no importance to the letters.

Their journey to Moscow was becoming a matter of necessity; irrespective of the sales to be effected, there was the trousseau to be ordered, and they expected to meet Prince Andrew who might arrive any day. The old prince was to pass the winter there, and Natacha was quite sure her lover had by this time come from abroad. So, as the countess meanwhile got no better, it was settled that the count and the two girls should go without her at the end of January.

BOOK EIGHT

CHAPTER XL

PETER, in spite of his entire faith in the truths that the Benefactor had declared to him, and of the deep gladness he had experienced during the early months of apprenticeship when he gave himself up with genuine enthusiasm to the task of self-regeneration, found that his new course of life, notwithstanding his efforts to persevere in it, had suddenly lost its charm when Prince Andrew was betrothed to Natacha, and within a short time after Bazdéïew died. Nothing remained to him but the dry bones of life: his house, his wife—who stood in higher favour than ever with her illustrious friend—his numerous but uninteresting acquaintance, and his duties at court with all their tiresome formalities. He felt an overwhelming weariness and disgust when he contemplated his life; he ceased to keep his journal, avoided the society of the brethren, haunted the club, and took once more to drinking and bachelor habits; indeed he was so much talked about that Countess Helen thought it incumbent on her to take him severely to task. Peter submitted on every point, and withdrew to Moscow in order that she might not be compromised by his reputation.

When he found himself there once more, in his immense house, with his cousins, the princesses, who were withering on the stem and turning to mummies, and the innumerable dependants who swarmed in every corner of it; when he had been to the chapel of the Virgin of Iverskaïa, blazing with the light of a thousand tapers burning devoutly in front of the holy images in their gold and silver frames; when he had crossed the great square of the Kremlin lying under its mantle of spotless snow; when he had once more seen the drivers and the shops of Kitaïgorod, and the old men and women of Moscow quietly vegetating in their old nooks without a wish beyond; when he had again taken part in the dinners and balls at the English Club—then he felt he had reached a haven. At Moscow, where he was at home in his own house, he had the comfortable

132

sensation of a man who, after an exhausting day, gets into a warm old dressing-gown, easy, though a little worn and greasy.

All the society he had left welcomed him back with open arms; his place had not been filled and was ready for him, and he had only to resume it, for all these good people thought of Peter as one of the best fellows living, eccentric, but genial and shrewd, a typical fine gentleman of the old Moscow stamp, absent-minded but generous, with a purse that was always empty because everyone dipped his fingers in it without scruple.

Performances got up for the benefit of incompetent artists, daubs and sculpture of the most wretched description, gipsy choruses, subscriptions for dinners, freemasons' charities, gifts for church purposes, the publication of expensive books—he was ready to help each and all. He could never say no, and would have completely ruined himself if two friends, to whom, indeed, he had lent a large sum of money, had not fortunately taken him in hand. At the club not a dinner or a soirée could be given without him. No sooner had he stretched his huge person on one of the divans, after emptying a couple of bottles of Château Margaux, than he was surrounded by an obsequious circle, talking and laughing and flattering him. If a dispute arose, his genial smile and some appropriate jest restored peace; and if he were absent even a masonic meeting seemed to fall dull and flat. At a ball, when partners were few, the ladies would invite him and he would dance. Married or girls, they all liked him, for without paying special attentions to one more than another, he was good-humoured to all: "He is charming," they would say; "he is of no sex." Peter was one of those good-natured retired Court dignitaries finishing his days in Moscow, of which there were hundreds.

How deeply he would have bewailed his fate if, seven years before, when he first returned from abroad, anyone had told him that he need not seek a path or invent a career: that his life lay before him clearly marked out, and that in spite of every effort he would never be any better than a dozen other men would have been in his place?—To be sure, he would not have believed it.

Was it not he who had so passionately longed to see Russia a republic; who had aimed at becoming a philosophical tactician; whose one regret had been that he was neither Bonaparte nor the man who should conquer him? Was it not he who had believed in the regeneration of mankind, and who had laboured

133

to reach the highest pitch of personal moral perfection? Was it not he who had founded schools and hospitals, and emancipated his serfs?

And what was he after all? The owner of a vast fortune, the husband of a faithless wife, a retired courtier, a member of the English Club, and the spoilt child of Moscow society; a man who loved eating and drinking above all things; and who now and then, very much at his ease, after a good dinner, exerted himself to find fault with the government.

It was a long time before it struck him that he was neither more nor less than a perfect specimen of the retired court-functionary, living without aims or responsibilities—of the type which, seven years ago, he had held in such contempt, and of which Moscow could furnish so many examples. Then he sometimes tried to comfort himself, assuring himself that his life would not go on long in this groove; but at once his memory would remind him of all the men of his acquaintance who had drifted into this club existence with all their hair and teeth, and had only come out of it minus both; and he thought of them with alarm.

Sometimes, again, his pride would try to persuade him that he was unlike the courtiers he contemned, these vapid, colourless, self-satisfied beings: "What proves it, is that I am dissatisfied, always dissatisfied with myself, always craving to find something that I can do for the good of mankind. But who knows!" he would add, with sincere humility, "but that they, too, like me, have sought to clear an independent path through life, and that the force of circumstances and of the conditions of existence—elements against which man is impotent—may not have brought them just where they have brought me?" And by dint of such arguments, by the time he had spent a few months in Moscow, he had ceased to despise—nay, had learnt to like, to respect, and to pity his companions in misfortune just as he pitied himself.

Then he ceased to have fits of despair and disgust at life; but the evil that tormented him, and which he vainly strove to thrust into the background, was always present to his mind: "What is the end and aim of life? Why are we born? What have we to do in this world?" he would ask himself a hundred times a day. But knowing by experience that his questions must remain unanswered, he put them aside as quickly as possible, taking up a book, or going off to the club, or to see a friend to pick up the day's gossip.

"My wife," he reflected, "who never in her life cared for

anything but her own handsome person, and who is one of the most stupid persons I know, passes for a wit, and everyone bows down to her.—Bonaparte, who was snubbed and laughed at when he really was a great man, is implored by the Emperor Francis to accept his daughter's hand, now that he is a contemptible parvenu and snob.—The Spaniards get their priests to return thanks to Heaven for their victory over the French on the 14th of June, while the French, through priests of the same creed, return thanks for their victory of the same date over the Spaniards.—My brethren, the freemasons, promise and vow that they will give up every worldly advantage for the good of humanity, and grudge a rouble at the offertory. They quarrel among themselves, and fret and toil to get the code of the Scotch order, which no one really cares about or understands— not even the man who wrote it out.—We all profess to obey the Gospel, we preach forgiveness of injuries and love of our neighbour, and to illustrate our precepts we build forty times forty churches in Moscow, while yesterday a deserter was knouted, and the representative of the sacred law of love and forgiveness gives the victim a crucifix to kiss before his execution!"

Such were Peter's reflections; and this all-pervading hypocrisy, hypocrisy accepted and sanctioned by everyone, enraged him each time as a fresh discovery. "I feel it, I see it," he would say to himself, "but how can I convince others? I have tried, but in vain; I am sure they all know it is as well as I do and are wilfully blind. Then so it must be, I suppose. But what ought I to do? What is to become of me?"

Like many men, and particularly many Russians, it was his misfortune to believe in goodness and right, and at the same time to see so clearly the force of evil that he had not the necessary vigour to take an active part in the struggle. This omnipresent lie, which tainted every task he undertook, paralysed his energies; and yet he must live and find work whether or no. It was such misery to him to feel the burden of these vital questions without finding any answer to them that, in order to forget them, he threw himself into the wildest dissipations.

He devoured books by the dozen, reading everything that came to hand, even while his man was helping him to undress at night; and after spending a day thus he would pass the next in idle gossip at the club or in drawing-rooms, and the evening between women and wine. Drink was daily growing upon him, and becoming alike a physical and a moral necessity; he gave himself up to it more and more, in spite of the warning of the doctors, who, in view of his corpulence, considered it dangerous to his health. He never really felt at his ease or cheerful till he had swallowed several glasses of spirits, and then he felt a genial warmth and benevolence towards his fellow-men which helped him to face his thoughts without too closely examining them. Then only did the Gordian knot cease to be an appalling mystery, nay, sometimes even seem easy to untie; then only could he say to himself: "I will put it aside, and think it out by and by."—But that "by and by" never came; when the matter recurred to his mind the enigma rose before him more terrible and more insoluble than ever, and he flew to reading to drive away intolerable thought.

He remembered having heard that soldiers in the trenches under fire would contrive some diversion to make them forget the danger; and he reflected that this is what we all do: that all of us, in our dread of life, try, like the soldiers, to forget it—some by ambition, politics and state-craft—others with women, wine, horses, and sport. "Thus," he concluded, "nothing is possible or, on the other hand, important! . . . Everything comes to the same in the end; all we have to do is to evade implacable reality, and never look it fairly in the face!"

CHAPTER XLI

PRINCE NICHOLAS BOLKONSKY had settled at Moscow early in the winter; his past life, his wit, and his eccentricity, combined with his anti-French and supra-patriotic opinions—which, in consequence perhaps of a collapse of the enthusiasm roused by the earlier acts of the young czar, were quite in the fashion at Moscow—to give him a position as an object of respect, and the leader of the opposition party.

But the prince was very much aged; a fact that betrayed itself in sudden naps, in a forgetfulness of recent events and keen remembrance of a long-past time, and in the childish vanity which made him accept with glee the role of a party-leader. Nevertheless, when he made his appearance at the hour of evening tea, in a short coat lined with fur and his hair powdered, when he fell into the vein of telling anecdotes of his youth in his usual dry, pithy manner, or of passing keen and bitter judgment on the events and men of the day, all who heard him listened with awe.

His enormous house, filled with furniture that dated from the middle of the last century; the servants, always in full livery; he himself, sharp, haughty, and keen-witted, the representative of a departed epoch; his gentle and timid daughter and the pretty Frenchwoman, who both regarded him with fear and reverence—all these elements composed an impressive whole, a strange but captivating picture. Visitors were apt to forget that each day as it passed did not consist merely of the two hours which they spent in the interesting society of the master of the house, but of two and twenty more, which dragged their weary length along over the family in private, and fell with all their weight on poor Princess Maria. She, deprived of her dearest joys—her talk with "the people of God," and the solitude which served as a balm to all her woes, and with no one she cared to associate with, gained nothing by their change of abode. She soon had not even any invitations, as her father refused to let her go anywhere without him, and he, on the ground of his health, would not stir out. Every hope of marriage had faded from her horizon, for his perversity and irritability towards all who might have become suitors for his daughter were only too marked. She had no friends; si her arrival at Moscow she had even learnt to think more c of the two women who had shared her affection: Madem le Bourrienne, whom, for various reasons, she thought it to keep at a distance; and Julia Karaguine, with whom had kept up a correspondence for five years, only to fin soon as they met again, that they had in fact nothing mmon. Julia, the heiress to a large fortune in consequenc he death of both her brothers, threw herself into worldly sures, and was looking out for a husband. Time pressed would soon be a decidedly mature maiden; now or neve must play her cards well; and she felt that her fate mus ealed as soon as possible. As each Thursday came roun cess Maria smiled sadly to think that, not only ther no letter to write, but her friend's weekly visit had e completely a matter of indifference to her. She i arily thought of the old Frenchman who refused t y the woman he admired, saying: "If she were my where should I spend my evenings?" She could o ret that Julia's presence had put an end to their effusiveness, and that now there was no one to whom she could pour out the griefs that every day made heavier to bear.

Prince Andrew was now daily expected; the time fixed for his marriage was drawing nearer, but his father was no better inclined to it: on the contrary, the subject was so sore that the mere mention of the Rostows vexed him beyond measure, and his always fractious temper became almost unbearable. The lessons Princess Maria taught her little nephew, now six years old, were an additional distress, for, to her horror and distress, she found herself liable to fits of temper painfully resembling her father's. How often had she had to repent of her violence! And her most earnest endeavours to make his baby tasks easy, and her anxiety to teach him all she knew herself, were nullified by the certainty that the child, scared by her vehemence, would answer all wrong. Then she would get confused in her explanations, raise her voice and grow angry, and dragging him roughly by the hand, would put him in a corner. Having inflicted the punishment, she would melt into tears and accuse herself of cruelty; and the little boy, trotting out of his corner without waiting for leave, would cry too, and kiss her hands, and hug her to comfort her.

Still, worst of all was her father's temper, which daily grew worse so far as she was concerned. If he had forced her to spend her nights in prayer, if he had beaten her, or made her hew wood and draw water, she would have submitted without a murmur; but this terrible tyrant was all the more cruel because he loved her; nay, by means of his affection he could wound and humiliate her in every possible way; and he delighted in proving her wrong on every point and on every occasion. The attentions he lavished on Mademoiselle Bourrienne had, during the last few months, been more marked than ever; and the preposterous notion that he might marry this foreigner, which had in the first instance occurred to him merely to annoy his daughter when Prince Andrew had asked his consent, evidently began to smile on his fancy; still, his daughter fondly persisted in believing it was only a new device to grieve and bully her.

One day, when she was present, the old prince, after kissing Mademoiselle Bourrienne's hand, drew her to him and embraced her. The princess coloured and left the room, persuaded that her father had done it to insult and vex her. A few minutes later, when Mademoiselle Bourrienne joined her, smiling and gay, she hastily dried her tears, and unable to contain herself, she loaded the Frenchwoman with reproaches.

"It is vile, base, monstrous to take such an advantage of weakness!" she exclaimed, unable to finish her sentence. "Leave my room," she cried loudly, and began to sob.

The next day her father made no comment on the scene, but she observed that the Frenchwoman was served first at dinner; and when the old butler unfortunately forgot this last whim of his master's, and handed the coffee to the princess first, the old man flew into a terrific rage. He flung his cane at the peccant butler, and declared he should be sent off to serve as a soldier that same hour.

"You forgot! you forgot my orders, when I told you myself? She is the first person in the house, now do you hear? She is my best friend. And if you ever allow yourself . . ." he added, turning to his daughter. "You . . . to forget yourself in her presence as you did last evening, I will teach you who is master here. . . . Go, leave the room, or ask her pardon!"

And Princess Maria apologised, and then, with great difficulty, extracted forgiveness for the hapless servant.

After such scenes as these, the poor girl went through agonising struggles between outraged pride as a victim, and the secret remorse of a Christian conscience. Her father, whom she dared to blame, was he not old and helpless? Feeling about for his spectacles, losing his memory, walking feebly, distressed to think that his senility should be observed, dozing off at meals, and nodding his old head over his plate when there was no one to amuse him. "God knows I have no right to condemn him!" she would say to herself, blaming herself for her first impulse to rebel.

CHAPTER XLII

THERE was at Moscow, at that time, a French doctor, a tall, handsome man, and very amiable, as his countrymen know how to be when it suits them, who had achieved a great reputation in the most aristocratic circles, where he was treated as an equal and a friend.

The old prince, though very sceptical of medical treatment, had consulted him by Mademoiselle Bourrienne's advice, and became so accustomed to Monsieur Métivier, that at last he saw him regularly twice a week.

On St. Nicholas's day all Moscow called at the prince's door to offer congratulations, but he was at home to no one but a small party of intimate friends whom he had asked to dinner, and of whom he had given a list to the Princess Maria.

Métivier, however, thought proper to run the blockade, and go in to see his patient, who was certainly in a diabolical temper. The Prince wandered from room to room, took up every word and pretended not to understand anything that was said to him, as though on purpose to find excuses for being angry. Princess Maria was only too familiar with this lowering storminess, ready at any moment to burst into fury, and as inevitable as the explosion of loaded fire-arms; she spent the morning in agonies of anticipation, but the tempest did not break out till the doctor came. Having yielded to his going into her father's room, she sat down with a book in her hand in the drawing-room, where she could hear what was going on in the study.

First she heard Métivier's voice, then the prince's, then both talked loudly together, and the door was flung open, revealing the doctor, evidently terrified, and behind him the old man in his dressing-gown, his face distorted by rage.

"You do not know what he would be at," he screamed, "but I know! — French spy! Bonaparte's creature! . . ." And he slammed the door in a fury.

Métivier shrugged his shoulders, and going towards Mademoiselle Bourrienne, who had rushed in from another room on hearing the noise, he said: "The prince is not quite himself to-day—a little bilious; but do not be uneasy. I will look in again to-morrow." Then he went away, advising perfect quiet, while through the door they could hear the prince in his slippers shuffling over the polished floor and his repeated exclamations: "Traitors! Spies! Treason on all sides! Never a moment's peace even in our own house!"

A few minutes later he sent for Princess Maria to receive all the brunt of the explosion. Was it not her fault, and no one's else, he said, that this spy had been admitted? Where was the list he had given her, what had she done with it? It was all her fault that he could neither live nor die in peace! "We must part, part at once; distinctly understand me, we part; I can bear it no longer!"

He was leaving the room, but fearing perhaps that she would not take his words seriously, he came back again with a great effort to seem calm. "Do not fancy," he said, "that I am speaking in a passion. I have weighed my words, and we must part. Find a home elsewhere, I do not care where." Then, forgetting the calmness he had put on for a moment, he shook his fist in her face, exclaiming: "To think that there should not be an idiot to be found to marry her!" And he rushed back into his own room, slammed the door, and sent for Mademoiselle Bourrienne. Then silence reigned for a while.

The six guests invited to dine arrived all together at about two o'clock. They were Count Rostopchine, Prince Lapoukchine and his nephew, General Tchatrow—an old comrade in arms of Prince Bolkonsky's—Peter, and Boris Droubetzkoï. They assembled in the drawing-room. Boris, who was at Moscow, on leave, had begged to be introduced to the prince, and had so far won his good graces that the old man made an exception in his favour, and received him in spite of his being a man of matrimonial age.

The Bolkonskys' house was not one of those which figured in what Moscow regarded as society; but the mere fact of being admitted to this exclusive circle was esteemed a most flattering distinction. Boris had fully appreciated this a few days previously, when the governor of the city had invited Count Rostopchine to dine with him on St. Nicholas's day— Boris happening to be present—and Rostopchine had declined the honour, saying: "I must go, you know, and worship the relics of Prince Nicholas Andréïévitch."

"To be sure," the great man had replied. "How is he?"

The little party assembled to wait for dinner in the spacious, old-fashioned drawing-room might have been a council of six deliberating on some important question, for they only spoke in subdued tones, and were sometimes silent. Prince Bolkonsky at length joined them, very taciturn and gloomy; his daughter, more nervous than ever, only replied quite shortly to his guests' remarks, and they saw at once that she was not attending to what was going on around her. The talk was left entirely to Count Rostopchine, who alternately gave them some item of Moscow gossip and of political news. Lapoukchine and old General Tchatrow said but little.

Prince Nicholas sat listening with the solemnity of a judge, and from time to time, by his silence, by a motion of his head, or by a word, gave them to understand that he took note of what was said. Politics was the principal topic, and it was easy to gather from the tone of the conversation generally that the conduct of the Russian government was unreservedly blamed, and that they all thought matters going wrong, and from bad to worse. The only limit the speaker set himself, or found set to his judgments, was when his unfavourable opinions involved him in personal reflections on the czar. They spoke of Napoleon's occupation of Oldenburg, and of the last Russian note, which was decidedly hostile to him in tone, and which had been sent to all the European powers.

"Bonaparte is treating Europe as a corsair treats a ship he has captured," said Rostopchine, quoting a phrase of his own that he had repeated several times during the last few days. "The long-suffering, or the blindness, of the great powers is really incomprehensible! Now it is the Pope's turn; Napoleon is doing all he can to upset the Catholic religion, and not a voice is raised! The czar is the only monarch who has protested against the occupation of the Grand Duchy of Oldenburg, and even he . . ." The count broke off, he had gone as far as any one might dare.

"He offered him another territory in exchange for Oldenburg," added Bolkonsky. "He takes grand dukes lightly, and dispossesses them as I should transfer my peasants from Lissy-Gory to Bogoutcharovo!"

"The grand duke bears his reverses with admirable fortitude and resignation," said Boris, putting his word in. He had been presented to the grand duke at St. Petersburg, and liked to let it be understood that he knew him. The prince flashed a glance at him, and was on the point of uttering some satirical remark, but it came to nothing. He probably thought him too young, and did not trouble himself about him.

"I read our protest, and was astonished to find it so badly written," said Count Rostopchine, with the cool assurance of a man who knows what he is talking about.

"What does the style matter if the language is emphatic?" said Peter, looking at him in frank surprise.

"My dear fellow, with an army of five hundred thousand men we might so well have afforded a little style!" replied Rostopchine, and Peter understood the force of his criticism.

"Everyone can blacken paper nowadays," said their host. "At St. Petersburg they do nothing else. My boy Andrioucha has written a whole volume of laws for the country. . . . No one can do anything but scribble."

Then the conversation flagged, but General Tchatrow, after many vigorous ahems, started it afresh.

"Did you hear what happened the other day at the review at St. Petersburg, and what the new French ambassador did?"

"Yes, I fancy I heard his reply to his majesty a good deal criticised."

"Well, judge for yourself. The czar condescended to call his attention to the regiment of grenadiers, and their splendid appearance as they marched past; the ambassador seemed perfectly indifferent, though it is said he was so bold as to remark that in France they did not trouble themselves about such trifles. His majesty took no notice at the time, but at the next review he simply ignored his presence."

All were silent. The emperor being implicated no comment was possible.

"Insolent brutes!" said the old prince. "You know Métivier? Well, I turned him out of my house this morning. He had been let in, in spite of my express orders, for I did not wish to see anyone. . . ." And he looked wrathfully at his daughter as he proceeded to give the history of his interview with the doctor who, as he declared, was nothing else than a spy; and he gave his reasons for thinking so—not very cogent ones to be sure, but no one ventured to dispute them.

When the champagne was poured out, at the same time as the roast was handed round, the company all rose to congratulate the master of the feast, and his daughter came round to kiss him. He looked at her from head to foot with a hard, spiteful stare, and put out his clean-shaved cheek; it was very evident that he had not forgotten the scene in the morning, that his determination was still the same, and that only the presence of his guests kept him from repeating his fiat.

At last, when coffee was served in the drawing-room, he unbent a little, and with quite youthful vehemence gave his opinion on the war that was threatening.

"Our struggles with Napoleon," he said, "will always be ineffectual as long as we insist on allying ourselves with Germany, and, as a fatal consequence of the treaty of Tilsit, have the affairs of all Europe on our hands. We ought never to have taken part either with or against Austria; we ought to confine our attention exclusively to the East. And as for Bonaparte, a firm demeanour and a well-guarded frontier are quite enough to keep him from again setting foot in Russia, as he did in 1807."

"But how can we possibly make war against France, prince?" asked Rostopchine. "How can we rebel against our masters —our demi-gods? Look at our young men, look at our ladies! The French are their idols, and Paris is their Paradise!" He raised his voice to command attention. "Everything is French — fashions, ideas, sentiment. You, you say, have turned out Métivier; but our ladies are on their knees to him. Yesterday, at an evening party, I saw five Catholics doing worsted-work on a Sunday, in virtue of a dispensation from his Holiness the Pope, but they hardly had any clothes on for all that, and might have been painted for the sign of a bath-house. How much I should have enjoyed, prince, taking Peter the Great's thick stick out of the Museum and breaking some of our young dandies' ribs with it, in the good old Russian fashion! . . . Their imbecile priggishness would soon have disappeared, I promise you!"

There was a pause, but the old prince nodded approbation, and smiled at his friend's outburst.

"And now good night, excellency; take care of yourself," said Rostopchine, rising with his usual abruptness and holding out his hand.

"Good night, my friend, your words are real music; I quite forget myself as I listen to you," and, gently detaining him, the prince offered him his parchment cheek. The rest, following Rostopchine's example, also rose.

CHAPTER XLIII

PRINCESS MARIA had not taken in a word of the conversation; she was possessed by one anxiety—the fear lest the constraint between her father and herself should be evident to their guests. She had not even paid any attention to Droubetzkoï's civilities, though it was his third appearance at the house. The prince accompanied his friends out of the room, and Peter came to her, hat in hand, and asked whether he might stay a few minutes longer.

"Certainly," she replied; and her anxious glance seemed to ask whether he had noticed anything. Peter, who was always sweetly amiable after dinner, smiled vaguely, and said:

"Have you known that young man long, princess?"

"What young man?"

"Droubetzkoï."

"No; only lately . . ."

"Do you like him?"

"Yes; he seems pleasant. But why do you ask me?" she said, still thinking, in spite of herself, of the scene of the morning.

"Because I have observed that a young man never comes to Moscow excepting in search of a rich wife."

"You have observed it?"

"Yes; he is always to be found within easy reach of an heiress. I can read him like a book. At the present moment he is in a state of doubt: he cannot make up his mind whether to give you or Miss Karaguine the preference; he is extremely attentive to her."

"He goes there a great deal, then?"

"Oh, yes! a great deal . . . In fact, he has invented a new way of paying court to a lady," Peter went on, with a good-humoured love of mischief, which he had often recorded against himself in his journal. "A man must be melancholy to please the young ladies of Moscow, and he is very melancholy with Miss Julia."

"Indeed!" said Princess Maria, who, looking into his kind face, thought to herself, "I should, I believe, be less miserable if I could confide in someone—for instance, in Peter. He has a noble nature, and I am sure could give me some good advice."

"Would you marry him?" Peter continued.

"Indeed, there are times when I would marry anyone—the first that offered," replied the poor girl, almost in tears, and in spite of herself. "It is so hard, so very hard, to love anyone and feel yourself a burthen on those you love—to be a trouble to them, and not to be able to help it; there is only one alternative, and that is to go away. . . . But where can I go?"

"What do you mean, princess; what are you saying?"

"Oh! I do not know what has come over me to-day," she said, unable to restrain her tears. . . . "But pay no heed to what I have said. . . ."

Peter's gay humour was gone; he pressed her kindly for some further explanation, and entreated her to tell him of her secret trouble; but she persisted in saying that it was nothing, that she had forgotten what was the matter; that her only trouble was her brother's approaching marriage, which she feared would lead to a quarrel between father and son.

"What do you know of the Rostows?" she went on, to change the subject. "I am told that they are coming to town; and I expect Andrew, too, from day to day. I should have liked them to meet here."

"What view does he take of the matter now?" asked Peter, meaning the old prince.

Princess Maria shook her head sadly. "Just the same as

ever; and there are only a few months now to the end of the year they were to wait. I wish I could have seen more of her. . . . You have known them a long time? Tell me honestly, and without reserve, what you think of her—quite frankly, would you? For Andrew is risking so much by going against my father in this matter that I should like to know. . . ."

Peter fancied that this pressing desire to know the truth, and nothing but the truth, betrayed some covert ill-feeling towards his friend's betrothed. Evidently Princess Maria counted on hearing some word of blame.

"I hardly know how to answer your question," he said, colouring very gratuitously in his anxiety to give her a true impression of his own feeling. "I have not analysed her character, so I cannot tell how far it is worthy; but I know that she is fascination itself. It is vain to ask me how, for I could not explain it."

Princess Maria sighed. This only confirmed her fears.

"Is she intelligent?"

Peter reflected. "Perhaps she is, perhaps not. But she does not care to make any display of it, for she is fascination itself, neither more nor less."

"I should like to love her with all my heart," said Princess Maria. "If you see her, pray tell her so."

"They will be here in a few days," said Peter.

She told him that she was fully determined to see Natacha as soon as possible after their arrival, and to do all she could to persuade her father to receive his future daughter-in-law with a good grace.

CHAPTER XLIV

BORIS, who had failed in finding a rich heiress at St. Petersburg, was following up the same game at Moscow, and he hesitated between the two best matches then open to him—Julia Karaguine and Princess Maria. In spite of her plain face the princess was the more attractive to him, but after the dinner, on St. Nicholas's day, it was in vain that he tried to approach the delicate subject; all his attentions were completely wasted, for Princess Maria hardly listened to him, and answered quite at random.

Julia, on the other hand, accepted his civilities with pleasure, though in a way of her own. She was seven-and-twenty; she was now very rich, but her beauty was not what it had been, though she herself was persuaded that, in spite of her mature years, she had never been handsomer or more bewitching; and her recently-acquired wealth encouraged her illusions. As her age made her less dangerous to men, they took full advantage of her dinners and suppers, and of the pleasant circle she gathered round her. without fear of compromising themselves or being ensnared by her. Men who, ten years ago, would have avoided her carefully, went there constantly now, regarding her no longer as a young lady on her promotion, but simply as a pleasant acquaintance, without any consideration of sex. Indeed, the Karaguines' receptions this year were the most brilliant and liberal of the season. Besides dinners and evening entertainments by special invitation, every evening a large party collected there, chiefly men; there was a capital supper at midnight, and they seldom broke up before three in the morning.

Julia never missed a ball, a performance, or a picnic; her dresses came from the first makers; at the same time she gave herself all the airs of a *blasée* woman of the world, affecting to have ceased to believe in friendship, love, or earthly happiness in any form, and to sigh only for peace "beyond the grave"! It might have been thought that she had suffered some cruel and terrible disappointment in love, or had lost some adored friend; but nothing of the kind had ever happened to her. She had, however, succeeded in persuading herself that her life had been a series of sorrows, and, by degrees, had made others believe it too. While she enjoyed herself thoroughly, and provided enjoyment for her acquaintance, she gave herself up to constant pathetic melancholy; but each one, after sympathising with her deeply, flung himself, heart and soul, into the spirit of the thing:—gossip, dancing, games of wit, and, above all, capping verses, which was a favourite amusement.

Some few of the younger men, and among them Boris, affected a more enduring interest in Julia's woes, and would talk with her by the hour of the vanity of this world, as they turned over the leaves of her albums of drawings, mottoes, and verses, on serious and sentimental subjects. She treated Boris with particular favour, compassionating his early disenchantment, and offering him the consolation of her valuable friendship—for she, too, had suffered so much! Her album had no secrets from him, and Boris drew in it on a blank page two trees side by side

147

with this motto: "Ye rustic trees—your branches cast darkness and melancholy around me." On another he sketched a coffin, with these lines:

> Death is our friend, our only hope of peace,
> For in the grave alone can sorrow cease.

Julia was delighted, and thought the lines exquisite; she responded by a passage from a novel she happened to remember:

"How enchanting is the smile of melancholy! It is like a gleam of light in the darkness, a half-tint between sadness and despair, heralding the dawn of consolation."

Boris, acknowledging the grateful appropriateness of the quotation, answered again in a stanza:

> Sweet nutriment of every sorrowing soul,
> The only joy my grieving spirit knows,
> Bland Melancholy, Hail! Thou can'st console;
> Bring respite from my solitary woes.
> Exert thy secret soothing charm,
> And turn my flowing tears to balm!

Julia frequently played the harp, and would choose, for her friend's special delectation, her most doleful nocturnes; he, on his part, read aloud to her the story of *Lisa*,[1] and emotion would often interrupt him in his reading. When they met in the gay world their eyes would say that they were alone to understand and appreciate each other.

Anna Mikhaïlovna was a constant visitor; she became Mrs. Karaguine's unfailing partner, and drew from the fountain-head all the information she could desire as to Julia's fortune. She soon found out that it consisted of two estates in the government of Penza, and some magnificent forest-land in that of Nijni Novgorod. As a humble and resigned waiter on Providence, she perceived in the ethereal sentimentality which served as a bond of spiritual union between her son and the wealthy heiress, an undoubted manifestation of the will of the Almighty.

"Boris always says that here alone can he find peace.—He has outlived so many illusions, and he has such a tender soul," she would say to the mother.

"Always sweet, but always sad, dearest Julia!" she added, to the daughter.

"My dear boy, I am devoted to Julia," she would say to her son. "I cannot tell you how much I love her—indeed, it is impossible to help loving her; she is a heavenly creature! And her mother, too; I am so sorry for her! I found her the

---

[1] A novel by Karamzine.

other day worried to death over her accounts and letters from Penza. They have plenty of money, but, as she has no one to help her in managing it, she is robbed and plundered on all sides."

Boris smiled faintly as he listened to these transparent hints, but he was greatly interested, all the same, in all that concerned Mrs. Karaguine's stewardship.

Julia calmly awaited her gloomy adorer's declaration, and had quite made up her mind to receive it with favour; but her entire lack of natural impulse, and too broadly betrayed desire to get married, added perhaps to the necessity it would entail on him of giving up a truer feeling, repelled Boris, and kept him from taking the decisive step. His leave was nearly at an end. Every evening, as he came away from the Karaguines', he had postponed his proposal till the morrow; but on the morrow, as he looked at Julia's reddened complexion, veiled under a sprinkling of powder, her languishing eyes and affected expression, ready at a moment's notice to cast off melancholy, and assume the rapture which his offer would certainly inspire, he felt his courage sink—nay, to so low an ebb, that the attractions of her fine estates and income, of which he already saw himself the master, were not enough to raise it. Julia saw his hesitancy; sometimes she even fancied that he had conceived an insurmountable antipathy towards her; but her feminine vanity soon rejected that hypothesis, and she then ascribed his shyness to the passion he felt for her. At the same time her sentimentality became touchy, and she had just made up her mind to take some decisive measure, when the unexpected arrival on the scene of Anatole Kouraguine cleared the way. Her melancholy vanished as if by magic; she was bewitchingly gay, and laid herself out to please him in every way she could think of.

"My dear boy," said Anna Mikhaïlovna to Boris, "I have it on the best authority that Prince Basil has sent his son here on purpose to make a match with Julia. I cannot tell you how deeply it grieves me, I am so fond of her.—What do you think of the matter?"

The idea of having wasted so much time and energy, of losing the fruits of these months of servitude, and of seeing a fortune of which he could make such good use fall into the hands of an idiot like Anatole, exasperated Boris. He firmly resolved to propose to Julia no later than the morrow. She received him with a careless smile, told him how much she had enjoyed some

149

party the night before, and asked him when he was leaving. Though he had come fully intending to be tender and sentimental and to declare his passion, Boris could not help taking a tone of complaint, accusing all women of frivolity, inconstancy and caprice, according to the humour they were in and their fancy for accepting the homage of the latest favourite. Julia, much offended, said he was quite right, for that nothing was more intolerable than sameness; and Boris was about to retort rather sharply when the prospect of quitting Moscow without having gained his point—a sort of defeat he was not accustomed to—checked the words on his lips. He looked down to veil the angry indecision of his eyes, and said in a low tone: "I did not come to quarrel with you, on the contrary . . ." He glanced at her to see if he might proceed, and met her feverish, anxious gaze fixed on him with eager expectation. "I can easily manage to see very little of her," he said to himself. "I am in for it, and must go on with it." He coloured a deeper crimson as he added: "You have of course guessed my feelings towards you. . . ."

Surely this ought to have been enough, for Julia was radiant with triumph, but she would not spare him a single word, and he was forced to say all that is usually said under the circumstances; that he loved her—that he had never loved any other woman with such passion—etc. etc. Knowing very well what she had a right to expect in return for the lands of Penza and the forests of Nijni, she extracted the price she desired.

"The trees whose branches shed shade and melancholy" were soon forgotten, and the happy couple, thinking only of their plans for the future and the arrangement of their luxurious home, paid innumerable visits and made ready for a splendid wedding at an early date.

CHAPTER XLV

COUNT ROSTOW left his wife, still ailing, at Otradnoë, and came to Moscow with Natacha and Sonia at the end of January. Prince Andrew was to arrive soon; they must prepare the trousseau, the property must be sold, the old prince must be called on, and his future daughter-in-law introduced to him. The Rostows' house was neither fitted up nor warmed for their reception, so the count accepted Maria Dmitrievna Afrossimow's pressing hospitality and went to her house, all the more willingly as he did not intend to make a long stay. So rather late one evening the four vehicles that conveyed the Rostows and their belongings turned into the court-yard of a house in the Old Stables Street. This house belonged to Maria Dmitrievna, who lived there alone, her daughter being married and her four sons with their regiments.

Age had not bent her: her loud voice and firm distinct utterance expressed her opinion frankly to all in turn, and her whole person was a standing protest against the weaknesses, passions, and impulses of human nature, to which she for one would not yield. She was up early every morning, slipped on a loose jacket and looked into every detail of household management; then, if it was a fête-day, she went out in the carriage, first to mass, and then to visit the prisons; but of this she never said a word. On other days, after finishing her toilet, she received every one without distinction of rank who came to appeal to her charity. This reception being over she dined; three or four pleasant intimates shared her plentiful and well-cooked meal, which was invariably followed by a game of boston. Later in the evening she sat knitting while someone read aloud to her—the newspaper or some new book. She never accepted invitations, with a few very rare exceptions in favour of some of the higher town functionaries.

She was still up when the Rostows' arrival made the great front door creak heavily on its hinges, and brought a rush of cold and snow into the hall. Standing at the threshold of the drawing-room, her spectacles low on her nose and her head held very high, Maria Dmitrievna examined her guests with her usual critical severity. She might almost have been supposed to be very much vexed with them, but her orders to the servants for the disposal of the new-comers and their luggage at once contradicted the idea.

"Is that the count's?—Here, then, this way," she shouted, without even stopping to bid them welcome, so anxious was she to see their trunks properly disposed of. "The young ladies' boxes—to the left.—Well, what are you doing with your mouths wide open?" she went on to the women-servants. "Get the samovar ready.—So here you are, and fatter and prettier than ever," she exclaimed, drawing Natacha forward, quite red with cold under her fur hood.

"Mercy, what an icicle! Take off your wraps,"—then turning to the count, who kissed her hand, "and you, too, perfectly frozen!—Bring some rum with the tea, and make haste.—Well, Soniouchka, and how are you?" she continued with the slightly supercilious affection she always displayed to Sonia.

When they had all taken off their furs and had gathered round the tea-table their hostess kissed each in turn.

"I am so glad to have you with me! . . . and it is high time, too," she added, looking at Natacha, "the old man is here, and her son is expected. We must become acquainted, we really must, but we can talk of that later . . ." She stopped short, with a glance at Sonia to convey that she did not choose to discuss the subject before her. "And who will you send for to call on you to-morrow?" she went on, and she counted on her fingers: "First of all, Schinchine, I suppose? Then Anna Mikhaïlovna,—a whimpering goose! Her son is here, and is going to be married. . . . And who next? Bésoukhow, he is here, too, with his wife . . . he ran away from her, but she has run after him; he dined with me last Wednesday. As to those children," and she indicated the two girls, "I will take them in the morning to say their prayers to the Iverskaïa Virgin, and then to stop at the 'Highway Robbers,'[1] for they have not clothes to their backs I am quite sure, and I cannot set them the fashions. There is something new every day; it is enough to make an old woman shudder. The other day I had good proof of it; a young lady had sleeves as big as barrels.—Well, and what business have you to do?" she added, looking stern again.

"Oh! a little of everything; the girls' clothes, to sell my house and land—in the suburbs, you know; so I shall ask your permission to make a short excursion so far—I will leave the children with you and spend a day there."

"Very well, they will be quite safe with me, I will answer for that; as safe as if they were wards of the empire. I will chaperon them, and scold them and spoil them," said Maria Dmitrievna, stroking Natacha's cheek, who was her favourite and her god-daughter.

The programme laid down for the next day was duly carried out; they first went to worship at the shrine of the Virgin, then they paid a visit to Madame Aubert Chalmé, the famous dress-maker, who stood in such awe of Maria Dmitrievna that, only to get rid of her, she sold her the prettiest thing in her show-room at a loss; however, on this occasion the chief part of Natacha's trousseau was ordered of her. When they got home again Maria Dmitrievna dismissed Sonia and took Natacha aside.

[1] A play on words.

"Now we can talk," she said. "I congratulate you; you have secured a charming man, and I am heartily glad for your sake; I have known him from childhood." Natacha coloured with pleasure. "I love him and all his people. Now, listen to me. The old prince is excessively unmanageable and he disapproves of this marriage, but Prince Andrew is not a child and can very well dispense with his consent. Only it is always painful to become one of a family that receives you grudgingly.— Conciliation is far preferable; set to work with hearty goodwill, and, as you are no fool, I feel sure that, with tact and gentleness, you can win them over and all will be well."

Natacha said nothing, not out of timidity, as her friend perhaps imagined, but because it wounded her deeply when any third person touched on her love affairs. Her passion for Prince Andrew was a thing so completely outside and above all everyday associations that she did not believe anyone could enter into her feeling about it. She loved him, he was all the world to her; and he loved her, and he was coming.—What did she care about the others?

"Maria, his sister, is a good soul, in spite of the saying about sisters-in-law having ugly quarrels; she would not hurt a fly. She asked me to let her see you; you might go there to-morrow with your father. Try to please her, you are the younger, you know, and at any rate you will have made acquaintance before he arrives—his father and his sister will have had time to become attached to you. Is it not so? Will not that be best?"

"Yes, I dare say," said Natacha, but not heartily.

CHAPTER XLIV

THIS advice, however, was taken; they were to call on the old prince. But Count Rostow went much against his will; he was very much alarmed at the idea of an interview, remembering only too vividly how the prince had taken him to task, on the occasion of calling out the militia, for not having furnished the regulation contingent of men; and this rating had come as the answer to an invitation to dinner! Natacha, on the contrary, dressed in her best, was in a radiant frame of mind: "It is impossible that they should refuse to be fond of me; such a thing never happened to me in my life; besides, I am ready to do anything and everything they can wish—to love the old man

153

because he is his father, and to love her because she is his sister—in short to love them all!"

They had scarcely got into the hall of the vast and gloomy Bolkonsky mansion, when the count could not help sighing deeply and murmuring:

"Merciful God protect us!"

His agitation was extreme, and it was in quite a subdued and humble voice that he asked to see the prince and Princess Maria. A footman hastened forward to announce them, but some strange confusion at once arose; the man who was taking the message was stopped by another at the door of the big drawing-room, and they stood whispering together; then the princess's maid came forward with a scared look and said something to them; and finally the old major-domo, with his puckered cross face, came back to tell the count that the prince could not have the honour of receiving them, but that Princess Maria begged they would go to her sitting-room. Mademoiselle Bourrienne came out to meet them, and led the way with effusive politeness to the princess's rooms. Princess Maria, crimson with shyness and emotion, advanced awkwardly to receive them, trying in vain to control her feelings. Natacha did not please her at the first glance; she thought her dress too fashionable, and herself too frivolous and vain; an obscure jealousy of the girl's beauty and youth, and of her brother's love for her, had from the first prejudiced her against Natacha, and the feeling had been brought to a head by the brief storm which the announcement of this visit had roused. The old prince had declared with many oaths that he did not want to see the Rostows, and that he would not see them; she might do as she pleased. It was in great fear, and trembling with agitation—dreading lest her father should commit some gross act of incivility—that she decided finally to ask them to pay their visit to her.

"I have brought my little singer to pay her respects to you, princess," said the count, bowing and looking round him in evident alarm lest the old prince should unexpectedly put in an appearance. "I am most happy, most flattered by your kindness in allowing her to make your acquaintance. . . . The prince is still so ill? That is very sad, really very sad.—Will you allow me," he said, after a few commonplace remarks, "to leave my daughter with you for about ten minutes?—I have some business in the immediate neighbourhood and will come back for her."

The count invented this errand on the spur of the moment, as he subsequently confessed, in order to give the future sisters-in-law an opportunity of talking to each other freely and frankly, and to avoid any risk on his own part of meeting the master of the house. His daughter guessed this; it piqued her pride and she coloured up; then, vexed with herself for blushing, she turned to the princess with a slightly defiant air. Princess Maria willingly agreed to the count's suggestion, hoping in fact to be alone with Natacha; but Mademoiselle Bourrienne was determined not to understand her meaning glances, and went on talking with bland volubility of the amusements of the Moscow season. Natacha, annoyed to begin with by the parley in the ante-room, and humiliated by her father's unconcealed alarm, was quivering and recalcitrant in every nerve; she involuntarily adopted an indifferent and reckless tone which jarred on Princess Maria, while to her the princess seemed stiff and cold.

A laborious conversation was kept up for about five minutes, and then a sound was heard of quick, short steps, and of slippers tapping and shuffling on the floor. Princess Maria turned white with terror; the door opened and the old prince came in, wrapped in a white dressing-gown, with a cotton night-cap on his head.

"Oh! Madam Countess—Countess Rostow if I am not mistaken, pray excuse me—I was not aware, God knows, that you had done us the honour of calling!—I came to speak to my daughter . . . that accounts for this costume.—Pray excuse it, countess! God knows, I had no idea you were here," he repeated with sharp, rude emphasis.

Princess Maria had risen and stood with downcast eyes, not daring to look at him or at Natacha, who had also risen from her seat. Only Mademoiselle Bourrienne continued to smile.

"Pray, excuse me; God knows I had no idea," the old man growled once more, and after staring at Natacha from head to foot he withdrew. Princess Maria and Natacha looked at each other in consternation, without saying a word or attempting any explanation; and this awkward silence confirmed and embittered their preconceived antipathy.

The count now returned, and Natacha made haste to take leave with an eagerness that was almost ill-mannered. She had taken a great dislike to this "old maid"; she was very much annoyed with her for having led her into such a false position, and above all for never having mentioned Prince Andrew:

155

"It was not for me to speak of him first—and before that Frenchwoman!" thought Natacha; while the same difficulty was tormenting Princess Maria. The princess, indeed, felt that she ought to say something about the marriage; but while, on one hand, she, too, felt uncomfortable in Mademoiselle Bourrienne's presence, on the other the subject itself was such a painful one that she did not know how to begin. At last, just as the count left the room, she went up to Natacha determined to speak, took both her hands and murmured: "One minute, dear Natacha—I must say—I must tell you how glad I am that my brother—has found happiness. . . ." She paused as though she were conscious of speaking falsely, and Natacha, who was looking at her with a rather satirical smile, at once understood this.

"It seems to me, princess, that you have chosen the wrong moment for speaking of the matter," she said, turning away with some dignity though tears started to her eyes. "What have I done? What have I said?" she thought.

When dinner-time came they waited a long time for Natacha; she was sitting in her room and sobbing like a child. Sonia stood by her side, kissing her hair.

"Natacha, what is there to cry for? What can it matter? It will all be forgotten!"

"But only think what a humiliation!"

"Forget it, my pet—it was no fault of yours—come, kiss me." Natacha put up her face and their lips met; then she leaned her tearful cheek against her friend's.

"I do not know—it is no one's fault—or perhaps it was mine; but it was frightful! . . . Oh, why is he not here?"

At last she went down; but she could not hide the fact that her eyes were red with crying. Maria Dmitrievna, knowing the reception Natacha and her father had met with, pretended not to notice how upset she was, and went on talking and laughing with her guests, in a loud voice as usual.

156

THE INVASION

CHAPTER XLV

THAT evening the Rostows went to the opera, where their hostess had secured a box. Natacha did not care to go, but as the kindness was meant especially for her she could not possibly refuse. She dressed and went into the drawing-room to wait for her father; there she caught sight of her own figure in a long mirror; she could not help stopping to look at the image, and it struck her as pretty—so pretty that she felt quite in love with it as she gazed.

"Oh God! if only he were here! . . . I should not be satisfied only to kiss him shyly, as I did when I was frightened at such a new sensation! . . . No, no, I should have thrown my arms round him and have clung close to his heart—I would have made him look straight, deep into my eyes with that keen gaze—I can see it now.—What do his father or his sister matter to me? It is he that I love, and no one else: his face, his eyes, his smile—a man's smile and a child's smile, too—I must not think of it—I had better forget it for a little while, for otherwise I can never bear to wait. . . ." And as she turned away from the glass she could hardly keep from sobbing. "How can Sonia love Nicholas in that calm placid way I wonder? How can she go on waiting with such patient constancy? I am not like her;—no, quite different. . . ." And she fixed her eyes on her friend, who was coming towards her playing with her fan.

In her mood of suppressed emotion and tenderness it was not enough to love and know that she was loved; she felt an aching impulse to throw her arms round her lover's neck and hear his lips utter the passionate words that were surging up in her own heart. During their drive, sitting by her father, she watched the street lamps that sparkled through the frozen panes, forgetting all that surrounded her, and giving herself up to a melancholy luxury of love and daydreams. Their carriage fell into the line, and gently drew up, with a dull sound of crunching snow, in front of the portico of the theatre; picking up their skirts Natacha and Sonia sprang out, while the old count slowly followed, supported by the servants. They all three made their way through the crowd that was pouring in, paying no heed to the shouts of the libretto-sellers, or the sounds of the orchestra which were vaguely audible through the closed doors.

"Natacha, mind your hair!" exclaimed Sonia, while the *capeldiener* [1] hastened to show them to their box. The music burst on their ears; the boxes filled with women in full-dress, and the stalls crowded with dazzling uniforms blazed before their eyes. A lady in the next box turned round and shot a look of feminine envy at Natacha. The curtain was still down; the overture was being played; Natacha and Sonia shook out their dresses, sat down in front, and looked at the boxes opposite. All these eyes directed on them—on their arms and shoulders, gave Natacha a mixed sensation of pleasure and discomfort which she had not felt for a long time, and which brought back to her memory a whole world of excitements, hopes, and remembrances associated with that feeling.

The two girls, both uncommonly pretty, and old Count Rostow, who had not been seen at Moscow for many months, soon became the centre of general attention. It was vaguely known that his daughter was to marry Prince Andrew, and that the Rostows had remained in the country ever since the engagement; so the chosen bride of one of the best *partis* in Russia was an object of the greatest curiosity.

Natacha, who had improved very much of late, was looking particularly well that evening, owing no doubt to the excitement she was going through, and which betrayed itself in the startling contrast between her exuberant life and youthfulness and her entire indifference to all that surrounded her. Her black eyes looked round at the crowd without resting on anyone, and her slender, small hand, lying on the velvet cushion in front of her, played mechanically with a programme.

"Look, I think that is Mrs. Alénine with her daughter," said Sonia.

"Mercy! Michael Kirilovitch is fatter than ever!" exclaimed the count.

"And do look at Anna Mikhaïlovna! what a thing she has on her head!"

"She is with Boris and the Karaguines—an engaged couple, that is very evident! Has Boris proposed?"

"What, did you not know Droubetzkoï was accepted?" said Schinchine, coming into the box.

Natacha, following the direction of her father's eyes, saw Julia, radiantly happy, sitting by her mother; a pearl necklace was displayed on her powdered throat. Boris's handsome head and shining hair were visible in the background; he leaned over

[1] A court servant employed in the imperial theatres.

158

his Julia and was murmuring something in her ear—evidently speaking of the Rostows.

"They are talking of us, of me . . ." said Natacha to herself. "He is bidding her not to be jealous of me—quite unnecessary, I am sure. If they could but know how little I care about them all."

Behind them was the green velvet structure that formed a setting for Mrs. Droubetzkoï's face, expressive of triumph no doubt, but of triumph tempered by resignation to the will of Providence. Natacha understood by experience that high-pressure atmosphere of joy and love which hangs about an engaged couple; her own sadness increased tenfold as she watched them, and the impression of the treatment she had endured that morning recurred to her mind with added bitterness. She turned her head away as if she were stung.

"What right has that old man to refuse to receive me?— But why do I let myself think of it? I will forget all these odious things till he comes." And she resolutely began to inspect the faces, known and unknown, that crowded the stalls. Exactly in the middle of the front row, with his back to the stage, reviewing the house, stood Dologhow in a Persian dress; his hair curled and frizzled out made a huge and strange-looking coiffure. Filling a most conspicuous place, and well aware that he was attracting the attention of everybody there, surrounded by the gilded youth of Moscow to whom he gave himself patronising airs, he seemed as much at his ease as in his own smoking-room.

Count Rostow touched Sonia's elbow to point out her former admirer.

"Would you have recognised him?—Where has he sprung from?" he asked Schinchine. "He had disappeared completely."

"Yes, completely. He went to the Caucasus, then he bolted; after that, they say, he was prime minister to some sovereign prince in Persia, and that he killed the Shah's brother—and now all the women have had their heads turned by Dologhow, the handsome Persian. Everything is Dologhow; he is the only thing to swear by; you are invited to meet him just as if he were some rare and dainty dish to be eaten! Dologhow and Anatole Kouraguine have made fools of them all!"

At this moment a tall and splendid woman came into the adjoining box. A thick plait of light hair lay like a diadem on her head; round her throat was a double row of large pearls, and her shoulders, displayed by a very low gown, were remarkable for their perfect form and whiteness. She was a long time settling herself, and shook out her rustling dress with a great deal of fuss. Natacha was admiring this magnificent person as a whole and in detail, when the magnificent person's eyes met those of Count Rostow and she bowed with a friendly smile. It was Peter's wife, Countess Bésoukhow. The count, who knew everyone, leaned over to speak to her: "Have you been long here? allow me the pleasure of kissing your hand in a few minutes. I am in Moscow on business and have the girls with me . . . I hear that Séménova is perfect in this opera.—And the count, is he here?"

"Yes, he meant to come," replied Helen, her eyes fixed on Natacha.

Count Rostow sat down again.

"Is not she beautiful?" he whispered to his daughter.

"Wonderfully beautiful," replied Natacha. "I can understand having a passion for her."

The overture being ended the conductor rapped out three strokes. Everyone settled into place, the curtain rose, and there was silence. Young and old, civilians and soldiers, and the women with bare arms and shoulders, covered with jewels —all alike turned their eyes on the stage, and Natacha followed their example.

CHAPTER XLVI

SIDE scenes representing trees framed the boarded stage; in the middle stood groups of girls in short petticoats and red bodices; one of them, who was remarkably stout and dressed in white, sat apart on a low stool leaning against a slope of green canvas; they were singing in chorus. When this was over the large girl in white came nearer to the prompter's box; a man in silk tights stretched over a huge pair of legs, a cap and feather on his head, and at his waist a dagger, went up to her and began singing a solo with much gesticulation. Then the lady in white had her turn; then both were silent; and presently, as the orchestra recommenced *da capo*, the man with the plume seized the damsel's hand as if he were about to count her fingers, and resignedly waited for the bar when they were to begin singing together! The audience clapped and stamped with delight, and the two singers representing, as it would seem, a pair of lovers, responded to the applause by bowing right and left by way of thanks.

To Natacha, fresh from the country and predisposed to be particularly thoughtful that evening, this performance was bewildering and purposeless. She could not follow the thread of the story or appreciate the subtleties of the music; all she saw was coarsely-painted canvas, men and women in extraordinary garments moving, speaking, and singing in a broad patch of blazing light. She knew what was aimed at, of course, but the absurdity and unnaturalness of the whole thing affected her with a feeling of shame and embarrassment for the actors even. She looked round for some trace of the same effect on the faces of her neighbours; but everyone, with eyes fixed on the stage, was watching the action of the play with growing interest, and expressing such extravagant enthusiasm that it struck her as artificial and affected. "I suppose it must be so!" she thought as she still looked down on the curled and oiled heads of the men below, at the low-dressed women in the boxes, and above all at her fair neighbour, Helen, who might almost have been supposed to have nothing on, and who sat placidly gazing at the scene, smiling with Olympian serenity, pleased with the full light that showed her off, and inhaling the steamy heat of the crowded house. Natacha gradually felt a sort of intoxication stealing over her to which she had long been a stranger; she forgot where she was, and the play going on under her eyes; she looked without seeing, while the absurdest and most fantastic ideas danced through her brain:—Should she, now, jump on to the stage and sing the air that the prima-donna had just finished; or give a tap of her fan to the little old man in the front row; or lean over Helen and tickle her back?

During one of the pauses which preceded each fresh number, the door of the stalls, close by the Rostows' box, opened softly to admit a late arrival whose steps could be heard in the passage. "Here comes Kouraguine!" whispered Schinchine.

Countess Bésoukhow turned round and Natacha saw her smile to a grand-looking officer in aide-de-camp's uniform who came towards their box with an air of ease and good breeding; she remembered having seen him at the ball at St. Petersburg. There was a conquering manner in his gait that might have been ridiculous if he had not been so superbly handsome, and if his regular features had not worn such a prepossessing expression of thorough cordial good-humour.

Though the curtain was up he walked quite leisurely along the carpeted way, his sword jingling slightly as it tapped his spurs, and his perfumed head held high but gracefully. He glanced at Natacha as he went up to his sister, and laying his hand on the shelf of the box nodded to her, leaned forward and asked her a question, with an evident reference to her pretty neighbour:

"Charming!" he said, clearly alluding to Natacha; and she felt it, though she did not hear it. Then he went on to his place in the front row, and as he sat down he gave a friendly nudge of the elbow to Dologhow, whom the others treated with envious deference.

"How much alike the brother and sister are!" said the old count. "And both how handsome!"

Schinchine began to tell him in a low voice of some recent intrigue of Kouraguine's, and Natacha did not lose a word of it—just because he had thought her charming.

The first act was over and the public began to go out and come in again incessantly.

Boris came round to the Rostows' box, accepted their congratulations with the utmost simplicity, and begged them in Julia's name to be present at their marriage. Natacha chatted with him quite gaily; and yet—this was that very Boris with whom she had once thought herself in love. But in the excited state she was in nothing seemed unnatural or extraordinary. The fair Helen smiled on everyone alike, and Natacha, as she talked to Boris, smiled like her.

Countess Bésoukhow's box was soon crowded with men of mark and talent who had evidently met there with a view to showing the world at large that they enjoyed the distinguished honour of her acquaintance. Kouraguine with his back to the stage, leaning, like Dologhow, against the barrier that divided off the orchestra, never took his eyes off the Rostows' box throughout the interval. Natacha felt sure that they were talking of her, and was flattered; she even turned a little so as to display her profile, which, in her private opinion, was the best view of her pretty face. Shortly before the second act Peter came in; the Rostows had not yet seen him—he looked sad and was stouter than ever. Taking no notice of anybody he made his way to the front. Anatole approached him and said something, eyeing and indicating the Rostows' box. Seeing Natacha he hastened forward and came to speak to her. Leaning on the barrier of the box, he talked smilingly to her for a long time. During her talk with Peter, Natacha heard a male voice in the box of Countess Bésoukhow, which she somehow felt to be the voice of Kouraguine. Looking round swiftly his eyes met hers. Indeed he did not take them off her, and they expressed such enthusiastic and even tender admiration that she was conscious and embarrassed at seeing him so near her and feeling that she attracted him without their being acquainted.

The scene of the second act was a cemetery full of graves and monuments, and in the middle of the background there was a hole to represent the moon. Night fell—by means of shades over the foot-lights—horns and double basses were muffled, and a crowd of supernumeraries in trailing black cloaks came forward from the side scenes. They proceeded to wave their arms, brandishing objects which, in the dim light, looked like daggers, when some others rushed on dragging with them the lady of the white robe—only now she was in blue. Happily for her they began to sing in chorus before they had gone far. They had no sooner done than three smart blows on the drum were heard behind the scenes; the men in black fell on their knees and intoned a hymn, accompanied by the vociferous plaudits of the spectators, who even interrupted their pious exercises more than once.

Every time Natacha looked down at the stalls she could not help seeing Anatole, who sat with his arm over the back of Dologhow's seat, and his eyes fixed on her; and without attaching any importance to the fact, she felt a thrill of pleasure at the idea that she could so bewitch him.

Countess Helen took advantage of the next interval to move; she turned her handsome shoulders on the count and beckoned him with her finger; then she began a confidential talk, totally ignoring the visitors to her box who had come to pay their respects to her.

"Pray introduce me to your charming girls," she said. "All Moscow is talking of them, and I have not yet made their acquaintance."

Natacha rose and curtsied to the superb countess; she was so much touched by the compliment that she could not help colouring.

"I mean to become quite a Moscovite," Helen went on. "What a shame to keep two such pearls hidden in the depths of the country!" The countess might well be called a fascinating woman: she had the gift of being always able to say the very contrary of what she thought, and above all the whole art of flattering with a perfectly natural grace. "You must allow

163

me, dear count, the pleasure of seeing something of these young ladies; my stay here, like yours, will, it is true, be but a short one, so we must make the most of the time. I have heard a great deal about you," she added to Natacha with her stereotyped, engaging smile, "at St. Petersburg, from my humble servant Droubetzkoï, and from my husband's very good friend, Prince Bolkonsky." She emphasised the fact to convey that she knew of Natacha's engagement; and to promote their further acquaintance she invited her to come into her box.

The third act took place in a brilliantly-lighted palace, decorated with full-length portraits of bearded knights. In the middle were two personages representing apparently a king and a queen. The king, after some gesticulation, timidly began a grand *scena*; this he got through, it must be said, with small credit to himself, after which he took his seat on a purple throne. The young lady who had first appeared in white and then in blue now seemed to have little more on than her shift; her hair hung loose, and she gave utterance to her despair in a song addressed to the queen; but the king having raised a prohibitive hand, a crowd of men and women with bare legs appeared from various corners and began to dance. The fiddles played a light quick tune; one of the dancers, who had large legs and lean arms, came forward from among her companions, and after retiring for a moment to arrange her bodice, took her stand in the middle and began to jump, clapping her feet together. The spectators applauded with all their might. A man, also barelegged, struck an attitude in the right-hand corner, cymbals and trumpets played faster than ever, and he, in his turn, sprang forward, leaping and kicking in the air; this was Duport, who was making 60,000 francs a year by cutting capers. The enthusiasm of the house, boxes, stalls and "gods," knew no bounds; there was a perfect storm of clapping, shouting and stamping, and the dancer paused to bow and smile. Then the ballet went on till the king made some observation in recitative and all the chorus replied; but suddenly a tempest came on to an accompaniment of minor scales and chords in the orchestra, the stage crowd dispersed on all sides, carrying off the damsel in the shift, and the curtain fell. Then the spectators shouted louder than before, calling Duport with indescribable vehemence. And by this time Natacha had not only ceased to think it strange, she was actually smiling at all she saw.

"Is not Duport quite admirable?" Helen asked her.

"Oh yes!" replied Natacha.

THE INVASION

CHAPTER XLVII

DURING the next interval the countess's door was again opened, and the cold draught was followed by Anatole, who bowed his way in, caréful not to disturb anything.

"Allow me to introduce my brother," said Helen, turning her eyes uneasily from Natacha to Anatole. Natacha looked round at the handsome young man whom she thought no less splendid near than he had seemed at a distance, and she smiled at him over her shoulder. He sat down behind her, and assured her that he had longed to have the pleasure of her.acquaintance ever since he had seen her at the Naryschkines' ball. Koura-guine could talk very differently to men and to women; with the latter he was always natural and unpretentious; and Natacha was agreeably surprised by his simplicity and frank kindliness of manner, so that in spite of all she had heard against him, she did not feel at all uneasy with him.

Anatole asked her what she thought of the opera, and told her of the fall that Séménova had had at the last performance. "Do you know, countess," he said suddenly in the tone of an old acquaintance, "that a fancy-dress procession is being arranged; you really must join in it. It will be very good fun. We are all to meet at the Karaguines'. Do come, too,—you will, will you not?" and his eyes smiled back at Natacha's smiling eyes and then glanced, still with a smile, at her shoulders and arms. She felt their gaze even when she was looking else-where, with a mixed emotion of gratified vanity and natural shyness. However, she turned her head quickly, trying to divert this impertinent curiosity to her face again, and then she could not help asking herself with some anxiety what had become of that instinctive coyness which had always stood as a barrier between her and other men, and which he apparently ignored. How had this stranger, in so short a time, put himself on such a footing with her? How was it that after these few minutes' conversation on indifferent matters she was conscious of discomfort at seeing him so close to her, and of a fear lest he should secretly seize her hand, or even bend forward and kiss her shoulder? Never before had any man given her this sense of audacious intimacy. She looked up with questioning eyes at her father and Helen, as though they could explain; but Helen was thinking only of her squire then in attendance; and her father's genial smile and accustomed good-humour seemed to say: "You are enjoying yourself? So much the better; I am very glad of it."

After a short pause, which Anatole took advantage of to fix his fine eyes on her face, Natacha, in order to break the silence, asked him whether he liked Moscow; but no sooner had she spoken than she coloured. She felt as if she were doing something improper by talking to him.

"I did not like it much when I first arrived," he said with a smile. "What makes the place pleasant is the presence of pretty women—don't you think so? And there was none here then. Come to the procession, countess; you will be the queen of beauty there—and, to pledge yourself irrevocably, give me that flower."

Natacha, though she did not take in all the significance of this speech, felt its outrageous audacity. Not knowing what reply to make she turned away, pretending not to have heard it. But the feeling that he was there—close to her, behind her—oppressed and worried her: "What is he doing?" she wondered. "Is he ashamed? or vexed with me? Is it my place to try to mend matters? . . ." Finally she could not help looking round, and was conquered at once by his winning smile, his perfect self-confidence and cordial warmth of manner. This irresistible attractiveness filled her with alarm by showing her, more clearly than ever, the absence of any barrier between herself and him.

The curtain rose again; Anatole went back to his stall with a complacent smile, and Natacha returned to her father's box, taking with her the impression of having had a glimpse into another world. Her lover, her visit that morning, her country life—all was obliterated from her memory.

In the fourth act a tall devil sang and played antics till he vanished through a trap. This was all she saw. She was agitated and upset; and it must be confessed that Kouraguine, on whom she involuntarily kept an eye, was the cause of her discomfort. As they were going out he reappeared, called up their carriage, and helped them in, taking advantage of the opportunity to press Natacha's arm just above the elbow. Startled and blushing she looked round, and met a glance of tender passion from eyes that glowed and smiled at her.

When they reached home they found tea waiting for them, and not till then did Natacha shake off her bewilderment and begin to understand what had happened. The memory of

Prince Andrew came upon her like a thunderbolt; her face tingled with shame, and she hastily fled to her own room: "Good God! How could I let him do such a thing! I am ruined, lost! . . ." she thought, in her horror. Covering her burning cheeks with her hands she sat thinking for a long time, but without succeeding in bringing order into the chaos of her impressions. Just now, in that great lighted theatre, where Duport in his short spangled jacket was jumping on the watered boards, while old men and young men, and even the placid Helen, with her preposterously low bodice and her imperious smile, shouted bravo till they were hoarse. Just now, under the influence of that intoxicating atmosphere, all had seemed obvious and natural; but here and now, alone with her conscience, everything was dark and confused.

"What ails me?" she asked herself. "What just now made me so uncomfortably conscious, and what is this remorse that torments me now?" Her mother, to whom alone she could have confessed and confided all she felt, was far away. Sonia would not have understood, and her straightforward and strict judgment would have been horrified. So Natacha was reduced to seeking the cause of her torments in her own heart.

"Am I really unworthy of Prince Andrew's love?" she wondered; and then she laughed at her own folly. "How absurd! I really am an idiot to ask myself such a question! It is nothing after all—it was not my fault; I did nothing to put such an idea into his head. No one will ever know anything about it, and we shall never meet again. I have nothing whatever to blame myself for, that is quite certain, and Prince Andrew may still love me just as I am—just as I am! But what am I? Oh, merciful God! why is he not here?" She tried to comfort herself, but a deeper instinct revived her doubts; in spite of all the reasons she could give herself, she felt that the first purity of her passion for her lover had vanished for ever; and imagination insisted on recalling to her memory every detail of her conversation with Kouraguine, every feature of his face, every movement of his person, and the handsome officer's impudent smile as he squeezed her arm.

CHAPTER XLVIII

ANATOLE KOURAGUINE had been sent away from St. Petersburg by his father because he was there spending 20,000 roubles a year, not to speak of an equal sum outstanding in debts, for which his creditors were incessantly dunning him. Prince Basil explained that he would pay half of these debts for the last time, on condition that Anatole should go to live at Moscow where he had procured a place for him as aide-de-camp to the governor, and that he should make up his mind to marry some rich heiress—Princess Maria, for instance, or Julia Karaguine. Anatole agreed, went to Moscow, and made himself at home in Peter's house. Peter, at first, did not make him particularly welcome; but he soon got accustomed to his presence, sometimes joined in his orgies, and often gave him money under pretence of it being a loan.

Schinchine spoke truly when he said that Anatole turned all the women's heads; mainly by his lordly indifference to ladies and avowed preference for gipsy girls and actresses—particularly for Mademoiselle Georges, with whom he was said to be on terms of the greatest intimacy. He was to be met at every supper-party, at Danilow's as well as at every other fast man's in Moscow; drank hard, and left all his companions under the table. He never missed a soirée or a ball, where he openly paid court to several married women of fashion, with whom he carried on a more or less pronounced flirtation. As to choosing a wife, he never thought of that; for an excellent reason known only to a few intimate friends—he was married already. A Polish farmer, on whom he had been billeted two years before, had forced him to marry his daughter.

But he soon deserted his wife, and persuaded his father-in-law, in return for a sum of money, to be paid periodically, to connive at his continuing to pass for a bachelor. He was perfectly content, unfailingly satisfied with himself and the rest of the world, unable to conceive of any other mode of existence, and convinced that he had only the merest peccadilloes on his conscience. His view of things was that the Providence, which had made the duck to swim, had bestowed on him, Anatole Kouraguine, the right to spend 30,000 roubles a year and to be everywhere, and at all times, first and supreme. This belief was so firmly rooted in his mind that it even spread to those who came into contact with him; everyone gave way to him, everyone lent him money, which he borrowed as a matter of course, and, no less as a matter of course, never repaid.

He was no gambler, he had no sordid love of winning; he lacked vanity, and was indifferent to the opinion of others; he had no tinge of ambition, and drove his father to despair by his crazy freaks, which injured his prospects, and by his perpetual mockery of all dignities and honours. On the other hand, he was not avaricious, but always ready to help a friend. He was simply devoted to pleasure and to women; he could not see what there was wrong or base in his tastes, and was incapable of calculating the consequences of his deeds or passions, to himself or to others. In short, he considered himself a blameless character, had a genuine contempt for a rogue and held his head high with a quiet conscience.

Most magdalens, whether men or women, have a secret and childish belief in their own innocence, based on their hope of forgiveness. "She shall be forgiven much, for she hath loved much." "He shall be forgiven much, for he hath enjoyed much!"

Dologhow, having returned to Moscow from his foreign exile, was living in the most splendid style on the strength of his adventures in Persia, playing high, and indulging in every form of dissipation. This was of itself enough to bring him and his old companion in folly together once more, and to enable him to take advantage of the intimacy for his own benefit. Anatole, who thought highly of his courage and intelligence, was sincerely attached to him, while Dologhow simply made use of Kouraguine as a bait to catch young men of wealth, though he took good care not to let him suspect this. Besides these interested motives, moreover, it was a pleasure to him—a habit, and almost a necessity, to have some pliant will under the control of his own.

Natacha had made a sudden and deep impression on Anatole. As he sat at supper after the opera, he enlarged with the unction of a connoisseur on the beauty of her arms, her shoulders, her feet, her hair, and announced his intention of devoting himself to her forthwith, without stopping to think what the result might be for both of them. Such vulgar considerations were not part of his programme.

"She is very pretty, my boy, but she is not for us," said Dologhow.

"I shall tell my sister to invite her to dinner," said Anatole. "What do you think?"

"Wait till she is married."

"You know I adore little girls; you can turn their brains in a moment."

"Take care; you have been caught by one little girl," said Dologhow, alluding to his marriage.

"For that very reason I cannot be caught a second time," said Anatole, with a hearty laugh.

CHAPTER XLIX

THE Rostows remained at home next day, and no one came to call. Maria Dmitrievna and the count had a long private conference; they were laying a plot to attack the old prince. Natacha guessed their scheme, and it piqued and troubled her. She expected every hour to hear that Prince Andrew had arrived, and sent twice in the course of the day to inquire. Vain hope! Suspense added to her dejection, and the painful impression left by her interview with Princess Maria and the prince lent a vague feeling of alarm . . . . to her fevered impatience. She fancied sometimes that Prince Andrew would never come back, or else that something fatal would happen to herself. She could not drift into daydreams as she was wont, for all the experiences of the last few days would intrude themselves. For the hundredth time she asked herself if she had indeed been guiltless, if she were as constant as ever; and she recapitulated, in spite of herself, every detail of that evening at the opera—every shade of expression in the face of the man who had produced an impression on her that was as terrible to her conscience as it was incomprehensible. On the surface she seemed brighter and livelier than ever, while in her heart she had utterly lost all happiness and peace.

On the Sunday morning Maria Dmitrievna proposed that the young people should go to service at the parish church. "I do not like fashionable church-going," she said. "God is everywhere the same. Our priest is a very excellent man, and the deacon, too, and the service is well performed; and I cannot see that a choir, or the concert music that is given in some churches, beseems the sanctity of the place! I do not approve of it—it is making things too pleasant."

Maria Dmitrievna kept Sunday as a high festival; her house was cleaned from top to bottom every Saturday; neither she nor her servants did any such work on the Lord's day, and everyone went to mass. She had some extra dish for dinner, and would give the servants a treat of brandy, with a goose or a sucking-pig. And nowhere was the influence of the day more distinctly legible than on the broad, full face, always serious though it was, of the mistress of the house.

After returning from mass they had coffee in the drawing-room, where the chairs had their work-a-day covers removed, and presently the carriage drove up to the door. Wrapped in her very best shawl, Maria Dmitrievna rose and announced that she was going to call on Prince Bolkonsky, to come to some explanation with regard to Natacha.

A few minutes later, Madame Aubert Chalmé came to try on Natacha's dresses, and she, only too glad of anything to divert her thoughts, withdrew with the dressmaker to her own room. At the very moment when she was standing before the long glass, her head turned over her shoulder to contemplate the back of the bodice—which was only tacked together, and had no sleeves—she heard her father's voice, and that of a lady, which, with strange excitement, she at once recognised as Helen's. She had not time to put her dress on again before the door opened and Countess Bésoukhow came in, more smiling than ever, in a violet velvet dress richly trimmed.

"Ah! my beauty, my charmer," she began, "I have come on purpose to tell your father that it is really monstrous to keep you here without seeing a living soul! I insist on your coming to me this evening. I shall have a small party—Mademoiselle Georges will recite for us. . . . If you do not bring your sweet girls," she went on to Count Rostow, who had just strutted in, "I shall positively have to quarrel with you. My husband is gone to Tver, otherwise I should send him to fetch you. . . . You will be sure to come, will you not? Without fail—at about nine?"

Then, with a civil nod to the dressmaker who knew her well, and made her a very low curtsey, she seated herself in an easy-chair near the mirror, and while she gave her skirts a graceful turn, she went on chatting in the most friendly way, going into ecstasies over Natacha's beauty and her pretty new dresses, speaking of a new one of her own, and recommending the girl to have one made exactly like it. "It is lovely, my dear; gauze with metallic lights. . . . But what does it matter after all, for everything you wear looks well."

Natacha beamed with delight; it was new life to her to listen to the flattery of this amiable countess, who had struck her at first as so imposing, so loftily inaccessible, and who now treated her with infinite cordiality. It quite turned her head. Helen was in fact perfectly sincere, but wished to attract Natacha to her own house; her brother had begged her to get her there; and she was eager to serve his interests; the idea of bringing her brother and Natacha together amused her. She had once upon a time been jealous of Natacha's attraction for Boris; but she had quite forgotten that, and honestly wished her new friend to have all she had herself. As she was leaving she drew Natacha aside.

"My brother dined with us yesterday," said she, "and we nearly died of laughing. He eats nothing and can only sit and sigh. . . . He is madly, quite desperately in love with you, my dear."

Natacha blushed crimson.

"How she colours up—dear child!—Well, be sure you come. Though you are in love, it is not a reason for shutting yourself up; even though you are engaged, I am sure your future husband would be charmed to think that you went out a little in his absence, rather than perish of dullness."

"Then she knows I am engaged," said Natacha to herself, "and yet she has talked and laughed about it all with Peter, who is right-mindedness itself!—Then there can be no harm in it."

Under Helen's influence, in fact, all that till now had terrified her, seemed quite a matter of course. "She is a really perfect lady and most charming, and evidently has taken a great fancy to me. Why should I not have a little amusement?" And she looked up at her wide-eyed, with some surprise.

Maria Dmitrievna returned to dinner: it was evident from her silence and absent manner that she had been defeated. She was too much agitated to speak calmly of her interview with the old prince, and would only say that all would be well, and that the count should hear more about it to-morrow. But when she heard of Countess Bésoukhow's call and invitation she said very plainly that she did not wish to have her in her house, and she strongly urged that there should be no intimacy with Helen. "However," she added to Natacha, "go, as you have promised. It will be a little amusement for you."

THE INVASION

CHAPTER L

THE count accordingly escorted the two girls to the Bésou-khows' that evening. Though the party was a very large one, the company was for the most part unknown to the Rostows, and the count was much annoyed to perceive that it consisted almost exclusively of men and women whose manners were stamped by conspicuous free-and-easiness. The young men, among whom many were French—including Métivier, who had become intimate in the house since Helen's return to Moscow, crowded round Mademoiselle Georges; the count, therefore, quite made up his mind not to play cards or leave the girls to themselves, but to take them away as soon as the French actress had done her recitation.

Anatole, who had placed himself near the door so as not to miss their entrance, went forward, bowed and followed Natacha, who at once felt that heady pleasure of gratified vanity mixed with vague alarm which she had experienced at the theatre.

Helen received her with effusive warmth, and complimented her loudly on her looks and her pretty dress. While Mademoiselle Georges withdrew to change her costume, the chairs were placed in rows, and everyone found a seat; Anatole was about to take a place by the side of Natacha when the count, who kept his eyes on his daughter, took the chair, so he was obliged to find one close behind them.

Mademoiselle Georges soon reappeared, draped in a crimson shawl fastened on the shoulders so as to display her fine, though large dimpled arms; she stood in the middle of the space left for her facing her audience, struck an affected attitude which was hailed by a murmur of enthusiasm, and after gazing round her with theatrical gloom, began to declaim a long soliloquy in French (from *Phèdre*) describing her guilty passion for her stepson. Raising and dropping her voice by turns, she lifted her head in defiant pride or, rolling her eyes, she gave utterance to deep hoarse chest-notes.

"Exquisite! divine! delicious!" was shouted on all sides. —Natacha, with her eyes fixed on the stalwart tragédienne, neither saw nor understood. She was only conscious of having been suddenly plunged once more into this strange mad world, immeasurably remote from reality; a world where good and evil, folly and reason, were all mingled in confusion. Startled and painfully excited, her nerves were quivering

173

with expectancy. The monologue being ended, everyone rose and approached the actress.

"How beautiful she is!" Natacha exclaimed to her father who, like the rest, was trying to get through the crowd.

"I cease to think so when I look at you," Anatole murmured in her ear so that she alone could hear. "You are too be-witching. From the first moment I saw you . . ."

"Come, Natacha," said the count, turning round.

She followed her father with a dazed look in her eyes.

Mademoiselle Georges recited several more pieces, and then bid the countess good night. The rest of the company were asked to adjourn to the ball-room. The count now wished to leave, but Helen besought him so earnestly not to spoil her little improvised dance by taking away the two girls that he yielded and stayed. Anatole at once engaged Natacha for a waltz, and all through it, as he clasped her waist and hand, he kept telling her how charming she was, and how much he loved her. During the "Caledonians," which they danced together, he at first stood silent, and she wondered whether she had not dreamed that he had been making love to her all through the waltz; but at the end of the first figure she felt the pressure of his hand once more, and she was about to remonstrate when the tender and confident expression of his eyes stopped the words on her lips: "Do not say such things to me, I am engaged —I love another," she said, looking at him.

"Why do you tell me that?" replied Anatole, who did not seem in the least disturbed by the statement. "What does it matter to me? I only know that I love you—that I love you to distraction.—Is it my fault if you are irresistible? . . . It is our turn to lead the figure."

Natacha looked about her, half scared, and was less calm than usual in her demeanour. After the "Caledonians" there was a country-dance, the "*Grossvater*," and again her father wished to leave; she begged him to let her dance this, and yet, turn which way she would she felt herself under the fire of Anatole's eyes. She went into a room where the ladies had left their wraps to pin up a flounce on her dress which had come unsewn, and was followed by Helen, who laughed at her as she spoke of her brother's sudden passion; they went together into an adjoining room where Anatole was standing; then Helen vanished and Natacha was alone with him.

"You know," he began, in pathetic accents, "that I cannot see you at home. Must I be condemned, then, never to see you? I love you—you cannot think how madly; and must I never . . ." He detained her as she was about to go on, and bent down with his face quite close to hers. His glowing and sparkling eyes looked straight into hers, and she tried in vain to escape their fascination: "Natacha," he whispered, clenching her hands in his—"Natacha!"

"I do not understand. I can tell you nothing," was what her bewildered gaze seemed to answer. His burning lips were pressed to hers, but suddenly he let her go.—To Natacha it was deliverance! The rustle of a dress and a footstep were audible at the door; it was Helen. Natacha saw her coming. Crimson and shuddering, she turned as if to ask some explanation, and went to meet the countess.

"One word, only one word," said Anatole.

She waited, for in truth she wanted him to say the word which would define the situation and give her something to answer. And again he repeated: "Natacha, one single word!" But he had no idea what that word was to be.

His sister joined them, and they all three returned to the ball-room. The Rostows declined to remain to supper, and took their leave.

Natacha lay awake all night, tormented by the problem she could not solve. Which of the two men did she love?—She certainly loved Prince Andrew; she had not forgotten her strong affection for him . . . but she loved Anatole too, beyond a doubt: "Otherwise, how could all this have happened? Could I have smiled in answer to his smile? When I did that it must have been because I loved him at once, at first sight. . . . That must mean that he is so good and generous and handsome that I could not help loving him. Oh! what am I to do? I love him and I love the other," and she said it again and again, without finding any issue from the overwhelming dilemma.

CHAPTER LI

MORNING brought back more commonplace cares and the usual bustle; the household got itself up and dressed, there was talk and stir, dressmakers and milliners played their accustomed parts, Maria Dmitrievna came out of her room, and they all met for breakfast. Natacha, with eyes that looked large after

175

her sleepless night, tried to read the glances of her companions, and did her utmost to seem her usual self.

After luncheon, which was her best time, Maria Dmitrievna settled herself in her arm-chair and called the count and Natacha to a conference.

"Well, my friends, after weighing the matter well, this is what I have to say: yesterday, as you know, I saw old Prince Bolkonsky. I spoke to him; he raised his voice and stormed, would you believe it? . . . But it is not easy to shut my mouth, and I had it all out with him from beginning to end."

"And what did he say?" asked the count.

"He—he is an old fool, and will not listen to anything; what is the use of talking to him? This poor child has been worried enough about him already. My advice is that you should finish your business here as soon as you can, and return to Otradnoë and wait. . . ."

"No, no!" cried Natacha.

"Yes, yes!" replied the old lady. "You must go, and you must wait. If you and Prince Andrew are here together a quarrel is inevitable; but if he is alone with the old man they will discuss things, and then Prince Andrew will go to fetch you."

The count saw that the plan was wise, and expressed approval. If the old man became more manageable the Rostows could always come back to Moscow, or even go to Lissy-Gory; in the opposite case, if he persisted in refusing his consent, the marriage could only take place at Otradnoë.

"What you say is quite true," he said. "And my only regret now is that I ever took Natacha to the house."

"There is no cause for regret. You could not have avoided paying him that mark of respect. . . . If he will not give in, that is his affair. The trousseau is all ready; why wait any longer? I will undertake to forward everything that has not yet been sent. I am very sorry to part with you, but it is far better so. Go, and God be with you all." Then she took a note from Princess Maria out of her bag, and handed it to Natacha:

"It is for you," she said. "The poor soul is afraid you may doubt her affection."

"Very true," said Natacha; "she does not love me."

"What nonsense! hold your tongue," said Maria Dmitrievna, very angrily.

"I ask no one's opinion. I know it; she does not love me," Natacha retorted, as she took the letter with an air of irritation and perversity that caused Maria Dmitrievna to look narrowly at the girl and frown.

"You will have the goodness not to contradict me, my dear; what I have said is true.—Go and answer the letter." And Natacha went without another word.

Princess Maria in a few kind lines expressed her regret at the misunderstanding that had come between them, and entreated Natacha to believe in her affection for the wife chosen by a brother for whom she would sacrifice anything and everything. Whatever her father's views might be, Natacha was not to think that he was ill-disposed towards her. "He is old and ailing," she wrote, "and you must excuse him; but he is thoroughly kind-hearted, and will not fail at last to love the woman who can make his son happy." She ended by begging Natacha to fix a time when they might meet.

Natacha sat down and mechanically wrote the two words: "Dear Princess," . . . then she laid down her pen. How was she to go on? What could she say to her after last evening?

"Yes, it is all over; everything is different now; I must refuse him. . . . But ought I?—This is dreadful!" And to escape for a while from these maddening thoughts she joined Sonia, who was busy choosing some patterns for worsted work.

After dinner she read the letter once more. "Is it really at an end—really and truly? Is the past quite and for ever effaced from my heart?" She was fully aware how strong her feeling had been for Prince Andrew; but now she was in love with Kouraguine; fancy painted in turns the happiness she had so often dreamed of as hers when she should be married to Bolkonsky, and the smallest incidents of the previous night, of which the mere remembrance fired her whole being: "Why may I not love them both?" she thought wildly. "That is my only hope of happiness. It is impossible to choose. How can I tell it—or, rather, how can I hide it from Prince Andrew? Must I say good-bye for ever to his love which so long has been my only joy?"

"Miss," said the maid, coming in mysteriously, "a man gave me this for you,"—and she held out a letter: "Only, for pity's sake . . ."

Natacha mechanically took the note, opened it and read it. She understood but one thing: that the letter was from him—from the man she loved.

"Yes, I love him. If I did not, could what happened have

taken place? could I hold this letter of burning passion in my hands?"

Tremulous with agitation, she devoured the contents; every line was the utterance of her own feelings. The letter, it must be said, had been composed by Dologhow, and ran as follows:

"Last evening decided my fate. You must love me or I die —there is no third alternative." Then Anatole went on to say that her parents would certainly refuse their consent for various secret reasons which he could tell her only; but that, if she loved him, it would be enough that she should say so, and no human power could interfere to prevent their happiness. Love conquers all! He would carry her off to the ends of the earth!

"Oh yes! I love him!" Natacha said to herself again and again, as she read these glowing words for the twentieth time, warming her own soul at the fire that burned in them.

Maria Dmitrievna had been invited to spend the evening with the Argharows, and she asked the girls to accompany her; but Natacha said she had a headache and retired to her room.

CHAPTER LII

It was late when Sonia came in. She went into Natacha's room and was surprised to see her lying asleep, still dressed, on the sofa. An open letter was on the table by her side. It caught Sonia's eye, and in her surprise she glanced through it, looking every now and then at the sleeping girl, and vainly trying to read some explanation in her face. It was calm and happy; while Sonia, white and trembling with terror, held her hand to her heart to save her pulses from choking her, and sank into an arm-chair in a flood of tears.

"How is it that I have seen nothing of this?" she wondered. "How can it have gone so far? Has she ceased to love Prince Andrew? And this Kouraguine! He is a villain; he is cheating her, that is quite clear. Oh, what will Nicholas say—good, honourable Nicholas, when he hears of this? That is what her agitated manner has meant to-day, and yesterday and the day before! . . . But she cannot love him; that is impossible. She has opened the letter without suspecting from whom it came, and she must have been deeply offended by it, I am sure. . . ."

She dried her eyes and went up to Natacha, examining her

closely; then she called her gently. Natacha awoke with a start.

"Ah! here you are back again!" she said, throwing her arms round her; then noticing her companion's troubled face, she herself put on an expression of embarrassment and defiance: "Sonia, you have read the letter!"

"Yes," murmured Sonia.

"Oh, Sonia!" she said, with a bright smile of happiness, "I cannot keep it from you any longer. Sonia, Sonia, dear little soul—we love each other; you see, he has written to me."

Sonia could not believe her ears.

"And Bolkonsky?" she said.

"Sonia, if only you could understand how happy I am! But you do not know what love is."

"Oh, Natacha!—and he, the other, have you forgotten him?" Natacha did not seem to hear. "Are you going to break with Prince Andrew?"

"I knew you would not understand! Listen to me," said Natacha vehemently.

"I will never believe it," Sonia went on, "and I tell you frankly I cannot understand it! What! For a whole year you love, and then, all of a sudden . . . Why, you have only seen him three times! . . . It is impossible; you are trying to take me in. What! In three days? Everything forgotten?"

"Three days! Why, I feel as if I had loved him for a hundred years. Sit down there and listen." She drew her close to her and kissed her warmly "I had often heard—and you, too, of course, that there was such a thing as love like this, but I had never felt it. . . . He is quite unlike the other! I had hardly seen him when I felt he was my master—that I was his slave. I was compelled to love him! Yes, I am his slave; whatever he commands I shall do. You cannot understand? Well, that is not my fault."

"But only think! I cannot let things go on like this. This letter sent in secretly; how could you take it or open it?" Sonia went on, quite unable to conceal her alarm or her disgust.

"I no longer have a will of my own, I tell you; I love him, and that is all!" cried Natacha with growing excitement.

"If that is the case, I will prevent it, I swear it; I will tell the whole story," said Sonia, and tears started from her eyes.

"For God's sake, do not do that! If you do I will never speak to you again. Do you want me to be miserable? do you want us to be parted?"

179

Sonia was ashamed of her terrors, though she pitied them. "What tie is there between you? What has he said to you? Why does he not come here, to the house?"

"Sonia, I entreat you do not torment me," said Natacha, without answering her question. "And for Heaven's sake remember that it is no concern of anybody's; I have trusted implicitly in you."

"But why all this mystery? Why does he not simply and honestly propose for you? Prince Andrew left you perfectly free. Have you reflected, have you tried to discern what these 'secret reasons' for his conduct can be?"

Natacha was startled, and fixed a blank look on Sonia's face: the question had never occurred to her, and she did not know what to say.

"His secret reasons?" she repeated. "He has reasons, and that is enough."

Sonia sighed and shook her head.

"If they were good ones . . ." she began; Natacha, guessing what she would say, interrupted her eagerly.

"Sonia, I ought not to doubt him, and you must not."

"Does he love you?"

"Does he love me?" said Natacha, with a smile of contempt at her friend's blindness. "You have read this letter—and you can ask!"

"But if he is a false man, devoid of honour?"

"He devoid of honour! You do not know him."

"If he is honourable," Sonia went on resolutely, "he ought to declare his intentions or cease to see you; and if you will not tell him so, I will: I will write to him, and tell papa everything."

"But I cannot live without him!" cried Natacha.

"I cannot understand either your actions or your words. Think of your father, think of Nicholas."

"I want no one, I love no one but him! How dare you speak of him as a man devoid of honour? Do you not hear that I love him? Go, go away; I do not want to quarrel with you. Yes, pray go; you see what a state you put me in! . . ."

And Sonia hastily left the room, fairly choking with distress.

Natacha sat down and wrote without further hesitation that answer to Princess Maria which she could not accomplish in the morning. She simply and briefly said that, as Prince Andrew had left her perfectly free, she was availing herself of his generosity; that after mature reflection she could but beg her to forget the past, and to forgive her if she had offended her; and she said that she could never be her brother's wife. At this moment all looked simple, clear, and easy.

The following Friday was the day fixed for the Rostows' departure for the country, and on the Wednesday Count Rostow went to inspect his estate in the neighbourhood of Moscow, accompanied by an intending purchaser.

On this same day Natacha and Sonia had been invited to a grand dinner at Julia Karaguine's, whither they were chaperoned by Maria Dmitrievna. Anatole, too, was there, and Sonia noticed that Natacha had some mysterious conversation with him, and that her agitation increased during dinner.

On their return home Natacha anticipated Sonia's questioning by saying in a coaxing tone, like a child that hopes to be praised:

"Well, Sonia, you will be glad to hear that we have come to an understanding—in spite of all the nonsense you talked about him."

"And what is the upshot of it? I am glad to see that you are not vexed with me; but tell me the whole truth."

Natacha paused to reflect.

"Ah! if you could only know him as well as I do. He said —he asked what were the terms of my engagement to Bolkonsky, and was so glad to learn that it only lay with me to break it off."

Sonia sighed: "But you have not broken it off yet."

"Suppose I have? Suppose everything were already at an end between Bolkonsky and me? Why do you think so badly of me?"

"I have not a bad opinion of you; I simply cannot understand . . ."

"Wait, and you will understand; you will see what sort of man he is; you will see! Don't think badly of him or me."

"I don't think badly of anyone. I love you all. But what would you have me do?"

Natacha's blind amiability could not mislead Sonia; on the contrary, she grew sterner and more stringent as her friend became more insinuating.

"Natacha, you begged me to say no more about the matter, and you yourself have reopened it. Therefore I have a right to tell you that I do not believe in him! Why so much mystification?"

"As suspicious as ever!" replied Natacha.

181

"I am afraid for you."

"What are you afraid of?"

"Afraid lest you are rushing to your ruin," said Sonia bravely, though she was frightened at her own words. Natacha's face took an evil expression.

"Very well; I will rush to my ruin, and the faster the better. It is no concern of yours. I shall be the sufferer, not you, I suppose?—Leave me—go—I hate you!" She marched out of the room, and all the next day she would neither speak to Sonia nor look at her.

She walked up and down her room and made spasmodic efforts to fix her attention on any kind of occupation; the fever that was consuming her was visible in her face. In spite of the painfulness of her position, Sonia never ceased watching her as she stood for a long time at one of the drawing-room windows; she seemed to be expecting something or someone, and waved a signal to an officer who drove past, and Sonia concluded that it must be Anatole. Then she was more on the alert than ever, and observed that Natacha was unusually excited during dinner and all the evening. She was absent-minded and replied incoherently to all that was said to her, leaving her sentences unfinished, and laughing for nothing or out of season.

After tea Sonia saw a maid-servant go into Natacha's room with a look of mystery; she crept up to the door and put her ear to the key-hole, guessing that she had received a second letter. It suddenly flashed upon her that Natacha was planning some dreadful scheme to be carried out perhaps within a few hours, and she knocked loudly at the door:—no answer.

"She means to fly with him! She is quite capable of it!" thought she in despair. "She was sad but determined to-day; and the other day, when her father went into the country, she cried at parting. . . . Yes, that is what it is: she means to fly with him—what ought I to do? The count is away! . . . Write to Kouraguine and ask for an explanation? But why should he answer me?—Write to Peter as Prince Andrew said in case of anything going wrong? but then she has broken with Bolkonsky, for she sent her reply to Princess Maria last evening! —Great Heavens!—What can I do?—Speak to Maria Dmitrievna?—But she has such perfect confidence in Natacha; it would be treachery!—And yet, come what may I must do something," she reflected as she stood in the dark passage. "It is my part now to show my gratitude for all the benefits they have heaped on me and my love for Nicholas. If I have to sit up three nights running I will not sleep a wink; I will not allow her to stir out, even if I keep her in by force; I will not let shame and dishonour come upon the family!"

CHAPTER LIII

ANATOLE had for some little time been living with Dologhow The idea of carrying off Natacha had been hatched by Dologhow and was to be put into execution on the very day when Sonia had registered her vow not to let Natacha out of her sight.

Natacha, on her part, had promised to be at the outer door of the servants' staircase at ten o'clock at night, to meet Kouraguine, who was to be waiting for her and take her *en troika* to Kamenka, a village about sixty versts from Moscow. There an excommunicated priest was to marry them, and after this they were to go on with fresh horses on the road to Warsaw, take the mail coach at the next stage, and get beyond the frontier. Anatole had provided himself with a passport, a permit for the mail and 20,000 roubles, which he had obtained from Dologhow and his sister.

The two witnesses to the marriage, Gvostikow, formerly a law clerk, and Makarine, a retired hussar, both creatures of Kouraguine's, were at Dologhow's lodging, taking tea in the ante-room; while the master, wrapped in an oriental travelling-cloak, with high, fur-lined boots, sat in the adjoining room, a large apartment hung with Persian rugs, bear-skins, and trophies of arms. He was at his desk, looking through bills, counting rouble notes packed in piles, and writing down sums on a sheet of paper: "You will have to give Gvostikow two thousand roubles."

"Well, let him have them," said Anatole, coming in from a room beyond where a man-servant was packing their portmanteaux.

"As to Makarka" (a pet name he gave to Makarine) "he is quite disinterested; he would throw himself into the fire for you.—That is all; our accounts are made up—look, is that right?" And Dologhow held out the sheet of paper.

"No doubt, it is all right," said Anatole, who had not listened to him, and whose smiling eyes gazed into vacancy and saw nothing.

Dologhow closed the desk: "Look here," he said with a mocking glance, "throw it up; there is still time."

"Idiot!" retorted Anatole. "Do not talk nonsense. If you knew—but the devil alone can know."

"I am quite in earnest—give it up. It is really no light matter that you are going in for."

"What, are you going to worry me again? Go to the devil!" and Anatole scowled. "I have no time to listen to your twaddle."

Dologhow looked loftily indignant: "Come, I am not jesting. . . . Listen to me."

Anatole came towards him with a visible effort to attend to his friend, whose influence was strong, in spite of himself.

"Listen for the last time, I beg of you. Why should I jest about it? Have I tried to put a spoke in your wheel? On the contrary, have I not arranged and settled everything; found you a priest, got the passport, and lent you the money?"

"Well, and I am very much obliged to you; do you think I am not grateful?" and he embraced Dologhow.

"I have done what I could to help you, but I am bound to tell you the truth; it is a dangerous game; and if you only think of it, it is an absurd one. You will carry her off? Very good. And what next? The secret will come out; it will transpire that you are already married, and you will be prosecuted as a criminal."

"Rubbish, rubbish; that is all rubbish! I thought I had made it clear to you," said Anatole, and with the dull persistency of a limited intellect he repeated, for the hundredth time, all the reasons he had already given. "I told you in the first place, if the marriage is illegal I shall not have to answer for it; and in the second, if it is legal it does not matter, for no one out of Russia will ever hear of it. Is that clear? So now, no more about it."

"Be advised; give it up. You will get into a mess and then . . ."

"Go to the devil!" cried Anatole, clapping his hands to his head. "Feel how it beats," he added, seizing his friend's hand and placing it over his heart.—"Oh! such a foot, my dear fellow! Such eyes!—A perfect goddess!"

Dologhow's hard glittering eyes were fixed on him with scorn: "And when the money is gone—what then?" asked he.

"Then," repeated Anatole, slightly dashed by the prospect suggested to him, "well, then—I don't know.—But we have

THE INVASION

talked long enough; it is time!" and taking out his watch he went into the inner room. "Have you nearly done?" he added, angrily addressing the servants.

Dologhow locked away his money, called a man-servant and desired him to bring in some supper, no matter what; then he joined Makarine and Gvostikow, leaving Anatole, who had thrown himself languidly on the divan and who was smiling vaguely and murmuring incoherent words to himself.

"Come and eat something!" he called to him.

"I do not want it," replied Anatole.

"Come, Balaga is here."

Anatole went into the dining-room. Balaga was a coachman, very famous as a driver of a *troika*, who had frequently supplied them with horses. During the six years that he had known the two young men, how many times had he brought them from Tver at daybreak, and taken them back from Moscow by nightfall again, where Anatole was in garrison. Many a time had he saved Dologhow from pursuit. How often had he driven them with parties of gipsies and ladies of no repute! How many good horses had he knocked up in their service, how many foot-passengers and hackney-coachmen had he run down! His masters, as he called them, always rescued him from the clutches of the police; they thrashed him now and then to be sure, and forgot him for hours, standing at the door during their orgies; but in return they would often give him as much champagne as he could carry, or better still, Madeira, his favourite liquor. He was in all their secrets, and knew of deeds of theirs for which anyone else would have paid a visit to Siberia.—In their orgies they had often made him drink and dance with the gipsies and so some thousands of roubles had found their way through his hands. Many times a year he risked his life and limbs in their service, and in their services he had ruined more horses than could ever be paid for by the money he had from them. He really loved them after his fashion, and he passionately loved driving at a mad pace of eighteen versts[1] an hour. He loved to upset a hackney-driver, to scare the foot-passengers into the ditch, to lay his long whip, as he passed, across the shoulders of a wretched peasant, who shrank back more dead than alive; to gallop tearing through the labyrinthine streets of Moscow, and to hear his masters urging him on with their wild cries and thick

[1] About twelve miles. The verst is 0.661 or rather less than two-thirds of a mile.

185

drunken voices: "Yes, they are real gentlemen!" he would say to himself with pride.

Anatole and Dologhow, on their side, thought a great deal of his skill as a Jehu, and liked him from sympathy. Balaga drove a hard bargain with everyone else, asking twenty-five roubles for a two hours' excursion, and very rarely condescending to drive, but generally sending one of his men. For "his masters" he himself would drive, and make no bargain beforehand. But when he happened to know through the house-servants that cash was plentiful in the house he would drop in early several times a month: bow to the ground before them, and implore them to help him out of some pressing difficulty. And always "his masters" made him sit down. "Please help me, Feodor Ivanovitch, sir, or your excellency," he would say, "I have got through all my horses; so please lend me what you can to go to the horse-fair with." And Anatole and Dologhow when flush of money, would give him a thousand or two roubles each.

He was seven-and-twenty; short, red-haired, blowzy, thick-necked, snub-nosed, with glittering eyes and a little square beard; he wore a blue cloth caftan lined with silk, over a fur coat.

He crossed himself as he came in, with his face turned to the right; then, holding out his tanned hand: "Hail to Fédor Ivanovitch!" he said.

"Good day, my good fellow."

"Hail to your excellency!" he added to Anatole, holding out his hand to him, too.

"Listen to me, Balaga: you love me? I ask you," said Anatole, patting him on the shoulder. "Well then, prove it to-night. What horses have you brought?"

"I have done as you told me—the mad ones—yours."

"Very good; and you will not mind killing them so long as we cover the distance in three hours?"

"But if I kill them how are we to get there?" said Balaga, smiling at his own wit.

"I will break your jaw for you, do you hear? No joking!" said Anatole with a ferocious glare.

"Why no joking? You might think I was a man to grudge trouble for my masters. . . . They will be made to go as fast as they can, and there's an end of it!"

"Good," said Anatole, "then sit down."

"Sit down," repeated Dologhow.

"I can stand, Fédor Ivanovitch."

"Sit down, no nonsense," said Anatole, pouring him out a

large glass of Madeira. Balaga's eyes twinkled at the sight of his favourite wine. After refusing at first, out of good manners, he ended by swallowing it at a gulp, and wiped his mouth with the tumbled red silk handkerchief which he always carried in the crown of his fur cap.

"And when do we start, excellency?"

"Well . . ." Anatole looked at his watch.—"Pretty soon. Don't be late, Balaga, whatever happens."

"It must depend on the start, little father; if we get off well, then . . . Did I not bring you from Tver to Moscow once in seven hours? You have not forgotten, excellency?"

"Only think," said Anatole, smiling as he remembered the incident, and turning to Makarine, who gazed at him with affectionate veneration. "Only think, he brought me from Tver one Christmas Day at such a pace that we were quite out of breath. It was not running, I swear, it was flying—and if we did not come on a whole row of carts and positively jump the two end ones!"

"But what horses they were! I had put in two young ones, with the light chestnut; and on my word, Fédor Ivanovitch," Balaga went on, "the mad creatures flew through the air for sixty versts. I could not hold them in; my fingers were quite stiff with cold. . . . I had to drop the reins. 'Look out for yourself, excellency,' says I, and I rolled over backwards into the sleigh. There was nothing for it but to let them go and hold on as best we could—and so we rushed on for three mortal hours. The near horse was the only one that was done for."

CHAPTER LIV

ANATOLE went for his wraps, and presently returned dressed in a short pelisse, with a leather belt and silver fastenings, and a cap trimmed with sable, knowingly stuck on one side so as to be most becoming to his handsome face. He looked in the mirror, came to the table and took up a glass full of wine:

"Well, my dear Dologhow, good-bye, thanks for all you have done for me—good-bye, you others, the faithful companions of my youth—farewell!"

Anatole knew, of course, that they were all coming with him, but he wanted to have a touching and solemn scene. He spoke slowly in a loud voice, with his chest thrown forward and standing on one leg.

"Take your glasses—you, too, Balaga. Yes, friends of my youth, we have lived, we have enjoyed ourselves, we have committed many follies together; and now, when shall we meet again? I am going abroad. Farewell, my children . . . To your good health, hurrah!" And swallowing the contents of his glass at one gulp, he flung it on the ground, where it flew into a thousand fragments.

"To your good health!" said Balaga, emptying his, and wiping his beard with his handkerchief. Makarine, with tears in his eyes, embraced Anatole: "Oh, prince! how sad that we must part!" he murmured.

"Now, let us be off!" cried Anatole. "One minute," he added as Balaga moved towards the door. "Shut the door and sit down." [1]

It was done. "Now, that is over, and off we go, my children." And he rose.

Joseph, his servant, handed him his money-bag and his sword, and they went out into the hall.

"Where is the pelisse?" asked Dologhow. "Here, Ignatka, go and ask Matrena Matféievna for the sable pelisse; I have heard about these abductions," he added in a lower tone. . . . "You will see, she will come running out more dead than alive, with nothing over her shoulders, and if you delay there will be tears: papa and mamma will put in an appearance . . . in short, wrap her in the pelisse and put her into the sleigh at once."

The servant came back with a pelisse lined with ordinary fox.

"Idiot! I told you the sable! Here, Matrëchka," he shouted with such force that his voice rang through the rooms.

A pretty gipsy, very pale and thin, with jet-black eyes, and hair in blue-black curls, came out hurredly, wrapped in a red shawl and carrying the sable fur.

"Well, here it is, then; take it.—I do not care!" she said in an ill-used tone that contradicted her words: she was afraid of her master. Dologhow threw the fox-lined cloak over her shoulders and pulled it round her.

"So," he said, turning up the collar, "and then so," and he drew it over her head so as to leave only a small portion of her face visible—"and last of all, so." And he pushed her towards Anatole, who kissed her lips.

"Good-bye, Matrëchka; my follies here are ended. Good-bye; wish me good luck!"

[1] A superstitious custom supposed in Russia to prosper a journey.

"God bless you, and give you every happiness!" said the girl with her gipsy accent.

Two *troikas* held by stable helps were standing at the door; Balaga mounted the first sleigh, lifted his arms very high and proceeded deliberately to sort the reins; Anatole and Dologhow got in behind him. Makarine, Gvostikow and a servant filled the second.

"Are you ready?" asked Balaga. "Leave go!" he cried, twisting the reins round his hand, and the sleighs were off, carrying them at a desperate pace along the Nikitski Boulevard.

"Hi, hi! Look out!" yelled the drivers as loud as they could. On the Arbatskaïa Square one of the sleighs got entangled with a carriage; there was a crash and a shriek, but it rushed on at the same mad rate till Balaga, with a powerful wrench, drew up short at the corner of the Old Stables Street.

Anatole and Dologhow got out and went up to the court-yard gate. Dologhow whistled and was answered, and a girl ran out to meet him.

"Come this way into the yard, or you will be seen; she is coming," said the maid. Dologhow stood in the gateway while Anatole, following the girl, went round the corner of the house; as he passed the front steps a tall man-servant suddenly stood before him.

"My mistress is waiting to see you!" he said in a bass voice.

"Who? Your mistress? . . . What do you want?" muttered Anatole in breathless amazement.

"Come. She desired me to show you in to her."

"Kouraguine, run for it! Treason!" shouted Dologhow, struggling with the door-keeper who was trying with all his might to shut him in. He succeeded at last in shaking the man off, seized Anatole by the arm as he came running across the yard, dragged him out into the street, and they both ran as fast as their legs would carry them to the corner where the sleighs were waiting.

CHAPTER LV

MARIA DMITRIEVNA had found poor Sonia in the corridor drowned in tears; had made her confess and gone straight to Natacha with her note to Anatole, which she had at once intercepted.

"Wretched girl! Shameless creature!" she exclaimed. "Not a word; I will not listen to you. . . ." She pushed away

189

Natacha who stood dry-eyed and amazed, watching her; and, seizing the key, locked the door of her room. Then she sent for the gate-keeper and desired him to admit anyone who might call at the house in the course of the evening, to lock the doors behind them and show them into the drawing-room. When Gavrilo told her that they had escaped she started up in great wrath and began walking up and down the room with her hands clasped behind her, considering what she ought to do next. It was near midnight when she took the key out of her pocket and went back to Natacha; Sonia was still sobbing outside the door.

"Maria Dmitrievna, pray, pray let me go in to her." Maria Dmitrievna opened the door without replying and walked in with a determined air; Sonia crept in after her.

"It is horrible, disgraceful, to have behaved so under my roof; but I will have some mercy on your father and tell him nothing!" she said, going towards Natacha, who was lying on the sofa as she had left her. Natacha did not look round; her stifled sobs alone betrayed the emotion that shook her soul. "A pretty thing, indeed," continued the old lady, "to be making assignations with your lover in my house! You have dragged yourself in the mud like any common hussy, and if I followed my own impulses—but I wish to spare your father, and I will tell him nothing. Happily for that man he got away; but I shall be able to find him! Do you hear me?" she added, and sitting down by the girl, she put her large hand under Natacha's chin and made her turn her face. She and Sonia were both startled at the sight; her eyes were dry and glittering, her lips set, and her cheeks looked hollow.

"Leave me alone. I don't care! I shall die!" She wrenched herself away with fierce violence and again hid her face.

"Natacha," said Maria Dmitrievna, "I wish you no ill. Lie there by all means if you prefer it; I will not touch you. But listen to me. I will not repeat what I think of your conduct; you know it. But what am I to say to your father, who will be here to-morrow?" Natacha's only reply was a gasp. "He is sure to hear of it, as well as your brother and your *fiancé.*"

"I have no *fiancé.* I have refused him!" cried Natacha, in a passion.

"That makes no difference. What will they say, do you think? I know your father—he is quite capable of fighting him; and then what will happen?"

190

"Leave me alone, go away. Why have you upset every-thing? Who asked you to interfere?" And Natacha, raising her voice, sat up and glared at Maria Dmitrievna.

"But what on earth were you aiming at?" said the old lady, provoked beyond endurance. "Were you kept under lock and key? What was there to prevent his coming here and seeing you in my drawing-room? Why should he elope with you as if you were a gipsy hussy? Do you really think we should not have caught you and brought you back?—As to him! He is a rascal, a villain!"

"He is worth all of you put together! If you had not inter-fered . . Good God! why has it come to this? Go away; get away, leave me." And she burst into tears, crying with the desperation of those who feel that they are the instruments of their own misery.

Maria Dmitrievna tried to soothe her, but Natacha shrieked at her: "Go, go, I tell you. You despise me and hate me!"

The old lady did not stir, however; she went on with her lecture, repeating how necessary it was to conceal this horrible scandal from her father, and impressing on her that no one need know if only she did not betray herself. Natacha said not a word; presently her tears ceased to flow and she took a feverish shivering fit. Maria Dmitrievna slipped a pillow under her head, covered her warmly with blankets, and left her, quite convinced that she would presently go to sleep. But sleep never came near her; her eyes remained wide open, her face was deadly white and she shed no more tears; Sonia, who came to look at her several times in the course of that long night, could not get her to speak a word.

The count returned early next day. He was in capital spirits; his sale had come to a happy conclusion; there was nothing to keep him in Moscow, and he was only anxious to get back to the countess whom he sorely missed. Maria Dmitrievna told him that his daughter had been very unwell the day before, and that she had sent for a doctor; but that she was now better.

Natacha remained in her room. Seated at the window, with pinched lips and fevered eyes, she watched the passers-by—carriages and foot-passengers—with eager anxiety, and turned round with hasty expectancy every time her door opened. She evidently hoped to hear something of Anatole, and thought he would come or write to her.

Her father's footstep startled her, but, seeing that it was he, her expression, which for a moment had brightened, relapsed into fractious coldness: she did not even rise.

"What is the matter, my darling? Are you ill?" he asked.

"Yes," she said after a pause. He questioned her anxiously, and asked her whether her depression were not the result of some painful difference between her and Prince Andrew; she reassured him on this point, and begged him not to worry himself. In this, indeed, Maria Dmitrievna confirmed her. Nevertheless, the count was not to be deceived, either as to the state of his daughter's health or the change that had come over her or the agitation which was only too legible in the faces of Sonia and his old friend. He suspected that some serious crisis had passed during his absence; but his fear of hearing anything to his daughter's discredit, or to depress his own exuberant good spirits, kept him from asking questions. He persuaded himself that it could be nothing of any importance, and only regretted that Natacha's indisposition should delay their return home for a few days.

CHAPTER LVI

SINCE his wife's arrival in Moscow, Peter had made up his mind to go away, partly in order to be as short a time as possible under the same roof with her; but the deep impression made on him by Natacha during the last few months also contributed to hasten his departure. He went to Tver, to see Bazdéïew's widow, who had promised him some papers and memoirs left by her husband.

On his return, he found a note from Maria Dmitrievna begging him to go and see her as soon as possible to talk over a serious matter relating to Bolkonsky and Natacha. For some time past, Peter had avoided being left alone with Natacha, for whom he felt a growing passion equally reprehensible in a married man and in her lover's best friend; but, in spite of his resolutions, Fate, it would seem, was bent on bringing them together. "What has happened? What have I to do with it?" thought he, as he dressed. "If only Andrew would come and get the marriage over!"

As he was crossing the boulevard someone called him.

"Peter! how long have you been back?" Peter looked round. A pair of fine greys, harnessed to a handsome private sleigh, were flying on and away from him, carrying off Anatole and his inseparable Makarine in a cloud of snow-dust. Anatole, whose fresh, florid face was half hidden in his beaver collar, was sitting in an attitude of classic elegance, and his cocked hat, with its white plume, set a little on one side and forward, displayed his curled and oiled hair, silvered with the finely powdered snow.

"God help me, but that is true wisdom!" said Peter to himself. "That boy never thinks of anything beyond the pleasure of the passing hour. Nothing troubles him; he is always in good spirits and in good humour. What would I not give to think and feel as he does!"

On reaching the house, the servant told him that Maria Dmitrievna would see him in her own room. As he passed through the drawing-room, he saw Natacha sitting at a window; her pale, worn features had an unwonted expression of set hardness. When he entered, she rose and frowned, and left the room with a brief greeting.

"What has happened?" asked Peter, as his hostess received him.

"Oh! pretty things have happened!" said she. "Fifty-eight years have I lived in this world, and I never knew anything so shameful!" Then, after binding over Peter to keep the secret, she told him that Natacha had broken with Prince Andrew without consulting her parents; that this was the consequence of an insane passion for Kouraguine, who was helped by Peter's wife. Natacha had altogether lost her head, and, during her father's absence, had agreed to elope with Anatole, and to be married to him privately.

Peter listened in open-mouthed astonishment, and could not believe his ears. How was it credible that Natacha—that sweet child to whom Bolkonsky was so passionately devoted—could have fallen in love with such an idiot as Anatole—who, as Peter knew, was already married—and be led so far as to break off with Prince Andrew, and to consent to an elopement. He could not understand it, and hardly could believe it.

Natacha's bright sweet face had no connection in his mind with such baseness, such cruelty and folly.

"They are all alike," and he thought of his wife. "I am not the only man who has become the victim of a depraved woman!" and his heart bled for his friend. What a blow this would be to his pride! And the more he felt for him, the deeper was his contempt and horror of Natacha, who, only a few minutes since, had walked past him wrapped in icy dignity. . . . How could he know, alas! that under this mask of rigid pride, the wretched girl's soul was steeped in despair, shame, and humiliation?

"Marry him?" he exclaimed. "But it is impossible; he is married already."

"Married!" echoed Maria Dmitrievna. "Oh! better and better! The villain! the scoundrel! And she sits waiting—hoping. . . . Well, she will wait no longer, for I will undertake to let her know of this."

Peter gave her all the details of this recondite business, and Maria Dmitrievna, after having relieved her mind by a broadside of abuse, begged Peter to persuade his brother-in-law to quit Moscow. She dreaded lest the count and Prince Andrew, who must soon arrive now, should challenge Kouraguine on hearing of his conduct, and her first aim was to conceal the whole business from those two. Peter, who had hardly had time to calculate all the consequences of the disgraceful plot, promised to do all she wished.

"So not a word to the count, you understand; if you see him, be on your guard, and I will talk to her. Will you stay and dine?"

The count came into the room not long after with a grieved and anxious face; his daughter had just told him of her rupture with Bolkonsky.

"It is a great misfortune, my dear fellow, when girls are left to themselves, and away from their mother. I am extremely sorry, I may confess, that I ever brought her here. Do you know, my dear fellow, what she has done? I may tell you. She has broken off her engagement to Andrew, without asking any advice. I never particularly liked the marriage, to be sure, though the prince himself is delightful; but it did not promise well for their happiness that they should not have his father's sanction; and Natacha will be sure to have offers, and to spare. What really annoys me is that this engagement has lasted now for some months, and that such a step ought not to be taken without a word to father or mother. . . . And so, of course, she is quite ill; God knows what ails her! Yes, my dear count, everything goes wrong in the mother's absence!"

Peter, seeing that he was quite overwhelmed, tried to change the subject, but the count always came back to it.

"Natacha is not very well," said Sonia, coming in; and she added with evident agitation, addressing Peter, "She would like to see you in her room. Maria Dmitrievna is there too, and begs you will go to them."

"Ah! you see, she knows you are intimate with Bolkonsky." said the count, "and she has some message to give you for him. Good God! if only everything had gone straight. Why must we . . . ?" and he hurried out of the room, clasping his hands over the thin grey locks that waved on his temples.

Maria Dmitrievna had told Natacha that Anatole was married. Natacha refused to believe it, and insisted on hearing the fact from Peter himself. Sonia told this to Peter as she led him along the corridor. Natacha was white, and seemed quite petrified; her inquiring glance was fixed on Peter's face with feverish anxiety as soon as he came into the room. She neither bowed nor even nodded, but looked into his eyes as if to read there whether he were a friend to Anatole or yet another foe; his personality as Peter Bésoukhow did not exist for her at that moment.

"He knows all about it," said Maria Dmitrievna. "Let him tell you, and you will see I have spoken the truth."

Natacha looked from one to the other, like a wild creature at bay between the hunters and the dogs

"Natacha Ilinischna," said Peter, looking down; for a passionate pity filled his soul with horror of the task laid upon him. "Whether true or false, it cannot matter, for . . ."

"Then it is false! He is not married?"

"No, it is true; he is married."

"And married some time since? Give me your word of honour."

"On my word of honour."

"Is he still here?" she asked in a husky voice.

"Yes; I have just seen him in the street."

She could say no more. With a wave of her hand, she implored them to leave her to herself.

CHAPTER LVII

PETER did not stay to dinner. When he left Natacha, he went in search of Kouraguine, whose very name made his blood boil and his heart beat till he could hardly breathe. He sought him everywhere—at the ice-hills, and in the gipsy quarter, and, finally, he went to the club, where everything was going on as usual. The members were assembling for dinner, and discussing the news of the day. A servant who knew his habits came to tell him that a table was ready for him in the little dining-room;

that Prince Michael Zakharovitch was in the reading-room, and that Paul Timoféitch had not yet come. Then an acquaintance who was talking gossip with his neighbour, interrupted himself to ask Peter whether it was true, as everyone was saying, that Anatole Kouraguine had carried off Miss Rostow. Peter laughed, and said it was pure invention, for he had that moment come from the Rostows'. Then he asked after Anatole: no one had seen him, but he was expected. He looked round with an odd sensation on this calmly indifferent crowd, so little suspecting what a turmoil there was in his soul; and he walked about the rooms till dinner was actually served; then, as Anatole had not come in, he went home.

Anatole was dining with Dologhow, discussing ways and means of renewing the enterprise that had failed, and of seeing Natacha. After dinner, he went to his sister to ask her to arrange another meeting; and when Peter came in after his fruitless search, his servant told him that Prince Anatole was with the countess, who had a great many visitors. Peter went to the drawing-room, but he did not go near his wife, whom he had not yet seen since his return, for at that moment he felt an intense aversion for her: he went straight up to Anatole.

"Oh! Peter!" said Helen. "Do you know what has happened to poor Anatole? . . ." But she stopped short. In her husband's face, his flashing eyes and resolute step she saw the fire of that fury of which she had had experience the day after his duel with Dologhow.

"Sin and depravity are always to be found at your side!" he muttered as he passed her. "Anatole, come with me: I want to speak to you."

The brother and sister exchanged glances. Anatole rose without a word; his brother-in-law took his arm, and hurried him out of the room.

"If you dare in my drawing-room. . . ." Helen began in a low tone, but Peter paid no heed. Anatole, though he followed him with his usual coldness, looked a little uneasy.

When they were in Peter's room he shut the door, and turning on Anatole looked him in the face: "You promised to marry Countess Natacha Rostow. . . . You were going to abduct her?"

"My good fellow," said Anatole, "it does not suit me to answer questions put to me in that tone." He spoke in French.

Peter's face, already colourless, was quivering with rage. He gripped his brother-in-law's collar with his powerful hand, and shook him till Anatole's terror was written in every feature. "But I tell you I must speak to you!" said Peter.

"Come, come, this is really monstrous!" said Anatole, now that he was released, as he pulled up his coat collar, which had lost a button in the struggle.

"You are a villain and a scoundrel!—I do not know what should keep me from cracking your skull with this!" cried Peter, in a frenzy, and lifting a large paper-weight which, however, he at once laid down again on his writing-table. "Did you say you would marry her? Answer."

"I . . . I . . . I do not think so. . . . In fact, I could not have promised such a thing. . . ."

"Have you no letters from her—any at all?" Peter went on, interrupting him and going very close to him. Anatole looked at him and hastily put his hand into his pocket, out of which he took a note-book. Peter seized the letter he handed him and pushing him aside with some force, he dropped on to a sofa.

"I will not touch you, do not be alarmed," he went on, in reply to a really terrified gesture of Anatole's. "First, the letters.—Next, you leave Moscow to-morrow."

"But how can I? . . ."

"Thirdly, you are never to breathe a word, not a syllable as to what has passed between you and the countess. I cannot compel you to silence it is true, but if you have a spark of decency left, you . . ."

He rose and walked up and down for a minute or two; Anatole sat at the table, scowling and biting his lips.

"You must surely understand that outside and beyond your pleasure there are the happiness and peace of others to be considered, and that you ruin a life to serve the ends of your amusement. Amuse yourself with women like my wife, if you choose; they, at any rate, know what you look for, and with them you are on even terms; they can defend themselves with the same arms that you use: the experience that comes of depravity. But to promise marriage to a young girl, to cheat her and rob her of her honour! Do you not see that it is like striking an old man or a child?"—Peter ceased and looked calmly at Anatole as if he expected a reply.

"Bless me! I am sure I do not know," said Anatole, who recovered his presence of mind in proportion as Peter cooled down. "I know nothing about it, and I do not want to know; but you have said things to me which, as a man of honour, I cannot allow to pass."

Peter looked at him in blank amazement, wondering what he was aiming at.

"Although there are no witnesses to your insults I cannot overlook . . ."

"You want satisfaction!" cried Peter ironically.

"At any rate you should withdraw your words—if you want me to follow your advice, that is to say—Hey?"

"I withdraw them, oh, yes! and beg your forgiveness," murmured Peter, involuntarily looking at the hole left by the button he had torn away. "I can even lend you money for your journey if you want it!"

Anatole smiled; and that mean, stereotyped smile, which he had so constantly seen on Helen's face, exasperated Peter: "Oh! they are a sordid and heartless race!" he exclaimed, as he quitted the room.

The next day Anatole left for St. Petersburg.

CHAPTER LVIII

PETER took an early opportunity of calling on Maria Dmitrievna and telling her that her wishes had been exactly carried out, and that Kouraguine had left Moscow.

He found the whole house in a commotion: Natacha was seriously ill, and Maria Dmitrievna confided to him, under seal of utter secrecy, that during the night, after she had heard that Anatole was married, she had poisoned herself with arsenic, which she had privately procured. But after taking a moderate dose she had been frightened, awakened Sonia, and told her what she had done. The most energetic remedies had at once been applied, and she was now quite out of danger; but, as she was too weak to travel, the countess had been sent for and was expected every minute. Peter met the count utterly scared and crushed; and Sonia, too, crying bitterly. Natacha herself was invisible.

He dined that day at the club; everyone was talking of the elopement that had failed of execution, but he persistently denied it. He felt convinced that his first duty was to smother up the whole disastrous business and save Natacha's reputation; he told all who would listen to him that she had simply refused his brother-in-law.

Prince Andrew's return filled him with alarm.

THE INVASION

The various reports in the town had at last come to the old prince's ears, thanks to Mademoiselle Bourrienne, and he insisted on seeing Natacha's note to his daughter; this had put him in the best possible temper, and he now awaited his son with joyful impatience.

A few days after Anatole's departure, Peter, in fact, received a few lines from Prince Andrew, begging him to call upon him. He had arrived the evening before, and his father had at once given him Natacha's letter, which Mademoiselle Bourrienne had filched from Princess Maria, and had told him the whole history of the elopement, embellished with various details of his own invention. Peter, who expected to find him in a state of despair, like Natacha, was amazed to hear him talking loudly, and even eagerly, in the adjoining room of a court intrigue of which Spéransky had been the victim. Princess Maria came out to receive him, and she sighed as she pointed to the door of her brother's private room. She seemed anxious to make some display of sympathy with Peter's distress, but he could read in her face her secret satisfaction at the breach, and the effect produced on her mind by Natacha's faithlessness.

"He declares that he expected it," she said. "No doubt his pride prevents his saying all he feels; but, be that as it may, he bears it with more philosophy than I could have expected."

"And is the breach final?" asked Peter. Princess Maria looked at him in amazement; she could not understand that there should be a doubt on the subject.

Peter went into the adjoining room; his friend, not in uniform, was standing in front of his father and Prince Mestchersky, and haranguing and gesticulating vehemently. His health was evidently quite restored, but there was a fresh line between his brows. He was talking of Spéransky and his unexpected exile, and of the treason ascribed to him, of which the news had but just reached Moscow.

"And the very men who a month ago extolled him to the clouds," said Prince Andrew, "even though they were incapable of appreciating his schemes, to-day impeach and condemn him. It is the easiest thing in the world to blame a man in disgrace, and make him responsible for the sins of others; for my part, I maintain that if any good has been done during the present reign it is due to him alone."

He paused a moment as Peter came in, a nervous thrill betrayed itself in his face, a sort of spasm of extreme irritation; but he added: "Posterity will do him justice!"

199

"Ah, here you are," he went on, turning to Peter. "And you are well? You have grown still stouter, I fancy."—And he returned to the subject of Spéransky, though the furrow on his brow deepened while he spoke.

"Yes, I am very well!" he said, in reply to Peter's inquiry, but in a careless tone, as much as to say: "What does it matter; who cares?" And after a few words with him on the bad state of the roads on the Russian side of the frontier, the people he had met who had asked after Peter, and Monsieur Dessalles, the Swiss tutor he had engaged for his boy, he once more joined with warmer interest in the discussion kept up by the two elder men.

"If there had been any treason there would be some proofs of a secret understanding with Napoleon, and those proofs would have been laid before the public. For my part, I never liked Spéransky, but I love justice!" Peter fully understood that his friend was feeling an irresistible impulse and need—such as he himself had often known—to heat himself and vent his heat on some indifferent matter, so as to forget, if possible, for a time the crushing burthen of his own thoughts.

Presently Prince Mestchersky left, and Prince Andrew took Peter by the arm and led him into his own room. A camp-bed had just been unpacked, and open trunks and cases were strewed about the room. Out of one of these he took a small packet carefully sealed. He said nothing and moved with short rough jerks; then looking up from the trunk he paused for a moment, looking gloomily at Peter.

"I was sorry to trouble you," he said, hardly opening his lips. Peter, foreseeing that he was about to speak of Natacha, could not keep his broad, kind face from betraying his pity and sympathy, and this only added to his friend's smouldering irritation. Andrew tried to speak firmly and frankly, but there was a forced ring in his voice. "I have received my dismissal from the Countess Natacha Rostow.—I heard vaguely something about a proposal, or to that effect, made to her by your brother-in-law. Is it true?"

"It is true, and it is not true . . ."

"Here are her letters, and a portrait of her," Prince Andrew went on, interrupting him. "Restore them to her—if you see her."

"She is very ill."

"She is still here, then? . . . And Prince Kouraguine?" he asked eagerly.

"He has been gone some days. She has been in great danger."

"I am sorry to hear of her illness. . . ." And a spiteful smile like his father's curled his pinched lips: "Then Prince Kouraguine did not after all condescend to give her his hand?"

"He could not—he is already married."

Prince Andrew laughed evilly— again reminding one of his father.

"And may I be informed where your brother-in-law is at the present moment?"

"He went to St. Peter's . . . I do not precisely know."

"Ah, well, it matters not. Pray tell Countess Rostow that she has always been, is still, perfectly free; and that I wish her all possible happiness."

Peter took the letters. Prince Andrew, who seemed to be considering whether he had said everything he wanted to say, or to be waiting for some further communication from Peter, looked into his face.

"Do you remember," said Peter, "a discussion we once had at St. Petersburg? . . ."

"Perfectly. We agreed that a woman, even though fallen, ought to be forgiven; but I never went so far as to say that I should forgive her if it touched me.—I cannot."

"But the case is quite different," said Peter.

Prince Andrew interrupted him vehemently:

"Oh, yes! Repeat my offer, show myself generous, and so forth, and so forth! Very noble, no doubt, but I do not feel that I can stoop to pick up Mr. Anatole's leavings!—If you wish to keep my friendship never mention her or this business to me again.—Now, good-bye. You will give her these letters, won't you?"

Peter withdrew and went in search of Princess Maria; she was with her father, who seemed in a better temper than usual. The mere sight of these two made him feel how bitterly and contemptuously hostile they were to the Rostows; he could not bring himself even to mention the name of the poor child, who could have preferred anybody to Prince Andrew.

At dinner the war, then imminent, was the subject of conversation. Prince Andrew talked incessantly, contradicting first his father and then Dessalles with a feverish fractiousness of which Peter knew the cause only too well.

CHAPTER LIX

In the course of the evening Peter went to fulfil his mission to Natacha; she was in bed, and her father was at the club. He gave the letters to Sonia and went to see Maria Dmitrievna, who was very eager to know how Prince Andrew had taken his disappointment. Sonia presently followed him.

"Natacha is bent on seeing Count Bésoukhow," she said.

"But how can he go to her room where everything is in disorder?"

"She is up and in the drawing-room," said Sonia.

Maria Dmitrievna shrugged her shoulders.

"Oh dear! when will her mother be here? I am at my wits' end.—Be careful what you say to her; do not tell her everything. She is such a pitiful object that I cannot bear she should be crushed."

Natacha, thin and white, but not looking at all broken as Peter had expected, was standing in the middle of the room. She hesitated as he came in, not knowing whether to go forward or to stand still. He hastened towards her, supposing that she would offer him her hand as usual, but she checked her impulse to do so, and with a choked sob, let her arms fall by her side. It was her usual attitude when she stood up to sing in the middle of the drawing-room, but how different now was the expression of her face!

"Peter Kirilovitch," she began abruptly. "Prince Andrew was your friend—is your friend," she corrected herself, for in this chaos of trouble she felt as though nothing still was as it once had been. "He told me to apply to you in case . . ."

Peter looked at her without speaking. Until this moment he had, in his own mind, loaded her with bitter reproach, he had even done his best to scorn and detest her; but now, as his pity for her grew, he blamed her less and less.

"He is here," she went on; "tell him that I beg—I beg him to forgive me!" Her voice broke under stress of feeling, but she shed no tears.

"Yes, I will tell him," Peter murmured, not knowing what else to say. Natacha, horrified to think of the meaning he might ascribe to her words, eagerly added: "Of course, everything is at an end, and I know it can never be mended, but I am miserable at the thought of how I have hurt him. Tell him to forgive me,—oh! let him forgive me!" and trembling violently, she dropped into a chair.

"Yes, I will tell him everything," said Peter, deeply moved; "but one thing I should like to know . . ."

"What is that?"

"Did you love that . . ." he hesitated and coloured, not knowing what name to give to Anatole.—"Did you love that wretch?"

"Oh! do not call him so!—I do not know . . . I know nothing now."

Pity such as he had never felt in his life, a passionately tender emotion, surged up in Peter's soul so suddenly that his eyes filled with tears and overflowed; he let them fall under his spectacles and hoped she might not observe them.

"Say no more about it, my child," he said, when he could control his voice; Natacha was struck by its pathos and sincerity. "Say no more!—I will tell him everything. But above all grant me one thing: Regard me as your friend; if at any time you want advice or help, or even feel that it would be a comfort to you to confide in a faithful heart—not now, of course, but when your own mind is calm and clear—remember me!" He took her hand and kissed it. "I shall be very happy to be of any use to you."

"Do not speak to me so—I do not deserve it!" cried Natacha, rising to leave him, but Peter detained her, he had something more to say; though, when he had said it, he was amazed at his own boldness.

"I must say to you, 'do not speak so,' for you have all your life before you still."

"No, no," she cried, "I have nothing;—all is over for me!"

"No. All is not over," Peter went on eagerly. "If I were anyone but myself; if I were the handsomest, the cleverest, and the best man living—if I were free—I would ask you on my knees, at this very moment, to bestow on me your hand and your love."

Natacha, who till now had not shed a tear, broke down completely; she looked in his face with grateful melancholy and hurried out of the room.

Peter, hardly able to check his own tears, also hastened away; he got into his wraps anyhow, and threw himself into his sleigh.

"Where to?" asked the coachman.

"Where?" thought Peter.—"Where can I go now? Not to the club certainly, to meet a crowd of heartless gossips!" Everything seemed mean and common in comparison with the impulse of love and compassion that had come over him, and the slow sweet gaze of her eyes through her tears.

"Home!" he said, throwing back his heavy bearskin coat, in spite of ten degrees of frost, to air his broad chest that was throbbing with exultation.

The night was exquisitely clear; above the dark and dirty streets and the tangled perspective of roofs, spread the deep vault of the sky bejewelled with stars. As he contemplated those remote and mysterious spheres, which seemed to have something in common with his state of mind, he forgot the abject squalor of the world. When they came out on the Arbatskaïa Square a wide horizon lay before him. Just in the middle blazed a pure luminary with a glorious train, surrounded by sparkling stars, that lay majestically displayed from the very margin of the earth; this was the famous comet of 1811—the comet which everyone believed to be a warning of endless woes and of the end of the world. It caused Peter no such superstitious terrors; his still moist eyes admired it with rapture. It looked to him like a bolt of flame that had rushed with giddy swiftness through measureless space to fall on that distant spot of earth and now remained quivering and blazing into infinitude. That heavenly glory dispersed the gloom of his soul, and gave him a foresight of the diviner splendours of another life.

BOOK NINE

CHAPTER LX

TOWARDS the end of the year 1811 the sovereigns, of Western Europe reinforced their armies and concentrated their strength. In 1812 these united forces, consisting of some millions of men, including the officers and commissariat, marched on the Russian frontier, while the Russians, on their part, marched to meet them. On the 12th of June the Western hordes entered Russia and war broke out.—That is to say, an event took place in diametrical opposition to all laws human and divine.

These millions of human beings rushed into the perpetration of every hideous crime: Murder, pillage, theft, fraud, forgery, treachery, incendiarism—the judicial annals of the whole world could not furnish so long or so black a list in the course of many centuries.—And yet those who committed them did not think of themselves as criminals!

What gave rise to this strange and monstrous state of things? Historians tell us, in all good faith, that the cause is to be traced in the insult offered to the Duke of Oldenburg, in the defiance of the continental blockade, in Napoleon's insane ambition and the Emperor Alexander's resistance; in blundering diplomacy and what not. If we are to believe them, a skilfully concocted note, written by Metternich, Roumiantzow or Talleyrand, between a court drawing-room and a rout, or a line from Napoleon to Alexander: "*Monsieur mon frère,* I am prepared to make restitution of the Duchy of Oldenburg, etc.," would have been enough to avert the war!

As may be easily supposed, this was the view taken by contemporary lookers-on. Subsequently, at St. Helena, Napoleon himself ascribed the conflict to the intrigues of England, while the English set it down to his insatiable ambition; the Duke of Oldenburg found the cause in the indignity to which he had been subjected; the merchant class, in the blockade which was ruining European trade; the old soldiers and commanders, in the need for finding them some employment; the legitimists, in the sacred duty of upholding constitutional principles; the diplomatic body, in the Austro-Russian alliance of 1809—which was no secret at the Tuileries—or the special difficulties in drawing up some memorandum—say number 178. All these reasons and a hundred others of a more trivial kind, and suggested by every variety of personal prejudice, may perhaps have satisfied the witnesses at the time; but to us, who are Posterity, who contemplate the event in all its magnitude, and who seek the true cause in all its terrible reality, they are wholly insufficient. We cannot believe that several millions of Christian men should have been ready to kill each other because Napoleon was ambitious, because Alexander was firm, because England was astute, or because the Duke of Oldenburg had been insulted. Where are we to find the connecting link between these facts and the very act and deed of battle and murder? Why were the natives of Smolensk and Moscow slaughtered and ruined in consequence of these events, by a swarm of invaders from the opposite side of Europe?

We are not writing history, and we cannot set to work to seek out the recondite first causes; we are satisfied to judge of events by a simple standard of common sense; and the more closely we examine them the more obvious do their true motives become. But whatever view we may take of those causes they still appear no less true or false if we compare their intrinsic triviality with the vastness of the events to which they ostensibly gave rise; we are driven to conclude that nothing but their cumulative force can account for the issue. Taken alone, Napoleon's refusal to withdraw his troops within the Vistula, or to reinstate the Duke of Oldenburg, seems to us no more sufficient than if we were told on the other hand: "If a French corporal had refused to fight, and a great many men had followed his example, the army would have been so much reduced as to render the war an impossibility."

No doubt if Napoleon had not taken offence at the concessions required of him, if England had not intrigued with the dispossessed duke, if the czar had not been deeply aggrieved, if the government of Russia had not been a despotic monarchy, if the various causes which led up to the French Revolution, the consulate and the empire had never existed—there would have been no war. But at the same time, if even one of this chain of circumstances had been missing, the sequel would not have followed.

Thus it was the sum total of them all and no one event by itself which entailed the fatal consequences. The war happened because it was bound to happen; and so it came to pass that some millions of men, ignoring all common sense and human feeling, started to march eastwards to slaughter their fellow-creatures, just as, some centuries before, unnumbered swarms had rushed down on the West, killing all on their way.

So far as their own free will was concerned, Napoleon and Alexander contributed no more by their actions to the accomplishment of such or such an event than the private soldier who was compelled to fight for them as a recruit or a conscript. Indeed, how could it be otherwise? For the fulfilment of their will, which apparently ruled the course of the world, the concurrence was needed of an infinite number of factors: all the thousands of individuals who were the active instruments of their purpose—all these soldiers, ready to fight or to transport cannon and victuals—had severally to consent to obey the orders of two feeble human units, and their obedience was the result of endlessly varied and complicated motives.

Fatalism is the only clue to history when we endeavour to understand its illogical phenomena; or, shall we say, those phenomena of which we see the causation but darkly, and which only seem the more illogical the more earnestly we strive to account for them

Each man lives for himself and has such play of free will as enables him to attain the end he may have in view. He has, and feels that he has, the power of doing or of not doing this thing or that; but as soon as it is done it is no longer in his hands: it has become a part of history, in which it finds its due place out of reach of chance and change.

The life of man is twofold—one side of it is his own personal experience, which is free and independent in proportion as his interests are lofty and transcendental; the other is his social life as an atom in the human swarm which binds him down with its laws and forces him to submit to them. For although a man has a conscious individual existence, do what he will he is but the inconscient tool of history and humanity. The higher he stands on the social ladder, the more numerous the fellow-beings whom he can influence, the more absolute his power, the more clearly do we perceive the predestined and irresistible necessity of his every action.

WAR AND PEACE

"The heart of a king is in the hand of God." Kings are the slaves of history.

History—that is to say the collective life of the aggregate of human beings—turns each moment of a monarch's life to account and bends kings to its own ends.

Although in the year of grace 1812, Napoleon was entirely convinced that it depended on his fiat alone whether the blood of nations should or should not be shed, he was, in fact, more subservient than ever to the mysterious promptings of history, which were driving him fatally onward while he still cherished the illusion of Free Will. And so, while they unconciously obeyed the law of the co-operation of forces, these men, marching eastwards in dense multitudes to slaughter their fellow-men, were moved by the combination of those numerous puerile reasons by which the common herd sought to account for this mighty migration. These, as we have seen, were the violation of the continental blockade, the squabble with the Duke of Oldenburg, the entrance of the troops into Prussia with a view to enforcing—Napoleon believed—an armed neutrality, his own reckless passion for war, and the habit of fighting which had grown upon him—added to the natural temper of the French and the general excitement caused by the magnitude of his preparations, their enormous cost and the consequent need for some indemnity; again, the intoxicating honours that had been paid him at Dresden, the diplomatic negotiations—which, though they were said to be conducted with a sincere desire to achieve a peace, only resulted in irritation—and fifty other pretexts more or less valid which, when combined, had finally no result whatever but that which was fatefully inevitable.

Why does an apple fall when it is ripe? Is it that its weight brings it down? Is it that its stalk withers? Is it that the sun has parched it and the wind torn it away? Or is it that the boy who eyes it as it hangs has an irresistible longing to eat it? Neither reason is enough by itself. The fall of the apple is the necessary consequence of all the causes brought about by the minute processes of organic nature. Hence the botanist who pronounces it to be the result of the decomposition of cellular tissue is just as much in the right as the boy who ascribes it to the potency and fulfilment of his desire.

In the same way, those were equally right and equally wrong who said that Napoleon went to Moscow because he had determined to do so, and that it became his ruin because Alexander had determined that it should—or those who should assert that a hill weighing several millions of hundredweights and undermined at the base, only fell in consequence of the last blow of the pickaxe given by the last labourer.

Those who are known as great men are really name-labels in history: they give their names to events, often without having so much connection with the facts as a label has. None of the acts of their so-called free will is a spontaneous act. It is bound up *a priori* with the march of history and human life, and its place has been appointed to it from all eternity.

CHAPTER LXI

NAPOLEON started from Dresden on the 4th of June. He had been there three weeks, surrounded by a court consisting of princes, grand-dukes, kings, and even an emperor. While he was gracious to those princes and kings who had earned his favour, he had given a lesson to those with whom he fancied he had cause for displeasure; he presented to the Empress of Austria gifts of pearls and diamonds of which he had robbed other sovereigns, and bestowed his tenderness on Maria Louisa (who considered herself his lawful wife though Josephine was at Paris), and left her inconsolable, it would seem, for his desertion of her. Notwithstanding the faith in the preservation of peace still entertained by the diplomatists, and their efforts to attain it; notwithstanding Napoleon's holograph letter to the czar beginning, "*Monsieur mon frère,*" and containing his assurance that he had no wish for war, with many concluding protestations of eternal regard and esteem, he was now on his way to join the army, and at every stage reiterated his orders to hurry on the march of the troops coming from the West to invade the East. He travelled in a close carriage with six horses, accompanied by his pages and aides-de-camp and a strong escort. His road lay through Posen, Thorn, Danzig and Königsberg; and in each of these towns thousands of inhabitants rushed to greet him with an enthusiasm that was not unmixed with terror.

Going on in the same direction as the army, he slept, on the 10th of June, at Wilkowiszky, in the house of a Polish count, to whom his advent had been announced; he then rejoined and outstripped the army, and arrived next day on the banks of the Niemen. There, putting on a Polish uniform, he went forward to examine the spot where the troops were to cross the river.

When he saw the Cossacks posted on the opposite banks and his eye looked out over the steppes which spread as far as the horizon between him and Moscow—the Holy City, the capital of an Empire which was like the Scythian Empire visited by Alexander the Great, he gave orders that the army was to advance the very next day—contrary to all the calculations of cabinets, and all the rules of strategy—and his troops crossed the Niemen on the day he had fixed.

Very early in the morning of the 24th he came out of his tent on the left shore of the river and stood watching through his field-glass, from the top of an escarpment, the progress of his armament which came forward, a living stream, out of the woods, and marched across the three floating bridges thrown over the Niemen. The army knew that the emperor was there, and tried to see him; and they no sooner caught sight of him on the top of the slope, in his greatcoat and cocked hat, a little apart from his staff and suite, than they threw their hats in the air with cries of: *"Vive l'Empereur!"* Thus, still pouring out of the forest where they had been encamped, they crossed the bridges in close ranks.

"We shall do something this time! When he takes things in hand he means business, by——! . . . There he is. *Vive l'Empereur!*—And are those the famous steppes of Asia?— A beastly country all the same, I say!—To our next meeting, Beauchet; I will keep the best palace in Moscow warm for you! Till we meet again; luck go with you!—Have you seen the emperor?—Brr!—If they make me Governor of India, Gérard, I will appoint you minister at Cashmere, that's a settled thing! —*Vive l'Empereur!* hurrah!—Look at the rascally Cossacks, how they run!—*Vive l'Empereur!*—Do you see him?—I have seen him twice as I see you, 'the little corporal'—I saw him give a cross to one of our old 'uns!"

These and a thousand such remarks were buzzing about the ranks of old and young alike; and every face was radiant with satisfaction at the opening of the campaign they had so anxiously looked for, and with enthusiastic devotion to the man in a grey greatcoat who stood up there on the hill.

On the 25th of June, Napoleon, mounted on a thoroughbred arab, galloped down to one of the three bridges, hailed on all sides with deafening acclamations. In fact he only endured

Crossing of the Niemen

these noisy demonstrations of affection because it was impossible to prohibit them; but it was very evident that they fatigued him and distracted his attention from the military question which at the moment was paramount in his thoughts. He crossed the pontoons, which trembled under his horses hoofs, and turned towards Kovno, preceded by his mounted guard, who made way for him through the troops. When he reached the banks of the broad river Vistula he stopped in front of a regiment of Polish Uhlans.

"*Vive l'Empereur!*" they shouted, as vehemently as the French soldiers, and breaking their ranks to get a better view of him.

He reconnoitred the river, dismounted, and took his seat on a log that was lying on the ground; at a wave of his hand a page, beaming with pride, stepped forward and handed him a telescope, which he rested on the lad's shoulder while he inspected the farther shore at his leisure. Then, after studying the map of the country which had been laid out before him, weighted with bits of wood, he murmured a few words without looking up, and two aides-de-camp rushed forward towards the Uhlans.

"What is it? What did he say?" they were all asking each other in the ranks of the regiment: The colonel had just received the command to find a ford and cross the river.

This colonel, an elderly and pleasant-looking man, begged the aide-de-camp to authorise his swimming across with all his regiment instead of waiting to seek a ford, and he fairly blushed and stammered with excitement as he preferred his request. A refusal would evidently have disappointed him bitterly; and the aide-de-camp hastened to assure him that the emperor could not fail to be pleased with such a display of zeal. The old officer, beaming with enthusiasm, waved his sword in the air with a shout of *Vive l'Empereur!* called on his men to follow, and dashed forward, spurring his horse; the beast refused, but he flogged it on; it took the leap and horse and rider plunged in, carried downwards by the strength of the current. All the men followed: those who were thrown clung to each other; several horses were drowned and not a few men; the rest swam on, holding on to their saddles or the horses' manes. They kept as straight a line as they could—and only half a verst farther down there was a ford—but they were too proud to spend themselves, and to die if need be under the eye of the little man sitting on the log, who did not even condescend to look at them!

When the aide-de-camp returned and presently took the

211

liberty of directing the emperor's attention to the self-devotion of the Poles, the man in the grey coat rose, called Berthier, and walked along the shore with him, giving him his orders and casting an indignant glance now and then at the men who, by drowning under his eyes, distracted his attention. It was nothing new in his experience to find that, from the deserts of Africa to the steppes of Muscovy, his presence was enough to turn men's heads and lead them to lay down even life for him. He remounted and rode back to his tents.

Forty Uhlans went to the bottom, though boats put out to the rescue. The greater part of the regiment were thrown back on to the bank they had left; only the colonel and a small following got safely across and scrambled up the opposite shore streaming wet. They had no sooner reached land than they cheered once more, and looked back at the spot where they had left Napoleon. Though he had disappeared, at that moment they were supremely happy.

That evening, after having sent two orders, one to hurry on the delivery of the forged banknotes intended for use in Russia, the other condemning a Saxon to be shot for having been found possessed of papers betraying the situation of the French army, he sent a third bestowing the cross of the Legion of Honour, of which he was the head, on the colonel of the Uhlans who had quite needlessly rushed into the most dangerous part of the river.— *Quos vult perdere Jupiter, dementat prius.*

CHAPTER LXII

THE Czar Alexander had already been more than a month at Vilna, where he gave all his time to reviews and manœuvres. Nothing was ready for war though it had long been foreseen, and it was to make preparations that the czar had come from St. Petersburg. There was no general scheme, and any decision as to which to choose of those that were proposed was farther off than ever, though his majesty had already been a month at headquarters. Each of the three divisions of the army had its general in command; but there was no commander-in-chief, and the czar did not choose to assume the functions. The longer he stayed at Vilna, the more slowly the preparations dragged on, and it even seemed as though the sole aim of those who surrounded him was to help him to forget the impending crisis, and make his stay as pleasant as possible.

After a series of balls and fêtes given by the Polish notables, by the magnates in office, and by the czar himself, one of the Polish aides-de-camp conceived the idea of a banquet and a ball in his majesty's honour, to be given by the whole staff. This plan was hailed with joy and accepted by the imperial guest; subscriptions flowed in, and a lady known to be in the czar's good graces agreed to do the honours. The 25th of June was fixed for the dinner, to be followed by a ball, a regatta, and fireworks; all to take place at Zakrety, a place in the neighbourhood belonging to Count Bennigsen, who placed it at the disposal of the committee.

Thus, on the day when Napoleon had sent his army across the Niemen, and his advance guard had driven back the Cossacks and invaded the frontier, the Emperor Alexander was dancing at a ball given by his staff officers!

The magnificent entertainment had brought together, it was said, all the handsomest women that had ever been seen. Countess Bésoukhow, who had come from St. Petersburg, eclipsed the more refined and elegant Polish ladies by the splendour of her sumptuous Russian beauty. The czar noticed her, and did her the honour of dancing with her once. Boris Droubetzkoï had left his wife at Moscow and was living at Vilna "*en garçon*" as he said; though he was not on the emperor's staff he was present at the entertainment in right of a round sum on the subscription list; he had gained considerable wealth, and promotion to various dignities, and no longer sought a patron, but held himself the perfect equal of his contemporaries of higher rank. He met Helen at Vilna, not having seen her for a long time, and having forgotten what had passed between them; but as she was now in favour of an important personage, and he lately married, they came together as old and good friends.

At midnight they were still dancing. Helen, finding no other partner to her taste, had asked Boris to dance the mazurka with her; they were the third couple. Boris, glancing with cool indifference at Helen's dazzling shoulders, rising above a gauze bodice of a dark shade spangled with gold, and talking of their former acquaintance, still kept an eye on his majesty, who stood near the door, speaking to one and another with the gracious benevolence of which he alone had the art. Presently he observed that Balachow, with whom the czar was on terms of intimacy, was waiting close to him, while he was speaking to a Polish lady. Alexander looked round inquiringly, and understanding that only some very serious motive could have prompted Balachow to take so great a liberty, he dismissed the lady with a bow and turned to him. As he listened, his face expressed the greatest surprise; he took his friend's arm and led him into the garden, not heeding the curiosity of the bystanders who respectfully made way for him. Boris had looked round at Araktchéïew, and noted how much he was disturbed by Balachow's proceedings, stepping forward a little way, as if he expected that the czar would invite him to join the conference. This little gesture made Boris understand that the minister of war was jealous of Balachow, and grudged him the good fortune of being able to communicate to his majesty some news apparently of the greatest importance. Finding that he was overlooked, he followed them at about twenty steps behind, into the illuminated garden, glancing furiously about him.

Boris, suddenly bitten with a desire to be one of the first to know this great news, told Helen that he would go to ask Countess Potocka to be their *vis-à-vis*; the countess was on the balcony, but just as he reached the spot he pulled up to make way for the emperor, who was coming in again with Balachow. Pretending not to have time to stand back, Boris squeezed himself against the doorpost and bowed low; and as he did so he heard Alexander say, in the indignant tone of a man who has been personally insulted:

"Across the frontier, and without having declared war! I will never sign a peace so long as a single foe remains on Russian ground." Boris fancied that the czar had felt some satisfaction in saying this and giving his feelings such explicit utterance, but at the same time he was evidently vexed at being overheard. "But do not say a word to anyone!" he added, knitting his brows.

Boris, understanding this as a hint to himself, looked down and again bowed. The czar went back into the ball-room, where he remained about half an hour longer.

Droubetzkoï having thus, by the merest chance, heard of the passing of the Vistula by the French army, took advantage of his good luck to make some important personages believe that he was often better informed than they were, which raised him considerably in their estimation.

The news fell like a thunderbolt, and coming in the middle

of a ball, after a month of expectancy, it seemed absolutely incredible. The czar in the first impulse of rage and indignation had exactly expressed his feeling in the exclamation overheard by Boris which, later, became famous.

At two in the morning he sent for Schischkow, his secretary, dictated an order of the day to the army, and a rescript to Marshal Prince Soltykow, in which he declared his solemn determination—in the very words he had used in speaking to Balachow — never to make peace so long as a foe remained on Russian ground.

Then he wrote a holograph letter to the Emperor Napoleon:

"*Monsieur mon frère,*—I learnt last evening that, in spite of the loyalty with which I have always adhered to my engagements with your majesty, your troops have crossed the Russian frontier. I have this moment received from St. Petersburg a note in which Count Lauriston announces that your majesty considered that war was declared between us from the moment when Prince Kourakine demanded his passport. The grounds on which the Duke of Bassano refused the passport gave me no reason to suppose that his demand could serve as a pretext for this aggression. In point of fact, my ambassador was never authorised to take such a step, as he himself explicitly stated; and as soon as I heard of it, I informed him how highly I disapproved, and ordered him to remain at his post. If your majesty is not bent on shedding the blood of our subjects for a misunderstanding,[1] and will consent to withdraw your troops from the Russian territory, I am ready to regard the past as nullified, and we may arrive at some compromise. In the opposite case, your majesty, I shall be compelled to repulse an attack so wholly unprovoked by me. It still rests with your majesty to avert the calamity of a fresh war.

"I remain, etc.,

"ALEXANDER."

---

[1] His majesty wrote in French, and here made the mistake of writing *mésentendu* for *malentendu.*

CHAPTER LXIII

On the 13th at 2 a.m. the czar sent for Balachow, read him this letter, and desired him to deliver it in person into the hands of the French emperor; he repeated the words he had used at the ball, and charged him to repeat them exactly to Napoleon. He had not written them in the note, feeling, with his invariable tact, that they were out of place at the moment when he was making a last effort to maintain peace; but he insisted on Balachow's repeating them accurately to Napoleon himself.

Balachow set out at once with a trumpeter and two Cossacks, and by daybreak had reached Rykonty, a village on the Russian side of the Niemen, occupied by the outposts of French cavalry. A subaltern of hussars, in a purple uniform and fur cap, shouted to him to stop; Balachow only went a little slower; the subaltern muttering an angry oath met him, and drawing his sword, asked him rudely whether he was deaf. Balachow gave his name, and the Frenchman, after sending one of his men to summon the officer in charge of the outpost, rejoined his comrades and paid no further attention to the Russian envoy. It was a strange experience for Balachow to be subjected in his own person and on his native soil to this insolent display of brutal force. In his constant intercourse with despotic power he was accustomed to be respected, and only three hours before he had been talking with the czar.

The sun was beginning to pierce the clouds, the air was fresh and dewy. The village cattle were being driven afield. Larks soared and sang, one after another, like the bubbles that rise spontaneously to the surface of the water. Balachow watched their flight as he waited for the French officer, and the men of his escort and the French hussars examined each other.

The French colonel, who was evidently only just out of bed, appeared at last, followed by two hussars, and riding a fine grey charger, sleek and well fed; his men, too, and their horses were smart and clean, and looked well groomed.

As yet the war was in its first stage, the stage of accurate full-dress and order as good as in time of peace, enhanced by a certain warlike smartness and the spirit and excitement which usually accompany the opening of a campaign.

The colonel could hardly swallow his yawns, but he was polite to Balachow, and fully understood his dignity. He led him past the outposts, and assured him that, as the emperor's head-

216

quarters were close at hand, there need be no delay in his being admitted to an audience. They rode through the village among groups of hussars, soldiers and officers, who saluted their colonel and stared at the Russian uniforms; beyond it, at a distance of about two versts, the general of division was encamped who was to conduct the czar's envoy to his destination.

The sun was now well up, and shone brightly on the fields and meadows. They had just passed a tavern, standing on a little hill, when they saw a party of officers riding towards them, led by a tall man on a black horse, with harness that glittered in the light. He wore a red cloak over his shoulders, and rode with his legs stiffened forward in the French fashion. From beneath his hat flowed a bush of black curls, and a plume waved in the air, while the gold braid of his uniform flashed and sparkled in the fierce glare of the midsummer sun.

Balachow was within a few yards of this theatrical-looking horseman, blazing with splendour and covered with jewels of all kinds, when the French Colonel Julner whispered in his ear: "The King of Naples!"

It was in fact Murat, though no one knew why, at this time, he was King of Naples. He himself, however, took the whole thing very seriously; so much so that the day before he withdrew from Naples, when he was out walking with his wife, on hearing some Italians shout "*Viva il Rè!*" he said sadly: "Poor souls! they little think that I am leaving them to-morrow!"

But notwithstanding his firm conviction that he was King of Naples, and that his subjects were bewailing his departure at the first beck of his august brother-in-law, he had gladly resumed his usual duties. "I made you king in order that you should govern in my way and not in your own!" Napoleon had said to him at Danzig, and like a fine young stallion that must frisk even in harness, he went galloping along the Polish high roads, decked out in the most gorgeous colours and splendid jewels, without caring, in his rampant high spirits, whither he was going.

When he saw the Russian general he tossed his curly head with a majestic air of royalty, and looked inquiringly at the French colonel, who explained to his majesty what Balachow's errand was, but could not succeed in pronouncing his name.

"De Belmacheve?" said the king, making a plunge with his unfailing presence of mind, where the colonel had hesitated and blundered. "Charmed to make your acquaintance, general," he added with a gracious bow; but as his majesty raised his

217

voice it lost its dignity, and he at once fell into the tone of jovial good-nature which was natural to him. He laid his hand on Balachow's saddle-bow and went on: "Well, general, it is war, I suppose. . . ." as if he regretted the fact, and had no pretension to pass judgment on it.

"Sire, my master the czar had no wish for war, and, as your majesty sees . . ." And Balachow dwelt with particular emphasis on the royal title, which he took every opportunity of repeating, perceiving from the comical delight on Murat's face that it was an agreeable novelty to him. *"Royauté oblige"*: a king must condescend; and Murat thought himself called upon to discuss affairs of state with Monsieur de Balachow, the Emperor of Russia's envoy-extraordinary. He dismounted. Then, taking Balachow's arm, he walked up and down with him, talking with an air of extreme importance. He told him, among other things, that Napoleon was much offended by the demand made upon him to withdraw his forces from Prussia, and more especially by the publicity given to the demand, which was an insult to the dignity of France. Balachow replied that there was no offence in that, for that . . . But Murat did not give him time to finish his sentence:

"Then by your account it is not the Emperor Alexander who has provoked the war?" he said abruptly, with a foolish smile.

Balachow explained the reasons which forced him to regard Napoleon as the aggressor.

"Well, my dear general, I only hope with all my heart that the emperors may settle matters between them, and that this war, which has begun by no connivance of mine, may come to a speedy conclusion." Murat ended after the fashion of a man who wishes to remain on good terms, even if his master must pick a quarrel.

He then inquired after the health of the grand duke, spoke of the time they had passed so gaily together at Naples; till, suddenly, remembering his majesty, he solemnly drew himself up, struck an attitude as he had done on the occasion of his coronation, and with a dignified wave of the hand said:

"But I will not detain you any longer; I wish you all success!" He fell back to join his suite, who were standing respectfully a little way off, and in a few minutes the scarlet cloak, with all its gold embroidery, the waving plume, and the sparkling jewels that reflected the suns ray's, were lost in the distance.

Balachow expected to find Napoleon within a short distance,

and went on; but on his arrival at the next village he was again stopped by the sentinels of Davoust's corps of infantry, and the general's aide-de-camp conducted him to the marshal's lodgings.

CHAPTER LXIV

DAVOUST, who was to the Emperor Napoleon what Araktchéïew was to the czar, was the very counterpart of the Russian, minus his cowardice; no less severe, and punctual in his official capacity, and, like him, knowing no way of displaying his devotion to his master but by acts of cruelty. Men of his stamp are as necessary in the machinery of administration as wolves are in the economy of nature; they always must exist, and manifest and justify their existence by the mere fact, trivial as it may seem, of their immediate intercourse with the sovereign. How, indeed, unless by some inherent necessity, can we account for the presence and influence of a man like Araktchéïew—cruel, coarse, and ill-bred—who would, for instance, pull a private's moustache close to the throne of Alexander, whose soul was tender and whose spirit nobly chivalrous?

Balachow found Marshal Davoust, with his aide-de-camp, housed in a barn and seated on a barrel, busied in checking and settling accounts. He might, no doubt, have found more comfortable lodgings, but he was one of those people who like to find life difficult, that they may have the better right to be morose and taciturn, and who on all occasions affect extreme haste and overwhelming cares.

"How is a man to see the cheerful side of life, I ask you, when he is harassed as I am with worries, and perched on a tub in a wretched barn?" was what the marshal's face expressed. The greatest pleasure to men of this kidney is, when they happen to meet anyone whose position in life is unlike their own, to make a great parade of perpetual and savage activity; and this was now Davoust's instinct as he saw Balachow, fresh and eager from his morning's ride, the lovely day, and his talk with Murat. He glanced at him over his spectacles, smiled contemptuously, without even a bow, and returned to his sums with a vicious contraction of his brows. The unpleasant impression his strange behaviour produced did not, however, escape the marshal's notice; he presently looked up, and coldly asked Balachow what he wanted.

The Russian, attributing this reception to Davoust's ignorance of his rank as aide-de-camp on the imperial staff, and his office as the czar's representative, hastened to explain his mission; but, to his great amazement, Davoust was stiffer and ruder than before.

"Where is your dispatch? Give it to me, and I will send it to the emperor."

Balachow replied that he had been enjoined to put it into his majesty's own hands.

"Your emperor's orders are carried out in your army, but here you must submit to our regulations." And to make the Russian general understand more clearly how completely he was at the mercy of brute force, the marshal sent for the officer on guard.

Balachow laid the packet containing the czar's letter on the table, which was simply a door, with the hinges still hanging to it, balanced on a barrel. Davoust read the address.

"You are quite at liberty to treat me politely or not, as you please; but I may venture to remind you that as I am one of his majesty's general's aides-de-camp . . ." Davoust stared at him, but did not speak; the annoyance, which was plainly legible on the envoy's face, evidently gave him the keenest satisfaction.

"You will have all due respect paid to you," he said at length, and, putting the dispatch in his pocket, he left the barn. A minute after, Monsieur de Castries, Davoust's aide-de-camp, came to fetch Balachow, and showed him to a lodging where he was to put up. The Russian general subsequently dined with Davoust, in the barn. The marshal told him that he was going away the next day, but that he, Balachow, was to remain behind and advance with the baggage-train. He was to have no communication with anyone except Monsieur de Castries.

At the end of four days of solitude and irritation, during which he learned only too surely his own insignificance and helplessness, feeling them all the more acutely by contrast with his all but sovereign power only a day or two ago; after travelling a few stages in the rear with Marshal Davoust's personal luggage, and in the midst of French troops—who pervaded the whole country—Balachow was conducted back to Vilna, now in the hands of the French, and re-entered the town by the same gate that he had left it by four days before.

THE INVASION

Next morning Monsieur de Turenne, one of Napoleón's chamberlains, came to announce to him that his majesty would grant him an audience.

A day or two previously sentinels of the Préobrajensky regiment had mounted guard at the door of the house to which Balachow was taken; now there were two French grenadiers, in dark blue uniforms and fur hats; a detachment of hussars and lancers and a splended suite of staff-officers were in waiting, expecting Napoleon to come out. They were standing at the foot of the balcony steps, near his horse, which was held by his mameluke Roustan.

Napoleon was receiving him in the same house where Alexander had given him his message.

CHAPTER LXV

THOUGH Balachow was well used to court splendour, he was amazed at the magnificence displayed in every detail by the French emperor. Count de Turenne led him into a large room crowded with generals, chamberlains, Polish magnates, most of whom he had ere now seen paying their court to the Emperor of Russia. Then Duroc came forward and told him that his majesty would see him before going out riding.

In a few minutes the gentleman-in-waiting begged him, with a courtly bow, to follow him into a little drawing-room, adjoining the very room in which he had received Alexander's parting injunctions; there he waited a short time. A quick, firm step was audible outside the door, which was thrown open, and Napoleon stood before him. He was dressed for riding in a dark blue uniform, over a long white waistcoat, which emphasised the rotundity of his shape, high boots, and doeskin breeches, tightly fitting his stout short legs; his hair was cut short, all but one long lock, which fell over his broad forehead. His thick white neck rose in strong contrast of colour from the collar of his uniform, and he was strongly scented with eau-de-Cologne. His face, still fresh and youthful, wore an expression of dignified and benevolent politeness. He walked rapidly, his head held high, and at each step gave a little nervous jerk. His whole thick-set figure, with square shoulders, deep chest and double chin, had the look of mature and settled dignity, which is often

221

to be seen in men of forty who have lived a life of ease: he seemed to be in an excellent humour.

Balachow bowed low and respectfully; the emperor nodded his head quickly in return, and at once began to talk as a man knowing the value of time, and who does not take the trouble to elaborate his speech, from a foregone conviction that what he says must be to the point and well said.

"Good day, general. I received the letter entrusted to you by the Emperor Alexander, and I am happy to see you." For a moment he took his fine eyes off Balachow's face; for the Russian in himself did not interest him in the least. His whole attention was concentrated, as usual, on the thoughts working in his brain, and he considered the outside world as of very small consequence generally, believing it to be wholly at the mercy of his will.

"I never wished for war—I do not wish it now," he went on, "but it has been forced on me. I am quite ready, even now,"—and he emphasised the words—"to accept any explanations you can offer." And he proceeded to state in a few concise words his dissatisfaction with the conduct of the Russian government.

His friendly and moderate tone deluded Balachow into a belief in his desire to maintain peace and to open negotiations.

"Sire, my master the czar . . ." he began with some hesitation, and much disconcerted by Napoleon's fixed inquiring gaze. "You are uncomfortable—be easy," was what those eyes seemed to say as they examined his uniform and sword, with the faintest possible smile. However, Balachow proceeded to explain that Alexander did not regard Kourakine's demand for his passport as a *casus belli*; that the ambassador had acted without orders; that the czar hoped to avoid war, and had no understanding whatever with England . . .

"Not yet," interrupted Napoleon; and then, as if fearing to betray himself, he nodded to the Russian envoy to proceed.

Balachow, when he had said all he had been desired to say, repeated that the czar would only open negotiations on certain conditions. Suddenly he stopped short: he had just remembered the words of the dispatch to Soltykow which he had been desired to repeat exactly to the French Emperor; they were quite clear to his memory, but a feeling he could not account for made him hesitate to utter them, and it was with some embarrassment that he added: "On condition that your majesty shall withdraw the invading army beyond the Niemen."

Napoleon observed his hesitancy; the muscles of his face twitched and the calf of his left leg trembled nervously. He did not move, but he spoke louder and faster. Balachow's eye was irresistibly caught by the strange trembling in the calf of the leg, and he observed that it increased visibly as his majesty raised his voice.

"I desire peace as sincerely as the Emperor Alexander. Have I not done everything in my power to preserve it these eighteen months? And for these eighteen months I have awaited explanations. Well, and what is it I am required to do before negotiations can commence?" And he emphasised the question by an energetic gesture of his small, plump, white hand.

"To withdraw your army beyond the Niemen, sire," replied Balachow.

"Beyond the Niemen!—Is that all?" said Napoleon, looking him straight in the face.

Balachow bowed respectfully. Instead of the demand of four months previously for the French to leave Pomerania, now they were only required to retire beyond the Niemen.

"You say," the emperor repeated, walking up and down the room, "that before negotiations can be opened I have merely to recross the Niemen! Do you know that, only two months since, I was required, in the same way, to recross the Oder and the Vistula!—and in spite of that you are still prepared to negotiate."

After a short silence, still pacing the room, he stopped in front of Balachow; his face seemed turned to stone, its expression was so stern and rigid, and his left leg still quivered spasmodically.—He himself, at a later date, said: "The twitching of my left calf is an ominous sign."

"Suggestions to abandon the Oder or the Vistula may be made to the Prince of Baden, but not to me!" he suddenly broke out. "Not if you were to give me St. Petersburg and Moscow would I accept your conditions! You accuse me of having begun the war—but which of us was the first to join his army? The Emperor Alexander. And you come to talk to me about negotiations, when I have spent millions, when you have allied yourself with England, and when your position is every day more critical! What is the object of your alliance with England? What advantage has it been to you?" he went on, evidently bent on proving his own justification and power, and the czar's blundering, instead of discussing the possibility or the conditions of peace. At first he pointed out the

223

advantageous position in which he stood, hinting at the same time that, in spite of his superiority, he would still vouchsafe to re-establish amicable relations with Russia; but as he warmed to his subject he was less guarded in his speech, and at length it was evident that his sole aim and end was to magnify himself and cast obloquy on the czar, while at the beginning of the interview he had seemed to wish the reverse.

"You have made peace with Turkey, I hear?"

Balachow bowed assent: "Yes, the peace is . . ."

But Napoleon cut him short. No one was to talk but himself.

"Yes, I know it," he broke in with that vehemence of speech and impatience of tone which are common among the spoilt children of Fortune. "Yes—I know: you have come to terms with the Turks without getting Moldavia and Wallachia. I would have given those provinces to your emperor, just as I gave him Finland! Yes, I would have made him a present of them, for I had promised them to him; and now he shall not have them. But he would have been glad to add them to his empire, and to extend Russia from the Gulf of Bothnia to the mouths of the Danube. Catherine the Great could have done no more!" he exclaimed, with growing excitement, and he repeated to Balachow, with but slight variations, what he had said at the meeting at Tilsit.—"And all that he would have derived from my friendship.—What a glorious dominion, what a glorious dominion!" He took a small gold snuff-box out of his pocket and eagerly sniffed the contents. "Ah! what a splendid empire the Czar Alexander *might* have had to govern!"

He looked quite compassionately at Balachow, but as soon as the general tried to speak a few words he began to talk again. "What could he want more or better than my friendship?" and he shrugged his shoulders.—"No: he has preferred to surround himself with my enemies, such as Stein, Armfeldt, Bennigsen, Wintzingerode!—Stein, a traitor banished from his own country; Armfeldt, a dissolute intriguer; Wintzingerode, a French deserter; Bennigsen, a better soldier than the others, but quite incompetent—Bennigsen, who was useless and helpless in 1807, and whose presence alone might have revived horrible memories in his mind!—If they were but men of some capacity one could make use of them," he went on, carried away by the arguments which crowded on his mind in support of his might and his right—in his eyes one and the same thing.—"But no; they are good for nothing, either in war or in peace. Barclay is the best of them they say, but I can hardly

think so judging from his first marches. . . . What do all these courtiers do? Pfuhl suggests, Armfeldt argues, Bennigsen criticises, and Barclay, when called upon to act, does not know which side to take! Bagration is the only thorough soldier of them all: he is stupid, but he has experience, a keen eye, and prompt decisiveness. . . . And then what part, let me ask you, does your young emperor play in the midst of all this incompetency? He is compromised at every turn, and held responsible for accomplished facts. A sovereign ought never to be with the army unless he is a general!"
—And he jerked out the words like a challenge to the czar, knowing full well that Alexander's chief ambition was to pass for a good military leader.—"Why the campaign was opened a week ago, and you could not even hold Vilna! You are cut in two, driven out of the Polish provinces, and your army is grumbling already!"

"Pardon me, sire," Balachow at last exclaimed, having followed this volley of words with some difficulty, "on the contrary, the troops are fired with the desire . . ."

"I know all about it," said Napoleon, again interrupting him. "All about it; do you understand?—I know the strength of your battalions as well as I know that of my own. You have not 200,000 men of all arms, and I have three times as many. I give you my word of honour"—he forgot perhaps that his word did not command implicit confidence— "that I have 530,000 men on this side of the Vistula. The Turks will be of no use to you; they are good for nothing. Indeed, they have amply proved it by making peace with you! As to the Swedes —they are predestined to be ruled by madmen: as soon as their king went out of his mind they chose another just as crazy— Bernadotte! For certainly it is sheer madness for Sweden to enter into an alliance with Russia!"—And Napoleon, with a spiteful sneer, sniffed again at his snuff-box.

Balachow, who had answers ready for everything, was unconciously gesticulating with impatience, without being able to check this deluge of words. With reference to the madness attributed to the Swedes, he might have pointed out that an alliance with Russia placed Sweden in the position of an island; but Napoleon was in that general state of irritation in which a man must talk and shout, simply to prove himself right to himself. The situation was becoming a painful one to the Russian: he feared that he was compromising his dignity as the czar's envoy by making no reply, while, as a man, he could not help shrinking into himself before this unreasonable fury. He knew quite well that all this rhodomontade was mere talk, and that Napoleon himself would be the first to be ashamed of it in a calmer mood; so he stood with downcast eyes, to avoid meeting those of the little man, of whose person he could only see the sturdy legs with their nervous restlessness.

"And when all is said, what do I care for your allies? I have allies too; the Poles — 80,00 men who fight like lions, and they will be 200,000 before long."

Thus lashing himself up by his own lies, and infuriated by Balachow's imperturbable calmness and silence, he went quite close up to him, stood exactly in front of him and with much gesticulation shrieked out in a harsh voice:

"I tell you, if you incite Prussia to join you against me I will blot it out of the map of Europe—and as for you, I will drive you beyond the Dwina and the Dnieper; I will restore the barrier between you and Europe that it has allowed to be felled in its folly and its blindness! Yes, that is what you have to look forward to, and what you have gained by alienating me!"

Then he again paced up and down the room, took out the snuff-box after having just put it in his pocket, and raised it several times to his nose, till stopping once more in front of the Russian general he looked at him with a satirical twinkle and murmured: "And yet, what a splendid realm your master *might* have ruled over!"

Balachow replied that the Russians did not take so gloomy a view of affairs, but counted on a sure triumph. Napoleon vouchsafed a condescending nod, as much as to say: "To be sure, it is your duty to say so; but you do not believe a word of it; I have convinced you to the contrary."

Allowing him this time to finish his sentence, Napoleon took a pinch of snuff and stamped on the floor: it was a signal, for at that moment the doors were thrown open and a gentleman-in-waiting offered the emperor his hat and gloves, bending respectfully as he did so, while another held out his pocket-handkerchief. He did not seem to see them.

"Give your emperor my fullest assurance," he said, "that I esteem him as entirely as I have always done. I know him, and highly appreciate his great qualities. I will detain you no longer, general; my answer to the czar will be placed in your hands." He snatched at his hat and went quickly to the front door; all the suite rushed downstairs to be ready to receive him at the foot of the steps.

THE INVASION

CHAPTER LXVI

AFTER this explosion of wrath and his last formal words, Balachow felt sure that Napoleon would not ask to see him again, but would rather avoid doing so, after allowing him, a humiliated envoy, to witness his ill-timed fury. But, to his great surprise, Duroc came to invite him to dine at the emperor's table that very day. Bessières, Caulaincourt and Berthier were also of the party.

Napoleon received Balachow very courteously, and no sign of awkward consciousness was visible in his good-humoured manner; on the contrary, he seemed to be anxious to put his guest at his ease. He was so convinced of his own infallibility that everything he did, whether conformable or no to the laws of right and wrong, could not fail to be good from the fact that he did it.

He was in the very best temper after his ride through Vilna, where the whole populace had come to meet him with acclamations, and where every window had been hung with flags and tapestry and filled with Polish ladies, bowing and waving their handkerchiefs. He talked to Balachow as cordially as though he were one of his own suite, of those who approved of his schemes and rejoiced in his successes. The conversation happening to turn on Moscow, he questioned him about the great capital, as a traveller might have done who was desirous of being informed as to a strange place he was about to visit, and with evident conviction that, as a Russian, his guest must be flattered at his interest in the place.

"How many inhabitants are there in Moscow—how many houses—churches? Is it really called Holy Moscow?" he asked; and when Balachow told him that there were more than two hundred churches:

"What is the good of so many?" he asked.

"The Russians are a very pious people," said the general.

"At the same time it is a fact that a great number of churches is commonly a sign of a backward stage of civilisation in a nation," Napoleon remarked, turning to Caulaincourt.

Balachow respectfully begged leave to differ:

"Every nation has its own customs," said he.

"Possibly; but there is nothing of the kind to be seen elsewhere in Europe, nowadays," Napoleon observed.

"I ask your majesty's pardon, but besides Russia there is Spain, where there are churches and convents innumerable."

227

This reply, which bore a covert reference to the recent defea
of the French in the Peninsula, made quite a sensation when it
was repeated at the court of St. Petersburg, as Balachow was
subsequently informed; but it fell flat at Napoleon's table, and
excited no remark. The dull faces of the marshals showed
that they had not seen the point of the allusion: "If that had
been witty," they seemed to say, "we should have discovered
it; so of course it was not!" Napoleon himself so little understood it that he asked Balachow, with much simplicity, to tell
him through what towns the most direct road lay from Vilna
to Moscow.

The envoy, who said nothing without deliberate intention,
told him that, as all roads lead to Rome, so all roads lead to
Moscow: that there were several routes, among others that
through Pultawa, which Charles XII had selected. But he had
not time to congratulate himself on this happy repartee before
Caulaincourt changed the subject to an enumeration of the
difficulties of the journey from St. Petersburg to Moscow.

Coffee was served in the emperor's private room; he seated
himself, and, as he raised his Sèvres cup to his lips, he pointed
out a chair to Balachow. There is a certain frame of mind
which usually, and involuntarily, comes over a man after dinner;
a pleasant mood in which he is happily satisfied with himself,
and prepared to think all men his friends. Napoleon was in
this comfortable humour; like any other mortal; he felt as
though all around him were alike and equally his adorers, not
excepting Balachow.

"This room, it seems," he began, addressing the Russian with
an amiable though ironical smile, "is that which the Emperor
Alexander also used. You must own, general, that the coinci-
dence is a strange one to say the least." And he appeared to
have no doubt that this consideration, as proving his evident
superiority over the czar, must necessarily be pleasing to his
guest.

Balachow made no reply but a bow.

"Yes, in this very room, four days since, Stein and Wintzingerode were holding council," Napoleon went on, still with that
satirical smile. "I really cannot understand why the czar
should have taken up my personal enemies—I cannot understand it! . . . Did it never occur to him that I might do
as much by him?" And his own speech revived the hardly
smothered furies of the morning. "Aye, and I will too; let
him know that!" he exclaimed, pushing aside his cup and rising.

"I will drive all his kith and kin out of Germany—out of Würtemberg, Baden, Weimar. . . . Yes, I will turn them out! He had better make a refuge ready for them in Russia."

Balachow made a movement intended to express both his anxiety to withdraw and the painful position in which he was placed by being obliged to listen and make no reply; but Napoleon did not notice it, and continued to treat him not as his enemy's ambassador, but as a man who could not but be devoted to him, and who must therefore rejoice in the humiliation of the sovereign whom he had formerly served.

"Why did the Emperor Alexander take the command of his armies? Why indeed?—War is my business—his business is to govern. Why did he take such responsibility on himself?"

Napoleon opened his snuff-box, took a turn in the room and then abruptly went up to Balachow, and smiling slightly, approached him, so firmly, simply, swiftly as if he were doing something not only important but agreeable to Balachow, lifted his hand to the face of this forty-year-old Russian general and taking him by the ear gave it a gentle tug, smiling only with his lips. "To have the ear pulled by the emperor," was reckoned one of the greatest honours at the French court. "Well, and you say nothing, you, the czar's admirer and courtier?" he asked in a sarcastic tone, intended to mark his conviction that, in his presence, it was out of the question that admiration could exist for anyone but himself.—"Are the horses ready for the general?" he added, nodding in answer to Balachow's bow. . . . "Let him have mine, *he has far to go.*"

Balachow, carrying a letter from Napoleon to the czar—the last he ever wrote to him—gave a full report of the reception he had met with;—and war broke out.

CHAPTER LXVII

Not long after his interview with Peter, Prince Andrew left Moscow for St. Petersburg. He said he was there on business, but, in fact, it was with a view to finding Kouraguine, whom he was bent on fighting. Kouraguine, being warned by his brother-in-law, made haste to depart, and got the minister of war to give him employment with the army in Moldavia. During this same visit to St. Petersburg Prince Andrew met Koutouzow, his old general. Koutouzow was delighted to see Prince Andrew, to whom he had always been much attached, and offered him an appointment on his own staff; he had just been nominated commander-in-chief of the forces in Moldavia, and was about to proceed thither. Prince Andrew accepted, and they set out together.

His purpose was to challenge Kouraguine to a duel; but for this some pretext must be found, otherwise Countess Natacha would be compromised. He tried to meet him somewhere, but in vain, for Kouraguine returned to Russia as soon as he got wind of Prince Andrew's arrival in Turkey.

However, life seemed more endurable in a new country, and under different conditions. Natacha's faithlessness had been a blow, all the more painful because he did his utmost to conceal how heavily it had fallen on him, and the scenes where he had been happy were now unendurable. Even more trying were the liberty and independence which in the past he had thought so precious. He no longer meditated on the ideas which the calm sky of Austerlitz had first brought to his soul, on the thoughts which he had once loved to talk out with Peter, and which had been the companions of his solitude at Bogoutcharovo, in Switzerland, and at Rome; he did not dare now to glance at the distant horizons of which he had had a glimpse, and which had looked so bright in their infinitude. The commonplace interests of daily life now absorbed him entirely, all the more since they were apart from those of the past. It seemed as though the limitless heaven that had then bent over his head had been transmuted to a dark and ponderous vault, narrowly circumscribed, and henceforth bereft, to him, of mystery and eternity.

Of the various occupations that lay under his hand, military duty was the simplest and most familiar. As general on staff service under Koutouzow, he surprised his chief by the punctuality and zeal he put into his work. Having failed to come across Anatole in Turkey, he did not think it necessary to follow him back to Russia; neither the course of time, nor the contempt he felt for Kouraguine, nor the reasons which told him that it was impossible for him to stoop to fight him, would keep him from provoking the quarrel the first time they should meet; nothing can keep a starving man from rushing at food. The sense of the wrong he had not avenged, and the wrath he had not vented, but which lay congealed at the bottom of his soul, poisoned the factitious calmness with which he fulfilled his many and various duties.

THE INVASION

When, in 1812, the news reached Bucharest of the war with Napoleon, Prince Andrew asked permission to exchange into the army on the eastern frontier. Koutouzow, to whom his zeal was a constant irritation, and who felt it a standing reproach to his own indolence, willingly acceded, and entrusted Bolkonsky with a mission to Barclay de Tolly.

On his way to join the army, which in the month of May was in the field at Drissa, he stopped at Lissy-Gory, which lay on his road. During the last three years, he had thought and felt so much, had gone through so many trials, and seen so many things in his travels, that it struck him strangely to find at Lissy-Gory the same kind of life as he had left there, unchanged in the smallest detail. He had hardly crossed the threshold of the great stone gateway of the avenue leading to the house, when he felt as though he were entering on enchanted ground, where slumber reigned supreme; in the house he found the same quietude, the same exquisite neatness, the same furniture and walls, the same perfumes, and the same faces, only a little older: Princess Maria, crushed, timid, and plain as ever, seeing her best years vanishing into the past without one ray of love or joy to mingle with her terrors and anxieties: Mademoiselle Bourrienne, on the contrary, enjoying every minute of her existence, and, as of old, spinning visions of hope for the future; she was still the same pert little person, with an additional modicum of insolence. The tutor Prince Andrew had brought from Switzerland, Monsieur Dessalles, wore a long coat of native cloth, and talked Russian after a fashion to the servants; but, otherwise, he had not altered since his arrival: a thorough good soul, pedantic, and somewhat narrow-minded. The old prince had lost a tooth; only one, but it left a conspicuous gap. In temper, he had not changed; his irritability and scepticism as to the genuineness of things in general had increased with advancing years. Only Nicolouchka, with his rosy cheeks and curly chestnut hair, had grown; when he laughed, the upper lip of his pretty mouth curled up just as his mother's had done. He alone rebelled against the yoke of the inevitable in this spellbound castle.

Nevertheless, though all on the surface was unchanged, the relations to each other of the inhabitants of Lissy-Gory had perceptibly altered. There were two parties, two hostile camps, which never could agree, but which consented to a tacit truce in honour of Prince Andrew's presence. One consisted of the old man, Mademoiselle Bourrienne, and the architect; the other

231

of Princess Maria, little Nicholas, his tutor, the old nurse, and all the women of the household.

During Andrew's stay at home they all dined together; but he soon perceived, from the general awkwardness of all the party, that he was being treated as a visitor in whose presence an exception is made. He was so fully aware of this that it made him, too, quite awkward, and he took refuge in utter silence. This tension of the atmosphere, too marked to be ignored, made his father sullen and taciturn; as soon as dinner was over, he withdrew to his own room. When Prince Andrew joined him there in the course of the evening, and tried to win his interest in the campaign carried through by young Count Kamensky, his father, instead of listening, broke out in abuse of Princess Maria's conduct, of her religious superstitions, and her hostility towards Mademoiselle Bourrienne—the only creature, he declared, who really cared for him. "His daughter made life a burden to him, and that was why he was never well, and she was ruining the child with her over-indulgence and absurd ideas!"

In his heart he knew full well that she did not deserve such a wretched life, and that he was her tormentor, but he knew, too, that he could never be otherwise, or cease to torture her.

"I wonder why Andrew, who sees everything, has not spoken to me of his sister," said he to himself. "Does he think I am a monster, an idiot, and have quarrelled about nothing with my daughter, simply to win the good graces of the French-woman? He does not understand; I must explain to him—he must know me better."

"I should never have alluded to the subject if you had not mentioned it," said Prince Andrew, in reply to this unexpected confidential communication, and he could not look his father in the face, feeling that he was condemning him for the first time in his life. "But since you ask me, I will be frank with you. If any misunderstanding has arisen between you and Maria, I cannot accuse her of any fault in the matter, for I know how much she reveres and loves you; if there is such a misunderstanding," he repeated, his temper gradually rising, as of late it had been apt to do, "I can only ascribe it to the presence of a woman who is utterly unworthy to be my sister's companion."

The old prince was sitting with his eyes fixed on his son, and a forced smile showed the gap left by the missing tooth, to which Prince Andrew could not get accustomed.

"What companion, my dear fellow? Ah! You have already talked it over."

"Father, I have no wish to pass judgment on your actions," replied Prince Andrew coldly; "you yourself have driven me to it. I have always said, and shall always say, that Maria is not to blame. It is the fault of those . . . in short it is that Frenchwoman's."

"What, you criticise me—you condemn me!" said the old man in a quiet tone, which even betrayed some embarrassment to his son's ear; then, suddenly springing to his feet, he cried out furiously:

"Get out of my sight—go! Never let me see you again! Go!"

Prince Andrew at once decided to leave the house without delay; but his sister implored him to give her one more day. The old prince remained invisible; no one was admitted to his room but Mademoiselle Bourrienne and Tikhone, and he asked repeatedly whether his son were gone.

Before setting out Prince Andrew went to see his boy. Nicholas jumped on to his knee and begged to be told the story of Blue-beard. He listened with absorbed attention; but suddenly his father stopped without finishing the story, and fell into a brown study, entirely forgetting Nicolouchka. He was thinking of himself, feeling with horror that he was concious of no remorse for his quarrel with his father, though they were about to part on bad terms for the first time. What shocked and distressed him still more was that, even for his child, he felt none of his usual tender affection.

"And what next? Tell me the rest of it," said the little boy; but his father, without answering, set him down from his knee and left the room. In fact, Prince Andrew, finding himself again in the midst of the scenes where he had once been happy, felt so disgusted with life that he thought only of getting away from these associations, and of making some fresh occupation for himself.

"Then you are really going, Andrew?" said his sister.

"Yes, I am free to go, thank God! I am only grieved that you cannot do so, too."

"Why do you say that, when you are going to the war—this dreadful war?" said Maria. "And he is so old—Mademoiselle Bourrienne told me that he had asked about you . . ." And her lips quivered, while large tears rolled down her cheeks.

Andrew turned away and did not answer.

"Good God!" he suddenly exclaimed, walking about the room, "to think that things and creatures so utterly contemptible can bring such misery on others!" His violence alarmed his sister, who understood that his remark applied not alone to Mademoiselle Bourrienne, but also to the person who had wrecked his happiness.

"Andrew, I entreat you," she said, lightly laying her hand on his arm and looking up with beaming eyes through her tears—"Do not fancy that sorrow is the work of man—he is but an instrument in the hand of God!" Her gaze, over and beyond her brother's head, was fixed on space, as if she were accustomed to see some familiar and beloved image there: "Sorrow is sent by Him; men are not responsible for it. If you think that anybody has sinned against you, forget it and forgive. We have no right to punish; and you, too, will some day understand the joy of forgiving!"

"Yes, Maria, if I had been a woman I should no doubt have thought so too. Forgiveness is a woman's grace; for a man it is different; he cannot, and he ought not to forget, nor to forgive," and though he had not thought of Kouraguine until that moment, all his unsatisfied hatred for the man rose up in his heart.

"When my sister can speak to me so," he said to himself, "it is sufficient proof that I ought long since to have had my revenge." He listened no more to her little sermon; he was picturing to himself, with envenomed satisfaction, the moment when he should meet Kouraguine, who, as he knew, was with the army.

Princess Maria tried to persuade her brother to remain only twenty-four hours longer; she was sure that her father would be grieved at his departing without their being reconciled. But he was of the contrary opinion; he assured her that their quarrel would only be embittered by delay, that his absence would be short, and that he would write to his father.

"Good-bye, then; remember that suffering is sent by God, and that men are not accountable for it." These were Princess Maria's last words.

"I suppose it must be so!" said Prince Andrew to himself, as he turned out of the avenue. "An innocent martyr, it is her fate to be victimised by a half-crazy old man, who is conscious of his cruelty, but who cannot now alter his nature! My boy is growing up, smiling at life; and he, like others, will dupe or be duped! And I am joining the army—what for? I have no idea, unless it is to fight with a man I despise, and so give him an opportunity of killing me first and laughing at me afterwards!"

Though the various elements of life were the same to him now as they had ever been, they had lost their unity and left only isolated and incoherent impressions.

CHAPTER LXVIII

By the time Prince Andrew reached headquarters it was the end of June. The first division, with which the czar was, held an entrenched camp on the Drissa. The second, which had been cut off, it was said, by a strong hostile force, had retired to take a fresh line of march and join it. Much dissatisfaction prevailed in both, in consequence of the general conduct of military matters; but it never occurred to anyone to apprehend a foreign invasion into the Russian provinces, or to conceive of war as extending beyond the western Polish territory.

Prince Andrew found Barclay de Tolly holding a position on the banks of the Drissa, at a distance of about four versts from where the emperor was established. As there was no village or town within reach of the camp, the numerous generals and court functionaries had taken possession of the best houses on both sides of the river, scattered along a line of about ten versts.

Barclay de Tolly received him with rigid coldness; he told Bolkonsky that he must refer him to his majesty for employment, but proposed to him meanwhile to remain on his staff. Kouraguine had left, and was at St. Petersburg; and Prince Andrew was really glad; he was thankful to have a short respite from the thoughts that his name always roused in his mind, and to be able to give himself up wholly to the absorbing interest of the war just beginning. Having no immediate duties he spent the first four days in riding about the camp, and acquired a very complete apprehension of the position by the aid of his own intelligence and by questioning those who could give him any useful information. What its advantages were remained to him an unsolved problem. His experience had taught him that the most learned and skilful tactics are often of very little value in practical warfare. He had seen this at Austerlitz, and since that day he had understood better than before that victory depends mainly on the power of anticipating and preventing unexpected movements by the enemy, and on the men who have to direct the operations of the army. To get the clearest possible light on this last factor he took every opportunity of studying the details of administration and character of the men and parties concerned in it.

During the emperor's stay at Vilna, the army had been broken up into three divisions: the first under the command of Barclay de Tolly, the second under Bagration, the third under Tormassow. The emperor had joined the first without assuming the functions of commander-in-chief, and his presence was merely announced in the order of the day without any further statement or remark. Nor had he with him any special staff, but only the ordinary staff at imperial headquarters. The chief officer was Quartermaster-General Prince Volkonsky, and attached to him were a crowd of generals, and aides-de-camp, of civil functionaries for diplomatic work, and a considerable number of foreigners, but there was no army staff. The emperor's personal circle included the following persons performing no functions; Araktchéïew, the ex-minister of war; Count Bennigsen, the senior general; the Czarevitch Grand Duke Constantine; Count Roumiantzow, the chancellor; Stein, who had been the Prussian minister; Armfeldt, a Swedish general; Pfuhl, who was chiefly responsible for the scheme of the campaign; Paolucci, a Sardinian refugee and general aide-de-camp; Woltzogen, and others. Though they were all attached to his majesty with no military functions in the army, they had so much influence that the general of division himself did not always know from whom a piece of advice, or an order under the guise of a hint, had emanated when given by Bennigsen, the grand duke, or anyone else; whether they were speaking on their own authority or expressing the czar's wishes; and whether they were to be obeyed or not. They were part of the stage accessories; their presence, and the czar's, was perfectly intelligible from their point of view, as courtiers—and every man becomes a courtier in the presence of his sovereign—and implied that, notwithstanding Alexander's refusal to accept the title of commander-in-chief, the control of the three divisions was in his hands; consequently, his immediate circle were, practically, his privy council.

Araktchéïew, the guardian of his person, was at the same time the mouthpiece of his orders; Bennigsen, who owned large estates in the government of Vilna, and whose one idea seemed to be to do the honours to his sovereign, had a high reputation as a soldier, and was held in reserve to replace Barclay de Tolly in case of need; the grand duke was there for his own pleasure; Stein as a councillor in virtue of the high esteem in which he was held; Armfeldt, Napoleon's most detested foe, was much listened to by Alexander—thanks to his calm assurance and intense conviction of his own merits; Paolucci was one of the phalanx because he was bold and decided; the generals aides-de-camp because they attended the czar everywhere, and finally—and this is the most important—Pfuhl, because after having conceived and elaborated the plan of the campaign, he had succeeded in getting it accepted in its entirety. He it was, in fact, who was conducting the war. Woltzogen was attached to Pfuhl because he was able to pass on his ideas in a more acceptable form than Pfuhl himself, a man of harsh manner, self-confident to the point of contempt for everybody else, and a cabinet theorist.

Besides all these high dignitaries, there were numerous subordinates, Russians and foreigners, adherents of their respective chiefs; the foreigners making themselves especially conspicuous by the audacity and variety of their military schemes: a natural consequence of serving in a country not their own.

In the vortex of opposite opinions which agitated this brilliant and haughty circle, Prince Andrew was soon able to discern the existence of several parties which evidently drifted asunder.

The first consisted of Pfuhl and his followers, the theoretical students of the science of war, who believed in immutable laws, in oblique attacks, and flank movements; their desire was that, in compliance with such hypotheses, the army should be withdrawn to the interior of the country; and they regarded every infringement of these imaginary rules as a proof of barbarism and ignorance—not to say of malicious intentions. This faction included the German princes, and indeed all the Germans: Woltzogen, Wintzingerode, and the rest.

Those of the second party, diametrically opposed to these, fell, as so often happens, into the other extreme; they clamoured to advance into Poland, and to start on no preconceived plan; they were bold and enterprising, and represented the national party, and consequently were all the more one-sided in discussion. It was composed of Russians: Bagration, Termolow, who was beginning to make his mark, and others. At that time there was a very current joke; Termolow, it was said, had one day requested the emperor to promote him to the rank of "German." The men of this party were never tired of repeating Souvorow's saying that it was useless to argue and stick pins into maps, that the point was to fight, to put the enemy to rout and prevent their getting into the country, and not give the army time to become demoralised.

The third party, to which belonged Araktchéïew, and in which the czar felt most confidence, were courtiers, mediators between the other two; not very military for the most part, and who thought and said what most men think and say who have no fixed ideas and are anxious not to betray the fact. Thus they were ready to admit that in a war against such a genius as Bonaparte—he was Bonaparte again to them—a thorough knowledge of tactics and the art of war was certainly indispensable; that Pfuhl no doubt was admittedly a master of it, but that the limitations of his judgment—the common fault of theorists—must prevent their having implicit confidence in him; that, in consequence, the opinions of his adversaries—men of the craft, men of action, whose experience was practical—must also be taken into consideration and therefore they must choose the happy middle course. They insisted that it was necessary to hold the camp at Drissa as Pfuhl had planned it, but to change the relative positions of the other two divisions. By this action, to be sure, neither of the ends aimed at was secured; nevertheless, the adherents of this party believed such a combination to be the best plan.

The fourth current of opinion was led by the grand duke, who could never forget his disappointment at Austerlitz when having made ready in parade uniform to rush on the French at the head of his regiment of guards, and to crush them, he unexpectedly found himself close under the enemy's fire, and only got out of the mêlée with the very greatest difficulty. The sincerity of this prince and his adherents was at once a good and bad thing; they dreaded Napoleon and his strength; they saw only impotence and weakness on their own side, and declared loudly: "Nothing but defeat will come of it all! Nothing but disgrace and reverses! We abandoned Vilna and then Vitebsk, and now we shall abandon the Drissa. There is only one rational course open to us: to make peace as soon as possible before we are driven out of St. Petersburg!"

This opinion found acceptance among the higher ranks of the army, in the capital, and with Count Roumiantzow, the chancellor, who, for other reasons of state, voted unhesitatingly for peace.

A fifth faction, again, were supporters of Barclay de Tolly, simply because he was minister of war and general - in - chief.

"In spite of all that can be said," was their verdict, "he is an honest and capable man; we have not a better. . . . As war, under divided authority, is out of the question, give him real power and he will show what he can do, as he did in Finland. We owe it to him that we still possess a well-drilled army, an army that could fall back on the Drissa without loss; all would have been lost if Bennigsen had been in his place; he displayed his incapacity in 1807."

The sixth set, on the other hand, cried up Bennigsen; no one, said they, was more prompt and well-informed than Bennigsen, and he would have to be employed after all. "The best proof is that the retreat on the Drissa was a series of blunders and failures — and the more the better; it will be evident then that we cannot go on so. What we want is not a Barclay but a Bennigsen! — Bennigsen, who made his mark in 1807, to whom Napoleon himself did justice, and to whose orders all will be ready to submit."

A seventh group included a considerable number of men such as are always to be seen round a young sovereign: generals and aides-de-camp devotedly attached to the man rather than to the ruler, honestly and disinterestedly worshipping him, as Rostow had worshipped him in 1805, and seeing nothing in him but graces and virtues. These lauded him to the skies for his modesty in refusing to undertake the chief command, while they blamed him for his exaggerated diffidence: "He ought," they said, "to put himself publicly at the head of the army, to select a formally constituted commander-in-chief's staff, to take counsel with theorists and practical veterans alike, and himself lead the soldiers, who are always excited to delirious enthusiasm by his mere presence."

Finally, the eighth and most numerous party, ninety-nine per cent of the whole, did not care whether the upshot were war or peace; whether the Russians acted on the offensive or remained entrenched by the Drissa or elsewhere; whether they were commanded by the czar in person, by Barclay de Tolly, Pfuhl, or Bennigsen. Their one sole aim was to catch pleasure on the wing, and get as much profit and amusement as possible. Here, too, it was easier than elsewhere or in time of peace, to put themselves forward and give themselves importance in the vortex of dark and tangled intrigues which were carried on at the imperial headquarters. One, to keep his place, upheld Pfuhl one day — and opposed him the next; and on the third, to escape responsibility and gratify the emperor, declared he had no opinions at all in favour of one plan more than another. A second, eager to find a footing, would take up some passing remark of the czar's and elaborate it at the next council, shouting, gesticulating, quarrelling, even on occasion calling out those who contradicted him, merely to attract the sovereign's attention and display his devotion to the public cause. A third would quietly seize a favourable opportunity, between two meetings of the council, to request and to obtain a gift in money as the reward for his loyal services, knowing full well that, under existing circumstances, it would be quicker to grant his request than to refuse it. A fourth would constantly, and as by the merest chance, come in the way of the czar, who found him always overburdened with business; while a fifth was ready to attack or defend every new opinion with equal vehemence and with more or less plausible arguments, only to get invited to dine at the emperor's table. The sole aim of all in this party was to gain medals and orders, rank and money; they devoted themselves to watching the fluctuations of imperial favour; no sooner had it taken a definite direction than this swarm of waiters on providence threw themselves into the scale, and so effectually, that the czar sometimes found it difficult to act on the opposite side. In fact the gravity of the danger in the immediate future, which gave a vague and feverish intensity to the general excitement—the whirl of intrigue, self-interest and conceit—and the perpetual collision of opinions and feelings—all lent weight to this, the most numerous party, so that it contributed largely to complicate and divert the march of events. This buzzing swarm, rising up as soon as any new question came under discussion without having settled the previous one, so deafened and bewildered everyone as to smother the voices of those who were prepared to examine it fully and honestly.

At the time when Prince Andrew joined the army a ninth party had just come into being and was beginning to make itself heard: a party of veteran statesmen of wisdom and experience, who agreed with none of those here described, but were competent to judge impartially of what was going on under their eyes in the staff at imperial headquarters, and who sought some way out of the general indecision and confusion. These thought and said that the chief mischief lay in the presence of the czar and his military court, which had imported this multiplicity of conventional and fluctuating ranks, convenient perhaps at court, but in the army absolutely fatal. The emperor's place was to govern the country and not to command the troops;

the only solution of the difficulty lay in his departure with his suite; his mere presence was an impediment to the movements of 50,000 men who were responsible for his safety; and in their opinion the worst general of division, if he were but free to act, was worth more than the greatest commander-in-chief who ever lived under the paralysing influence and presence of the sovereign.

Schichkow, the secretary of state, one of the most influential leaders of this faction, aided by Balachow and Araktchéïew, concocted a letter to the czar in which, presuming on the liberty they were allowed of discussing the war operations as a whole, they respectfully begged him to return to the capital, and to excite the enthusiasm of his subjects, stirring them up by his speeches to rise in defence of the country, and fanning the flame of that spirit which, in fact, became a main cause of the triumph of Russia, and which his majesty's presence at Moscow undoubtedly encouraged. Alexander decided to follow the advice thus offered and leave the army.

CHAPTER LXIX

It was before this letter had been laid before the czar that Barclay informed Prince Andrew at dinner, that he was to call on Bennigsen at six that afternoon, as his majesty had expressed a wish to question him himself with regard to affairs in Turkey. That morning a report—subsequently proved to be erroneous—had reached headquarters of an offensive movement on the part of Napoleon, and that same day Colonel Michaud, in a tour of inspection with the czar of the defences of Drissa, proved to him that this camp, which had been planned by Pfuhl, was not merely useless, but might be the ruin of the Russian army

Prince Andrew went at the appointed hour to Bennigsen's quarters: a house on a small private estate on the banks of the Drissa. He there found only Czernichew, one of the imperial aides-de-camp, who told him that the czar had gone out for the second time with General Bennigsen and Marquis Paolucci, to reconnoitre the entrenchments, since serious doubts had arisen as to their value.

Czernichew was reading a novel in the window-bay of a room which had formerly, no doubt, been a ball-room; there was an organ in it, piled with rolls of carpet; in one corner Bennigsen's

241

aide-de-camp, exhausted by fatigue or by the supper he had just eaten, was asleep on a bed. There were two doors from the room; one led into a small study, and the other into a drawing-room, where many voices were audible, talking German chiefly but occasionally French. There, by the emperor's orders a meeting had been convened—not a council of war, for Alexander disliked such definite designations—but a committee of those whom he wished to consult at this critical moment. These were Armfeldt the Swede, Woltzogen, Wintzingerode—whom Napoleon always called the French deserter—Michaud, Toll —who, indeed, was no soldier—Baron Stein, and finally Pfuhl, the mainspring of it all, whom Prince Andrew had ample opportunity of studying, for he arrived after Prince Andrew, and stood some minutes talking to Czernichew.

Though he had never seen Pfuhl before, he felt at once as though he knew him quite well; he wore the Russian uniform, but with a singularly bad grace, and his appearance was of a common stamp with that of Weirother, Mack, Schmidt, and fifty other theorising generals whom Bolkonsky had seen at work in 1805; but Pfuhl seemed to have united in himself all that characterised the class, and, to Prince Andrew, was a perfect and complete specimen of the German theorist. He was short and thin, but square-shouldered and strongly built, with broad bony shoulder-blades; his face was deeply wrinkled, and his eyes deep-set. His hair, combed smoothly and carefully over his temples, hung over the nape of his neck in little ragged tufts. His expression was anxious and sour, as if everything he met caused him alarm. He held his sword clumsily and asked Czernichew where the emperor was. It was evident that he was in a hurry to get through all ceremony, and be seated in front of the maps on the table, where he would be in his element. He listened with a sarcastic smile to the history of the emperor's inspection of the entrenchments which he had devised, and could not help growling between his teeth: "Idiots! everything will be lost . . . and a pretty state of things that will be!" Czernichew introduced Prince Andrew, adding that Bolkonsky had just come from Turkey where the war had ended so successfully. Pfuhl scarcely condescended to look at him: "You have seen a good specimen of tactics then!" was all he said, with crushing scorn, and he moved towards the next room.

Pfuhl, at all times cross-grained, was more so that day than ever, in consequence of the criticism to which his defences had been subjected. This brief interview, with his reminiscences of Austerlitz, was enough to enable Prince Andrew to form a fairly just estimate of the man. Pfuhl was evidently one of those men of one idea, who would go to the stake on the assurance they derive from their faith in the infallibility of some principle. Such natures are found among the Germans, who alone are capable of entire confidence in an abstract idea; as for instance in science, that is to say in their assumed knowledge of an absolute truth. A Frenchman will be completely self-assured because he considers himself personally irresistibly charming to men and women; an Englishman because he knows himself to be a citizen of the best-conducted state in the world and therefore, by being an Englishman, whatever he does must be undoubtedly right. An Italian is self-assured because he gets excited and easily forgets himself and others; and a Russian because he knows nothing and wants to know nothing, and disbelieves in the possibility of anything being known. But a German is self-assured more firmly, more unpleasantly, more obstinately than anybody, because he knows "the truth"— science, which he invented himself and which to him is "the absolute truth."

Pfuhl was, in fact, a believer in the theory of oblique attack as deduced from the wars of Frederick the Great, and everything in modern campaigns which did not accord with this theory was, in his eyes, so monstrous a blunder and so preposterous a mistake that such barbaric combination did not, in his opinion, deserve serious consideration as warfare.

In 1806 he had been the principal organiser of the campaign which culminated at Jena and Auerstedt, and even that failure had not convinced him of the evils of his system. On the contrary, he still insisted that it was entirely due to the neglect of certain rules, and was fond of repeating with gratified irony: "I knew the whole thing would go to the devil!" Pfuhl's passion for theory led him so far as to lose sight altogether of its practical ends; he had an intense aversion to its application and never would pay any attention to that.

The few words he spoke to Czernichew and Bolkonsky à propos the present war were in the tone of a man who foresees catastrophe and does not even deplore it. The melancholy little curls that hung over his coat collar and the neatly-combed locks on his temples seemed to harmonise with the tone of his words. He went into the farther room and his loud scolding voice was soon audible above the others.

CHAPTER LXX

PRINCE ANDREW had hardly turned his head when Count Bennigsen rushed through the room, nodding to him as he passed into his study, and giving the aide-de-camp some orders. He had come on in front of the czar to make some arrangements and receive him on his arrival. Czernichew and Bolkonsky went out on the steps: the emperor was dismounting. He looked tired, and walked with his head bent; it was evident that he was bored to death by Paolucci, who was haranguing him with extreme vehemence; he went forward hoping to cut the Italian short, but he, red with excitement and oblivion of etiquette, followed him closely without ceasing:

"As for the man who advised the entrenchment of that camp, of the camp at Drissa"—Paolucci went on, while the czar went up the steps, gazing at Prince Andrew whom he could not recognize—"As for him, sire," Paolucci went on, unable to check himself, "I see no alternative but a lunatic asylum or the gallows."

Alexander, without paying the smallest heed to these words, bowed graciously to Bolkonsky, whom he had at length identified.

"I am delighted to see you," he said. "Go in there where they are all assembled and await my commands."

Baron Stein and Prince Peter Mikhailovitch Volkonsky followed the czar into the little room, and the door closed upon them. Prince Andrew, authorised by the sovereign, went into the larger room where the council was assembled. Then Prince Peter Volkonsky, who was at the time the head of his majesty's immediate staff, brought in some maps and plans, and laying them on the table stated, in order, the various questions on which the emperor desired to take the advice of the council; news—afterwards proved false—had just been received that the French were preparing to surround the camp at Drissa.

Count Armfeldt was the first to speak; he proposed to ward off the difficulty by drawing up the whole army at some point, to be determined on, between the high roads to Moscow and to St. Petersburg, and there to await the foe. This proposal, which was altogether beside the question laid before the council, was made obviously with the sole object of showing that he, too, had a preconceived plan of action, and that he took the first opportunity of detailing it. The scheme, upheld by some and talked down by others, was one of those vague projects which seem to be made without any reference to the influence of events on the course of the war. Young Colonel Toll criticised it hotly, and pulling a manuscript out of his pocket he asked leave to read it. It was a minutely elaborated plan, in every respect precisely the reverse of Armfeldt's and Pfuhl's. This Paolucci attacked, arguing in favour of acting on the offensive, which would put an end to suspense, and at any rate get the army out of "this trap," as he designed the camp at Drissa. Pfuhl and his interpreter, Woltzogen, had kept silence through all this stormy debate; the former confined himself to jerking out inarticulate interjections, and sometimes even turned away with a contemptuous look, as if to emphasise the fact that he would never stoop to refute such a pack of nonsense. Prince Volkonsky, as president, appealed to him in his turn and begged him to give his opinion, but all he would say was that it would be useless, as the others obviously knew better than he did what remained to be done.

"You have your choice," he said, "between the position so wisely chosen by General Armfeldt with the enemy in your rear, and the attack suggested by the Italian gentleman; or, again—which would perhaps be best—an honest retreat!"

Volkonsky, frowning at this outburst, reminded him that he, Volkonsky, represented the emperor. Pfuhl rose, and with increasing warmth went on:

"Everything has been spoilt and muddled. You thought you could improve on my scheme, and now you appeal to me! I can only tell you to carry out to the letter what I have suggested, on the plans I have laid down," and he rapped his bony fingers on the table.—"Where is the difficulty? There is none! Stuff and nonsense! Child's play!" And going up to the map he rapidly went over various points, proving as he proceeded that no chance of war could cause his plan to fail, or nullify the advantages of the camp; that he had foreseen and provided for everything; and if the enemy should, in fact, surround it, they would rush on their own destruction.

Paolucci, who could not speak German, asked him a few questions in French; and, as Pfuhl spoke that language very badly, Woltzogen came to the rescue, and translated with great volubility Pfuhl's explanations—all intended to show that the difficulties they were at this moment endeavouring to meet were solely due to the inexact execution of his plan. At last, like a mathematician who will waste no more time on proving a problem he has solved, and of which the solution to him seems obvious, he ceased speaking and left his ideas to be explained in French by Woltzogen, who turned to his chief from time to time, saying—"Do you not think so, excellency?" And Pfuhl, heated by the contest, invariably replied with increasing annoyance:

"Of course. It is beyond dispute."

Paolucci and Michaud meanwhile were attacking Woltzogen in French, and Armfeldt was speaking to Pfuhl in German, while Toll explained it all to Prince Volkonsky in Russian.

Prince Andrew looked on and said nothing.

Of all these various personages Pfuhl was the one who most attracted his sympathy: this man, with his preposterous self-confidence and irascible but determined temper, was the only one of them all who asked nothing for himself, who had no hatreds, and who merely wished to see the execution of a scheme based on long years of study. He was ridiculous, no doubt, and his irony intolerably disagreeable, but in spite of it all, it was impossible not to respect his single-minded devotion to an idea. Nor did his speech betray the sort of panic which his adversaries could not, with all their efforts, conceal. This very general feeling—of which there had been no symptom in the councils of 1805—was now the result of the proved genius of Napoleon, and was perceptible in the most trivial arguments. To him all things were thought possible; he might even be able to attack them on all sides at once, and his name alone was enough to demolish the soundest reasoning. Pfuhl alone spoke of him as a barbarian, and only to be ranked with the rest of those who opposed his theory. And, in spite of his self-assurance, his bad-tempered German irony, he was pitiable with his smoothly brushed temples and the little tufts of hair sticking out at the back of his head. Besides his respect for Pfuhl, Prince Andrew felt a vague kind of pity; for, to judge from the tone of the others, from Paolucci's speech to the czar, and above all from some expressions the learned theorist himself let drop, it was clear that they all anticipated his impending overthrow. It was evident that under this bitter and scornful sarcasm lay angry despair at losing this sole opportunity of applying and verifying his system on a grand scale, and of proving its merits to the world at large.

The discussion was a long one and waxed hotter and noisier; degenerating at last into personalities, and coming to no practical issue. Prince Andrew, as he stood in the midst of this confusion of languages, schemes, suggestions, and counter-suggestions, could not help being amazed at all he heard. During his own career of active service he had often thought over what was called the science of warfare—a science which, in his opinion, did not and could not exist; and he had come to the conclusion that military genius was a mere conventional phrase. These ideas, hitherto but vaguely formed in his mind, had, during this day's debate, found ample confirmation, and had assumed in his mind the aspect of irrefutable truth.

"How," thought he, "can a theory and a science be supposed to exist under unknown conditions and circumstances, and when the forces brought into play can never be accurately determined? Can anyone guess what the relative position of our army and the enemy will be twenty-four hours hence? Have we not seen again and again that, thanks to some resolute madman, 5000 men have held their ground against 30,000—as they did at Schöngraben—or a force of 50,000 have given way and fled before 8000—as they did at Austerlitz, merely because one single coward started the cry of: 'We are cut off!'—Where is the science, when everything is vague and depends on an endless variety of circumstances, whose resultant force cannot be calculated even for a single minute, since that minute itself can never be foreseen? Armfeldt declares that our communications are cut off; Paolucci says that we have got the foe between two fires; Michaud says that the weak point of the Drissa camp is having the river behind it; Pfuhl proves that that constitutes its strength!—Toll has one plan, Armfeldt another: they are equally good and equally bad, for the merits of each one can only be discovered in the moment of execution and the evolution of events.—They all talk of military genius. Is the man a genius who contrives to keep his army supplied with biscuit, and sends one regiment to the right and one to the left? No. They only call a man a genius when he is successful and powerful, and because a crowd of toadies, on their knees, as they always are before Power, attribute to him certain qualities which, after all, are not those of true genius. The contrary is the fact. All the best generals I have known are stupid and absent-minded: for example, Bagration—and Napoleon thinks him the best of them all! Look at Napoleon himself. Did I not see his conceited and limited expression at Austerlitz?—A good leader need not be a genius, or have any superior characteristics; on the contrary, the loftiest and noblest qualities of man—love, poetry, tenderness, an inquiring and philosophical scepticism—must lie out of his ken. He must be narrow-minded, absolutely convinced of the importance of the task before him—this is indispensable, for otherwise he will lack patience; he must keep aloof from all affections, and know no ruth; never pause to reflect, never ask himself what is just or unjust . . . on these conditions only can he be a perfect general. Success, even, does not depend on him, but on the private who shrieks: 'We are lost!' or the man who shouts: 'Hurrah!' —only the soldier who serves in the ranks can be convinced of his own efficiency."

Prince Andrew was quite lost in these meditations when Paolucci's voice suddenly recalled him to himself: the council was breaking up.

The next day, on parade, the czar asked him where he wished to be appointed; and Prince Andrew sank past redemption in the estimation of the court circle, by begging to be sent on active service instead of requesting a place near his majesty's person.

CHAPTER LXXI

NOT long before the commencement of hostilities Nicholas Rostow received a letter from his parents, informing him of Natacha's illness and her rupture with Prince Andrew: "she broke off the engagement herself," it said, "without consulting us." They implored him to retire from the service and return home. In his answer he expressed his deep regret at his sister's illness and the breach with her fiancé, and assured them he would do what he could to fall in with their wishes; but he never dreamed of asking leave.

"Adored friend of my soul," he wrote privately to Sonia, "honour alone forbids my returning to be with you all. Now, on the very eve of war, I should feel disgraced, not only in the eyes of my comrades, but also in my own, if I were to prefer happiness to duty and devotion to my country. But this, I believe, will be our last separation. As soon as the campaign is over, if I am still alive and you still love me, I will give up everything here and fly to you and clasp you for once and all to my loving devoted heart."

This was the exact truth; the war alone had prevented his

marriage. The autumn at Otradnoë with its hunting, the winter with its carnival festivities, and his love for Sonia, had raised visions of peaceful happiness and quiet scenes which till then he had not known, and which smiled upon him more and more: "A perfect wife, sweet children, a capital pack of wolf hounds, ten or a dozen leash of swift borzois, the estate to manage, neighbours to entertain, and an active share in the functions of the nobility." But it was of no use to think of it; the war required his presence with his regiment, and it was in his nature to submit to such a necessity without recalcitrancy, fully content with the life he led and which he made pleasant to himself.

He had been hailed with joy by his fellow-officers on his return from his furlough; he had next been entrusted to buy horses for the regiment and brought back some well-selected beasts from Little Russia. Everyone was satisfied, and he was warmly commended by his chiefs. During this short absence he had been promoted to the rank of captain, and when his regiment was called upon to serve he found himself in command of his old squadron.

War had begun, pay was doubled; the regiment was sent into Poland and there joined by fresh officers, soldiers, and horses, and it was gay with the enthusiasm and bustle always to be seen at the beginning of a campaign. Rostow, fully appreciating the advantages of his position, gave himself up entirely to the pleasures and duties of the service, though he knew full well that the time would come when he must leave it.

For many reasons of state and of policy, not to mention others, the troops were moved from Vilna, and every yard of their retreat gave rise to fresh complications in the staff—interests, passions, and intrigues of every kind. So far as the Pavlograd hussars were concerned the retreat was effected in beautiful weather, with abundant supplies, and all the ease and comfort of a pleasure-trip. If there were despair, discouragement and above all intrigues at headquarters, that was their affair; in the ranks no one cared where they were going or why they went. The only regrets the retreat gave rise to were for the quarters where life had been so pleasant, and the pretty Polish girls. If it ever occurred to an officer to think that the future did not promise much good he made haste, as a soldier should, to cast away dull care and be jolly, and to concentrate his attention on the work in hand so as to forget the general situation. The camp was at first pitched at a short distance from Vilna; there was plenty of fun to be had among the Polish landowners with whom the officers made acquaintance, and in constant preparations for being reviewed by the czar or someone high in command.

Then the order came to fall back on Sventziany and to destroy all victuals that could not be carried away. The hussars had a vivid recollection of Sventziany, which, when they had last been in quarters there, had gone by the name of "the drunkards' camp." The conduct of the troops, who in foraging victuals and necessaries had taken possession of horses, vehicles, carpets, and everything that had come in their way, had given rise to serious complaints. Rostow, too, remembered the place only too well, having had to dismiss his quartermaster the very day of his arrival and been at a loss what to do with his men, who were as drunk as owls, and who had, without his knowledge, brought away five tuns of strong old beer!

From Sventziany the retreat was continued as far as Drissa; and from Drissa farther still, towards the Russian frontier.

On the 13th July the Pavlograd regiment had a sharp encounter with the foe; on the previous evening it had suffered under a furious gale of wind with heavy rain and hail, the precursor of the violent storms and tempests which were so unusually frequent in the course of the year 1812. Two squadrons had bivouacked in a field of rye which the horses and cattle had trampled till there was not a grain of corn left in the ear; it was raining in torrents. Rostow and a young officer he had taken under his protection, named Iline, had sought shelter under a hurdle hut run up in great haste. Another officer, whose face was literally hidden behind a gigantic pair of moustaches, rushed in, overtaken by the squall.

"I have come from headquarters," he said. "Have you heard, count, of Raïevsky's exploit? . . ." And he told him the details of the battle of Saltanovka. The moustached officer, whose name was Zdrginsky, made his story graphic; to hear him you might have thought that the dike at Saltanovka was at least as important as the pass of Thermopylæ, and that General Raïevsky's conduct in going forward on to the dike with his two sons was comparable to that of the heroes of antiquity. Rostow paid no particular attention to the narrative; he smoked his pipe, wriggled a little as the water every now and then trickled coldly down his back, and looked at Iline out of the corner of his eye. There was the same relation between the lad of sixteen and himself now, as, seven years ago, had bound him to Denissow. Iline had quite a feminine adoration for Rostow, who was his idol and pattern. Zdrginsky could not impart the fire of his enthusiasm to Nicholas. He sat in gloomy silence, and it was easy to see by his face that the whole story was particularly displeasing to him. Did he not know, only too well, by his experience of Austerlitz, and the war of 1807, that men always lied in their reports of military deeds—nay, that he himself lied in speaking of his own prowess? Did he not know, too, that in battle nothing really happens exactly as we fancy, and as we describe it afterwards? So the story annoyed him, and yet more the narrator, for he had an unpleasant habit of leaning over the person he was addressing and putting his face so close as almost to touch him; besides which he took up too much room in the tiny hut. "In the first place," said Rostow to himself, as he fixed his eyes on the speaker, "the crush and confusion on the dike must have been so great that even if Raïevsky rushed forward with his sons it could have had effect only on the ten or twelve men who were nearest to him.—As to the rest, they certainly would not have noticed who he was; or, if they did, it would have affected them but little, since at the moment their first care was the preservation of their own skin, and consequently the parental heroism cannot have mattered to them. . . . And after all, the fate of the country did not hang on that dike! It came to much the same thing whether we took it or let the enemy have it; and it was not Thermopylæ, whatever Zdrginsky may think, so what was the point of the sacrifice? Why put his sons in the front? I should not expose Pétia so; no, nor even Iline, though he does not belong to me and is a good little fellow;—on the contrary, I should have taken care to keep them out of harm's way." But he took good care not to give utterance to these reflections; experience had taught him that such frankness was useless, since, as this rhodomontade was all to the honour and glory of the Russian army, of course he must pretend to believe it implicitly, and he did not hesitate to do so.

"This is unbearable!" Iline presently exclaimed, guessing that Rostow was but ill-pleased. "I am wet to the skin; the rain is diminishing. I shall look for shelter elsewhere." And he and Zdrginsky went out together.

Not five minutes afterwards, Iline came back again, splashing through the mire. "Hurrah! Rostow, come along. I have found a place. There is a tavern two hundred yards away, and some of our men are there already. We can get dry there, and Maria Henrikovna is there too."

Maria Henrikovna was a pretty little German whom the surgeon of the regiment had married in Poland, and now took with him wherever he went. Whether this was because he could not afford to set up housekeeping, or because he did not like to part with her during the early months of their married life, no one knew. Be that as it may, the surgeon's jealousy had become an inexhaustible joke to the hussar officers. Rostow threw his cloak round him, called Lavrouchka and ordered him to follow with his baggage; then he and Iline set out, slipping in the mud and splashing into puddles; but the rain was lighter, the storm was passing over, and the lurid flashes of lightning rent the darkness at longer intervals.

"Rostow, where are you?" shouted Iline.

"Here, all right," said Rostow. "What a flash!"

CHAPTER LXXII

THE surgeon's *kibitka*[1] was standing at the door of the tavern, where five officers had taken shelter. Maria Henrikovna, a pretty, fair creature, but rather stout, was sitting on the bench in the place of honour in her dressing-jacket and night-cap, and partly screened her husband, who lay stretched behind her, fast asleep. They were all laughing and talking as the new-comers went in.

"You seem very jolly here!" said Nicholas.

"Well, you are in a nice mess, you two!" was the reply. "Perfect waterspouts! Do not swamp our drawing-room. Take care, don't spoil Maria Henrikovna's dress!"

Rostow and Iline looked about for a corner where, without insulting that lady's modesty, they might get into dry clothing. This they found in a part of the room divided off by a partition; but it was already occupied by three officers who entirely filled it. They were playing cards by the light of a tallow candle stuck into a bottle, and declined to make way. Maria Henrikovna, however, took pity on them; she lent them a petticoat, which they hung up as a curtain, and with Lavrouchka's help, behind its folds, they at length got out of their soaked garments.

With some difficulty, they lighted a fire in a broken-down stove; a board was found somewhere, and propped up on two

[1] A travelling-carriage or cart with a tilt.

saddles, and covered with a saddle-cloth. A samovar was un-packed, a basket was opened in which there was half a bottle of rum, and Maria Henrikovna was requested to preside. They all gathered round her; one offered his white pocket-handker-chief to wipe her pretty hands; another laid his pelisse under her feet to preserve them from damp; a third hung his cloak across the window to keep off the cold; and a fourth waved off the flies that might have awakened her husband.

"Let him be," said Maria, with a timid smile; "let him be; he always sleeps hard after a night ride."

"Impossible!" said the officer. "We must take good care of the doctor; one never knows what may happen, and he will do as much for me when he cuts off a leg or an arm for me."

There were but three glasses, and the water was so dingy and yellow that it was impossible to tell whether the tea were too strong or too weak. The samovar only held enough for six glasses, but no one complained; nay, they thought it very good fun to be served in turn, in order of seniority, and to accept the scalding liquid from Maria Henrikovna's plump hands, though her nails, it must be owned, left much to be desired on the score of cleanness. They all seemed—and, indeed, were—in love with her that evening; even the card-players came out of their nook and left their game, to be attentive and amiable to her. Thus surrounded by handsome young men, Maria Henrikovna was radiantly content, in spite of her alarm at the slightest movement on the part of her sleeping husband.

There was but one spoon, but to make up for that, there was plenty of sugar; only, as it would not melt, it was agreed that Maria should stir each glass of tea in turn. When she handed Rostow his glass, he put in some rum and held it out to her.

"But you have put no sugar in!" she said, laughing. To see the good humour of the whole party, it might have been thought that everything that was said was exquisitely witty and funny.

"I do not want any sugar; I only want you to dip your spoon in my tea with your pretty fingers."

Maria Henrikovna was nothing loath, and looked round for the spoon, which someone else had meanwhile taken possession of.

"Never mind, dip your little finger in; I shall like that even better," said Rostow.

"But it will burn me," said Maria, colouring with pleasure.

Iline took up a pail of water, threw in one or two drops c rum, and brought it to her.

"Stir that with your finger," said he, "and I will drink every drop of it!"

When the samovar had been drained to the bottom, Rostow took a pack of cards out of his pocket, and proposed that Maria should play *écarté* with one of them. They drew lots for the honour, and it was agreed that the winner, drawing the king, should kiss the lady's hand, and that the loser should devote himself to heating the samovar again for the surgeon's tea.

"But supposing Maria Henrikovna herself should draw the king?" said Iline.

"Well, as she is our queen, her orders shall be obeyed in the matter."

They had scarcely begun when the doctor's touzled head made its appearance over his wife's shoulder; he had been awake a minute or two, and had heard all the fun going on around him; but it was evident from his forlorn and sulky expression that he did not find it amusing. Without taking any notice of the officers, he dolefully scratched his head, and asked to be let out of his corner; they let him pass, and he went out, followed by a Homeric roar of laughter. Maria Henrikovna could not help reddening till the tears came into her eyes; but she was not the less bewitching in the opinion of her admirers. When the doctor came in again, he told his wife, who had ceased smiling, and sat anxiously awaiting her doom, that the rain was over, and that they must get into the kibitka again for fear their effects should be stolen.

"What an idea!" exclaimed Rostow. "I will put an orderly in charge—two if you like."

"I will mount guard myself!" cried Iline.

"Thank you very much, gentlemen," said the doctor grimly. "You have all had plenty of sleep, perhaps. I have spent two nights without rest." And he sat down sulkily by his wife's side to see the end of the game. The surgeon's expression, as he fiercely watched her every movement, only added to the amusement of the other men, who could not keep from laughing, and racked their brains to invent more or less plausible excuses for their merriment. When he at last carried off his pretty better half, they lay down, wrapped in their damp cloaks; but they could not sleep, and kept up their jests for a long time after at the doctor's fright and the lady's enjoyment; some even went out on the steps to overhear, if they could, what was going on in the kibitka. Rostow tried several times to get to sleep, but each time he was roused by some fresh sally, and they all began talking again, with hearty shouts of laughter—laughter without either rhyme or reason, like a parcel of children.

CHAPTER LXXIII

No one had yet been to sleep, when, at about three in the morning, the quartermaster came in with orders that the regiment was to start at once for Ostrovna, a town a little farther on.

The officers got ready in a hurry, but did not stop talking; the same samovar was once more heated to boil the same yellow water; but Rostow went off to see his squadron, without waiting for tea. It was not raining. Day was breaking; the clouds were slowly dispersing. It was very damp and cold, and this was the more chilling because his uniform had not had time to get dry. As they passed the kibitka, Iline and Rostow glanced into it. The surgeon's legs came out from under the wet apron; in a corner, resting on a pillow, was his wife's little nightcapped head, and they could hear her heavy breathing.

"She is really a nice little thing!" said Rostow to his companion.

"Charming!" exclaimed Iline, with all the conviction of sixteen.

Within half an hour the squadron were standing in their ranks along the road. The order was given to mount, and the men, crossing themselves, leaped into their saddles. Rostow put himself at their head.

"Forward!" he cried, and the hussars started, four abreast, to the noise of their horses' hoofs trampling in the mud and the clatter of their sabres; they followed in the wake of the infantry and artillery, along the high road, between the lines of birch-trees.

Violet-grey clouds, still crimson in the east, floated swiftly across the sky; day grew apace. The grass in the ditches was now visible, all wet with the night's rain, and sparkling drops hung from the drooping branches of the birch-trees. The soldiers' faces were more plainly distinguishable. Rostow and Iline were riding along the little avenue formed by two rows of trees on one side of the road. Nicholas was fond of changing his horse in the course of a day's ride, mounting a cossack horse

instead of the regimental charger. He was a lover and connoisseur of beasts, and had lately purchased a fine sorrel nag,
with a white mane, from the steppes of the Don, which nothing
could outstrip, and which he rode with intense enjoyment;
so he now trotted on, thinking of his horse, of the surgeon's
wife, of the dawning day, without once reflecting on the enemy
that might be down on them at any moment.

Formerly, he would have felt afraid of marching on to battle;
now, he had no fears. Had custom inured him? No; but he
had learnt to control himself, and to think of anything rather
than of that which might have seemed the most pressing at
such a moment: the danger, namely, that lay before him. All
his efforts, all the reproaches he had heaped upon himself for
his cowardice, had not, during the early years of his service,
conquered the terror which instinctively came over him; but
time had insensibly worked the change. So he took his way
with calm indifference under the trees, pulled a leaf as he passed,
stroked his horse's shoulder with his toe, and held out his pipe
when it was empty to the hussar behind him, without turning
round; he might have been riding out for a morning airing.
He felt real pity for Iline's anxious and excited face, which expressed so many conflicting emotions; he knew by experience
that state of feverish apprehension, that anguish of anticipating
terror and death, and he knew that time was the only remedy.

The sun had no sooner struggled up above the bank of clouds
than the wind fell; it seemed hushed in respect at the glorious day
that dawned after so wild a night. A few drops were still falling,
but now vertically. The fiery orb as it rose higher was hidden
for a minute behind a strip of cloud, and rent the upper edge
to blaze forth once more in full splendour; the landscape shone
in beauty, the verdure glistened brightly—and then, like an
ironical comment on this glory of life and light, they heard in the
distance the first growl of cannon.

At what distance Rostow had not time to guess, when an
aide-de-camp from Count Ostermann-Tolstoï rode up from
Vitebsk at a gallop, and communicated an order to advance as
rapidly as possible.

The squadron soon outrode the infantry and artillery—who
also went at double-quick pace—down a hill, through an abandoned village, and up the opposite slope, men and horses bathed
in sweat.

"Halt!" cried the colonel of division: the squadron formed
in line.

"Left! forward!" The hussars made their way along the front to the left flank of the position, behind the Uhlans who were to lead the attack. On the right the infantry reserve were placed in dense columns; over their heads, on the heights, the cannon gleamed against the sky in the slanting rays of the morning sun. Below, in the hollow, the enemy's columns and artillery were briskly exchanging shots with the Russian outposts.

The rattle of musketry, which Rostow had not heard for many a day, exhilarated him like martial music; he listened with pleasure to the *rap, tap, ta-ta, tap* that incessantly fell on his ear, singly or in louder unison with irregular rests and outbursts of renewed vigour; like a child trampling on crackers.

The hussars waited motionless for about half an hour; then the heavy fire began. After speaking a few words to the colonel of the regiment, Count Ostermann and his suite rode to the rear of the squadron, and away towards a battery posted a few yards off. A few minutes later the order was given to the Uhlans to form for the attack, and the infantry in front parted to let them pass. Down the slope, and away at a round trot, their pennants flying from their lances, they rode towards the French cavalry which had just turned the left shoulder of the hill.

As soon as they had started the hussars were brought forward to take their place and cover the battery. A few spent bullets passed over their heads, whistling and sighing through the air. This noise, as it came closer, increased Rostow's eager, high spirits. Perched as high as he could sit on his saddle, he could look down on the whole field of action, and anxiously followed every movement of the Uhlans. As they came into collision with the French horse there was a moment of confusion, under a cloud of smoke; then he saw that they were driven back on the left, and mixed up with them and their sorrel chargers were the compact blue masses of French dragoons on dappled-grey horses.

CHAPTER LXXIV

ROSTOW's practised eye at once understood what was happening: the Uhlans, broken up by the enemy, were scattered and flying, and coming nearer and nearer. He could already distinguish the movements of the men, though they looked small in the distance—he could see them clash, struggle and flourish their sabres.

Rostow watched the scene as he might have watched a hunt; his instinct told him that if the hussars were to attack the dragoons now at once the French would give way; but it was now or never: a second later would be too late. He looked round; a captain was by his side—his eyes, too, fixed on the struggle.

"Andrew Sévastianovitch," said Rostow, "we could knock them over? What do you say?"

"No doubt of it, for . . ."

But Rostow did not wait for the end of the sentence; spurring his horse, he set off at the head of his men who, as if stirred by the same impulse, did not wait for orders to follow him. Nicholas had no conscious reason for doing as he did, and hardly knew how he did it: the action was unpremeditated and instinctive, as it might have been out hunting. He saw the enemy galloping in some disorder at a short distance off; he felt that they would make no stand, and that, come what might, the moment must be seized, for that once past it would be gone for ever. The singing of the bullets was so exciting, his horse was so difficult to hold in, that he was carried away by impulse, and he heard the tramp of his squadron close behind him as they pelted down the hill. On the level below they broke into a gallop, faster and faster as they got nearer to the Uhlans, whom the French were pursuing. On seeing the hussars, the front ranks of the dragoons hesitated and paused, stopping the way to those behind them. Rostow, giving his cossack steed his head, rushed on to the attack like a huntsman cutting off the line of a wolf. One Uhlan checked himself in his flight; a man on foot threw himself on the ground to escape being crushed; a riderless horse plunged into the middle of the hussars, and then the larger number of the French dragoons turned and were off at top speed.

Just as Rostow spurred his horse in pursuit a bush stood in his path, but his good beast took it at a bound, and Nicholas had hardly settled himself in his seat again when he was close

The larger number of the French dragoons turned and were off at top speed

on the enemy's heels. A French officer, to judge from his uniform, was galloping a few feet ahead of him, bent over his horse's neck and beating him with the flat of his sword. Half a second later Rostow's charger rushed down with all his force, his breast-bone on the Frenchman's crupper, nearly upsetting him; Rostow mechanically raised his sabre and let it fall on the foe. But, in the very act, the fire that had carried him so far was extinct as if by magic. The officer had gone down, more from the collision and his own alarm than from the blow dealt him by his assailant, which had only wounded him very slightly above the elbow.

Rostow pulled up to look for the man he had hit; the luck-less dragoon was hopping along on one foot, unable to disengage the other from his stirrup. He blinked his eyes and frowned, as if apprehending a second blow, and glanced up and down in undisguised alarm at the Russian hussar. His boyish face, pale and mud-stained, with light blue eyes, fair hair and dimpled chin, was far indeed from the type of countenance one would expect to meet on a battle-field; it was not the face of a foe, but the simplest, most innocent face to grace a peaceful home. Rostow was still wondering whether he was really going to finish him, when the lad said: "I surrender!" Still hopping and unable to free himself he allowed some Russian hussars to disengage his foot and help him into his saddle again. Many of his comrades, like himself, had been taken prisoners; one of them, streaming with blood, was still fighting to recover his horse; another, supported by a Russian, was clambering on the victor's charger to sit on the crupper behind him; the French infantry were still firing as they retreated.

The hussars now promptly returned to their position, and Rostow as he followed them had a painful impression of a weight on his soul; it was but vague and ill-defined, a sort of compunction that he could not account for, which he had felt in taking the young officer prisoner, and still more in hitting him.

Count Ostermann-Tolstoï came to meet the conquerors, sent for Rostow, thanked him, told him that he should report his heroic exploit to his majesty, and recommend him for the cross of St. George. Rostow, who had expected on the contrary to be blamed and reprimanded, since he had acted without orders, was greatly surprised; but that background of distressed feel-ing, which was really acutely painful, prevented his entire satisfaction.

"What is it that is worrying me?" thought he, as he turned

away. "Not Iline? No, he is safe and sound! Have I done anything wrong? No, nothing of that kind! . . . It is the little Frenchman with his dimpled chin. I hesitated a moment before striking him.—I remember it still! . . ."

The prisoners, under guard, were just setting off; he went up to them to look once more at the young dragoon, and saw him mounted on a hussar's horse, with a very scared expression. His wound was trifling; he smiled shyly at Rostow and waved his hand, and Rostow felt a discomfort that was almost shame.

All that day and the next his fellow-officers observed that, without being fractious or sullen, he was silent, pensive, and absent-minded; that he drank without enjoyment and preferred to be alone, as if some fixed idea weighed upon his mind.

He was thinking of the "heroic exploit" which had earned him the cross of St. George, and by which he had gained a reputation for valour. There was to him an impenetrable mystery in the affair. "Then they are more afraid than we are?" thought he. "And this—and nothing more than this —can pass for heroism? But it does not seem to me that love of one's country has anything to do with it.—And my blue-eyed prisoner, what share has he in the responsibility?—How terrified he was! He thought I was going to kill him! Why should I kill him? And although my hand trembled, I am to have the cross of St. George all the same! I can make nothing of it, absolutely nothing!"

But while Nicholas Rostow was lost in such reflections, puzzling himself with questions to which there was no solution, Fortune had suddenly turned her wheel in his favour. He was promoted after the fight at Ostrovna to the command of two squadrons of hussars; and henceforth, when a brave officer was in request, he always had the preference.

CHAPTER LXXV

On hearing of Natacha's illness Countess Rostow, though still ailing, had set out for Moscow with Pétia and all her servants; she settled into their town house, whither the rest of the party had already moved.

Natacha's illness took so serious a form that happily for her and for her parents, all the causes that led to it—her misconduct and the breach with Bolkonsky—were cast into the background. She was in too critical a state to allow of her estimating her own fault in the matter: she ate nothing, did not sleep, grew thinner every day, and coughed incessantly; the doctors told her parents that her life hung on a thread. After this their one idea was to alleviate her suffering. All the leaders of science were called in to see her, singly or in consultation; laid their heads together, criticised each other, talked French, German, and Latin, and prescribed the most antagonistic remedies, adapted to cure every complaint that they ever had heard of.

It never struck them that the disease from which Natacha was suffering was not within the power of their science; that not one of the ills that crush humanity, in fact, ever can be; since every human being has a constitution of his (or her) own and bears within himself his own peculiar malady, unknown to medicine and often highly intricate. It is not to be traced exclusively to the lungs, the liver, the heart, or the spleen; it is not specified in any treatise; it is simply the outcome of one or another of the numberless complications which arise from a disorder of one of these organs. Physicians who spend their lives in prescribing for the sufferers, and are paid for doing it, will not admit this; how can they?—And even if they did, how could the magician cease to work his spells? How should they think themselves other than indispensable when they are so in fact, only in a different way from what they fancy. At the Rostows', for instance, if they were of any use it was not because they made their patient swallow a variety of mixtures, for the most part noxious, though their effect in small doses was almost inappreciable, but because their presence was a satisfaction to the aching hearts that loved and watched over Natacha. This is where the strength of the physician lies, be he a quack, a homœopath, or an allopath. He supplies the perennial demand for comfort, the craving for sympathy that every human sufferer feels, and of which the germs exist in the child. See a baby that has given itself a blow; it runs to its mother or its nurse to be kissed and have "the place" rubbed; and it actually suffers less for the pity and caress.—Why? Because it feels that they are bigger and wiser than itself, and have it in their power to help it.

So the doctors were of a certain use to Natacha when they assured her that she would be better after taking the pills and the powders from the shops in the Arbatskaïa, which were put up in a neat little box, costing one rouble and seventy copecks, and were to be dissolved in boiling water, and taken every two hours.

And what would have become of Sonia and the count and countess if they had had nothing to do but to fold their hands, instead of carrying out every order to the letter: of giving the mixture at regular intervals, insisting on a morsel of chicken being eaten, and attending to all the thousand little things which give occupation and comfort to those who have the care of the sick? How could the count have borne this anxiety about his darling child if he had not been able to look forward to sacrificing several thousand roubles, and taking her abroad at any cost for change of air and the opinion of foreign celebrities? What would he have done if he could not have had the pleasure of telling his friends how that Métivier and Feller had made a mistake, how that Frise had hit the nail on the head, and Moudrow had exactly understood Natacha's case? And what would the countess have found to occupy her if she might not have scolded her daughter when the child rebelled against the rules laid down for her?

"You will never get well if you do not do as you are told and take the pills regularly," she would say with a kind of impatience which made her forget her anxiety. "You must not play any tricks with an illness which, as you very well know, may lapse into pneumonia." And she really found comfort in speaking this learned word, which she did not understand,— and, God knows, there are many like her.

Sonia again, what would she have done if she had not been able to say that she had never had her clothes off for three nights, to be always at hand to carry out the doctor's orders, and that even now she slept with one eye open, so as to be ready to administer the pills out of the gilt paper box. And even Natacha herself, though she was convinced she should never get well, and did not wish to live, found much satisfaction in all the sacrifices that were made for her, and in taking her medicine with due punctuality.

The doctor came every day, felt her pulse and looked at her tongue, and laughed and talked a little, taking no notice of her forlorn looks. When he left the room the countess would hurry after him; he put on a grave face, shook his head, and tried to persuade her that he hoped for wonders from the last remedy; that they could but wait and see; that the malady was as much mental as . . . But then the countess, who refused to allow herself to recognise this, would slip his fee into his hand and go back with a lighter heart, to sit with the invalid.

The serious symptoms were a total loss of appetite and sleep,

and an almost incessant cough, with an apathy from which
nothing could rouse her. The doctors, saying that she could not
get on without constant treatment, kept her in the unwhole-
some air of the city, and the Rostows were consequently obliged
to remain in Moscow throughout the summer of 1812. However,
in spite of this, and of the infinite number of bottles and boxes
of pills, drops, and powders—of which Mrs. Schoss, who was a
fervent believer, made a complete collection—youth at length
got the upper hand: the small incidents of daily life gradually
healed over Natacha's griefs; the acute suffering which had
wrung her heart glided into the past, and by degrees her strength
came back.

CHAPTER LXXVI

NATACHA became calmer, but she did not recover her spirits.
Indeed, she avoided everything that might have amused and
cheered her—balls, parties, theatres, concerts; even when she
smiled there seemed to be tears lurking in the background.
She could not sing. At the first sound of her own voice she
broke down; tears choked her; tears of repentance, tears for
the memory of that happy time, now for ever past. Song and
laughter seemed sacrilege to her sorrow! As to flirtation, she
never thought of such a thing; as she truly said, she cared no
more for any man than she did for Nastacia, the old buffoon.
A secret scruple prohibited all pleasure in her life; she could
feel no interest in the thousand small occupations of a girl's
round of happy heedlessness and trivial hopes. What would
she not have given to recall one day of that past autumn at
Otradnoë, with Nicholas, for whom her heart yearned with
terrible anxiety! But alas! All that was gone, and for ever.—
Her presentiments had not deceived her. Her freedom of that
time and her aspirations after unknown joys were over and
done;—and yet she had to live.

Instead of thinking, as she had then been apt to do, that
she was better than others, she now took a pleasure in humbling
herself, and wondering what the gloomy future could have in
store for her. She tried to give no one any trouble, and as to her
personal comfort, she never even thought of it. She commonly
kept aloof even from the family circle, and only seemed quite
at her ease with Pétia, who could sometimes make her laugh

She rarely went out, and of those who now and then came to
see her, the only person she cared for was Peter. It would have
been impossible for anyone to show more discretion, tenderness,
and tact than Count Bésoukhow; she felt it without thinking
about it, and it naturally made his society pleasant to her.
But she did not appreciate it at its full worth; she was so convinced that in his commonplace good-nature Peter found it no
effort to be kind to her. Nevertheless she noticed from time
to time that he seemed ill at ease, particularly when he feared
lest the conversation should revive painful associations; but she
ascribed this to his kind-heartedness and his native bashfulness.
He had never again alluded to feelings the confession of which had
escaped him that day in the stress of intense emotion, and she
thought no more of it than of the soothing words with which we
try to comfort an unhappy child. Never supposing it to be
anything but a form of consolation, it never came into her head
to imagine that love, or even a pure and sublimated friendship,
such as she knew could sometimes exist between a man and
a woman, could come of their intimacy—not, indeed, because
Peter was a married man, but because the moral barrier which
had so completely given way between her and Kouraguine,
stood firm and rigid between her and Peter.

It was towards the close of the midsummer fast, before
St. Peter's day, that a neighbour from Otradnoë, Agrippina
Ivanovna Bélow, arrived at Moscow to worship at the shrines of
the martyrs. She asked Natacha to join in her devotions, and
Natacha gladly consented, in spite of the doctor, who prohibited
early exercise; and, to make more serious preparation than was
customary in that household, she said that she could not be
satisfied with the three shorter services, but should accompany
Agrippina to all the services—vespers, matins, and high mass,
throughout the week. The countess encouraged her religious
fervour. She hoped in her heart that prayer might prove a
more efficient remedy than the efforts of science, and, without
confiding in the doctor, she gave way to her daughter's wish,
and put her in charge of Bélow, who, when she went to call
Natacha at three in the morning, found her already up for fear
of being late.

Having hastily dressed in her shabbiest gown, she slipped on
her oldest cloak, and, shivering with the chill of night, they made
their way through the empty streets in the cold pale light of
dawn. In obedience to the advice of her zealous friend, she
attended the services not in her own parish, but at another

church, where the priest was esteemed for a particularly pure and austere life. The worshippers were few. Natacha and Agrippina followed the service with deep devotion, kneeling in front of the image of the Virgin which stood between the choir and the congregation, and fixing their eyes on the blackened figure, lighted at this mystic hour by quavering tapers, and the first streaks of day peeping through the windows. And a feeling of humility was born in her soul which she had never before known, of abasement in the presence of Something supreme and incomprehensible. When she could follow the words pronounced by the choir or the officiating priest, her aspirations found utterance in the common prayer; when she failed to catch the sense, she told herself submissively that the desire to know was an outcome of pride; that she ought to be content to believe and trust in the Lord, whom she felt at this moment to be the Sovereign of her soul. She prayed and crossed herself, imploring God with fervour, enhanced by her sense of iniquity, to forgive her her sins, most of all she abandoned herself in prayers of penitence. She rejoiced to find in herself a sincere will to amend, and a power of foreshadowing the possibility of a pure and happy life in the future. And leaving the church at a still early hour, she would meet no one on her way home but the masons going to their work, and the gate-porters sweeping the streets in front of the still sleeping houses.

This sense of regeneration possessed her throughout the week, and the happiness of receiving Communion and tasting the Lord seemed so exquisite, that she only dreaded lest she should die before that thrice-happy Sunday.

But the longed-for day dawned in due turn; and when Natacha came back from the Communion service, in her white muslin gown, she felt, for the first time after many weeks, at peace with herself and the life before her.

The doctor, when he paid his usual visit, bid her continue the powders he had prescribed a fortnight since:

"Go on taking them very regularly," he said, with a smile; he was honestly convinced of their efficacy. "Be quite easy," he added to the countess, skilfully hiding in his palm the gold piece she had slipped into it; "she will soon be singing and dancing again. This last prescription has done wonders; she is very much better."

The countess spat for luck, looking at her nails,[1] and went into the drawing-room, greatly cheered.

[1] A ceremony vulgarly supposed in Russia to ward off the evil eye.

CHAPTER LXXVII

By the beginning of July the most alarming reports of the progress of the war had reached Moscow; the czar had issued a manifesto, and was on his way to the capital; it was said that he had left the army because it was in danger; that Smolensk had capitulated; that Napoleon had not less than a million of men with him; and that nothing but a miracle could save Russia.

The manifesto was received on the 23rd of July, but, as it had not yet been printed, Peter promised to dine with the Rostows on the following day, and bring a copy of it from Count Rostopchine, with the proclamation appended to it.

The next day was a Sunday, a perfect summer day, oppressively hot even by ten in the morning, the hour at which the Rostow family were in the habit of attending mass in the chapel of the Hôtel Rasoumovsky. Everyone was suffering from lassitude and that general nervous sensitiveness and uneasiness which is so commonly the result of a very hot day in a great city. This state of tension gave acuteness to every impression: the light colours of the people's dresses, the cries of the street vendors, the dusty leaves of the trees along the boulevard, the clatter on the pavement, the noisy music and dazzling white trousers of a regiment marching to parade, and yet more the scorching heat of the July sun. All the rank and fashion of Moscow had met at a private chapel, for most of the nobility, anticipating serious events, had remained in town instead of spending the summer on their estates.

Countess Rostow stepped out of her carriage, and a footman in livery marched before her to make way for her through the crowd. Natacha, who was following her, presently heard a young man whom she did not know, say to his neighbour rather loud:

"Yes, it must be the Countess Natacha; she is much thinner, but she is even handsomer than she was!"

Then she fancied—but that she often did—that she heard the names of Bolkonsky and Kouraguine, for she felt as though everyone who saw her must discuss what had happened. Stung to the quick and painfully agitated, she nevertheless walked on, in her lilac dress, with all the more calmness and dignity because in her heart she was dying of shame and grief. She knew she was handsome, but her beauty no longer gave her the

266

satisfaction she had formerly felt; and this bright, sultry day seemed, on the contrary, to turn it to bitterness and vexation: "One more week gone," she said to herself, "and so it will always be. The same dreary and melancholy life,—I am young and handsome—I know it. . . . I was very naughty, but now I am good—I know that, too. . . . And the best years of my life must be wasted without profit to anyone."

She took her place by her mother's side, and looked round at the people and the dresses near her, criticising, from sheer force of habit, the appearance of her neighbours and their way of crossing themselves.—"And they are criticising me no doubt!" she said to herself as an excuse. But at the first chant of the service she shuddered with horror, as she compared these idle thoughts with those she ought to have had after that day of her communion. Had she not sullied the bright purity of that impression for ever?

A venerable old priest performed the service, with the gentle impressiveness that brings peace and rest to all who pray. The holy gates were closed, from behind the curtain, which was slowly withdrawn, a mysterious voice murmured a few words. Natacha's eyes involuntarily filled with tears, and her whole being thrilled with soft and languid emotion.

"Teach me what I ought to do!" she murmured. "Teach me to school myself, and above all to correct myself of my faults!"

The deacon, coming forth from the iconostasis [1] and taking his place in front of the holy gates, pulled his long hair out of the neck of his dalmatic, and making the sign of the cross, said solemnly:

"Let us pray to the Lord in unison!" Natacha mentally responded: "Let us pray without difference of rank, and without hatred, all united in brotherly love!"

"Let us pray that He may grant us the world above and the salvation of our souls," said the priest, and Natacha replied from the bottom of her heart: "Let us pray to attain the world of the angels and of all the spiritual beings who dwell above us."

At the prayer for the army she besought the Lord for her brother and for Denissow; at the prayer for all who travel by land or by water she thought of Prince Andrew, and implored forgiveness for the wrong she had done him; at the prayer for

---

[1] The iconostasis is the screen on which the holy images are placed in the Greek Church.

those who love us she interceded for those near and dear to her, understanding for the first time how cruelly she had wounded them; at the prayer for our enemies she wondered who her enemies could be, and could think of none but her father's creditors. Nevertheless, one name always rose to her tongue at this petition—that of Anatole; and though he, to be sure, had not hated her, she prayed for him with double fervour as for an enemy. She never could think of him or of Prince Andrew with any calmness except in these moments of devotion, for then only did the fear of God get the better of her impulses towards them both. At the prayer for the Imperial Family and the Holy Synod she crossed herself devoutly, telling herself that, since she was forbidden to doubt, she ought to pray fervently for the Holy Governing Synod without knowing what it meant.

"Let us each and all commend ourselves and each other, at each moment of our lives, to the holy keeping of our God and Saviour Jesus Christ," the priest went on; and Natacha, carried away by the impetus of religious fervour, responded ardently: "Take me, O Lord! take me to Thee!"

To see her it might have been thought that she was on the point of being lifted heavenwards by an invisible power, and delivered once for all from her regrets, her faults, her hopes, and her remorse. The countess, who had been watching her rapt expression and glistening eyes, was praying on her part that God would vouchsafe to help and comfort her darling child.

In the middle of the service, contrary to the usual custom, the sacristan brought in the wooden stool on which the book was commonly laid from which the priest recited the prayers, kneeling, on Whit-Sunday, and placed it in front of the holy gates. The officiating priest, with his violet velvet cap on his head, came down the altar steps and knelt down, stiffly; his example was imitated by the astonished congregation. He was about to read the prayer, composed and distributed by the holy synod, beseeching God to deliver Russia from the foreign invasion.

"O Lord Almighty, O Lord Deliverer!" he began in clear unemphatic tones, the voice of the Greek priesthood, which appeals so powerfully to Russian hearts—"We humbly implore Thy infinite mercy, trusting in Thy love. Hearken to our prayer and come and succour us! The enemy brings consternation on Thy children and would fain make the world a waste; rise Thou up against him! The wicked have contrived to destroy Thy land, and to bring Thy faithful Jerusalem, Thy beloved Russia, to naught, to defile Thy temples, upset Thy altars, and profane Thy sanctuaries. How long, O Lord, shall the sinners triumph? How long shall they defy Thy laws? Lord, hearken unto them that call upon Thee. Let Thine arm maintain our very pious autocrat Czar Alexander Paulovitch, and may his faithfulness and meekness find grace in Thine eyes. Reward his virtues, which are the bulwarks of Thy well-beloved Israel. Inspire and bless his resolutions, his undertakings and his deeds; strengthen his rule by Thy omnipotent hand, and give him the victory over his enemies, as Thou didst to Moses over Amalek, to Gideon over Madian, to David over Goliath! Protect his armies, uphold the bow of the Medes under the arms of those who have gone forth in Thy name, and gird them with Thy strength in the fight. Arm Thyself with the shield and lance and rise up and help us! Send down confusion on those who wish us evil so that they may be scattered by the armies of the faithful even as the dust is scattered by the wind, and give Thy angels strength to disperse them and pursue them. Let their secret plots be turned against themselves in open day; let them fall into the net that they have laid; let them go down before Thy slaves that we may tread the foe underfoot. Lord! Thou canst save great and small, for Thou art God, and man can to nothing against Thee.

"Lord God of our fathers! Thy grace and mercy are everlasting; turn not Thy face from us by reason of our iniquities, but vouchsafe to forgive our sins in the plenitude of Thy goodness. Create in us pure hearts and a righteous spirit; strengthen our faith and hope; inspire us with mutual love, and unite us in defending the inheritance that Thou hast given us and our fathers, to the end that the sceptre of the wicked may not rule in the land of the people which Thou hast blessed.

"O Lord God, we trust in Thee; let us not be confounded, nor our hope in Thy mercy be deceived. Give a sign that our enemies and the enemies of our holy religion may see, and be put to confusion and perish. Let the nations of the earth see and believe that Thy name is THE LORD and we are Thy children. Show Thy mercy upon us and deliver us. Send joy to the hearts of Thy slaves, strike our enemies and throw them under the feet of the faithful. For Thou art the help and the strength and the victory of those that trust in Thee.

"Glory be to the Father, and to the Son, and to the Holy Spirit, now and for ever and ever. Amen."

Natacha, highly strung and agitated as she was already, was deeply moved by this prayer. She listened eagerly to the passages alluding to the victories of Moses, Gideon, and David, and to the destruction of Jerusalem, and prayed with a fervent emotion, though hardly understanding what it was that she was asking of God, When it came to entreating for a pure spirit for herself, for confirmation of faith, for plenitude of hope and brotherly love, she put her soul into the petition; but how could she ask God to let her trample her enemies under foot, when, but a few minutes ago, she had only wished she had any, that she might love them and pray for them all? How, on the other hand, could she question the rightness of the prayer that the priest had just read on his knees? Devout terror came over her as she thought of the punishments that come upon sinners; she prayed fervently for pardon, for them, and for herself; and it seemed to her that God had heard her prayer, and that He would grant her peace and happiness in this world.

CHAPTER LXXVIII

SINCE that night when Peter had carried away the remembrance of Natacha's grateful eyes—since that night when he had gazed at the comet blazing in space—a new horizon lay before him: the contemplation of human nothingness and folly ceased to fill his mind. The terrible and sinister problems which constantly rose up before him vanished as if by magic at *her* image. Whether he were talking, or listening to the most trivial matters, or hearing an account of some base action or monstrous absurdity, he did not feel so terrified as he used; he had ceased to ask himself why men toiled and tormented themselves; when life, in itself so short, led only to the unknown. He pictured her as he had then seen her, and his doubts were dissipated; the thought of her lifted him up to an ideal and pure sphere where sinners and righteous were not, but only beauty and love, the sole final causes of existence. Whatever sordid and base deeds he might happen to see, he said to himself: "What does it matter to me if a man who has robbed the state and czar is heaped with honours, since yesterday she smiled on me, she begged me to go there again to-day, since I love her—and not a soul will ever know it!"

Peter still lived in the gay world, drank as hard as ever, and

270

led a perfectly idle life. But when the news from the frontier became daily more alarming, when Natacha's health was much improved, and ceased to give him the pressing anxiety which was the excuse for his constant visits, a dull irritability that had no visible cause took possession of him—a presentiment that some great change was coming into his life, that a catastrophe was imminent—and he sought with eager curiosity for some prophetic indications of it.

One of the brethren of his craft had pointed out to him a prophecy in the Apocalypse that had been applied to Napoleon. In chapter xiii., verse 18, it is written: "Here is wisdom. Let him that hath understanding count the number of the beast: for it is the number of a man; and his number is six hundred three score and six." And at verse 5 we find: "And there was given unto him a mouth speaking great things, and blasphemies; and power was given unto him to continue forty and two months."

By collating these sums with the alphabet, regarding the first nine letters as units, and the rest as tens, thus:—

a	b	c	d	e	f	g	h	i	k	l	m	n	o
1	2	3	4	5	6	7	8	9	10	20	30	40	50

p	q	r	s	t	u	v	w	x	y	z			
60	70	80	90	100	110	120	130	140	150	160.			

If the words "Le Empereur Napoléon" were constructed by the cipher, the sum total of the figures added together would be 666.[1] Hence Napoleon was the Beast spoken of in the Apocalypse. Moreover, by adding the figures corresponding in the same cipher to the French words *quarante-deux*[2] (42), the period of years set for his power, the sum of 666 is again brought out, which indicated that the year 1812, as being the forty-second year of his age, would be the last of his rule.

This manner of divination captured Peter's fancy; he was constantly trying to guess what would put an end to the power of the Beast, otherwise called Napoleon; and he endeavoured to calculate the answer to the mysterious question by this process. He worked at it with the words "*L'Empereur Alexandre*" and "*La Nation Russe*," but the added numbers did not give the fatal total. One day when he was puzzling, still without success, over his own name, changing the spelling and

[1] 20, 5,—5, 30, 60, 5, 80, 5, 110, 80,—40, 1, 60, 50, 20, 5, 50, 40.
[2] 40, 110, 1, 80, 1, 40, 100, 5,—4, 5, 110, 140.

dropping the title, it struck him that in a prophecy of this kind his nationality ought to find mention; still he only made it 671, 5 too many. This 5 represented the letter e; he dropped the e in the article and brought out *L'Russe Bésuhof*,[1] the figures amounting to 666.

How and why should he be so directly connected with the great event foretold in the Revelation? Though he could not comprehend it, he never for a moment doubted the fact. His love for Natacha, the appearance of Antichrist, the advent of the comet, the invasion of Russia, the discovery of the sum 666 in Napoleon's name and in his own—all this concurrence of singular facts gave rise to a painful ferment in his soul, which, when it reached its height, could not fail to snatch him forcibly from the futile life which weighed upon him, and lead him to accomplish some heroic action and attain some great happiness!

He had promised to carry the manifesto to the Rostows, so on that Sunday morning he went to call on Count Rostopchine to ask him for a copy; there he met a courier who had that instant come from headquarters; he was an old acquaintance, and one of the most indefatigable dancers at the Moscow balls.

"Do me a service," said his friend. "Help me to deliver some of these letters."

Peter was willing; among them was one from Nicholas Rostow to his parents. Count Rostopchine gave him a copy of the emperor's proclamation, and of the order of the day as forwarded from the army, with the last "bill of the play"[2] he himself had issued. As he glanced through the orders of the day, and the lists of those killed, wounded, or promoted, Peter observed the name of "Nicholas Rostow decorated with the order of St. George of the 4th class for his conduct at the affair of Ostrovna," and, a few lines lower down, Bolkonsky's appointment as colonel of the regiment of light horse. Anxious to let his friends have the good news of their son's splendid achievement as soon as possible, he at once sent off the letter and the order of the day, although Prince Andrew's name figured on the same page; he would take the proclamations himself later.

His conversation with Rostopchine, whose look of absorbed

[1] The letter of the Russian alphabet commonly written kh or ch—in Bésoukhof, for instance—is more often pronounced like the German, ch, a very sharp h.

[2] *Affiche* (placard), the name by which Count Rostopchine's proclamations were popularly known.

concentration betrayed deep anxiety—his friend the courier's thoughtless report of bad news from the army; a rumour that spies had been discovered in Moscow itself; an anonymous broadsheet that was passing from hand to hand, announcing that Napoleon intended to occupy both capitals before the autumn; and the expectation of the czar, who was to arrive on the morrow, all contributed to keep Peter's excitement at fever-heat; and it had been steadily increasing ever since the night of the comet, when war had been proclaimed. Had he not been a member of a society which preached perpetual peace, he would have taken active service without hesitation; even the sight of those Muscovites who had set the example, and who were *chauvins* to the last degree, though they made him feel half ashamed, would not have kept him from following their example. At the same time, his passivity arose, in the first place, from a conviction that *L'Russe Bésuhof*, whose number was the same as that of the Beast, and who had been predestined from all eternity to the grand task of destruction, ought to be content to wait and watch for this coming.

CHAPTER LXXIX

THE Rostows were accustomed to gather a few friends together to dine with them on Sunday, so Peter went somewhat early to be sure of finding them alone.

He had grown immensely stout during the last few months, and if he had not had a Herculean frame, and consequently carried the weight of his bulky person with some ease, he would have looked positively monstrous. Puffing and murmuring something to himself, he mounted the stairs without being asked by his coachman whether he should wait, for the latter knew that his master never left the Rostows before midnight. The servants hastened to help him to lay aside his cloak, hat and stick, which, by a habit he had acquired at the club, he always left in the ante-room.

The first person he saw was Natacha; or rather he heard her before he saw her, for she was practising solfeggio in the big drawing-room. Knowing that she had not been singing since her illness, he was both surprised and glad. He opened the door softly, and found her walking up and down the room as she sang; she still wore the lilac silk dress she had put on to go to mass in; when she got to the end of the room she turned, and finding herself suddenly face to face with Peter's broad countenance, she blushed and came to meet him.

"I am trying to sing, you see. It is something to do," she hastened to add, as if to excuse herself.

"And you are quite right to take it up again," replied Peter.

"I am so glad to see you; I am so happy to-day," she went on as eagerly as before. "Nicholas has had the cross of St. George given him, and I am so proud of him."

"I know it. It was I who sent you the order of the day. But I am interrupting you; I will leave you and go to the sitting-room."

"Count," said Natacha, detaining him, "am I wrong to sing?" And she coloured deeply as she looked in his face.

"No. Why should it be wrong? On the contrary. . . . But why should you ask me of all people?"

"I don't know," said Natacha, speaking quickly. "But it would grieve me deeply to do anything you should not approve. I have absolute confidence in you. You cannot imagine how highly I value your opinion, or how much you have been to me! I have seen," she went on, not noticing that Peter was much embarrassed and reddening in his turn, "I saw *his* name in the order of the day: Bolkonsky"—but she spoke the name in a low voice as if she feared to lack strength for her whole confession—"Bolkonsky is in Russia again—on active service. . . . Do you think he will ever forgive me? Do you think he will always, always think hardly of me? Tell me—do you think so?"

"I," said Peter, "I think he has nothing to forgive. If I were in his place . . ."

The same words of love and compassion that he had before spoken were rising to his tongue, but Natacha did not allow him to finish his sentence.

"You," she cried. "Oh, that is different! I do not know a better or a more generous man than you—such a man does not exist! If you had not helped and comforted me then, and now, still—I do not know what would have become of me!" Her eyes filled with tears, which she hid behind her music, and turning away abruptly she began her scales and her walk once more.

At this moment Pétia came running in; he was now a pretty lad of fifteen, rosy-cheeked, with rather thick, ruddy lips; he was like Natacha. He was being prepared to enter the university; but lately, and in secret, he had made up his mind with his comrade Obolensky to be a hussar. He put his arm through that of his namesake to get him to discuss this great scheme, and begged him to tell him whether it were in any way possible. But the bigger Peter listened so little that the boy was obliged to pull him by the sleeve to attract his attention.

"I say, Peter Kirilovitch, how is my business getting on?"

"Ah! to be sure, you want to go into the hussars? Yes, I will mention it this very day."

"How d'you do, my dear fellow?" piped the count. "Have you brought us the manifesto? My little countess heard a new prayer this morning, at mass at the Rasoumovskys', and says it is very fine."

"Here is the manifesto; and the latest news is that the czar will be here to-morrow. A meeting extraordinary of the nobility has been convened, and they talk of fresh levies of ten in every thousand. And now, allow me to congratulate you."

"Yes, indeed! God be thanked! And what news from headquarters?"

"The army is still retiring, they have reached Smolensk already," replied Peter.

"Dear me, dear me! And the manifesto?"

"I forgot. . . ." And Peter felt in all his pockets, but in vain, while he kissed the countess's hand as she came in, and still kept his eye on the door, hoping to see Natacha reappear. "I really do not know where I have hidden it; I must have left it at home. I will run and see."

"But you will be late for dinner!"

"So I shall; all the more because my carriage has gone home."

Natacha now came in; her face wore a pathetic and softened look, and Peter, still hunting for the manifesto, brightened at the sight of her; Sonia meanwhile had carried her search into the ante-room, and returned in triumph with the papers, which she had at last found carefully tucked into the lining of Bésou-khow's hat.

"We will read all that after dinner," said the count, who looked forward to it as a great treat.

They had some champagne to drink the health of the new Knight of St. George, and Schinchine brought all the gossip of the town; the old Princess of Georgia was ill, Métivier had made himself scarce, a hapless German had been mistaken by the populace for a French spy and seized, but Count Rostopchine had released him.

"Yes, yes, they are all being taken up," said the count. "I have been advising the countess not to talk French. This is not the time for it."

"And do you know," said Schinchine, "that Prince Galitzin has engaged a Russian in order to learn the language? It seems to be quite dangerous, by his account, to be heard speaking French in the streets."

"What about the militia, Count Peter Kirilovitch; of course you will have to mount a horse?" said the count to Peter, who was silent and thoughtful, and did not immediately understand what he was talking about.

"Ah! The war. To be sure. But I am no soldier you see. . . . And the whole business is so strange—so extraordinary, that I am quite at sea. My tastes indeed are anything rather than military; however, under the circumstances, there is no knowing!"

When dinner was over and the count settled comfortably in his arm-chair, he gravely requested Sonia, who was supposed to read aloud remarkably well, to read out the manifesto:

"To our chief capital, Moscow:

"The enemy has crossed the frontiers of Russia with an innumerable host, and is about to devastate our beloved country —etc. . . ."

Sonia read on in her clear treble, and the old count listened with his eyes shut, groaning at certain passages. Natacha glanced inquiringly at her father and Peter by turns; Peter, feeling her eyes on him, avoided looking her way; the countess jerked her head to express disapprobation at the more solemn passages in the proclamation, for to her they meant only one thing: that her son would be in danger, and that the danger would not be over for a long time to come. Schinchine, listening with a covert smile, was evidently preparing some epigram by the time Sonia should have done reading, on the old count's reflections, or on the manifesto itself, if nothing more obvious should come within range of his satire.

After reading the phrases relating to the danger that threatened Russia, to the hopes that the czar founded on Moscow, and especially on its chivalrous nobility, Sonia, whose voice trembled a little from the consciousness of having an audience, came to the concluding sentence:

"We shall hasten to place our person in the midst of our people at Moscow our capital, or wherever else in our empire it may seem necessary to lead the deliberations and place ourself

276

at the head of our forces—both of those which are now checking the advance of the enemy and of those which are about to be formed to strike at him wherever he shall intrude. May the woes with which he hopes to crush us be visited on him alone, and may Europe, freed from the yoke, glorify Russia!"

"Well said! That is well said! Speak the word, sire, and we will sacrifice all without a regret!" exclaimed the count, opening his eyes which twinkled through tears; and he sniffed, as if he were smelling at a bottle of salts.

Natacha sprang up and threw her arms round her father's neck with such a flash of spirit that Schinchine dared not laugh at this patriotic outburst.

"Papa, you are splendid!" she exclaimed as she kissed him; and she glanced at Peter with involuntary self-consciousness.

"Bravo! That is what I call a female patriot!" said Schinchine.

"Not at all," retorted Natacha, indignant and offended. "You must always laugh at everybody and everything; but this is too serious to be made game of."

"Made game of!" cried the count. "He has only to speak the word, one single word, and we shall rise in a mass. We are not Germans!"

"Did you observe," said Peter, "that he says, 'to lead the deliberations . . .'?"

Pétia, of whom no one was thinking, went up to his father.

"Now is the time," he began bashfully, and speaking in a voice that varied between roughness and shrillness, "to tell you, papa and mamma—it is as you choose, of course, but . . . you really and positively must let me be a soldier, because I cannot . . . I cannot . . . and there's an end of it!"

The countess raised her eyes to heaven and clasped her hands; then turning to her husband with an ill-used air, she said: "Well, he has made a clean breast of it."

The count's excitement had suddenly calmed down.

"What next?" he said. "What nonsense! a pretty soldier on my word! . . . And first and foremost you must learn your lessons."

"It is not nonsense," persisted Pétia. "Fédia Obolensky is younger than I am and he is to be a soldier; and as to learning lessons, I could never do it now, when . . ." he hesitated and blushed up to the roots of his hair: "when the country is in danger."

"Come, come. Enough of this folly!"

"But, papa, you yourself said you were ready to make any sacrifice!"

"Pétia, be silent!" cried the count, glancing uneasily at his wife, who sat pale and trembling, and looking at her youngest born.

"But, papa, I assure you—and Peter Kirilovitch can tell you . . ."

"And I tell you it is folly! Why, your nurse's milk is not dry on your lips, and you want to be a soldier!—Folly, nonsense, I tell you. . . ." And the count rose to go to his own room, taking the manifesto with him so as to get it well into his head before taking his afternoon nap. "Peter Kirilovitch," he added, "come, and we will smoke."

Peter, embarrassed and vacillating, was under the spell of Natacha's eyes, in which he had never seen so bright a light as at this moment.

"Thank you very much—but I think I must go home."

"What! Home? Why, did you not mean to spend the evening with us? We so seldom see you now!—And that child"—added the count with perfect simplicity, "she never is so bright as when you are here."

"Yes—but the fact is, I forgot . . . I have something that must be attended to, at home . . ." Peter murmured.

"If that is the case, *au revoir*," said the count, and he left the room.

"Why are you leaving? What is troubling you?" asked Natacha, looking Peter straight in the face.

"Because I love you!" was what he could have said; but he stood in awkward silence, staring at the floor. "Because it would be better if I did not come here so often . . . Because . . . No, simply because I have something to attend to. . . ."

"Why?—tell me, I entreat you!" said Natacha, resolutely—but she broke off suddenly, for their eyes had met with startled and conscious meaning.

Peter vainly tried to smile: it was a painful and tremulous attempt; he kissed her hand and went away without speaking another word: he had made up his mind that he would never set foot in the house again.

THE INVASION

CHAPTER LXXX

PÉTIA, after this repulse, shut himself into his room and shed many burning tears; however, none of the party noticed his red eyes when he reappeared at tea-time.

The czar arrived next day. Some of the servants asked leave to go and see his progress through the city. Pétia took a long time dressing that morning, doing all he could to settle his collar and brush his hair like a grown-up man. Standing in front of his glass, he wriggled and grimaced, squaring his shoulders and knitting his brows; at length, satisfied with his own appearance, he slipped out of the house by the back-stairs, without breathing a word of his plans to anyone.

He had quite made up his mind: he would somehow, and at any cost, get at the czar. He would apply to one of the gentlemen-in-waiting—he supposed the emperor to be always surrounded by dozens—would explain that he was Count Peter Rostow; that, young as he was, he was fired with a desire to serve his country, and fifty other fine things which, in his opinion, ought to produce an irresistible effect on the gentleman in question. Although he relied to some extent for success on his baby face and the surprise it would certainly excite, he tried, nevertheless, by the arrangement of his collar and his hair, to give himself the importance of a grown man.

As he went through the streets, however, he got more and more interested in the sight of the crowd that was gathered round the walls of the Kremlin, and thoughtless of keeping up appearances as a man of mature age. He was obliged, too, to keep his elbows at work to save himself from being too much hustled. When he at last reached the Trinity gate the crowd, not aware of his patriotic intention, drove him so effectually against the wall that he was forced to stand there, while the carriages, one after another, rolled through the vaulted archway. Close to Pétia, and, like him, penned fast by the crowd, were a fat woman of the lower class, a footman, and an old soldier. He was beginning to be impatient, and made up his mind to struggle forward, without waiting for the end of the line of vehicles, so he tried to release himself by giving his stout neighbour a vigorous elbow-thrust.

"Now there, young gentleman!" exclaimed the woman, furiously. "Can't you see that no one is stirring? Where on earth do you want to poke your nose in?"

"Oh! if it comes to fighting for room, I'm your man!" added the footman, pushing Pétia into a corner, where the smells were then doubtful. The unlucky boy wiped his face, which was streaming with perspiration, and tried to set up his collar, but the heat had taken out all its stiffness, and he wondered, with dismay in his heart, whether any chamberlain, seeing him in such a plight, would allow him to come within speech of the emperor. He could not get out of that cursed alley and put himself to rights a little. He could, no doubt, have appealed for rescue to a general who was a friend of his parents, and who had just passed him in his carriage; but that, he thought, would have been undignified in a man.

At last the crowd surged forward, carrying Pétia with it as far as the great square, which was also full of starers. They thronged every spot, even the roofs of the houses. Having got there he could hear the frenzied pealing of bells, and the confused roar of the human tide that flooded every nook and corner of the vast space.

Suddenly every hat was in the air and the mass of people swayed forward. Pétia, squeezed almost flat, and deafened by the thunder of cheers, vainly tried, by standing on tiptoe, to see the cause of the excitement.

He saw all round him beaming or agitated faces; close to him stood a market-woman, her cheeks bathed in tears; "My little father! My angel!" she cried, wiping her eyes with her hand.

The crowd, checked for an instant, now moved on again. Pétia caught the infection and entirely lost his head. Pushing and fighting right and left, he shouted hurrah! with the rest, and was ready to be the death of his neighbours, who on their part returned his blows with interest, cheering and yelling at the top of their voices.

"This is the czar then," thought he. "How could I ever have dreamed of speaking to him myself!—It would be too audacious!" Nevertheless he went on fighting his way, and at last he could see, just ahead, an open space spread with red cloth. The mob, checked in front by the police, at this point ebbed again. The czar was coming out of the palace to go to the church of the Assumption. At this instant someone dealt Pétia such a blow in the ribs that he fell back fainting. When he came to his senses, he found himself supported by a priest, apparently a sacristan, whose head was bald all but a lock of grey hair that hung down the back of his neck; this unknown friend held him up on one arm, and with the other was trying to protect him against the pushing of the throng.

"Here! a young gentleman has been crushed," he kept saying. "Take care—look out—he is crushed to death, I believe!"

When the emperor was lost to view within the church porch, the crowd loosened, and the sacristan managed to get Pétia as far as the Czar cannon (one of the sights of Moscow). There he was again almost stifled by the dense press of people who took pity on him, some unbuttoning his coat, while some hoisted him up to the block of stone on which the gun stood, and showered abuse on those who had handled him so roughly. Pétia soon recovered; his colour came back, and the brief discomfort had procured him a post of vantage on the plinth of the cannon. From here he hoped that he might see the czar; but he had forgotten his petition; he had but one wish: to see *him*.—Then, and not until then, could he be happy.

During high mass, with a *Te Deum* in honour of his majesty's return and. the peace with Turkey, the crowd perceptibly thinned; the sellers of *kvass*, gingerbread, and poppy-seed—which Pétia liked best of all—began to wander about, and groups collected here and there in the open square. A woman stood lamenting a rent in her shawl and expatiating on its cost, while another was declaring that silks ere long would be at ruinous prices. Pétia's deliverer, the sacristan, was disputing with a civil functionary as to who was assisting his eminence in performing the services. Two young fellows, munching filberts, were laughing with a couple of girls. But to all these various conversations, which at any other time would have been extremely interesting to Pétia—especially that of the four young people—he now turned a deaf ear. Perched on the stone block, all his thoughts were merged in devotion to his sovereign; the impulse of passionate loyalty which had supervened on the panic and physical pain he had gone through, lent solemn emotion to this hour of his life.

Suddenly the roar of cannon was heard from the quay. The crowd rushed off to see where and how they were being fired, and Pétia would have followed, but the sacristan who had taken him in hand would not allow it. The cannon were still thundering when a party of officers, generals, and gentlemen-in-waiting, hurried out of the church: all took off their hats, and the gapers who had been running to the quay, ran back again. Then four officers in splendid uniforms, blazing with stars, made their appearance.

"Hurrah! Hurrah!" the crowd yelled and bellowed.

"Where is he? Which is he?" asked Pétia breathlessly, but he got no answer. No one could attend. So he fixed his eyes—so full of tears that he could scarcely see—on one of the magnificent four, although it was not the emperor, and with all the vehemence of his young enthusiasm shouted a tremendous hurrah, vowing to himself that in spite of every obstacle he would be a soldier.

The crowd closed up behind the emperor, and when he disappeared into the palace, slowly broke up. By this time it was late. Though Pétia had had no food, and the perspiration streamed down his face, he never thought of going home; he took up a position among a small group of idlers in front of the palace; he would wait for what might happen, and he gazed with envy not only at the dignitaries who arrived in carriages to take their place at the imperial table, but even at the men in uniform whom he could see passing to and fro behind the windows, to wait upon them.

During the banquet Valouïew, looking out on the square, observed to his majesty that the people of the city were waiting outside, and seemed to be anxious that he should show himself once more. When dinner was over the czar, who was still eating a biscuit, came out on the balcony. Some of the crowd calling him "father," others "our angel. Hurrah!" And the women, and even the men, and Pétia too, shed tears of devotion. A piece of the biscuit the czar held in his hand broke off and fell between the ironwork of the balcony on to the ground at a coachman's feet; the man picked it up, and those standing near him fell upon the happy possessor to snatch a share. The emperor, seeing this, had a large dish of biscuits brought out and threw them down one by one. Pétia's eyes were almost starting out of his head, and in spite of his fear of again being crushed he, too, rushed forward to catch one of the cakes that the czar's fingers had touched. Why?—He did not know, but he felt that he must. He ran, upsetting an old woman who was on the point of seizing one, and though she screamed desperately, got it before her; then he set up a wild hurrah, but alas! in a very hoarse voice.

The czar withdrew and the people dispersed.

"You see it was worth waiting for," said one and another, fully content, as they went away.

Happy as he was, Pétia did not like to go home and feel that the day's enjoyment was over. So he went off to his friend Obolensky, who was of his own age, and about to join the army. Finally, however, he was obliged to go home, and he no sooner got in than he solemnly told his parents that if they did not consent to his wishes he should run away. The old count had to give way; but before giving his formal sanction he went next day to inquire from competent authorities how and where he could send him on service without exposing him to unnecessary danger.

CHAPTER LXXXI

On the morning of the 15th of July, three days after the emperor's arrival, a crowd of carriages were drawn up in front of the Hotel Slobodski. The reception-rooms within were thronged: in one the nobility were assembled; in another the merchants who had been decorated with orders. The former was full of excitement: the most notable of the Moscow aristocracy were seated on high-backed chairs, round a table, over which hung a full-length portrait of the Czar Alexander; others were walking up and down the room in eager conversation. Though their uniforms resembled each other in type, many of them dated from the reign of Peter the Great, others from those of Catherine and Paul, while others were of recent make; and this gave a motley appearance to the party, most of whom Peter knew more or less well, having met them at the club or at their own houses. The elders especially were strange to look upon: toothless, or blind, and bald, clumsily fat, or as lean and parched as mummies, they sat silent and motionless, or if they rose to move, always ran up against someone. Their faces wore the most various expressions; some looked anxiously expectant of some great and solemn event; some beatifically smiling at the remembrance of the last game they won at boston, or of the good dinner Pétroucha the cook had sent up, or of some other no less important detail of daily life.

Peter, who had got into his court uniform with no small difficulty, as it was too tight for him, was pacing the room in the greatest agitation. The convocation simultaneously of the nobles and the merchant class—real states-general—had revived in his mind his old opinions as to the *contrat social* and the French Revolution; for, though he had for a long time ceased to think of them, they were not the less deeply

283

implanted in his soul. The words of the manifesto, in which the czar had said that he was coming to deliberate with his people, confirmed him in his views, and it was with a firm conviction that the reform he had so long hoped for was about to come to pass, that he listened to what was being said by others; though he could trace no echo there of his own ideas.

The manifesto had been read and hailed with enthusiasm, and the meeting separated to talk matters over. Besides the usual subjects of conversation Peter heard a discussion as to the places reserved for the marshals of the nobility on the occasion of his majesty's arrival, a ball to be given in his honour, the advantages of division into governments or into districts, and so forth; but as soon as the war was mentioned—the real object of the meeting—everyone seemed vague or bewildered, or for the most part lapsed into prudent silence.

A middle-aged man in the uniform of a retired navy captain was talking in a loud voice to a group, including Peter, that had gathered round him to hear what he had to say. Count Ilia Andréiévitch, in his caftan of the time of the Empress Catherine, moved about smiling and recognising many of his friends. He, too, paused to listen to the orator with much satisfaction, signifying his approval by nodding his head. It was easy to see from the faces of his audience that the speaker was bold in his utterances; the more peaceful or timid presently dropped away, slightly shrugging their shoulders. Peter, on the contrary, found a flavour of liberalism in his speech, differing no doubt from that which he himself professed, but which nevertheless pleased his ear. The navy man spoke with a burr, and the ring of his voice, though it was rich and melodious, betrayed a rakishness as well as a habit of command.

"What can it matter to us," he said, "that the inhabitants of Smolensk have offered to levy a force of militia for the czar? Does their vote make a law for us? If the nobility of Moscow thinks it necessary, it has other means of displaying its devotion. We have not yet forgotten the calling out of the militia in 1807. —Thieves and swindlers were the only persons who benefited by it." Count Rostow stood smiling bland assent.

"Have the militia ever done the country any service, I ask you? None.—They destroy our fields and that is all they do. Recruiting is far preferable; in any other way what you get is neither a peasant nor a soldier, it is unmitigatedly corrupt! . . . The nobility does not bargain over life; we will all go out if we are required and take recruits with us, the czar has

only to speak the word and we will all die for him!" the speaker
ended with an energetic flourish.

Count Rostow, highly excited, nudged Peter with his elbow,
and Peter, burning to speak, stepped forward, though not
knowing precisely what he had to say. He had not time to
begin before an old senator, with a look of keen intelligence,
took up the parable with the determination of a man inured
to debate and to presiding over discussions: he spoke quietly
but very distinctly.

"I believe, sir," he began, "that we have met not to decide
whether it will be most in the interest of the empire to levy
recruits or to add to the militia. . . . What we have to do is
to respond to the proclamation our sovereign has done us
the honour of addressing to us, and to leave it to his supreme
authority to decide between recruiting and . . ."

But Peter interrupted him. He found an outlet for his excitement in the indignation he felt at the speaker's narrow and too
legal views of the functions of the nobility; without stopping to
consider the full import of his own words, he began talking with
feverish vehemence, larding his discourse with French phrases
and literary language.

"Pray excuse me, excellency," he said, addressing the senator—
he knew him intimately, but thought it proper to assume an
official tone—"though I cannot share the views of the gentleman"—he hesitated: he was longing to call him "the honourable
gentleman opposite," but he went on—"whom I have not the
advantage of knowing, I imagine that the nobility are invited
not merely to express their sympathy and patriotism, but also
to deliberate on such measures as may prove beneficial to the
country. I believe, too, that the czar himself would be ill-
pleased to find that we regarded ourselves merely as owners
of peasants whom we could bring in our train as '*chair à canon*'[1]
when he has appealed to us for support and advice."

Several of the bystanders, startled at such daring, and frightened by the senator's contemptuous smile, dropped out of the
circle, and Rostow alone approved of Peter's speech, it being
his way to be always ready to agree with the last speaker.

"Before discussing such questions," Peter went on, "we
should do well to ask the czar, with all respect, to inform us of
the exact number of our troops and the state of our armies;
then . . ."

But he got no farther. He was loudly interrupted on three

[1] Cannon fodder. A famous saying of Napoleon's.

sides at once, and had to break off at this point. The most determined of his opponents was a certain Stephen Stépanovitch Adrakcine, often his partner at boston, and very much his friend when a game of cards was at hand; but not like himself at all to-day, whether by reason of his uniform, or perhaps because he seemed furiously angry.

"Allow me to point out to you," he began with some violence, "that we have no right to make any such request. And even if the Russian nobility had the right, the czar could not answer the question, since the movements of our army must depend on those of the enemy, and the number of our soldiers on the exigencies of tactics. . . ."

"It is not a time for discussion, we must act," another man threw in—a man known to Peter as having met him among the gipsies; this gentleman's reputation, indeed, was anything rather than fair, but he, too, was completely metamorphosed by his uniform. "The war is actually in Russia; the foe is marching down to devastate our country, to desecrate the tombs of our fathers, to carry away our women and children" —here the orator struck his breast.—"We will rise as one man to defend the czar our father. We Russians are not the men to grudge our blood in the defence of our faith, of the throne, and of the country! If we are the true children of our beloved native land, let us have no more of dreaming. We will show Europe how Russia can rise and fight as one man!"

This orator was warmly applauded, and Count Ilia Andréïévitch was again one of those to demonstrate his approval.

Peter was anxious to be allowed to say that he, too, was prepared to make any sacrifice, but that above all it was most important to know how things really stood before the remedy could be applied. But they would not give him a hearing; they shouted and interrupted him again and again; some even turned their backs as if he were the common foe; they formed into knots that broke up and re-formed, all talking at once; the excitement was indescribable. It did not arise, as might have been supposed, from the irritation produced by Peter's words, which were by this time forgotten, but from that instinctive craving which incites a crowd to find a visible and tangible object on which to vent its hatred or admiration. Consequently, the hapless Peter now became the object of general aversion. Several speeches, some full of point and very well expressed, were made after that of the retired seaman, and were heartily applauded.

Glinka, the editor of a newspaper—*Le Messager Russe*—declared that "hell alone could fight against hell.—We must not be content," said he, "to stand like children, smiling at the lightning and the pealing of the thunder."

"Hear, hear! That is the way to put it. We must not sit smiling at the thunder and lightning!" was echoed through the whole audience to the remotest corner, with noisy acclamation; while the old nobles seated round the table looked at each other and at their neighbours, their vacant faces betraying nothing but that they found the room dreadfully hot. Peter, painfully agitated, felt that he had gone on the wrong tack, but he did not therefore give up his convictions. His anxiety to set himself right, and still more to show that at this tremendous juncture he, too, was prepared to do all that was required of him, prompted him to make a last effort to be heard: "I said," he began again as loud as he could, "that it would be easier to make sacrifices when we knew what was needed. . . ." But no one would listen, and his voice was drowned in the general tumult. One little old man only leaned forward to attend to what he was saying, but he turned away again, attracted at what was being said on the opposite side.

"Yes, Moscow must be surrendered! Moscow must be our sacrifice! . . ."

"He is the foe of the human race. . . ."

"I insist on being heard. . . ."

"Pray take care, gentlemen, you are crushing me completely . . ." was to be heard on all sides.

CHAPTER LXXXII

AT this moment Count Rostopchine came into the room, in his general's uniform, with a ribbon across his shoulder, and the crowd at once made way. Keen eyes and a strongly-moulded chin were the characteristic features of his face.

"His majesty is now coming," he said. "I think that under the circumstances there is no time to waste in debating; the emperor has condescended to invite us to meet him—us and the great merchants of the city. Millions of roubles are waiting for him there . . ." and he nodded in the direction of the room where the merchants were sitting. "And on our part we ought to propose to call out the militia and not spare ourselves. It is the least we can do."

The old lords, sitting round their table, held consultation in an undertone; groups again formed and discussed it, and then each gave his vote.

"I agree," said one.

"I am of the same opinion," said another, not to repeat his neighbour's words; and the thin voices of the old men, distinctly audible one by one in the silence that had succeeded the tumult, had a strange, almost a melancholy effect. Then the secretary was desired to write out the following resolution: "The nobility of Moscow, following the example of those of Smolensk, offer a contingent of ten men in every thousand, fully equipped."

The elders rose as if they were thankful to have got rid of a heavy anxiety, pushing back their chairs with a good deal of noise and stretching their stiff old legs; each seized on the acquaintance he happened to meet, and taking his arm, proceeded to walk about the room, talking.

"The Czar! The Czar!" was presently the cry, and they rushed to the entrance. His majesty walked down the large room between two closely-packed rows of men, all bowing low with a mixed expression of veneration, curiosity, and anxiety. Peter heard the emperor's description of the danger that threatened the state, and his expressions of confidence in his faithful nobles. Then the resolution just passed by the nobles was communicated to his majesty.

"Gentlemen," said Alexander, in a broken voice, "I never doubted the devotion of the Russian nobility, but this day it has surpassed my expectations. I thank you in the name of our beloved country. Gentlemen, let us act in concert—time is precious!" He broke off, and the assembly gathered round him with enthusiastic cheers.

"Yes, yes. That is the point.—There is nothing so precious as the word of the sovereign!" repeated old Count Rostow through his tears; but he had hardly heard and put his own interpretation on everything.

The czar then proceeded to the next room, where the merchants were expecting him; he stayed there about ten minutes. Peter saw him come out with tears of emotion in his eyes; he heard afterwards that he had actually wept and ended his address in a choked voice. Two of the merchants came in with him; one of them Peter knew; he was a great contractor; the

288

other was the mayor, a lean, yellow-faced man with a peaked beard. Both were in tears; the burly contractor, especially, fairly sobbed as he said: "Our lives, our fortunes,—command them all, sire!"

Peter himself was possessed by one idea: his wish to prove that he was ready and glad to make any sacrifice; he reproached himself bitterly for his constitutional speech, and was only anxious to efface the impression it had left. Hearing that Count Mamonow was prepared to levy a regiment, he then and there announced to Count Rostopchine that he would furnish a thousand men and provide for their maintenance.

Count Rostow went home and wept as he told the countess all that had passed; then, finally giving his consent to Pétia's desire, he went to put his name down on the list of the hussar regiment.

The czar left Moscow the next day. The Moscow nobles packed away their court uniforms, and settled back into their ordinary habits and places at home or at the club, giving orders to their various stewards to take the necessary measures for supplying men to the militia, and themselves wondering at the liberality of their promises.

BOOK TEN

CHAPTER LXXXIII

WHY did Napoleon make war on Russia? Because the fates had decreed that he should go to Dresden; that he should have his head turned by flattery; that he should put on a Polish uniform; that he should feel the subtle intoxication of a fine June morning; and finally, that he should allow himself to fly into a passion, first before Kourakine, and next before Balachow.

Alexander, feeling that he had been personally insulted, refused to negotiate; Barclay de Tolly devoted all his care to the conduct of the army, intending to do his duty and to win a reputation as a great commander; Rostow, as we know, had rushed down upon the French because he had found the temptation to a mad canter across an open plain irresistible—and thus it was that each in his degree, and in accordance with his natural disposition, habits, and ambitions, played his part in this memorable war. Their alarms, their vanities, their joys, their criticisms—all the impulses that arose from what they believed to be their free will, were the unconscious instruments of history, and contributed, though they knew it not, to a result of which the magnitude is only now appreciable. And this is always the lot of the active agents of history, who are less free, in fact, in proportion as their social rank is higher.

The men of 1812 have vanished from the scene; their personal interests have left no mark; only the historical effects of that time are now visible, and we can see how Providence led each individual, acting from his own point of view, to co-operate to a colossal end, of which certainly neither Alexander nor Napoleon had the faintest preconception.

It would be idle at this day to speculate on the immediate causes of the disasters of the French: on one hand there were, obviously, their invasion of Russia too late in the year and the total lack of any preparation for a winter campaign; on the other, the aspect given to the war by the virulent hatred of the foe to which the Russians were worked up, and the destruction by fire of their own towns. An army of 800,000 men, one of the finest the world has ever seen, commanded by the most brilliant leader, and led against an army of not half the strength under inexperienced generals, evidently could not have succumbed to any but these two causes. But what we now see so clearly was not understood by contemporaries, and the struggles of the Russians and of the French themselves all tended to nullify their chances of escape.

The writers of certain French histories of the year 1812 have taken elaborate pains to prove that Napoleon was fully aware of the risk he was running in undertaking this expedition, and in dispersing his troops over the plains of Russia; that he was anxious to fight a pitched battle; that his marshals besought him not to go beyond Smolensk, etc. Russian authors, on the other hand, dwell with no less emphasis on the scheme which, as they say, was laid down from the first for decoying Napoleon—after the manner of the Scythians—into the very heart of the empire, crediting the plan, some to Pfuhl, some to some unknown Frenchman, some to Toll, some to Alexander himself; and to support the statement they bring forward a goodly array of hypotheses and inferences from the facts and events themselves. But these theories obviously belong to the category of untrustworthy hearsay, which the historian cannot rely upon without neglecting the truth; and indeed the facts, as they stand, contradict them. Not only during the whole course of the war was there no desire of the Russians to entice the French into the interior of their country, but everything was done to stop them from the time they first crossed the frontier; and as for Napoleon, not only did he not fear the dispersal of his troops over the enemy's country, but was pleased with every step taken in advance, as if it were a triumph; and very lazily, not as in former campaigns, sought to give battle.

For what is the first state of things as we see them? The Russian armies cannot communicate; they are striving to combine, though that combination can secure them no benefit —especially if the object is to tempt the foe into the interior; the camp on the Drissa is fortified in obedience to Pfuhl's views, with the evident intention of holding it; the czar is with the army, certainly not to lead a retreat, but to encourage the soldiers by his presence, and to defend every inch of ground against foreign encroachment—nay, he vehemently reproaches the general, who steadily continues to retire. How then is it to be supposed that he ever for a moment imagined that Moscow would be set on fire, or that the enemy had already entered Smolensk?—Then his indignation breaks out when he learns that no pitched battle has been fought, though the armies have succeeded in effecting a junction, and that Smolensk has been taken and burnt. The troops and the people are no less infuriated by this continual retreat;—and all this time events take their course, not haphazard nor yet by virtue of a deep-laid plan, which no one believes in, but as the outcome of intrigues, ambitions, and efforts of the most opposite kind, in the hands of men who act only for their own ends or without any ends at all.—What, in fact, is actually being done? In the hope of uniting the armies before being forced to fight, the Russians try to concentrate on Smolensk, closely followed by the French. The manœuvre fails, because Barclay is a German and unpopular, because Bagration, who commands the second division, hates him and refuses to put himself under the command of a man who is his junior in the service, and so delays the junction of the forces as long as possible. Then the czar's presence, instead of rousing enthusiasm foments discord, and nullifies all unity of action; Paolucci, whose ambition is to be made commander-in-chief, gains influence over him; Pfuhl's scheme is abandoned and the chief command is given to Barclay de Tolly, though, at the same time, his authority is limited, as he does not inspire implicit confidence. As a result of these squabbles at headquarters and of the commander-in-chief's unpopularity, it is impossible to fight a decisive engagement, and while this gives rise to much general annoyance, with a hatred of all Germans, it rouses patriotism to frenzy.

Matters were in this state when the czar withdrew from the army on the pretext—the best that could be put forward—of fanning the enthusiasm of the two great capitals to a white heat, and his visit to Moscow trebled the organisation of national resistance. Although the czar was gone, the commander-in-chief's position became daily more critical; Bennigsen, the grand duke, and a whole swarm of generals hung on his heels to watch his proceedings, and, at need, to keep him up to the mark; but Barclay de Tolly, feeling himself more and more under the constant surveillance of "the czar's eyes," waxed all the more cautious and avoided giving battle. This prudence was severely blamed by the czarevitch, who even went so far as to hint at treason, and presently insisted on a pitched battle. Lubomirsky, Bronnitzky, Vlotzky, and others made so much noise about the matter that Barclay, under the pretence of important despatches to be delivered to the czar, sent away the Polish generals one by one and then boldly defied the grand duke and Bennigsen.

Finally, in spite of Bagration's opposition, the armies combined at Smolensk. Bagration arrived in his carriage at the house occupied by Barclay de Tolly, who put on his scarf to receive him and to report progress to his senior officer. Bagration, in a fit of patriotic abnegation, expressed his entire submission to Barclay, which did not, however, prevent him entertaining opinions diametrically opposed to those of the commander-in-chief. He put himself into direct correspondence with the czar, by his majesty's desire, and wrote as follows to Araktchéïew:

"In spite of my sovereign's command I cannot remain any longer with the minister"—as he chose to designate Barclay: "for God's sake, send me away, no matter where; give me only a regiment to command, but get me out of this; headquarters swarm with Germans who make life unendurable to the Russians; the whole thing is an utter mess. I fancied I was to serve the emperor and the country, but as it is I serve no one but Barclay, and that, I frankly confess, I refuse to do." Bronnitzky, Wintzingerode, and the rest still sowed dissension between the commanders-in-chief and thus prevented all unity of action. Preparations were made, nevertheless, to attack the French before Smolensk; a general was sent to reconnoitre the position, but he, being inimical to Barclay, spent the day with a regimental colonel, and when he returned criticised the field of battle which he had not even seen.

While all this intriguing and debating was going on over the position where the battle was to be fought, and while the Russians were trying to find out where the French were, the enemy had fallen upon Névérovsky's division and fought their way to the very walls of Smolensk. This left the Russians no choice; to save their communications they had to fight, whether they liked it or not. The battle was fought; thousands were slain on both sides, and Smolensk was evacuated, in spite of the czar's commands and the will of the nation! The town was set on fire by the inhabitants, who had been cheated and deceived by the governor. Ruined and desperate, they made their way to Moscow, there to set an example to their brethren and stir up their hatred of the enemy. All this while the Russian army was retreating, and Napoleon advancing in triumph, never suspecting the danger which hung over him;—and thus, against all expectation, was his ruin brought about, and the salvation of Russia.

CHAPTER LXXXIV

THE day after Prince Andrew's departure, Prince Bolkonsky sent for his daughter.

"Now I hope you are satisfied: you have made me quarrel with Andrew, which was what you wanted. As for me, I am saddened and grieved; I am old, weak and lonely. . . . But that is what you wished. . . . Go away!"

He sent her out of his room, and it was more than a week before she saw him again, for he fell ill and did not leave his study. Princess Maria observed to her great surprise that Mademoiselle Bourrienne was no longer in and out as of old; her father would be attended by no one but old Tikhone.

At the end of a week he was convalescent, and fell into his regular routine once more, looking after his building and his gardens; but his intimacy with Mademoiselle Bourrienne had ceased entirely. Though he was, as usual, cold and distant to his daughter, he seemed to express by his conduct: "You vilified me to Andrew, you made me quarrel with him about this Frenchwoman; now you may see that I want nobody— not her any more than you."

Princess Maria spent a part of each day with her little nephew, listening to his lessons, giving him some herself, and talking with Dessalles; the rest of her time she devoted to reading, chatting with the old nurse and with her pilgrims, who still came to see her up the back-stairs.

She thought of the war as women think of such things: that is to say, she was anxious for her brother, and deplored the cruelty of men who slaughter each other; but she attached no more importance to this war than to those that had preceded it. Dessalles, who watched its progress with keen interest, now and then expressed his views of it, and kept her up to the latest intelligence. The pilgrims, too, confided to her all their terrors, telling her their version of the myth of Napoleon's being Anti-christ; and the fair Julia, now Princess Droubetzkoï, wrote her letters full of effusive patriotism.

"I must write to you in Russian, my dear friend, for I hate

the French and their language, which I cannot even bear to hear spoken. We are now at Moscow, and everybody is in a state of indescribable enthusiasm for our beloved emperor. My poor husband has to endure hunger and privations in Jewish inns, and my letters from him add to my excitement.

"You have heard, no doubt, of Raïevsky's heroism—embracing his two sons, and saying, 'I will die with you, but we will not give way! . . .' And though the enemy was twice as strong, we did not give way! We pass our time here as best we may, and make the best of a bad business. Princesses Aline and Sophie come to see me every day, and we three poor 'grass widows' talk of edifying subjects as we ravel out lint. You, alone, my dear Maria, are wanting," and so forth.

If Princess Maria had no adequate idea of the vital importance of the events that were going forward, the fault was her father's; he never spoke of them, but affected to know nothing about them, and would laugh at Dessalles and his sensational news, when they met at dinner. His cool and indifferent tone gave his daughter blind confidence, and, without thought, she accepted everything he told her.

The old man was full of energy and activity. During the month of July, he planned a garden and laid the first stone of a new house for his numerous retainers. Still, one symptom distressed Princess Maria: he hardly slept at all, and changed his room night after night: he would have his camp-bed placed in the gallery, or even in the dining-room, or sometimes he would sleep in an arm-chair in the drawing room, lulled by the voice of Pétroucha, the young servant who now filled Mademoiselle Bourrienne's place as his reader.

On the first of August, he received a letter from Andrew, who had already written one to beg his forgiveness, asking him to forget all he had dared to say to him, and the old prince had sent him a few affectionate lines in reply. In this second letter, Prince Andrew gave him a detailed account of the occupation of Vitebsk by the French, and of the events of the campaign, of which he sketched the plan with all the issues it might ultimately entail; and he ended by urgently entreating him to retire from the scene of the impending struggle—which was getting nearer every day to Lissy-Gory—and to move at once to Moscow.

Dessalles, who had just heard that the French were at Vitebsk, announced it at dinner to the old prince, thus reminding him of his son's letter.

"I had a letter from Prince Andrew this morning," he said to his daughter. "Have you read it?"

"No, father," she said timidly. How, indeed, could she have read the letter when she did not even know of its existence?

"He writes about this war," her father went on, with the scornful smile he always put on when he alluded to the subject.

"It must be extremely interesting," said Dessalles. "The prince, of course, is fully informed. . . ."

"Of course!" cried Mademoiselle Bourrienne.

"Go and fetch it," said the prince; "it is on my little table under the paper-weight."

Mademoiselle Bourrienne rose with eager haste.

"No, no," he said, frowning. "Do you go, Michael Ivanovitch. . . ."

Michael Ivanovitch obeyed, but he had scarcely left the room when the prince got up impatiently, and, throwing his napkin on the table, muttered: "He never can find anything; he will turn all my papers topsy-turvy!" and hurried after him.

Princess Maria, Mademoiselle Bourrienne, and little Nicholas looked at each other, but said nothing, and presently the old man returned, followed by Michael Ivanovitch. He had in his hand the letter and the plans of the new building; he laid them by his plate, and finished his dinner without reading the letter.

When they had gone into the drawing-room, he gave it to his daughter, who, after reading it aloud, looked at her father; but he affected to be absorbed in his plans of the new building, and to have heard nothing.

"What do you think of it all, prince?" asked Dessalles.

"I—I?" said the prince sharply, without looking up.

"The scene of war may come quite close to us," Dessalles went on.

"Ha! ha! ha! The scene of war? I have said already, and I say it again, the scene of war is in Poland, and the enemy will never come beyond the Niemen."

Dessalles looked at him blankly; the Niemen! When the enemy had already reached the Dnieper. No one but the princess, who had forgotten her geography, could accept her father's statement.

"When the snows melt they will all be swallowed up in the Polish swamps. Bennigsen ought to have marched into Prussia long ago; matters would have turned out very differently," he went on; his mind evidently was running on the campaign of 1807.

THE INVASION

"But, sir," said Dessalles, more timidly than before, "in this letter—we hear that Vitebsk is in the hands of the French . . ."

"In the letter?—Ah! yes, to be sure . . ." and his face clouded. "To be sure, he writes . . . The French were beaten, somewhere—I forget where . . . near some river."

Dessalles looked down:

"Prince Andrew does not mention that," he said gently.

"Does not mention it?—I did not invent it, that is quite certain."

After this there was a spell of silence.

"Well, well, Michael Ivanovitch," said the old man suddenly, "explain to me how you propose to remedy this error in our plan."

Michael Ivanovitch needed no second bidding, and the prince, after listening for a few minutes, left the room with an angry glare at Dessalles and his daughter. Princess Maria caught a look of pained astonishment on the tutor's face, but she dared not ask him the cause of it, or even guess at it. The much discussed letter was left on the drawing-room table; Michael Ivanovitch came to ask for it in the course of the evening. Princess Maria gave it to him; and though the question was, she felt, an awkward one, she asked what her father was doing.

"Oh! he is very busy," replied the architect, with a polite but sardonic smile that chilled her blood. "He is very full of the house-building . . . he read a little, and now he is rummaging in his desk. . . . Very likely he is making his will." For some time past the prince had found a favourite occupation in arranging the papers which were to see light after his death.

"And he is sending Alpatitch to Smolensk, did you say?" asked she.

"Yes. Alpatitch is ready to start, and is only waiting for orders."

CHAPTER LXXXV

THE architect found his patron seated in front of his bureau in a rather theatrical attitude, with his spectacles on, and a shade over his eyes. He held in his hand a large paper book, in which he was reading over his "Notes"—as he called the document which was to be sent to the czar after his death; the remembrance of the time when he had written them had brought

297

tears into his eyes. He took his son's letter and slipped it into his pocket; then he sent for Alpatitch and gave him his instructions:

"First of all," he said, looking through the list of things that he wanted from Smolensk, "you are to buy me eight reams of letter-paper, do you hear, eight reams, gilt-edged like this pattern; some sealing-wax, and some varnish;—then give my letter to the governor in person," and while he talked he never ceased walking up and down. Then he told him not to forget the locks for the new house, to be made on a pattern of his own invention, and a large paper-case to contain his will and his "Notes." He had been talking for about two hours when he suddenly sat down, closed his eyes and fell asleep for a minute; but he was aroused by Alpatitch, who moved to leave the room. "Very well," he said. "Go now; if I want anything more I will send for you."

Then he went back to his desk, arranged his papers neatly, and sat down to write the letter to the governor. By the time he had written and sealed it, it was growing late; he was succumbing to fatigue and sleep; but he felt that he should not be able to rest, since melancholy thoughts would keep him awake as soon as he was in bed. He called Tikhone and went round the rooms with him to make up his mind where he would have his bed placed for the night. Every corner was looked at and measured, but no spot could be found to suit him; his usual place, particularly, he could not endure to think of; he seemed afraid of it; perhaps by reason of the depressing thoughts he had suffered from there. At length, after much deliberation, he decided on having it made up in the drawing-room, in a space between the wall and the piano where he had never yet slept. Tikhone was ordered to put the little camp-bed there, and did so at once with the help of one of he men-seravnts.

"Not like that—not so!" cried the old man, pulling it to him, and pushing it about.

"Well, perhaps I shall get a little rest," and he allowed his faithful attendant to undress him.

Having got out of his coat and trousers with some difficulty, he sat down on the bed and seemed lost in the contemplation of his withered, yellow shanks. He paused and hesitated before making the final effort to raise them and stretch them out. "Good God! what a weight," he muttered. "Why do you not make a quicker end of me, 'vous autres,'—of me and my miseries? Why can't you let me go? . . ." At last, with a deep sigh, he got his legs up in front of him. But he had no sooner lain down than the bed began to shake and rock under him; it almost seemed as though the thing were alive and moving itself; this was the case almost every night. The prince opened his eyes which he had just closed.

"No rest, no rest, curse them all!" he exclaimed in a rage, as if he were anathematising someone.—"But was not there something of importance that I put aside to think of at my leisure in bed?—The locks? No, I have ordered them. It was not that. What was it that I forgot just now when Princess Maria and that idiot Dessalles were talking such nonsense?—Something—and then I think I put something in my pocket. After that?—I cannot remember.—Tikhone, here; what were we talking about at dinner?"

"Of Prince Andrew . . . ?"

"That will do; hold your tongue. . . . I know, my son's letter. Yes, Princess Maria read it, and Dessalles was speaking of Vitebsk—I will read it now."

He had it brought to him and made Tikhone place the little table on which his lemonade and his candle stood, close to the bed, then he put on his spectacles and read his son's letter with great attention. Then only, in the silence of the night, by the dim light of the candle under its green shade, did he at last, for a moment, understand the importance of the news it contained: "The French are at Vitebsk? In four marches they can reach Smolensk—they are there perhaps by this time! . . . Here, Tichka! . . ."

Tikhone started up. "No, never mind—it is nothing!" said his master; he slipped the letter under the candlestick and closed his eyes. . . .

He sees the rushing Danube, the shores overgrown with gigantic reeds, the Russian camp under a brilliant sky; himself —a young general, gay and vigorous, going into Potemkin's tent; and the mere reminiscence revives his passionate jealousy of the favourite in all its virulence . . . he hears once more every word that had been spoken at that first interview!—He sees by his side a sallow woman of middle height and stout figure—our mother the empress!—She smiles an him—speaks to him—and at the same instant behold the face is changed; she lies on her state bier, surrounded by burning tapers, . . . and the sharp words he had with Zouboff at the coffin side about the right to kiss her hand.

299

"Oh! if I could only go back to that time, if the present might vanish, and if 'they' would but leave me in peace!" the old man muttered in his dreams.

CHAPTER LXXXVI

DURING the conference between the prince and his steward, Dessalles had gone to the princess, and had respectfully represented to her, on the strength of her brother's letter, that it was certainly unsafe to remain at Lissy-Gory, only sixty versts distant from Smolensk and but three versts off the high road to Moscow. Therefore, as the state of her father's health prevented his taking the necessary steps to secure their safety, she would do well to send a letter by Alpatitch to the governor of the province, begging him to let her know the real state of affairs, and to tell her whether there were any danger in remaining in the country. Dessalles, indeed, wrote the letter, Princess Maria signed it, and gave it to Alpatitch with orders to return without losing a moment.

Alaptitch, thus amply instructed, was at last ready to be off, and he got into a large kibitka with a leather hood and three stout roans harnessed abreast.

The bells of the harness were stuffed with paper to muffle them, for the old prince never allowed one to be heard on his domain; but Alpatitch, who liked the tinkle, fully intended to set them going as soon as he was far enough away from the house.

His own people, including a clerk, a cook, two old women, and a boy-servant, all crowded round him. His daughter packed in his eiderdown pillows in chintz covers, and one of the old women stealthily shoved in a large parcel, as the steward, respectfully assisted by one of the stablemen, was getting in.

"Hallo, hallo! What is all that? Women's fussiness! Oh! women, women!" he exclaimed as he seated himself, in a voice as harsh and breathless as his old master's. After giving his parting instructions as to work and the building, he took off his hat and crossed himself three times—in this, it must be said, strangely unlike his master.

"If there is anything wrong, the very least danger, you will come back at once, won't you, Jakow Alpatitch?" said his wife, who was frightened out of her wits at the rumours of war. "For Heaven's sake have pity on us here!"

"Oh! women, women!" he growled once more, while the kibitka made its way by the side of the fields, which he inspected with the eye of a connoisseur. The rye was just turning yellow; the oats, still green, stood thick and strong; the summer wheat, unusually fine this season, rejoiced the steward's heart, and he looked at it with pride. The harvest was being reaped on all sides; and as he went on he rehearsed in his mind all his schemes for sowing and cropping, wondering every now and then whether he had forgotten any of the prince's commissions.

He stopped twice to bait his horses, and reached the town in the evening of the 16th of August. On the road he met several baggage-trains, and even some detachments of marching soldiers; and as he got nearer to Smolensk, he fancied he heard cannon at a considerable distance, but that did not trouble him. What surprised him far more seriously was to see a camp pitched in a fine field of oats which the men were mowing down, no doubt to feed their horses; but he was absorbed in business and calculations, and ere long had forgotten the incident. For more than thirty years his sole interest in life had lain in carrying out his master's wishes; thus anything which had no direct bearing on that did not appeal to his mind; in fact, scarcely existed so far as he was concerned.

When he reached the suburbs he pulled up at an inn kept by one Férapontow, with whom he commonly lodged. This Férapontow had once upon a time bought, through Alpatitch, on easy terms, a wood belonging to Prince Bolkonsky, and the sale by retail had proved so profitable that by degrees he had built a house, and an inn, and now did a large business in flour. He was a peasant of about forty, black-haired, pleasant-looking, with a portly stomach, thick lips, a flat nose and prominent bumps over his thick brows, which he commonly knit. He was standing with his back against his shop door, in a coloured shirt and a waistcoat.

"Good evening, Jakow Alpatitch; you are a welcome sight. So you are coming into town when others are getting out of it?"

"How is that?"

"They are afraid of the French—the idiots!"

"Old wives' gossip!" said Alpatitch.

"That is what I tell them. I tell them that orders have been given that he is not to be let in; so of course he will not get in!—And those rascally peasants take advantage of the panic to charge three roubles for a goods van!"

Jakow Alpatitch, who listened without marking, interrupted

him to order a feed of hay for his horses; then, after some hot tea, he went to bed.

All night through regiments were marching past the house; but Alpatitch heard them not, and next morning he went as usual to transact his business in the town. The sun shone brightly, and at eight in the morning it was quite hot. "What lovely weather for the harvest!" thought the steward. The growl of cannon and rattle of musketry were audible at daybreak outside the town. The streets were full of soldiers and of coach-drivers going and coming as usual, while the shop-keepers stood at their open doors. Mass was going on in the churches. Alpatitch made his usual round, went into the different law courts, called at the post-office, and at the governor's; wherever he went war was the word; the enemy was down on the town they said; everyone was questioning everyone else and trying to reassure his neighbour.

Outside the governor's residence Alpatitch found a large gathering; there was a detachment of Cossacks on guard, and the grand functionary's travelling-carriage. On the steps he met two gentlemen, one of whom he knew as having been the head of a district.

"It is past a joke!" he was saying vehemently. "For a bachelor it is all very well; only one to look after, a mere trifle! —but with thirteen children, and all their fortune at stake! . . . What are the authorities about, to let things come to such a pass that there is nothing before us but ruin? Such villains deserve hanging!"

"Come, come! Take it calmly!"

"What do I care if they hear me? Let them hear me! We are not dogs to be treated so."

"What you, Jakow Alpatitch? What brings you here?"

"I have come, by his excellency's orders, to see the governor," said the steward, drawing himself up with pride, and putting his hand into his waistcoat—a gesture he always used when speaking of his master. "I am to ascertain the true state of affairs."

"Go and ascertain it by all means. You will find that there is not a carriage or a cart to be had.—You hear that noise?— Well, then. . . . The scoundrels have led us into ruin!"

Alpatitch shook his head sadly, and went on; the waiting-room was full of women, merchants, and clerks. The door of the inner room was opened; everyone rose and pressed forward. An official came out, looking very scared; he spoke a few words to one of the merchants, called a burly clerk with an order round his neck, and carried him off with him in a hurry, without paying any heed to the questions and looks that followed him. Alpatitch took a front place, and when, presently, the same official reappeared, he held out the two letters, put his left hand, in due form, inside his waistcoat, and spoke:

"For Baron Asch, from General Prince Bolkonsky," he said, with such solemn significance that the man turned round and took the letters he held out to him. A few minutes later the governor sent for Alpatitch.

"Tell the prince and princess," he said, hurriedly, "that I know nothing, and that my orders—here . . ." he added, giving him a printed paper. "The prince, I see, is ill. I advise him to go to Moscow; I am going there myself. Tell him . . ." but he did not finish the sentence: an officer, covered with dust and sweat, rushed into the room, and said a few words in French. The governor's face expressed extreme dismay.

"Go—go," he said, nodding to Alpatitch, who immediately left the room. All the waiting crowd, eager for news, looked at him with anxious inquiry.

As he hurried back to his quarters he listened more attentively to the firing, which was certainly nearer. The printed document ran as follows:

"I can assure you that at present no danger threatens the town of Smolensk, and it is not likely that it will. I, on one side, and Prince Bagration on the other, are advancing to unite there on the 22nd of this month, and the combined armies will then co-operate to protect their fellow-countrymen and the government under your jurisdiction; until by their efforts they shall have repulsed the foe, or until not a soldier is left to fight. So you see that you may with perfect confidence re-assure the inhabitants of Smolensk, for when two armies as brave as ours are prepared to fight, victory is certain. (Order of the day, from Barclay de Tolly to Baron Asch, Governor of Smolensk.—1812.)"

The streets, however, were full of anxious faces. At every turn carts were to be met coming out of the court-yards of the houses, loaded with movables, furniture and household goods of every description, and all making their way to the gates of the town. Some, ready to be off, were standing in front of the shop next to Férapontow's, the women were wailing and crying, and exchanging last words, while a cur barked and leaped round the horses' heads.

Alpatitch turned into the inn-yard and went up to his conveyance with unwonted briskness; the coachman was asleep. He roused him, desired him to put the horses to, and then went into the house. In the owner's room he could hear children squabbling, women shrieking, and above them all Férapontow's harsh, angry tones. The cook was rushing about the hall like a frightened hen.

"He has been beating her, beating the missis to death," she screamed.

"Why?"

"Because she begged and prayed him to let her go. 'Take me away,' says she—'do not leave me to die, me and the children,—Everyone is going; why do we stop?'—and he gave her such a thrashing! Oh dear, oh dear!"

Alpatitch, not caring to hear any more, merely nodded his head, and went on to the room where his purchases had been stowed.

"Wretch, monster!" yelled a pale woman, with torn clothes, holding a child in her arms, who rushed out on to the landing and flew downstairs. Férapontow was following her, but, seeing Alpatitch, he pulled up short, settled his waistcoat, yawned, stretched his arms, and went into his room with him.

"What, are you off?"

The steward examined his parcels, and made no reply, merely asking for his bill.

"Presently—time enough. Tell me, what is the governor doing? Is anything settled?"

Alpatitch told him that the baron had spoken in very vague terms.

"It will be good for our trade, do you know that?" said the man. "Sélivanow sold some flour to the army the other day at nine roubles a sack.—Will you have some tea?"

While the horses were being put to, Alpatitch and his host drank some tea, talking amicably of the price of corn, of the approaching harvest, and the fine promise of the crops.

"It seems to me," said Férapontow, "that there is less noise out there now. Our men have got the best of it, no doubt. They declared that they would not let him in: so we are strong enough, of course. Matveï Ivanovitch Platow pitched eighteen thousand of them into the river the other day."

The steward settled his score; the tinkling of the bells of his kibitka, which had been taken out of the inn-yard, and was now standing in front of the house, attracted him to the window; he looked up and down the street on which the sun was shining hotly, and there was scarcely any shade; it was long past noon.

Suddenly a strange, shrill, far-off whistle rushed through the air, followed by a sharp thud, and after it the noise of a cannonade that made all the windows rattle. Alpatitch went down into the street just as two men fled past the house towards the bridge. Now the hissing flight of bullets was to be heard on all sides with the clatter of their falling, and the bursting of shells which were pouring on the town; but the inhabitants did not heed them much; the firing outside the walls disturbed them far more. This was the bombardment of the town by one hundred and thirty guns, which Napoleon had ordered at 5.0 p.m.

Férapontow's wife, who was still sobbing in a corner of the coach-house, suddenly became quite calm; she went out into the gateway to get a better view of what was going on, and to stare at the passers-by, whose curiosity was roused by the noise and shell. The cook and the shop-clerk from next door joined her, and all three stood watching the projectiles with eager interest as they flew above their heads. Then some men came round the corner of the street, talking excitedly.

"What tremendous force!" said one. "The roof, ceiling, everything was smashed to powder."

"And it ploughed up the ground like a boar with his snout," said another.

"I had just time to jump out of the way, or I should have been made mincemeat of," added a third.

The crowd stopped them, and they gave a full account of how some of the shot had fallen close to them; and all the time the shrill ring of bullets and the hum of bombs and shell grew louder and faster; but nearly all flew over the roofs.

At last Alpatitch got into his carriage; his host was attending to his last arrangements when the cook, with her sleeves turned up and arms akimbo, came out and went down to the street corner to listen to what was being said, and stare, too, at the exciting scene.

"What the devil are you gaping at there?" cried Alpatitch roughly. At the sound of this despotic call, she turned and came hurrying back again, dropping her red petticoat which she had been holding up. At this instant the ominous whistle sounded so near that it might have been a bird flying close to the ground; there was a flash in the very street, a tremendous explosion, and then a dense cloud of smoke. The cook fell groaning in the midst of a circle of pale and terrified faces. Férapontow ran forward; the women all shrieked and fled, the children cried, but the woman's screams sounded above them all.

In less than five minutes the street was deserted; the poor girl, whose ribs had been broken by a piece of the shell, had been carried into the inn-kitchen. Alpatitch and his coachman, with Férapontow's wife and children and the gate-keeper, had all in their terror taken refuge in the cellar. The hollow roar of cannon and rush of grenades did not cease, and mingled with the cook's moans. Férapontow's wife tried in vain to quiet her baby and get it to sleep, while she questioned everyone who came in to know what had become of her husband; she heard that he had gone to the cathedral, where the inhabitants had flocked in crowds to demand that a procession should go round the town with the miraculous image of the Virgin.

As dusk fell the cannonade died away; the evening sky was shrouded by a dense cloud of smoke, though here and there, through the rents, the silver crescent of a new moon was seen. The incessant thunder was followed by a lull; but in a very few minutes a noise was heard of trampling crowds, with groans and shrieks, and the sinister crackling of fire. The poor cook had ceased her wailing. Soldiers came hurrying down the street, no longer in well-ordered file, but like a swarm of ants escaping pell-mell from an upturned ant-hill. Some rushed into the inn-yard, to get out of the way of a regiment that barred the road by having suddenly turned in its flight. Alpatitch came out of the cellar and stood in the gateway.

"The town has surrendered!—Get away as fast as you can," cried an officer; adding, as he saw his men coming out of the yard: "I forbade you to go into the houses."

Alpatitch called his driver and told him to mount the box. All Férapontow's family came out one by one into the yard, but when the women saw the lurid glare of the conflagration, very visible in the twilight, they broke out into lamentations, which found an echo in cries of anguish in the street. Alpatitch and the coachman, under the shed, disentangled the reins and straps with trembling hands; at last the vehicle moved off. As the steward passed Férapontow's open shop he saw a dozen or more soldiers still filling large sacks with flour and sunflower seeds. The owner came rushing in, and was on the point of flying at them in fury, but he stopped short, tearing his hair, and his rage vented itself in a sort of sobbing laugh.

"Take it, take it, children!" he said. "Anything rather

than that it should fall into the hands of those fiends!" and he himself seized the sacks and flung them out into the street. A few of the soldiers were frightened and fled; the rest quietly continued their work of plunder.

"Russia is lost, Alpatitch, ruined and lost!" exclaimed Férapontow. "I shall go, too, and help make the fire. . . ." And he rushed out into his yard.

The road was so crowded that Alpatitch could not move; Férapontow's wife and children had got into a cart, and, like him, were waiting for an opportunity to make a start.

It was a dark but starlight night by the time they had reached the slope down to the Dnieper, advancing inch by inch. There again they had to pause, the way was stopped by soldiers and vehicles. Close·to the cross-roads where they pulled up, the last remains of a house and some shops were still burning; the flame fitfully dying out in dense black smoke and then blazing up again brighter than before, and lighting up minutely with a malignant glare the figures of the speechless and terrified bystanders. Shapes passed to and fro in front of the fire, and cries and wailing mingled with the crackle of burning timber; soldiers were coming and going in the fiery glow; two of them, helped by a man in a cloak, were dragging a blazing beam into the yard of the next house, and others were bringing in armfuls of hay.

Alpatitch got out of his kibitka and joined a group who were staring at the destruction of a granary, where the flames were licking the walls; one side presently gave way, the roof fell in and the burning joists crashed down.

At this instant a voice called him by his name.

"Good God! excellency!" he exclaimed, recognising Prince Andrew, who, mounted on a black horse, kept just behind the crowd.

"What are you doing here?"

"Excellency," said the steward, melting into tears. "I—I —Is all lost?"

"What are you doing here?" repeated the prince.

A shaft of flame suddenly shot up to heaven and revealed his pale, worn face. Alpatitch briefly told him what he had come for, and the difficulty he had in getting out of the town.

"Tell me, excellency," he said once more. "Is there no chance for us?"

Prince Andrew did not reply, but he took out his note-book, tore out a leaf and wrote in pencil, on his knee, these few words. to his sister:

"Smolensk is abandoned. The enemy will be in Lissy-Gory in a week at latest. Go at once to Moscow . . . Let me have a line by express messenger to Ousviage to tell me that you are off." He had just given the note to Alpatitch and was adding a few verbal instructions, when a staff-officer, followed by his orderlies, addressed him in a strong German accent:

"You, a colonel!" he said, "and you can look on while the houses are being set on fire under your very eyes!—What is the meaning of it? You will have to answer for this!" It was Berg, who had found a berth as adjutant on the staff of the general in command of the infantry of the first army's left flank, and found it, as he often said, a pleasant and advantageous position.

Prince Andrew looked at him, but answered never a word; he went on speaking to Alpatitch:

"Tell them that I shall wait for an answer till the 10th. If I do not hear that they are gone by that time, I shall be obliged to leave everything and go to Lissy-Gory."

"A thousand apologies!" Berg now put in, having just recognised the prince. "But I have strict orders, otherwise I should not have ventured—you know I am punctually obedient! A thousand apologies!"

There was an appalling crash; the fire suddenly seemed extinct; only whirling clouds of smoke rolled up—then another crash; the huge building reeled and fell in, with a noise like the crack of doom. The crowd yelled with wild excitement; the fire flew up again in a burst of flame, lighting up the ghastly faces of those who had planned it. The man in the cloak waved his arm, shouting:

"Hurrah!—It is done, my boys! It is blazing well now!"

"That is the owner of the store!" said one and another in a low voice.

"So you understand, Alpatitch," said Prince Andrew, taking no notice of Berg, who stood petrified by the scene. "Tell them just what I say — good-bye"; and spurring his horse he rode off.

THE INVASION

CHAPTER LXXXVII

FROM Smolensk the Russians continued to retire, closely followed up by the enemy. The regiment under Prince Andrew's command marched along the high road and past the turning which led to Lissy-Gory, on the 10th (22nd) of August. For three weeks past the heat and drought had been terrific. Heavy clouds occasionally veiled the sun, but they soon passed over, and he set, evening after evening, behind a thick mist of dusky crimson. The uncut crops shed their seed and withered standing in the fields, while the cattle, bellowing with hunger, vainly sought a blade of grass in the scorched meadows and dried-up marshes. There was no respite save at night, and then only in the woods; the refreshing balm of dew had no effect on the parched land. On the high road huge pillars of dust blinded the soldiers from the moment they started at daybreak. The baggage-trains and artillery took the middle of the road while the infantry tramped along the side paths, through the hot, choking dust which the night dews had no power to lay. It clung to the soldiers' feet and caked on the wheels of the wagons, and hung round and over them like a cloud, getting into the eyes, the nostrils, and above all the lungs of man and beast alike. As the day went on, the scorching sandy curtain grew more and more dense, till the sun was seen through it as a globe of blood-red fire. Not a breath of air came to stir the suffocating atmosphere, and the men stopped their noses and covered their mouths to be able to breathe at all. As soon as they reached a village everyone rushed to the well, and the poor creatures fought for a drop of muddy water, which was swallowed with avidity.

Prince Andrew devoted himself to his regiment and the health and comfort of his men. The burning and evacuation of Smolensk, by fanning his hatred of the invaders, marked an epoch in his life, and the virulence of his hatred enabled him to forget his own griefs. His kindness and affability made him dear to his subordinates, who always spoke of him as "our prince." With his subalterns and men he was invariably gentle and friendly; they knew nothing of his past life; but when chance threw him in the way of an old acquaintance his whole nature rebelled; like a hedgehog, he would be all spines, and his demeanour would become cold and haughty. He revolted from all that recalled the past, and whenever he found it necessary to think of it, restricted himself to being scrupulously just.

Everything, indeed, looked dark before him. On one hand Smolensk, which he was convinced might have been held, had been abandoned on the 6th (18th); on the other his father, decrepit and ailing, had been forced to leave Lissy-Gory, the home that the old man had built and arranged to his own taste and that he loved above everything in the world. It was well for Prince Andrew that his regimental duties diverted his mind from these gloomy thoughts, by constantly claiming his most minute attention.

His detachment reached Lissy-Gory on the 22nd; he had heard, two days previously, that his father and sister had left for Moscow. There was nothing to tempt him to visit the place; but an impulse to snatch a bitter joy by reviving his sorrowful memories made him decide to ride round that way.

Leaving his men to march on, he turned off towards the village where he was born and had grown up. As he passed the pond where the washer-women were usually to be seen singing and chattering over their work, he was surprised to find it deserted; the little raft lay half under water, half hauled up on the bank; there was not a soul in the watchman's hut, and weeds were sprouting in the garden; calves and colts were disporting themselves in the pleasure grounds; the windows of the orangery were broken; some of the tubs were upset and several of the trees dead. He called Tarass, the gardener, but no one answered. Turning the corner of the greenhouse he perceived that the paling of the orchard was broken down and that the branches of the plum-trees were stripped of their fruit. An old peasant whom he could remember for years as sitting outside the gate, was now sunning himself on the old prince's favourite bench. He was plaiting bass-shoes, and a skein of the bark hung, ready to his hand, on the trunk of a fine magnolia half dead of drought. As he was perfectly deaf he did not hear Prince Andrew's approach. The prince rode up to the house; some old lime-trees that had stood in front of it had been felled; a piebald mare and her foal were capering about the flower-beds at the bottom of the steps and among the clumps of roses. All the shutters were closed excepting one on the ground floor; a small boy, who seemed to be on the watch, catching sight of the horseman vanished indoors.

Alpatitch had remained alone at Lissy-Gory after seeing off all the family; he was studying the *Lives of the Saints* when the

Burning of Smolensk

child rushed in to announce the arrival of the young master. He hastily buttoned up his coat and ran out, his spectacles still on his nose; and without saying a word he flew down to meet Prince Andrew and burst into tears. But he at once turned away, ashamed of his weakness; and controlling his voice, gave him a full account of the state of things. All that the house had contained of any value had been sent to Bogoutcharovo, with a hundred *tchetverts* of wheat; but the summer's crops of hay and corn, which were wonderfully fine that year, had all been cut by the troops before they were ripe. The peasants were all ruined, and some of them had also moved to Bogoutcharovo.

"When did my father and sister leave?" asked Prince Andrew who had listened absently to his lamentations, and who concluded that his family were at Moscow.

"They set out on the 7th (19th)," said Alpatitch, never doubting that he knew that they were at Bogoutcharovo, and then, going back to business again, he asked him for further orders. "There is still some corn left; am I to give it up on having a signed receipt for it?"

"What ought I to say?" thought Prince Andrew, looking down at the old man, whose bald head shone in the sun; he read in his face that he himself knew how useless it was to ask —that he only did so to cheat his own sorrow.

"Yes," he said. "You can let them have it."

"You see the state the garden is in. I could not help it; three regiments marched in to find quarters. The dragoons especially behaved . . . I took down the name of the officer in command to lodge a complaint. . . ."

"And what are you going to do now?" said his master. "Do you mean to stay here?"

Alpatitch looked up at him, and raising his hands to Heaven he said devoutly:

"He is my Protector. . . . His will be done!"

"Well, good-bye," said Prince Andrew, bending down to the faithful old man. "But go away; take what you can carry, and tell all the peasants to make their way to our place in Riazan, or even to the estate near Moscow."

Alpatitch, weeping bitterly, clung to him for a moment, but Prince Andrew gently released himself and went off at a gallop down the avenue.

He passed the old man again, sitting in the same place and still absorbed in his industry—it reminded him of a fly on a

311

dead man's face. Two little girls, who had no doubt come out of the orchard house, stopped short as they saw him: they held up their skirts, which were quite full of the plums which they had gathered. They were so much alarmed that the elder, seizing her companion's hand, dragged her hastily away, and they hid behind a birch-tree without stopping to pick up the still green fruit that dropped from their laps. Prince Andrew looked another way and pretended not to see them, for fear of frightening them more — he could not bear to see the pretty things so terrified.

The sight of these two children had suddenly roused a new phase of feeling in his spirit—a soothing and, so to speak, restful sense of the existence of other interests in life, outside and apart from his own, but equally human and equally natural. These little persons evidently cared for nothing at this moment but the safe possession and enjoyment of the half-ripe plums, and their chief point was to escape detection;—Why should he interfere with the success of their enterprise? He could not resist the temptation to look back at them, and he saw them run out of their hiding-place now that the danger was over, and scamper barefoot over the grass, with their frocks held high, laughing and chattering in their shrill childish voices.

Prince Andrew, much refreshed by his ride away from the dust of the high road, soon came up with his men, who had stopped to rest near a pool of water. It was two in the afternoon; a broiling sun scorched the soldiers' backs through their black cloth uniforms, and the dust, hanging over them like a cloud of smoke, muffled the ring of their voices. There was no wind. As he rode along the dike, a faint puff of damp marsh air fanned his cheek and made him long to plunge into the water, all muddy as it was. The little pond, whence shouts of laughter fell upon his ear, was overgrown with weeds and slime, and at this moment was so crowded with soldiers bathing that the water washed up to the footpath; their white bodies, with hands, faces, and necks burnt to a brick-red, were wriggling and leaping in the green miry pool like fishes in a watering-pot. This frisky enjoyment, and the peals of thoughtless laughter, gave him an obscure feeling of pity and regret.

A fair youngster, a man of the third division, with a strap fastened below the calf of his leg, crossed himself, stood back a pace to get a better leap, and plunged in head foremost; a sergeant with tousled hair was stretching his weary limbs in the water, snorting, and pouring it over his body with hands blackened up to the elbow. There was a noise of gurgling and splashing water mingled with shouts of merriment; and in the pool and on the bank nothing was to be seen but a medley of human limbs—human flesh, white, firm, and healthy, with muscles as hard as steel. Timokhine, whose nose was redder than ever, was sitting on the grass wiping himself with care; he was half ashamed of being caught so by his colonel, but thought he had better sing the praises of his bath.

"It is really very nice, excellency, you should take a dip yourself."

"The water is dirty," said Prince Andrew, making a face.

"They will make way for you; they will clear it out," cried Timokhine; and running all naked to the pond, he cried out to the men:

"The prince wants to bathe, children!"

"What prince?"

"Why, our prince of course; who the deuce else?"

"Our prince," shouted several. And they all began to make such a stir that Prince Andrew had the greatest difficulty in persuading them that he would far rather have a douche in a barn.

"Flesh and blood—*chair à canon!*" said he to himself, as he looked down his own body from head to foot; and he shuddered as he remembered that mass of human creatures splashing in the dingy pool, though he hardly let himself think of the impression of terror and horror that the sight had made on him.

Bagration had written the following letter to Araktchéïew, dated from his camp on the Smolensk road and written on the 7th (19th) of August. Knowing full well that it would be read by the czar he had weighed every word—as thoroughly, that is to say, as his intelligence allowed.

"To Count Alexis Andréïévitch: The *minister* will, no doubt, by this time have reported to you the surrender of Smolensk to the enemy; everyone is distressed beyond words, and the whole army is in despair at the evacuation, without any useful result, of so important a place. I, for my part, entreated him most urgently; indeed, I wrote to him about it. I give you my word of honour Napoleon was as completely surrounded as if he had walked into a sack, and might have lost half of his army instead of capturing Smolensk. Our troops fought and are fighting as they always do. I held out more than five and thirty hours with 15,000 . men and I repulsed the enemy; but *he* would not hold out fourteen hours. It is a blot and a disgrace to our armies, and after this he is not worthy to live. If he has reported that our losses are heavy it is false—four thousand killed and wounded at most . . . that is all. The enemy, on the other hand, has suffered most severely.

"Why could he not hold out two days longer? The French would certainly have been the first to give way, for they had not a drop of water. He had solemnly promised me that he would not retire, and then suddenly he sends me a message to say he is withdrawing that very night.

"This is not war. At this rate we shall lead the enemy on to the gates of Moscow.

"I am told that you are thinking of making peace. God forbid! After such immense sacrifices and such mad retreats it is not to be thought of. You will have all Russia down upon you, and we shall be ashamed to be seen wearing her uniform. Since things have come to such a pass we must fight as long as Russia can stand; as long as she has a man!

"One man ought to command and not two. Your minister may be a very good minister, but as a general it is not enough to say he is bad—he is atrocious! And the fate of the country is in his hands! My brain is frenzied with rage—pardon my plain speaking. It is perfectly certain that any man who can counsel peace at such a moment and take the minister's part is no friend to the czar, and only hopes for our ruin. I am writing you the strict truth. Bring out the militia in all haste.

"Mr. Woltzogen, the aide-de-camp, does not command the confidence of the army: far from it—he is suspected of favouring Napoleon, and he is the minister's prime counsellor. So far as I am concerned, I obey as implicitly as any corporal, though I am his senior in rank. It is a constant grievance to me; but being, as I am, devoted to my sovereign and benefactor, I submit—though I lament that he should have placed his armies in such hands. Would you believe that in the course of this retreat we have lost by fatigue, and scattered in various hospitals, no less than 15,000 men; if we had advanced this would never have happened. Tell all who will listen to you that our Mother, Russia, will accuse us of cowardice, for we are handing over the country to the rabble and so fomenting hatred and revenge in the hearts of her children. What are we afraid of? It is no fault of mine if the minister is timid, undecided, crotchety, and dilatory—a combination of every defect. The army is depressed, and loads him with abuse."

314

THE INVASION

CHAPTER LXXXVIII

THERE are, we opine, two categories under which we may classify all the various and widely different ways in which men live their lives; the first, including those in which form is more important than fact; the second, those in which fact rules supreme over form. For instance, we may compare country life, or provincial life, or life even in a city like Moscow, with life in St. Petersburg; and more especially with the life of fashionable drawing-rooms which is everywhere and always the same.

From 1805 to 1812 Russia was fully occcupied with quarrelling and making it up again with Napoleon, and making and unmaking constitutions; while in the drawing-rooms of Anna Paulovna and Countess Helen no perceptible change had taken place, and all wore the same aspect and complexion as of old. At Anna Paulovna's everyone was as much astonished as ever at Napoleon's successes, and the general submission of the sovereigns of Europe was still regarded as a wicked conspiracy intended solely to disturb and annoy the Russian court circle, of which Anna Schérer considered herself the uncontested representative. In Helen's house, where Roumiantzow was a constant visitor—speaking of her as a remarkably clever woman —the same enthusiasm for "the Great Man" was still as fashionable in 1812 as it had been in 1808, and the rupture with France was spoken of as a matter of regret, though, of course, it must soon end in peace.

When the czar came to St. Petersburg after quitting the army, an unwonted excitement was perceptible in these rival centres; indeed, hostile demonstrations were attempted, but the two houses kept true to their colours. Anna Paulovna would receive no Frenchmen but a few blue-blooded legitimists, and her patriotic zeal proscribed the French theatre, which—said she—cost the country as much to keep up as a regiment. At her house the movements of the army were eagerly watched, and the most favourable reports of the Russian troops were repeated there.

In Helen's, on the contrary, where the French were numerous, every hint at peace on Napoleon's part was noted, the rumours as to the enemy's barbarities were discredited, and the advice of those who spoke of removing the court and the seat of government to Kazan was denounced as premature. In their opinion

315

the war was simply a demonstration; hence peace must soon be concluded; and they were fond of repeating a saying of Bilibine's—a diligent hanger-on now at the house where every man of mark had to be, or to have been, seen—to the effect that "critical questions could not be settled by gunpowder, but only by those who had invented it." There was much wit and laughter there, though of course with due discretion, at the patriotic excitement in Moscow which had culminated during the czar's visit to the elder capital.

At Anna Schérer's, on the other hand, this enthusiasm roused such admiration as Plutarch felt for his heroes. Prince Basil, who still held various important places, was the link that united the rival factions. He was at home alike with "my good friend Anna Paulovna," and in "my daughter's diplomatic circle"; and it occasionally happened that in oscillating between the two, he got entangled in his talk, expressing in one house the opinions which he ought to have kept for the other.

At Anna Schérer's one day, not long after the czar's return, Prince Basil who had been censuring Barclay de Tolly very severely, ended by confessing that, as matters then stood, he should find it extremely difficult to name the man who could fill the post of commander-in-chief. Another familiar visitor, who was commonly known as the "man of distinguished merit," said that he had that day seen the commandant of the St. Petersburg militia inspecting volunteers at the office of the ministry of finance, and ventured to suggest that he possibly was the man whose fate it might be to satisfy the requirements of all parties. Anna Paulovna smiled sadly: "Koutouzow," she said, "did nothing but involve the czar in worries."

"Yes, I told them so in the chamber of nobles," said Prince Basil. "I told them that his election as general of militia would give his majesty no satisfaction; but they would not listen to me. They have a mania for petty squabbling. And why? Simply because they want to ape the ridiculous enthusiasm of Moscow," he went on, forgetting that this speech, which would have found approval in his daughter's drawing-room, would certainly be frowned at in Anna Schérer's. He was immediately conscious of it, and tried to set himself right.

"Is it fitting, I ask you, that Count Koutouzow, the oldest general in the Russian army, should preside there in person? He will get nothing by that move.—And then, honestly, how can a man be appointed commander-in-chief who has absolutely no manners, who cannot sit a horse, and who goes to sleep at a council? Can anyone say that he covered himself with glory at Bucharest? I will not allude to his military qualities; that would take us too far. But in such critical circumstances how can we put our trust in a helpless old man who can hardly see? What sort of commander-in-chief can he be? He is good for nothing but to play blind-man's buff, for he really cannot see."

No one replied to this vehement attack, which was delivered on the 21st of July, when Prince Basil was still on the safe side; but a few days later, on the 29th, Koutouzow received the title of prince. This mark of favour, which it may be said only indicated a desire in high quarters to be rid of Koutouzow, did not at all disturb Prince Basil; but it had the effect of making him more cautious in his utterances. On the 8th of August, a council was held consisting of Soltykow, Araktchéïew, Viasmitinow, Lopoukhine and Kotchoubey, to discuss the progress of the campaign. They came to the conclusion that its failure so far was due to the division of power, and after brief deliberation it was decided, in spite of the czar's small liking for Koutouzow, to place him in command as general of the army and commandant of all the district occupied by the troops. And the appointment was confirmed the same evening.

On the following day Prince Basil was at Anna Paulovna's with the "man of distinguished merit," who was very anxious to be civil to him as he wanted his interest to procure him a place as curator of an institution for young girls. Prince Basil marched into the room with an air of triumph, and said, as if his fondest hopes had been crowned with fruition:

"Well! You have heard the great news? Prince Koutouzow is marshal in command, all differences are settled,—I am heartily glad. At last there is something like a man!" he went on, with a challenging glance at the audience.

The "man of distinguished merit," though he was a candidate for a place, could not forbear reminding the orator of the opinions he had expressed only a short while since. It was a double breach of good manners, for Anna Paulovna, too, had received the news with eager satisfaction.

"But, prince," he said, unable to check himself, and using Prince Basil's own words, "they say he is blind."

"What next! He can see well enough," said the prince, talking quickly in his hoarsest bass and clearing his throat energetically—this was his favourite resource when he was at all embarrassed.—"He can see well enough, take my word for it; and I am glad that the czar has given him an amount of power over the troops and over the country, too, which no commander-in-chief has had yet. He is a second autocrat."

"God grant he may prove so!" sighed Anna Paulovna.

The "man of distinguished merit," little skilled as yet in the ways of courts, fancied he could flatter the old maid by upholding her former opinion. He hastened to add:

"But they say that the czar signed the appointment much against his feelings; and that he coloured like a girl when he told Koutouzow that the honour was awarded him by his sovereign and his country."

"Perhaps his feelings had nothing to do with the case," observed Anna Paulovna.

"Not at all, not at all," cried Prince Basil, who now would not hear a word against Koutouzow. "That is impossible; the czar has always appreciated his splendid qualities."

"Then God grant that Koutouzow may really wield the power, and allow no one to put a spoke in the wheel," said Anna Paulovna.

Prince Basil, understanding her allusion, added in a low voice:

"I know for certain that Koutouzow insisted, as a *sine quâ non*, that the czarevitch should be recalled. I can tell you what he said: 'I could not punish him if he did wrong, nor reward him if he did right.' Oh! he is a man of keen foresight. I have known Koutouzow this many a long day."

"But it is even said," the "man of distinguished merit" persisted, "that his highness exacted a promise from his majesty not to join the army on any account."

He had scarcely spoken when Prince Basil and his hostess exchanged a pitying glance at such inconceivable want of tact, and turned their backs as if they were moved by one spring, both sighing deeply.

CHAPTER LXXXIX

WHILE all this was happening at St. Petersburg, the French, having left Smolensk behind them, were steadily approaching Moscow. Thiers, in writing his narrative, endeavours, like other historians of Napoleon, to palliate the errors of his hero by asserting that he was led on to Moscow against his will. This might be true if it were possible to assign the will of a single man as the cause of events affecting the whole world; and in that case these historians would be as right as the Russian historians who state that Napoleon was decoyed onwards by the skill of the Russian generals. In studying previous events as a process of incubation of the facts which were their ultimate outcome we may often detect a certain connection between them which only makes them seem more complicated. When a good chess-player has lost a game and is fully persuaded that the fault was his own, he sets aside the blunders he may have committed during the progress of the game to examine what mistake he made at the beginning, of which his adversary took advantage to compass his defeat. The game of war— a much more elaborate matter—is influenced by the conditions under which it is carried out; and far from being within the power of one single will, it is the outcome of the friction and shock of all the thousand wills and passions which are brought into play.

Napoleon, after quitting Smolensk, tried, but vainly, to force a pitched battle on the Russians, first at Dorogobouge near Viazma, and then at Czarevo-Saïmichtché; various circumstances prevented the Russians from confronting him till he reached Borodino, within 112 versts of Moscow. At Viazma Napoleon gave the order to march on the ancient Asiatic capital of the empire, the Holy City of Alexander's subjects. Moscow, with its numberless pagoda-like churches, excited his imagination. He set out from Viazma on his little cream-coloured horse, followed by his body-guard, his aides-de-camp and his pages; Berthier, the chief of staff, lingered behind to question a Russian prisoner with the help of Lelorgne d'Ideville, but he soon overtook his master and pulled up close in front of him with a radiant look of satisfaction.

"What is it?" asked Napoleon.

"A Cossack, sire, who has just been taken prisoner, says that Platow's division is joining the main body of the army, and that Koutouzow is appointed commander-in-chief. The rascal has a long tongue and seems intelligent."

Napoleon smiled, ordered that the Cossack should be mounted, and had him brought to him that he might have the pleasure of questioning him himself. Some aides-de-camp galloped off to carry out his instructions and in a minute Denissow's serf, whom he had handed over to Rostow, our old friend Lavrouchka, with his shrewd face somewhat flushed by liquor, in his uniform as an officer's servant, and riding a French cavalry charger, trotted up to Napoleon, who bid him ride by his side that he might cross-question him at his leisure.

"You are a Cossack?" he asked.

"Yes, highness."

"The Cossack," says Thiers, in telling the story, "not knowing to whom he was speaking—for there was nothing in Napoleon's appearance to suggest the dignity of the sovereign to an oriental mind—talked with the utmost readiness of the state of affairs then existing."

Lavrouchka was drunk, or not far from it; having failed to provide his master's dinner the day before, he had been well thrashed and sent off to lay hands on the poultry in the next hamlet; there, having been led into rashness by the pleasures of pillage, he had been caught by the French. Lavrouchka's life had been one of varied experience; he was one of those perfectly cool hands who are up to every conceivable trick, who can always make a good guess at their superior's worst impulses, and can measure at a glance the length and breadth of their trumpery vanity. Now, face to face with Napoleon, whom he at once recognised, he set to work to win his good graces; he was no more shy in his presence than in that of Rostow, or of the quarter-master with the cat in his hand; for, as he had nothing to lose, what could they take?

So he reported as fully as might be what was said in the Russian ranks; but, when Napoleon asked him whether they thought they could beat Bonaparte, he smelt a rat, frowned, and considered.

"If the battle is fought soon," said he, with a suspicious glance, "it is possible that you will win; but if there is no fighting for the next three days it is likely to be a long job."

This oracular reply was translated to the emperor by Lelorgne d'Ideville as follows: "If the battle were fought within three days the French would win, but if it were postponed till later, God knows what might come of it." Napoleon who was in a particularly good temper for the moment, listened with a smile and had the words repeated to him. Lavrouchka, observing this, still made believe not to know who he was.

"We know very well that the French have their Napoleon who has beaten everybody; but he won't find us so easy to deal with!" he went on, with an involuntary burst of patriotic boastfulness which the interpreter passed over in silence, only translating the first half of the sentence for his majesty's benefit.

"The young Cossack's speech made his puissant companion smile," says Thiers.

Napoleon rode forward a few paces and spoke to Berthier.

THE INVASION

He wished, he said, to see the effect produced on this son of the steppes of the Don by being told that he was addressing the emperor—that very emperor who had written his victorious name on the Pyramids of Egypt. Lavrouchka, quite understanding that Napoleon expected to see him awed by the information, affected terrified astonishment: opened his eyes, put on a bewildered face, and assumed the expression he was wont to wear when he was led off for a flogging in punishment of some delinquency. "Hardly had the interpreter revealed the fact," says Thiers, "than the Cossack, speechless with amazement, said not another word, but rode on with his eyes fixed on the conqueror whose name had reached even his ears across the steppes of the East. All his loquacity was staunched, and gave way to silent and awestruck admiration. Napoleon, after making him a present, gave him his liberty, 'like a bird restored to the fields that are its home.'"

His majesty went on his way, his head full of Moscow, which reigned supreme in his imagination, while "the bird restored to the fields that are its home" rode back to the Russian outposts. His thoughts ran on the wonderful romance he was prepared to tell his comrades; for he was not the man to relate facts as they had happened, and speak the unvarnished truth. He asked the Cossacks he met on his way where his regiment now was. It formed part of Platow's detachment, and late in the day he arrived at Jankow, where his squadron were bivouacked, just as Rostow and Iline were mounting to reconnoitre the neighbourhood. Lavrouchka was then and there ordered to accompany them.

CHAPTER XC

PRINCESS MARIA was not at Moscow, and out of all danger, as her brother supposed.

When the steward had returned from Smolensk the old prince roused himself from a kind of lethargy. He assembled all the militia and wrote to the general in command that he had quite made up his mind to remain at Lissy-Gory and to defend it to the last extremity, leaving it to him to take measures or not as he chose, for the protection of a spot where "one of the oldest Russian generals was preparing to die or be taken prisoner." He then solemnly announced to his household his firm determination not to quit Lissy-Gory! As to his daughter, she, he said, was to take the little prince to Bogoutcharovo, and he set to work to arrange for their immediate departure with Dessalles. Princess Maria, excessively alarmed by this feverish energy supervening on several weeks of apathy, could not bear to leave him alone, and for the first time in her life refused to obey him. She said she would not go, and so exposed herself to a violent storm; her father in his rage accused her of endless imaginary crimes, loaded her with the bitterest reproaches, accused her of having poisoned his existence, of having made him quarrel with his son, of having suspected him of the most abominable misdeeds — and finally dismissed her from his presence, saying she might do whatever she pleased, that he would have nothing more to say to her, and that he never would set eyes on her again. Princess Maria, however, was only too thankful not to have been placed in the carriage by force, and in this slender concession read proof positive of her father's covert satisfaction at her having made up her mind to stay under the same roof with him.

The day after his grandson's departure the old man got himself into full dress, and announced his intention of waiting on the general in command. His carriage was at the door, and his daughter could see him, blazing with orders, making his way to an alley in the grounds where he was about to review the peasants and servants whom he had put under arms. Sitting at her window she was listening to catch his various orders, when suddenly she saw some men running with faces of horror from the garden towards the house; she flew out, and was just turning into the alley when she saw, coming towards her, a party of the militiamen, and in their midst her father, whom they were carrying along, while his helpless feet dragged on the gravel. She went forward; the dancing lights through the foliage of the lime-trees at first prevented her seeing clearly the change in his features. As she got closer it was a fearful shock: his hard, set expression had turned to one of weakness and humility. On seeing his daughter, his lips moved helplessly, but only gave out a hoarse, inarticulate sound. They carried him into his room, and laid him on the divan, which only lately had been to him the object of such frenzied horror.

A doctor was fetched from the village, and bled him the same night. The whole right side, he said, was paralysed. As a residence at Lissy-Gory was every day more unsafe, Princess Maria had the invalid carried to Bogoutcharovo, and sent her little nephew to Moscow in the care of his tutor.

His majesty went on his way his head full of Moscow

THE INVASION

The old man lived for three weeks in his son's house, still in the same state. His mind was gone; he lay motionless, almost lifeless, constantly murmuring inarticulate sounds; and it was impossible to tell whether or no he was aware of what was going on around him. He seemed to wish to express some desire which no one could guess at. Was it some sick man's whim, or the fancy of a weak brain? Did he want to speak of business; his own or the country's? No one could discover.

The doctor maintained that this irritation meant nothing, and was due solely to physical causes; but Princess Maria was sure that it was not so: and the old man's increased agitation when she was present confirmed her in this belief. There was no hope of his recovery, and to move him was impossible, for there would have been a risk of his dying on the road. "Oh! and would not death be preferable to life in this state?" thought Princess Maria. She never left him day or night, and, it must be confessed, she watched his slightest movements, not for a sign of improvement, but often, on the contrary, to read a warning of the end. And what was still worse—nor could she conceal it from herself—since her father's illness all her secret aspirations and hopes, now so long set aside, had suddenly revived in her soul: dreams of an independent life, full of new joys, and freed from the yoke of her father's tyranny; of loving and being loved, and knowing the happiness of married life, haunted her fancy like snares of the devil. In spite of every effort to drive them out they returned upon her again and again, and she often caught herself picturing and planning an altogether different existence when *he* should be gone. To resist temptation she had recourse to prayer, kneeling and fixing her eyes on the images of the saints; but her devotions lacked fervour and faith. Her feelings were drawn away by another current—the tide of active life, harder, but free, and in utter contrast to the moral atmosphere which had surrounded and imprisoned her till now. Prayer had hitherto been her one and sole consolation, now she was under the charm of a more practical life.

There was some danger, too, in remaining even at Bogoutcharovo; the French were coming nearer, and a neighbouring estate had just been laid waste by pillage.

The doctor insisted that the sick man should be moved; the *Maréchal de Noblesse* even sent a special messenger begging Princess Maria to leave as soon as possible; the local head of police came in person to tell her that there were French troops only forty versts away; "the enemy's proclamations had been sent out to all the neighbouring villages, and if she did not go immediately he could not answer for the consequences."

She finally made up her mind to go on the 15th of August; the whole of the 14th was spent in giving orders and making preparations, and she passed the night, as usual, without undressing, in a little room next to her father's. She could not sleep, and frequently went to the door to listen; she heard him moaning and faintly groaning while Tikhone and the doctor lifted him and changed his position. She would have liked to go in, but fear held her back; she knew by experience how much any appearance of alarm annoyed her father, who always looked away when he saw her anxious eyes involuntarily fixed on him; and she knew that her intrusion in the middle of the night, at an unusual hour, would occasion extreme irritation. And yet she had never felt so pitifully towards him as at this minute. A complete revulsion had taken place in her feelings; she really dreaded losing him, and as she let her memory dwell on the long years they had spent together, his every act seemed to her fancy a proof of his affection. If a vision of her future liberty intruded on the pathetic retrospect, she shut it out at once with horror as a suggestion of the evil one. At last, wearied out, and hearing no more stir, she fell asleep towards morning, and did not wake till late.

The sharpening of apprehension, which often accompanies our awakening, at once brought home to her consciousness the predominant thought of our life; she listened, and hearing nothing but the usual constant murmur in the next room, she said to herself, with a weary sigh:

"Still the same thing—always the same! But what is it I want then? What else should it be? I wish him to die!" she exclaimed, disgusted with herself. She hastily rose, made her toilet, said her prayers, and went out on the steps. The horses were being harnessed, and the last small baggage was being packed into the carriage. It was a soft, dull morning; the doctor came up to her.

"He seems a little better this morning," he said. "I was looking for you; he speaks more intelligibly, and his head is clearer. Come, he has been asking for you."

She turned pale, and leaned against the door-post. Her heart beat painfully; the mere idea of seeing him and speaking to him, when she had just been indulging in such guilty thoughts, was a painful mixture of pleasure and misery and shame.

"Come," said the doctor again.

She followed him, and went close to her father's bed. He was lying on his back, propped up on pillows; his lean bony hands, with their network of knotted blue veins, were laid before him on the sheet; his left eye was glassy and fixed, the right drawn and haggard, his lips and brow were set; his face was extraordinarily wrinkled, and his feeble, shrunken look was pitiably pathetic. His daughter kissed his hand; and his left hand pressed hers; he was evidently needing her. He did this once or twice, and his brow and lips quivered with impatience.

She looked at him in alarm. . . . What did he want? She placed herself where he could see her with his left eye, and he was calmer at once. Then he made a desperate effort to speak, and at last his tongue moved; at first in inarticulate sounds, but soon he pronounced a few words anxiously and painfully, and looking at his daughter with timid entreaty—he was so afraid of not being understood. The almost ludicrous difficulty he had in speaking made Princess Maria look down to hide the convulsive sobs she could scarcely control. He repeated the same syllables several times, but she vainly tried to gather their sense. The doctor at last thought he made out that he was asking her if she were afraid; but the prince shook his head.

"He means that his mind is not easy," said Princess Maria, and her father with an affirmative nod drew her hand towards him, and pressed it to his breast, now here, now there, as if trying to find the best place for it.

"I am always thinking of you," he said, almost distinctly, and glad to have been understood; then, as she bowed her head to hide her tears, he stroked her hair, and said:

"I called you all night."

"If I had but known . . . I was afraid to come in."

He pressed her hand. "Then you were not asleep."

"No," she said, shaking her head. In spite of herself his weakness influenced her, she seemed to be trying to speak as he did, and to have the same difficulty in expressing herself.

"My little daughter,"—or "my little darling"—he murmured. Princess Maria could not be quite sure which; but his look assured her that it was something tender and kind, a thing she had never known before. "Why did you not come in?"

"And I was wishing him dead!" thought the poor girl.

"Thank you, my child! my dear child, thanks—for everything—forgive—thanks!" and two tears rolled from his eyes. "Call Andrioucha," he said, with a sudden puzzled look.

"I have had a letter fròm him," replied Maria. He looked at her in surprise.

"Why, where is he?"

"With the army, father, at Smolensk."

Then there was a long silence; he lay with his eyes shut, but presently he reopened them and nodded, as much as to say that he knew now and remembered everything.

"Yes," he said, slowly and distinctly. "Russia is lost— they have lost her!" and he sobbed.

He grew calmer, however, and closed his eyes, making a slight motion of his hand, which Tikhone understood, for he wiped the old man's tears away, while he murmured again some confused words. Was he speaking of Russia, of his son, his grandson, his daughter? No one could make out. A happy inspiration helped Tikhone: "Go and put on your white gown; I like it . . ."

"That is it," said the prince, turning to Princess Maria.

At these words she broke into such a violent fit of weeping that the doctor led her out of the room to recover herself, and to finish the arrangements for their departure. The old prince went on talking—of his son, the war, the czar, frowning angrily, and raising his hoarse, feeble voice, till suddenly a second and final stroke of paralysis silenced him.

The day had cleared, the sun was brilliant; but Princess Maria, standing on the balcony, was not thinking of it; she was conscious of nothing but a sudden gush of tenderness for her father, whom she had never in her life loved as she did at this moment. She went down the steps and towards the pond, across the avenue of lime-trees that her brother had lately planted.

"Yes, I wished him dead!" she exclaimed aloud in her agitation. "I wanted it to end quickly that I might rest.—But what good will rest be to me when he is gone? . . ."

She walked round the garden and back to the house, and as she went up to the door she saw coming towards her a stranger walking with Mademoiselle Bourrienne, who had refused to leave Bogoutcharovo. The gentleman was the *Maréchal de Noblesse*, who had come in person to impress on Princess Maria the need for departing. She listened, but she did not heed, asked him into the dining-room, offered him breakfast, and gave him a seat by her side. But a minute after she got up again and went to her father's room. The doctor stood in the doorway.

"You cannot come in, princess—go—go away," he said, authoritatively. She went back into the garden and sat down on the very edge of the pond, where she could not be seen from the house. How long she remained there she never knew. Suddenly a sound of hasty footsteps on the gravel roused her from her reverie; it was Douniacha, her maid, who had been sent to look for her, and who stopped short, startled at seeing her there.

"Come, princess,—the prince . . ." said she brokenly.

"Coming,—I am coming," cried Princess Maria, who set off running towards the house without waiting for the maid to finish her sentence.

"Princess," said the *Maréchal de Noblesse*, who was waiting for her at the entrance, "God's will be done!—You must bear it and submit!"

"It is not true—leave me, leave me!" she cried desperately.

The doctor tried to hold her back, but she pushed him aside and passed on.

"Why do they all try to stop me, why do they all look so frightened?" thought she. "I do not want them; what are they all doing here?"

She threw open the door of her father's room; it was flooded with light now, whereas it had always been kept darkened; a feeling of intense terror came over her. The old nurse and some other women were standing round the bed; they stood aside as she came in, and as they separated she could see the stern, calm face of the dead. She stood rooted on the threshold. ·

"He is not dead—it is impossible!" said she to herself.

Controlling her terrors with a great effort she went to the bed and pressed her lips to her father's cheek; but the contact made her shudder and start back; all the tender feeling that had surged up in her soul vanished before the horror and dread of that which lay before her.

"He is gone, he is gone,—and this horrible thing is in his place!—A dreadful mystery that freezes and horrifies me!" murmured the poor woman. . . . She covered her face with her hands and fell senseless into the arms of the doctor, who had followed her.

The doctor and Tikhone superintended while the old women laid out the body. They tied up the jaw that it might not stiffen with the mouth open, and fastened the legs together to keep them straight. They dressed the prince in his uniform with all his decorations and laid him on a table. Everything went on as usual in such cases. The coffin was ready by night-fall; the pall was laid over it, wax-tapers were lighted all round; the floor was strewn with juniper, and the reader began intoning the Psalms. The neighbours, and even many strangers, came in numbers and crowded round the coffin—for all the world like horses that shy and tremble at the sight of a dead horse, for they, too, were afraid—the *Maréchal de Noblesse*, the village overseer, the women of the household and farms, gazed with round eyes and panic-stricken faces, and crossed themselves before kissing their patron's cold stiff hand.

CHAPTER XCI

THE old prince had never had any liking for Bogoutcharovo; the peasants were quite unlike those of Lissy-Gory in language, costume and manners; they always said that they were origin-ally natives of the steppes. The prince did full justice to their laborious habits, and would have them over to Lissy-Gory for the harvest, or to dig a pond or a ditch; but he did not like them on account of their rough manners. Prince Andrew's residence among them, his reforms, his schools, his mitigation of the taxes, instead of civilising them had only fostered the native rusticity, which their old master always said was their most characteristic trait. The most extraordinary fables found credence among them: at one time they believed that they were all to be enlisted as Cossacks on service, and were to be made to accept a new religion; then, remembering the oath made to Paul I., in 1797, they would discuss the freedom he would have secured to them and which the owners of the fief had denied them; while some expected the return of Peter III., who was to rise again to govern in seven years' time. Then all would be free; everything would be legitimate, and reduced to such simple elements that there would be no laws at all! Mean-while the war with Napoleon and the French invasion were bound up in their minds with their confused notions of Anti-christ, the end of the world, and full and perfect liberty.

There were in the neighbourhood of Bogoutcharovo some large villages belonging to private owners or to the crown, but the proprietors rarely lived on their estates; consequently there were but few house-serfs, or men knowing how to read and write, so that among this peasantry the myths of national popular romance, whose origin is so often a mystery to the contemporary writer, had a particularly deep and contagious effect. For instance, about twenty years previously, the peasants of Bogoutcharovo, led away by those of the adjoining country, had migrated as one man, like a flock of birds of passage, to the south-east, to find certain fabulous streams whose waters were said to be always hot. Hundreds of families sold everything they possessed and set out in caravans; some bought their freedom, others simply ran away. Numbers of these poor wretches were severely punished and sent to Siberia, others perished on the way from frost and want of food; the rest came back, and the movement calmed down and died out, as it had begun, without any apparent cause.

At the present moment, in the same way, certain similar notions were abroad among the peasants; and those who had any intimate dealings with the populace knew full well that in 1812 it was pondering over various mysterious influences, which only needed a favourable opportunity to act with direct and increased violence.

Alpatitch, who had moved to Bogoutcharovo only a few days before the old prince's death, noticed an obscure ferment among the serfs there, whose manners and ways were curiously unlike those of their brethren at Lissy-Gory, though they were only sixty versts apart. While, at Lissy-Gory, the peasants were ready to desert their homes and leave them to the tender mercies of plundering Cossacks, here they clung to the soil and kept up a correspondence with the French; nay, some of Napoleon's proclamations were to be seen in their hands. The old steward had learned, through some faithfully devoted servants, that a man named Karp, who was very influential among his equals, and who had just come back from driving a train of crown cattle, was telling his friends that the Cossacks were destroying all the villages that had been deserted, while the French, on the contrary, respected them. He was told, too, that another peasant had brought from the nearest town a proclamation from a French general, which stated that no harm would be done to those who remained in their houses, that ready money would be paid for everything that was taken; and to prove his statement he displayed the 100-rouble notes he had received for his hay.—How could he know that the notes were forgeries?

Finally—and this was the most important point of all—Alpatitch found out that, on the very day when he had ordered the overseer of the village to levy a due supply of carts and horses to move Princess Maria's luggage, the peasants had met in council and announced their determination not to stir out of the village. But there was no time to be lost; the *Maréchal de Noblesse*, who had come on purpose to Bogoutcharovo, had insisted that the Princess must leave at once, saying that he would not answer for her safety beyond the next day—the 16th of August; in fact, in spite of his promise to attend the prince's funeral, he was prevented doing so by a sudden march on the part of the French, which only gave him time to carry off his family and a few of his more precious possessions.

Drone, the overseer or *starosta*, whom his deceased master had always called Dronouchka, had now for nearly thirty years been at the head of the hamlet of Bogoutcharovo. He was one of those men—strong in mind as much as in body—who, having once come to a man's estate, live to be seventy without a grey hair or a lost tooth, as strong and vigorous as they were at thirty.

Drone had been invested with his functions as headman of the village soon after the famous exodus to the "hot waters," in which he had started with the rest; he had now filled the post with blameless integrity for twenty-three years. The serfs feared him even more than they did their master, who treated him with respect and called him in jest "the minister." Drone had never been known to be ailing or drunk; never did he seem to be tired in spite of the most exhausting labour and nights without sleep; and, though he could neither read nor write, he never made a mistake in his accounts, nor in the number of *pouds* of flour which he carried in huge wagon-loads to sell in the neighbouring town, nor the quantity of wheat yielded by the fields round Bogoutcharovo. It was to this man that Alpatitch gave the order to supply twelve horses for Princess Maria's carriages, and eighteen carts with beasts to convey the furniture and luggage. Although the serfs' dues were paid in money, Alpatitch did not suppose that there could be any difficulty in executing this demand, since the village contained two hundred and thirty households, most of them in easy circumstances. But Drone simply looked down and said nothing as he listened to these instructions, which Alpatitch supplemented by telling him to which of the serfs he had best apply for the necessary horses and vehicles. The *starosta* replied that the horses belonging to the men he named were out. The steward mentioned some others.

"They have no horses now; they have hired them out to the government," replied Drone; "as for the rest, they are worn out with work, and bad food has killed a great many; so it is impossible to collect even enough for the carriages, much less for the baggage-carts."

Alpatitch, greatly surprised, looked fixedly at Drone. If Drone were a pattern overseer, he on his part was a first-rate steward; he understood at once that these replies were not the expression of Drone's own feeling, but that of the commune, which was evidently carried away by a tide of new notions. He knew, too, that the peasants hated Drone, as a serf richer than themselves, and that at heart the overseer was halting between two camps—the owners and the serfs: of this he saw the symptoms in his undecided looks. He went up to his subaltern with despotic impatience:

"Listen to me," he said. "No more nonsense of this kind! His excellency Prince Andrew gave me orders to see you all off the place that there may be no collusion with the enemy. Indeed, the czar has issued orders to that effect. Those who stop to bargain with the enemy are traitors—do you understand?"

"I understand," said Drone, without looking up.

But Alpatitch was not satisfied.

"Drone, Drone," he said, "this will bring you to no good," and he shook his head. "Be advised by me.—Do not be obstinate.—I can see straight through you, I can even see three *archines* under your feet, and you know it!" He took his hand out of his waistcoat and flourished it theatrically towards the ceiling. Drone looked at him askance, not without uneasiness, but at once fixed his eyes on the floor again. "Throw over all this folly; tell them all to pack up their chattels and start at once for Moscow. . . . And mind the carts are here to-morrow morning for Princess Maria.—As for you, do not go to the meeting again. Do you hear?"

Drone fell on his knees.

"Jakow Alpatitch, in God's name take the keys yourself."

"I simply tell you," Alpatitch repeated, sternly, "to give up your scheme. You know I can see into the earth under your feet."

For his skill in the management of bees, and in knowing the precise moment for sowing oats, with his twenty years of service under the old prince, had, as he knew, gained him a reputation as a sorcerer, and the ability to see yards into the ground was commonly considered as belonging to a sorcerer. Drone got up again and was about to speak, but Alpatitch stopped him.

"Come, tell me what you have got into your head! Heh? What did you really hope to do?"

"But what am I to do with the villagers?" said Drone. "They will not listen to reason, I have told them . . . ."

"Are they drinking?"

"They are quite unmanageable, Jakow Alpatitch; they have staved in a second barrel."

"Well, then, listen to me. I will go and fetch the head of the police, and you meanwhile go and tell them to have done with all this nonsense and find carts."

"Very good," replied Drone.

Jakow Alpatitch said no more; he had ruled over the peasantry too long not to be well aware that the best way to win was not to admit the possibility of resistance. So he feigned to be satisfied with Drone's submission; but he nevertheless took steps to secure the support of the authorities.

The evening came, but no carts. A noisy crowd had met outside the village tavern, and decided unanimously on refusing to supply them and on turning all the horses loose in the forest. Alpatitch therefore at once gave orders that the vehicles which had brought his goods from Lissy-Gory should be unloaded, and his horses kept ready for Princess Maria, while he hurried off to apprise the district authorities of the state of affairs.

CHAPTER XCII

PRINCESS MARIA had kept her room since her father's funeral, and had not admitted a soul to see her, when her maid came, and speaking through the closed door, told her that Alpatitch wished to have her orders as to her departure. This was before his interview with Drone. The princess was lying on the sofa, and she answered that she was not going to leave Bogoutcharovo at all—not to-day—never; and only begged to be left in peace. Stretched at full length, with her face to the wall, her fingers wandered idly over the leather cushion on which her head rested, mechanically counting the buttons, while her uncontrolled thoughts came back again and again to the same set of ideas: Death, the irrevocableness of God's decrees, the sinfulness of her own soul—the sinfulness of which she had been conscious during her father's illness, and which kept her from praying. . . Thus she remained a long time.

Her room faced the west, and the rays of the setting sun fell aslant through the windows; they suddenly lighted up the cushion on which her eyes were fixed, and diverted the current of her thoughts; she rose, smoothed her hair, and instinctively breathed more freely in the fresh evening breeze.

"So you may enjoy the beauty of the sky in peace now?" she said to herself. "He is dead—no one will interfere with you for the future!" She sank into a chair and laid her head on the window-sill.

She presently heard her name spoken again in an affectionate tone, from the garden side of the window; turning round she saw Mademoiselle Bourrienne, in a black dress, who came up to her, kissed her, and melted into tears. Princess Maria remembered all her past dislike, all her jealousy of the Frenchwoman, and the change that had taken place in her father during these last weeks when he would not have Mademoiselle Bourrienne come near him. "Was that not sufficient proof of the injustice of my suspicions? What right have I—I who wished him dead—to judge my neighbour?" And a vivid picture rose up in her mind of her companion's painful position, treated by her with marked coldness, dependent, nevertheless, on her kindness, and obliged to live under a stranger's roof in a foreign land. Pity gained the day; she looked up timidly and held out her hand. Mademoiselle Bourrienne grasped it eagerly and kissed it, weeping; then she dilated on the terrible loss they both had suffered: "The princess's permission that she should share her sorrow, their reconciliation under this common loss would be her only consolation. Her conscience was clear—and he, now above, would surely do justice to her affection and gratitude!" Princess Maria heard the sound of her voice, and looked up at her now and then, but paid no particular heed to what she was saying.

"Dear princess," Mademoiselle Bourrienne went on, "I understand that you have not thought—that you cannot yet think of yourself; my feelings compel me to think for you.— Has Alpatitch spoken to you of leaving?"

Princess Maria did not answer; her mind was too bewildered to take in what was said, or who it was that was to leave.

"Leaving? Why? What do I care now?" she was thinking to herself.

"Perhaps you do not know, dear Maria, that we are not safe here; we are surrounded by the French.—If we were to set out

we should undoubtedly be stopped, and God alone knows . . ."
Princess Maria looked at her blankly.

"Oh! if only you could know how utterly I do not care. I am not going away from him. . . . Talk to Alpatitch about it if you like. I will have nothing to say to it."

"I have talked to him about it. He hopes to get us off to-morrow; but in my opinion we had better stay where we are; it would be too dreadful to fall into the hands of the troops or of the insurgent peasantry!" And she drew out of her pocket a proclamation issued by General Rameau, advising the inhabitants not to desert their homes, and promising them, if they remained, the protection of the French authorities. "It seems to me that we cannot do better than apply to this general, for he will certainly treat us with all possible consideration."

Princess Maria read the paper and her face changed spasmodically.

"Where did you get this?" she asked.

"They probably heard that I was French!" said Mademoiselle Bourrienne, reddening.

Princess Maria, without another word, left the room, went into her brother's study and called Douniacha.

"Send Alpatitch or Drone to speak to me," she said, "I do not care which; and tell Amalia Karlovna (Mademoiselle Bourrienne) that I wish to be alone.—We must go—go as soon as possible!" she exclaimed, horror-stricken at the idea of any dealings with the French.

What would Prince Andrew say if such a thing were to happen? The mere thought that she, the daughter of Prince Nicholas Bolkonsky, should ask protection of General Rameau and lay herself under obligations to him, made her shudder and turn pale and red with outraged pride and anger. Her imagination conjured up every detail of the humiliation she must endure: "The French would make themselves at home here, in this house, in Prince Andrew's room—and turn over his letters and papers to amuse themselves; Mademoiselle Bourrienne would do the honours, and in their charity they would give me a corner to shelter in! . . . The soldiers would tear open my father's newly-made grave to steal his crosses and orders! . . . I should hear them boasting of their victories over the Russians, and expressing their false sympathy with my sorrows!" She instinctively adopted the feelings and views of her father and brother; for was she not their representative, and must she not behave as they would have behaved in similar circumstances? And as she sat trying to form a clear idea of the situation, of the exigencies of life, the need, nay the desire to live, which she had believed that her father's death had crushed out of her for ever, suddenly rushed back upon her with renewed force.

Greatly disturbed and excited, she catechised old Tikhone and the architect, but neither of them could tell her whether Mademoiselle Bourrienne had spoken the truth as to the vicinity of the French. The architect was half asleep, and would only smile and answer vaguely without committing himself to an opinion—a habit he had acquired during fifteen years of subserviency to the old prince. Tikhone's sad and weary face wore a stricken look of grief, but he answered all the princess's questions with dull submission; the sight of her seemed to increase his sorrow. At last Drone came into the room, bowed to the ground and stood in the doorway.

"Dronouchka," she said, addressing him as an old and faithful friend—for was he not the good Dronouchka who, when she was a child, had never failed to bring her home honey-cake whenever he came from the fair at Viazma, and to give it to her with a smile?—"Dronouchka, to-day, after the misfortune . . ." tears choked her utterance.

"We are all under the right arm of God!" said Drone, with a sigh.

"Dronouchka," she began again with an effort, "Alpatitch is away; I have no one to turn to—tell me, is it true, as I hear, that we cannot get away?"

"Why not, princess—you can always get away."

"I am assured that it would be dangerous to attempt it, on account of the enemy; and I, my good friend, know nothing; I do not understand!—I am quite alone. . . . But I feel I must go as soon as possible; to-night, or by daybreak to-morrow."

Drone did not at once reply, but stole a glance at her. Then he said:

"There are no horses; I told Jakow Alpatitch so just now."

"Why not?"

"It is the hand of God, to punish us. Some have been taken by the troops, some are dead—it has been a bad year. And the horses would not so much matter if we do not die of hunger ourselves.—For three days sometimes there is nothing to eat. —We are ruined, all ruined."

"The peasants are ruined? Have they no more corn?" asked Princess Maria, in astonishment.

"There is nothing for it but to die of hunger," Drone repeated. "As to carts, there are none."

"Why was I not told, Dronouchka? Can we not help them? I will do all I can. . . ."

It seemed so strange to her that at a time when her heart was tender and overflowing with grief, the rich and the poor should be dwelling side by side and the rich doing nothing to succour the poor. She had a general idea that there was always a reserve of corn, and that this reserve was distributed on occasion to the serfs; she knew, too, that neither her father nor her brother would have refused to give it to their serfs in need, and she was ready to take the responsibility on herself.

"We have corn belonging to the master, to my brother, have we not?" she went on, anxious to know how matters really stood.

"The master's corn has not been touched!" said Drone, proudly. "The prince said it was not to be sold."

"Then give the serfs what they need. I authorise you to do so in my brother's name." Drone only sighed. "Give it all away if necessary; and tell them, in my brother's name, that all we have is theirs too."

Drone gazed at her in silence.

"For God's sake, little mother," he cried at last, "deprive me of my place. Tell me to give up the keys; I have done my duty honestly for twenty-three years! . . . Take back the keys I entreat you!"

Princess Maria, startled, and not understanding the cause of his request, assured him that she had never doubted his fidelity, and would do everything in her power for him, and for the peasants, and then she dismissed him.

CHAPTER XCIII

An hour later Douniacha came to tell her mistress that Drone had returned to say that he had assembled the serfs by the princess's orders, and that they were waiting till she came.

"But I never sent for them!" said Princess Maria, quite amazed. "I merely desired Drone to distribute some corn."

"Then, princess, our mother, send them away without going out to them," said Douniacha. "They are deceiving you and that is the whole matter. When Jakow Alpatitch comes back we shall get away quite quietly; but for God's sake do not go out and show yourself."

"They are deceiving me, you say?"

"I am sure of it. Ask old nurse, she will tell you the same thing: they do not want to leave Bogoutcharovo; that is their notion."

"No, no, you are mistaken, you have misunderstood.—Fetch in Drone."

Drone said, as Douniacha had said, that he had assembled the peasants by the princess's orders.

"But, Drone, I never gave such an order; I desired you to distribute corn and nothing more."

Drone sighed. "They will go away again if you wish it," he said hesitatingly.

"No, no. I will go out and explain matters myself."—And Princess Maria went down the steps, in spite of the entreaties of Douniacha and the old nurse, who followed a little way behind her with the architect.

"They fancy, I dare say, that I am giving them the corn to bribe them to remain here, while I go off and leave them to the tender mercies of the French," said she to herself, as she walked on. "But I will tell them that, on the contrary, they will find houses and provisions, too, on the Moscow estate. . . . Andrew, I am sure, would have done even more in my place."

There was a stir in the assembled crowd as she appeared on the scene, and they instinctively took off their hats. It was quite dusk; Princess Maria walked on, looking at the ground; the heavy folds of her black dress encumbered her steps; she stopped in front of the mixed mass of faces old and young; their number intimidated her, and prevented her recognising them. She did not know what she had meant to say. Finally, controlling her hesitancy with an effort, her sense of duty gave her presence of mind.

"I am glad to see you all here," she began, without looking up, and her heart beat painfully. "Dronouchka tells me that the war has ruined you; we have all fared alike. You may rely on my doing all that lies in my power to help and relieve you. I must go, for the enemy is coming nearer . . . and besides—but in short, my friends, I give you everything. Take our corn. I only care that you should not want! If anyone tells you that I gave it you as a bribe to stay here, it is false. On the contrary, I implore you to leave, carry off all that you have, and go to our estate near Moscow. There, I promise you, you shall want for nothing—you shall find food and lodging."

She paused and sighs rose here and there from the crowd.

"I am acting on behalf of my dear father. He was a good master, you know," she added, "and of his son—my brother."

She paused again. No one spoke.

"The same misfortune has fallen on us all, so let us share all that is left to us. What is mine is yours," she ended, and she looked in their faces. Their eyes were fixed on her and every face wore the same expression—an expression which she could not read. Was it curiosity, devotion, gratitude, fear? Impossible to discover.

"We are grateful to you for your kindness," said a voice at last. "But we will not have his highness's corn."

"Why not?" said Princess Maria. No reply. She noticed that their eyes fell before hers, and repeated: "Why do you refuse it?" Still silence. She felt that she was getting agitated; but turning to an old man resting on his staff, she addressed herself directly to him: 'Why didn't you answer? Is there anything else I can do for you?" The old man looked away and bending as low as he could he muttered: "Why should we take it? We do not want corn? You want us to sacrifice and leave everything, and we do not choose to do so."

"Go—go by yourself!" said several voices, and the same expression sat on their faces: it was neither curiosity nor gratitude, that was quite clear, but an angry and obstinate determination.

"You have not understood my meaning," said Princess Maria with a melancholy smile. "Why do you object to go when I promise you that you shall be lodged and fed?—If you stay here the enemy will ruin you."

But the cries and murmurs of the crowd drowned her voice.

"We will not stir.—Let them ruin us.—We do not want your corn, we refuse to take it!"

Princess Maria tried vainly to make herself heard; this inconceivable obstinacy surprised and frightened her; she bowed her head and slowly bent her steps towards the house.

"She thought she could take us in, did she?—She is a sly one, she is!—Why should she want us to abandon the village? —Let her keep her corn, we don't want it!" cried one and another, while Drone, who had followed his mistress, was taking her orders. She was more than ever determined to quit the place, and repeated her commands that horses should be found; then she withdrew to her own room again, where she lost herself once more in painful reflections.

THE INVASION

CHAPTER XCIV

SHE sat for a long time that night with her elbows on the window-sill. A confusion of voices came up from the insurgent village; but she had ceased to think about the serfs, and did not care to guess at the meaning of their strange conduct. She could think of nothing but her grief, which, after this interval of anxiety for the present, had become "the past." She could now remember, weep, and pray. The breeze had died away after sunset, and night spread still and restful over the face of nature. The hubbub of voices gradually died away; then the cock crew as the full moon slowly rose above the lime-trees in the garden. Mists of dew shrouded the more distant objects and peace reigned in the village and in the house.

Princess Maria sat there dreaming: of the past, so lately past, of her father's illness and last moments—still keeping far from her the scene of his death which she felt she had not the courage to face in all its details at this silent and mysterious hour. She vividly pictured to herself the moment when he had the first stroke, and was held up under the arms and dragged along the garden of Lissy-Gory, mumbling something with his powerless tongue, twitching his grey eyebrows and gazing anxiously and timidly at her. "Even then he was wanting to say something to me. He was always thinking of having something to say to me." She remembered that night just before his attack; that night some presentiment of evil had kept her from leaving him at Lissy-Gory in spite of his wish. She had not slept, and had gone on tiptoe to listen at the door opening into the greenhouse whither her father's bed had been moved that night. He talked of the Crimea, of warm nights, of the empress. Then she had heard him talking in a feeble voice to Tikhone. She was sure he had wanted someone to talk to: "Why did he not send for me? Why would he never allow me to take Tikhone's place?—I ought to have gone in boldly. I am sure I heard him speak my name twice; he was weary and out of spirits, and Tikhone could not know! I remember he spoke of Lise then as if she were still alive, and Tikhone reminded him that she was no longer there, and he cried out 'Old fool!' He must have been in terribly low spirits. I heard from behind the door as he grunted and stretched himself out on the bed and said loudly 'My God!' Why did I not go in then? What would have happened to me? And perhaps he would have felt easier then; have said those words to me then." And the poor soul repeated aloud the last few tender words her father had spoken to her on the day of his death, and burst into sobs. This relieved her aching heart. She could see every feature of his face—not as she had seen it ever since her infancy, the face which terrified her, however far off; but that thin face with its piteous, submissive look over which she had bent to hear what he was murmuring, close enough, for the first time, to count the deep lines in it.

"What could he mean when he called me his 'little darling'? What is he thinking of now?" she wondered. A sudden craze of terror came over her as when her lips had touched his cheek, cold in death. She fancied she saw him as she had seen him last, lying in his coffin with his face bound up; and the terror and invincible horror that the picture inspired, made her tremble from head to foot. She tried in vain to shake it off by prayer; with widely staring eyes fixed on the moonlit landscape and the black shadows, she expected to see the hideous vision rise before her. Still she was riveted to the spot by the solemn silence and magic charm of the night; she felt petrified.

"Douniacha," she murmured. "Douniacha!" she cried hoarsely with a desperate effort.—Then, tearing herself free from the spell, she ran out of the room, meeting the women-servants who came hurrying up at her cry.

CHAPTER XCV

ON the 17th of August, Rostow and Iline, accompanied by Lavrouchka,—who, as we have seen, had been dismissed by Napoleon—mounted to ride out from their bivouac at Jankovo, about fifteen versts from Bogoutcharovo, to try some horses Iline had just purchased and find fodder in the neighbouring villages. For the last three days the hostile armies had lain about equally distant from Bogoutcharovo; the French vanguard and Russian rear-guard might at any moment come into collision there; so Rostow, as a captain careful of his men's wants, was anxious to be the first to lay hands on the victuals that might probably be found there. Rostow and Iline, both in capital spirits, also looked forward to having some fun with the pretty servant-girls who would very likely have remained behind at the prince's château.

As they went they catechised Lavrouchka concerning Napoleon, laughing heartily at his story, or they ran races to test the quality of their newly-acquired steeds. Rostow had no suspicion that the village through which they were riding belonged to the man who had been so near marrying Natacha. He had outridden Iline, who, on overtaking Rostow, reproached him for leaving him so far behind.

"Why," cried Lavrouchka, "if I had not been afraid of putting you to shame I could have distanced you both, for this Frenchy"—as he called the beast he was riding—"is a real wonder!" They now drew in, and rode at an easy pace up to a barn round which a crowd of peasants had assembled.

Some of the men took their hats off when they saw the officers; others merely stared. Two tall old serfs with wrinkled faces and shabby beards came hiccuping out of the tavern, and staggered towards them, singing at the top of their voices.

"These are nice folks!" said Rostow. "Have you any hay?"

"And as like as they can stare?" added Iline.

"A joll-ly, jolly fell-l-low," sang one of the old men with a bland smile.

"And who are you?" asked a peasant in the crowd, addressing Rostow.

"We are French!" said Iline with a laugh. "This is Napoleon himself"—and he pointed to Lavrouchka.

"Get along! You are Russians," said the man.

"Are there many of you behind?" asked another.

"Yes—a strong force," said Rostow. "But what are you all doing out here? Is it a holiday?"

"The elders have met to discuss the affairs of the commune," said the serf, and he moved away.

At this instant two women and a man with a white hat came towards them along the high road.

"The one in pink is mine! Beware of touching it!" cried Iline, seeing one of the girls coming boldly towards him: it was Douniacha. "What do you want, pretty one?" he added, smiling.

"The princess wishes to know your name and that of your regiment."

"This is Count Rostow, captain of hussars; as for me, I am your obedient humble servant."

"A jolly fel-l-low," the tipsy serf repeated, gazing at them with stolid curiosity. Douniacha was followed by Alpatitch, who was standing hat in hand.

"May I trouble your highness for a moment," he began,

putting his hand inside his waistcoat with a polite flourish not unmixed with contempt, perhaps for the officer's extreme youth. "My mistress, the daughter of General Prince Nicholas Bolkonsky, lately deceased, is in a very critical position—and it is all owing to the brutality of these ruffians," he added, referring to the mob that had gathered round them. "She begs you will go to speak with her—it is only a few steps farther on, and will be pleasanter I think. . . ." And he pointed to the two drunkards who were spinning round like gadflies about the horses.

"Ah! Jakow Alpatitch! It is you yourself. You must excuse us, you must excuse us," they said, still smiling idiotically. Rostow could not help looking at them and smiling as they did.

"Unless, to be sure, they amuse your excellency!" observed Alpatitch loftily.

"No, there is nothing amusing in such a sight," said Rostow, moving on. "What is the matter here?"

"I have the honour of explaining to your excellency that these low creatures will not allow their mistress to quit the property, and are threatening to take her horses out of the shafts. Everything has been packed since the morning, and the princess cannot start."

"Impossible!" exclaimed Rostow.

"It is the exact truth, excellency."

Rostow dismounted and gave his horse in charge to his orderly; then, questioning the steward as he went, he made his way to the house. Princess Maria's offer of corn on the previous evening, and her discussion with Drone, had made matters so much worse that Drone had definitely gone over to the serfs, had given up his keys to the steward, and refused to obey his summons. When the princess had given orders that the horses should be put to, the peasants came up in a mob and declared that they would take them out again and keep her there, "for everyone," they said, "was forbidden to desert his home." Alpatitch had tried in vain to make them hear reason. Drone had kept out of sight, but Karp had repeated that they would oppose Princess Maria's departure since it was contrary to orders: but that if she remained they would serve and obey her as they had always done.

Princess Maria, however, had made up her mind to go, in spite of the arguments of Alpatitch, of the nurse and the other women; the horses were actually being harnessed when the sight of Rostow and Iline, cantering along the high road, turned all their heads; the stable-men, taking them for the French, fled as fast as their legs would carry them, and the house rang with lamentations. So Rostow was hailed as a deliverer.

He went into the drawing-room where Princess Maria, scared and terrified, was awaiting her doom. She had lost the power to think even, and at first could scarcely understand who he was, and why he had come. But his appearance and manner and the first words he spoke, sufficed to reassure her and show her that he was her fellow-countryman, and a man of her own rank in life. She gazed at him with her large pathetic eyes, and addressed him in a husky and trembling voice.

"What strange streak of fate," thought Rostow to himself, "has thrown me in the way of this poor soul, crushed with grief and left unprotected, at the mercy of a mob of coarse insurgent serfs?" He could not help colouring the picture with a hue of romance, and he looked at her with much interest while she told her story. "What sweetness and dignity in her expression and features!"

When she told him of the scene that had taken place on the day after her father's funeral her feelings were too much for her; she turned away as if she feared he might think she was trying to excite his pity beyond reason. But when she saw tears sparkling in his eyes, too, she thanked him with a grateful look—one of those full, deep looks which redeemed her plainness.

"I cannot tell you, princess, how sincerely glad I am of the chance that has brought me here and which allows me to put myself entirely at your service. You can start at once—I give you my word of honour no one shall dare hinder you. I only ask your permission to serve as your escort. . . ." He bowed as low as if she had been a princess of the blood, and led the way to the door.

His respectful politeness seemed to imply that he would gladly have made further acquaintance with her, but that delicacy forbade his taking advantage of her difficult position and her sorrow to prolong the interview. Princess Maria herself understood it so.

"I am most grateful to you," she said in French. "I still hope that I have been the victim of no more than a misunderstanding; and above all I hope you will find no one actually guilty." She broke down into tears. "Pray forgive me," she added quickly.

Rostow himself had to hide his emotion, and after bowing once more he went out.

343

CHAPTER XCVI

"WELL, is she pretty? My pink one is delicious! Her name is Douniacha," cried Iline, as Rostow returned. But the expression of his captain's face silenced him; his chief and hero was evidently in no mood for jesting, for he glanced crossly at the young fellow and hurried off towards the village.

"I will teach them—the ruffians!" muttered Rostow. Alpatitch, striding after him, had great difficulty in overtaking him.

"What steps has your highness condescended to take?" asked the steward humbly.

"What steps, idiot!" said the hussar, shaking his fist at him. "What have you done, I should like to know? The serfs are in revolt and you stand looking at them; you cannot even make them obey. You are a rascal! I know your sort, and I will have you all flayed alive!"

And then he went off again at top speed, as if he were afraid of venting all the rage that seethed in his heart. Alpatitch, swallowing down his sense of undeserved obloquy, kept up with him as best he could, and as they went delivered himself of sundry reflections as to the insurgent serfs. He tried to make Rostow understand that, owing to their stiff-necked obstinacy, it would be both dangerous and useless to try to coerce them without the support of an armed force, and therefore it would be better to get that first.

"I will show them what an armed force means. They shall see, they shall see!" Nicholas repeated, not thinking of what he was saying. Full of his violent and impetuous indignation he marched resolutely up to the crowd still standing round the barn. Though Rostow had no fixed plan of action, Alpatitch foresaw a happy result from this daring proceedure. His firm cold manner, added to the set wrath of his face, showed the peasants that their hour of reckoning had come. Even during Rostow's absence and interview with Princess Maria a certain lack of cohesion had become perceptible; several who were beginning to feel uneasy had remarked that the officers were really and truly Russians, and would certainly be angry at their having delayed the young mistress. Drone, who was of this opinion, did not hesitate to express it loudly, but Karp and his party took him to task.

"And how many years have you been feathering your nest out of the village pickings?" cried Karp. "You are a good

344

one to talk.—You have buried a pot of money somewhere, and you will just dig it up and be off. What do you care if our houses are pillaged?"

"We know that the order was given," said another. "We were not to desert the village, or carry anything away, not even a grain of wheat; and that's all!"

"Your booby of a boy ought to have been taken for a soldier, but you did not like it, and it was my Vania that they caught and shaved," said a little old man furiously.

"There is nothing left for us but to die.—Yes, to die! . . ."

"I have not yet been discharged from my duties," said Drone.

"Exactly so, of course not; you are not turned off yet—but then you have filled your pockets!"

When Karp saw Rostow coming, followed by Iline, Lavrouchka, and Alpatitch, he went to meet him with his finger stuck into his belt and a smile on his lips. Drone, on the contrary, sneaked behind the others, and the crowd closed up again.

"Hi! you fellows, which of you is the *starosta?*" asked Rostow, walking straight up to them.

"The *starosta?* What do you want with him?" asked Karp. He had not time to finish his sentence when his cap flew into the air and he was half stunned by the blow that had hit it off.

"Hats off—rebels!" cried Rostow, in a voice of thunder. "Where is the *starosta?*" he repeated.

"The *starosta*—he wants the *starosta.*—Drone Zakharovitch, you are wanted," said one and another in subdued tones, while one by one the caps were removed.

"We are not rebels; we are only obeying orders," Karp went on, feeling himself still supported by a few of the men.

"We have to obey the council of elders . . ."

"How dare you answer me, villains!" cried Rostow, taking Karp, who was a big man, by the collar. "Here, hold him fast!"

Lavrouchka rushed forward and gripped his hands. "Shall I have our men up from the bottom of the hill?" said he.

Alpatitch turned to the serfs and desired two of them, by name, to give their waistbands to tie Karp's hands; the men obeyed in silence.

"Where is the *starosta?*" repeated Rostow. Drone, pale and scowling, at last made up his mind to come forward.

"It is you, is it?—Here, Lavrouchka, this one too," said Rostow decidedly, as if there could be no demur to his order.

And in point of fact two other men at once came forward, as Drone himself untied his belt to tie his own hands.

"As to the rest of you," Rostow went on: "Listen to me, all of you. Go home this instant, and do not let me hear another word."

"We have done no harm, we have only made fools of ourselves, that is all."

"Well, I told you so,—it was against orders," murmured several of the serfs at once, reproaching each other.

"I gave you due warning," said Alpatitch, who felt himself master of the situation once more. "It was very wrong, very wrong of you, my children!"

"Yes, Jakow Alpatitch, we have made fools of ourselves," they said, and the crowd quietly dispersed. They all went home, while the prisoners were taken up to the court-yard of the house; the two drunkards followed them.

"That is the style for you!" said one of them to Karp. "Now I can have a good look at you.—Did you ever hear anyone speak so to his betters? What on earth were you thinking of?"

"You are a fool, that is the long and short of it, a downright fool!" said the second with a sneer.

In the course of a couple of hours horses were found for the baggage-wagons and the serfs were carrying and packing the various goods, superintended by Drone, who had been released by his mistress's request.

"Take care of that!" said a peasant-lad, tall and pleasant-looking, to a companion, who had just taken a dressing-case from one of the maids. "It cost a lot of money—don't go pitching it into a corner or tying it anyhow; it might be scratched. Everything must be done thoroughly and well . . . there, like that! Covered with hay and matting it will be quite safe."

"Oh! the books, the books! what a load of books!" said another, bending under the weight of the cases out of the library. . . . "Don't push!—Mercy, what a weight! What beautiful books, to be sure, and what big ones!"

"The man who wrote those did not stop to play!" added the boy, pointing to some dictionaries lying one upon another.

Rostow, not wishing to intrude on Princess Maria, did not go into the house again, but waited to see her as she passed through the village. When the carriages started he mounted, and rode the twelve versts as far as Jankovo where the troops were encamped. When they stopped to change horses, he respectfully took leave of her and kissed her hand.

"You overwhelm me," he said in reply to her effusions of gratitude. "Any inspector of police would have done as much. If we had only peasants to deal with, the enemy would not have got so far into Russia," he added, awkwardly; and then, to change the subject, he went on: "I am only too happy to have had an opportunity of making your acquaintance. Adieu, princess. Allow me to wish you all possible happiness and to hope that we may meet again under more favourable circumstances."

Princess Maria's face brightened; she was deeply touched, and she felt that he deserved her best thanks, for, without him, what would have become of her? Must she not inevitably have been a victim to the insurgent mob, or have fallen into the hands of the French? Had he not exposed himself to the greatest dangers to protect her, and had not his kind and noble soul felt for her sorrow and her painful situation?—The sight of his honest, friendly eyes filling with tears when she had spoken to him, never left her mind. As she bid him good-bye she was so strangely moved that she asked herself whether she were not in love with him already. No doubt she felt some shame in confessing to herself that she had been suddenly captivated by a man who probably would never love her; but she comforted herself with the reflection that no one would ever know it, and that there could be no sin in cherishing secretly, and all her life through, this first and last love. "It was decreed that he should come to Bogoutcharovo to help me, and that his sister should refuse to marry my brother," said she to herself; and she saw the hand of God in this concatenation of events, and nursed a silent hope that the happiness of which she had thus caught a glimpse, might some day be a reality.

She, on her part, had made a pleasing impression on Nicholas, and when his comrades, who had heard of his adventure, laughed at him and teased him by congratulating him on having gone to look for hay and found one of the richest heiresses in Russia, he got seriously angry; at the bottom of his heart he confessed to himself that no better luck could befall him than to marry this gentle princess. Would not such a match be a joy to his parents, and make the clinging creature who regarded him as her deliverer perfectly happy?—For of that he felt instinctively certain.—On the other hand, would not her splendid fortune enable him to repair his father's? . . . But then what of Sonia, and the pledge he had given her?—This it was that worried him and made him irritable when he was laughed at about his excursion to Bogoutcharovo.

CHAPTER XCVII

KOUTOUZOW, having accepted the post of commander-in-chief, remembered Prince Andrew Bolkonsky and sent for him to appear at headquarters. He arrived at Czarevo-Saïmichtché on the day when Koutouzow was holding his first general review He dismounted in the village and sat down on a bench outside the priest's house to wait for "his serene highness," as the general was now commonly called. From the open country outside the village military bugle-calls rang out, almost drowned in the cheers and acclamations that hailed the new commander. About ten yards away from Prince Andrew two of Koutouzow's servants—one his courier and the other his house-steward—were taking advantage of the fine day and their master's absence to enjoy an airing.

At this moment a lieutenant-colonel of hussars rode up: a little dark-complexioned man, with an enormous moustache and thick whiskers; seeing Prince Andrew he stopped and asked him if this were his highness's headquarters and whether he would pass soon.

Andrew said that he was not on the commander-in-chief's staff, and that he himself had but just arrived. The hussar then turned to one of the servants, who answered with the lofty contempt which the servants of the commander-in-chief commonly affect in addressing an officer.

"Who?—His highness? He will be here by and by. What is your business?"

The lieutenant-colonel smiled under his moustache at the man's impertinent tone; then, throwing his bridle to his orderly, he dismounted, went up to Andrew and saluted him. Bolkonsky returned the salute and made room for him on the bench.

"You are waiting for him, too, then?" said the new-comer. "They say he is very accessible, which is a good thing!" he went on, and he spoke with a strong burr. "If we had those sausage-eaters to rule over us there would be no end to the muddle; it was not for nothing that Yermolow asked to be ranked as a German. Let us hope that the Russians will have a word in the matter now. The devil alone knows what they were at with all this retreating. . . . Have you gone through the campaign?"

"Not only have I gone through it," replied Prince Andrew, "but it has cost me all I held dear: my father, who is just dead, broken-hearted, not to mention my house and property.— I belong to the government of Smolensk. . . ."

"You are Prince Bolkonsky, perhaps?—I am delighted to make your acquaintance. I am Lieutenant-Colonel Denissow, better known as Vaska Denissow," said the hussar, shaking Bolkonsky warmly by the hand and looking at him with sympathetic interest. "Yes, I heard all about it," he added after a short pause. "It may be all right, but it is hard on those who pay the piper.—So you are Prince Bolkonsky? I am so very glad to make your acquaintance," and he shook his head with a half-melancholy smile and again pressed his hand.

Prince Andrew knew of Denissow through Natacha. This reminiscence, reviving in his mind the painful thoughts which during the last few months had begun to fade away, was at once painful and pleasurable. He had gone through so much since then—the evacuation of Smolensk, his short visit to Lissy-Gory, and the news of his father's death—that those past griefs did not so often recur to his memory, and had lost their keenest edge of pain. To Denissow, too, the name of Bolkonsky brought back a remote and romantic past,—the evening when, after supper, Natacha had sung, and he had declared his passion, he hardly knew how, to the girl of fifteen. He smiled as he remembered that romance and his love; but at once reverted to the one subject which at the present time interested and absorbed all his thoughts: a scheme for the campaign, which he had elaborated during the retreat, being on service on the outposts. He had laid it before Barclay de Tolly, and now he hoped to introduce it to Koutouzow's attention. His plan was based on an opinion that, as the French lines covered a wide extent of ground, the first object must be to attack them in front so as to check their advance, and at the same time break through them so as to intercept their communications. "They cannot keep up such a wide range of operations," he said. "It is out of the question. Give me 500 men and I will cut my way through them—on my word of honour. There is but one way of settling them and that is by guerilla warfare."

Denissow had risen to give emphasis to his discourse in his usual excitable manner when he was interrupted by the shouts and cheers that came, louder than ever, from the parade-ground, mingling with martial music and singing, and coming nearer and nearer. At the same moment the trampling of horses was heard at the end of the village street.

"Here he comes!" cried a Cossack, on guard at the door of the house.

Bolkonsky and Denissow rose and went towards a company of soldiers which formed Koutouzow's guard of honour, and they saw, at the farther end of the street, the commander-in-chief riding a small bay horse and followed by a numerous staff of general officers. Barclay de Tolly, also on horseback, rode by his side, and a crowd of officers were prancing and shouting round them. Then Koutouzow's aides-de-camp hurried forward to precede him into the court-yard of the house. The commander-in-chief was impatiently driving his heels into the flanks of his weary steed, which had fallen into an amble under the weight he carried; and his rider saluted right and left, raising his hand to his white military cap, which was bound with white and had no peak.

He drew rein in front of the guard of honour, a company of picked grenadiers, most of them wearing stripes and medals, who presented arms; for a moment he said nothing but looked at them keenly. Then a sardonic smile curled his lips, he shrugged his shoulders and turned to the generals and officers who stood near him.

"To think," he murmured with a gesture of surprise; "to think that with men like those we have retired before the enemy! —Well, good dây, general!" and he went in through the gateway, passing close to Prince Andrew and Denissow.

"Hurrah! hurrah!" shouted those left outside.

Koutouzow had grown very much stouter and heavier since Prince Andrew had last seen him; but his blank eye, his deep scar, and his bored expression had not altered. A whip hung from a narrow strap across one shoulder over his military cloak. He gave a deep sigh of relief as he rode into the court-yard, like a man glad to rest after having made an exhibition of himself. He took his left foot out of the stirrup, leaning forward heavily, frowned as with difficulty he got it up on to the saddle, bent his knee and let himself slip with a low groan into the arms of the Cossacks and aides-de-camp who waited to support him.

When he had landed on his feet he glanced about him with his half-shut eye, and perceived Prince Andrew, whom he did not at once recognise; then he walked forward, a little

350

For a moment he said nothing but looked at them keenly

unsteadily. As he reached the bottom of the steps he again looked hard at Prince Andrew, and, as often happens with old men, took a few seconds to put a name to the face which had at once struck him.

"Ah! Good day, prince; how do you do, my good friend? —Come in, come this way," he said, as he slowly toiled up the wooden steps that creaked under his weight. Then he unbuttoned his uniform and sat down on a bench, saying: "And your father?"

"I had news of his death only yesterday," said Bolkonsky.

Koutouzow glanced up with a look of startled alarm, took off his cap, and crossed himself.

"Peace be with him! God's will be done to us all!" he said, and sighed deeply. "I loved and esteemed him," he added, after a short silence; "I feel with you sincerely in your sorrow."

He put his arms round Prince Andrew, and held him tightly clasped to his broad bosom. Andrew could see the old man's lips quivering, tears stood in his eyes.

"Come in, come to my room and we will talk," said Koutouzow. He was trying to rise, propping himself up with his hands on the bench, when Denissow boldly went up the steps, in spite of the comments of the aides-de-camp, and straight to the commander-in-chief. Koutouzow, still leaning on his hands, watched him with some annoyance. Denissow mentioned his name and explained that he had a matter of great importance to the welfare of the country to lay before his highness. Koutouzow folded his hands over his stomach with a particularly cross expression and said indifferently: "The welfare of the country? What in the world can it be? Go on."

Denissow coloured like a girl—the blush looked strange under his thick moustache and bibulous complexion. However, he went on without wincing, and explained his scheme, whose main feature was to cut through the enemy's lines between Smolensk and Viazma; he knew every inch of the ground, for he had lived there. The fervour and conviction he threw into his statement gave prominence to the merits of the plan.

Koutouzow sat looking at the ground, glancing uneasily now and then at the adjoining cottage, as if he were expecting something unpleasant to appear from thence. And presently a general came out with a large portfolio under his arm.

"What is it?" Koutouzow asked, in the very middle of Denissow's arguments. "Are you ready?"

351

"Yes, highness," replied the general.

Koutouzow shook his head sadly, as much as to say that one man really could not do everything, and went on listening to the hussar.

"I give you my word of honour as an officer," said Denissow, "that I will break through Napoleon's lines."

Koutouzow interrupted him: "Is not Kirylle Andréïévitch, of the commissariat, a relation of yours?"

"He is my uncle," said Denissow.

"Ah! we were very good friends," said Koutouzow gaily. "Very good, stay here on my staff. . . We will talk all this over again to-morrow." He dismissed Denissow with a nod, and held out his hand for the papers brought to him by Konovnitzine.

"Would not your highness be more comfortable in a room?" said the general-in-waiting. "There are plans to be looked at and papers to be signed." And another aide-de-camp came to the house door, and said that the commander-in-chief's rooms were quite ready. But Koutouzow frowned; he did not intend to go indoors till his work was done.

"No," he said. "Bring out a little table,—and you stay here," he added to Bolkonsky.

While the general on duty was making his report, the rustling of a silk dress was heard through the half-open door of the house. Prince Andrew looked round and caught sight of a pretty young woman, in a pink gown, with a lilac kerchief on her head; she had a tray in her hand. The aide-de-camp whispered to Prince Andrew that this was the mistress of the house, the priest's wife; that her husband had already greeted his highness, receiving him with the cross in his hand; that she now wished to bid him welcome by offering him bread and salt.

"And she is very pretty," added the officer with a smile.

Koutouzow heard the last words and turned round. The general's report consisted mainly of severe strictures on the position taken up by the Russian army at Czarevo-Saïmichtché, and Koutouzow let him read on, with the same absence of mind as he had bestowed on Denissow, and, seven years since, on the discussion of the council of war the night before Austerlitz. He only heard because he had ears, and so could not help it, in spite of a scrap of tarred hemp which he kept stuffed into one of them.[1] It was easy to see that nothing could surprise or

[1] A popular remedy for toothache in Russia.

interest him, and that he merely submitted to listen to the end as he might have sat through a thanksgiving *Te Deum*. What Denissow had said was sensible and wise; what the general was saying was sensible and wise; but Koutouzow scorned sense and wisdom: they could not in his opinion solve the difficulty; what would finally cut the knot was, he believed, something quite apart and different from these two qualities.

Prince Andrew watched his face with interest, as it expressed first utter boredom, then curiosity as he heard the rustling of a petticoat, and finally a submissive readiness to do what was expected of him. It was very obvious that though he seemed to contemn Denissow's intelligent loyalty to his country, it was only because he was old and had seen too much of life.

He would only pronounce himself on one single point: when the general on duty presented for his signature an order desiring the colonels of regiments to indemnify the inhabitants for the havoc committed by the soldiers—an order that had been drawn up in consequence of the complaints of a farmer whose green oats had been cut—Koutouzow pinched his lips and shook his head.

"Put it in the fire," he said. "Once for all, my dear fellow, pitch all such rhodomontade into the fire. The corn must be cut and the wood must be burnt just as it is wanted. I do not order it, nor even authorise it, but it is out of my power to prevent it or to pay for it. . . . If you chop the wood the chips must fly!"

He glanced through the report once more.

"Oh!" he sighed, "that German preciseness!"

CHAPTER XCVIII

"Is that all?" he said, when he had signed the last paper, and rising with difficulty, drawing up his thick, wrinkled neck, he went to the house door. The priest's wife, crimson with shyness, snatched up the tray with the bread and salt, and went up to Koutouzow with a low curtsy. Koutouzow winked his eyes and chucked her chin.

"A very pretty woman!" said he. "Thank you, my dear, thank you."

He took out a few gold pieces and laid them on the tray. "Are you comfortable here?" he asked her, as he went into the room that had been made ready for him, and the mistress of the house followed him smiling.

The aide-de-camp invited Prince Andrew to breakfast with him; half an hour later Koutouzow sent for him. Bolkonsky found him lounging in an easy-chair with his coat unbuttoned, reading a French novel, *Les Chevaliers du Cygne*, by Madame de Genlis.

"Sit down," said Koutouzow, marking his place with a paper-knife and laying his book aside. "It is very sad, very sad indeed; but remember, my boy, I am a second father to you."

Prince Andrew told him what little he knew of his father's last hours, and described the state in which he had found Lissy-Gory.

"What a pass they have brought us to!" exclaimed Koutouzow suddenly, with much agitation, as he thought of the situation of the country. "But the time is coming!" he added vehemently. Then, not wishing to dwell on so exciting a subject, he added: "I sent for you to keep you here with me."

"I am sincerely grateful to your highness," said Prince Andrew. "But I am not fit now for staff-service." Koutouzow, seeing that he smiled as he spoke, looked at him with anxiety. "Besides," continued Bolkonsky, "I am fond of my regiment. The officers are attached to me, and I believe my men have a real affection for me, so I should be sorry to part from them. If I decline the honour of remaining near your person, pray believe that . . ."

A kindly, though slightly sarcastic twinkle, brightened the old man's big face; he interrupted Andrew:

"I am sorry for it, for you would have been of service to me. But you are right; it is not here that men are wanted; if all our advisers, or would-be advisers, would do as you do and serve with their regiments, it would be an immense gain. I remember your conduct at Austerlitz,—I can see you now with the flag in your arms!"

A faint flush of pleasure rose to Prince Andrew's face; Koutouzow drew him down to him and embraced him, and again Andrew saw that his eyes were full of tears. He knew that the old man's tears lay near the surface, and that his father's death naturally prompted him to be particularly friendly and affectionate; at the same time the allusion flattered and gratified him excessively.

"Go your own way, and God be with you!—I know it is the path of honour!—You would have been a valuable aid to me at

Bucharest," he presently resumed. "I had no one to send . . . Yes, they abused me handsomely down there, for the war first and then for the peace. And yet each came about in due season, for all things come to those who have patience.—And there, as here, advisers swarmed. Oh! those counsellors!—Why, if we had listened to them we should not have made peace with Turkey, and the war would not be at an end now! Kamensky would have been ruined, if he were not dead.—Kamensky, who must go storming fortresses with 30,000 men! To take a fortress is a small matter, but to carry a campaign through successfully is quite another thing. That is not to be done by assaults and attacks only; patience and time are needed. Kamensky sent his soldiers to take Roustchouk while I, with nothing but time and patience, took more strongholds than he did and made the Turks eat horseflesh! . . . Take my word for it," he added, slapping his breast and shaking his head, "the French shall have a taste of it, my word for that!"

"But we must give them battle though?" said Prince Andrew.

"Of course we must if everyone insists upon it; but, mark my words, the two best men are Time and Patience. They will win in the long run; only our advisers do not see that side of the question, that is the worst of it! Some are for one thing and some for another; and what is to be done? What is to be done, I say?" he repeated, as if he expected a reply, and his eyes shone with a shrewd deep look. "I will tell you, my dear boy, what is to be done,—and what I am doing: When in doubt, do nothing." And he spoke the words with slow emphasis. "Well, good-bye, my friend; remember that I feel for you in your sorrow with all my heart; to you I am not prince, nor the commander-in-chief, but your father! If you ever want anything, come to me. Good-bye," and once more he embraced him.

Prince Andrew had not left the room before Koutouzow sank back in his arm-chair with a sigh, and went quietly on reading *Les Chevaliers du Cygne*.

It was a strange and unaccountable fact that this interview greatly soothed Prince Andrew; he returned to his regiment much easier as to the course of events generally, and entirely trustful in the man who had taken them in hand. There was something inspiriting in the old general's complete freedom from self-interest, in his having outlived his passions and gained experience as their outcome; in his intelligence—in the sense of apprehension of facts and co-ordination of inferences—having given way to a philosophical contemplation of events. Bolkonsky left him with a conviction that he would be equal to the charge imposed on him: he would invent nothing and make no schemes, but he would listen and remember all he heard; he would know how to make use of it at the right moment; he would hinder nothing that might be of any use, and permit nothing that might do harm. "He sees that there is something stronger than his will: the inevitable progress of events; he watches them, appreciates them at their true value, and can view them from outside, irrespective of his own share in them. He inspires confidence because, in spite of his French novel and his French proverbs, a Russian heart beats under his uniform; his voice trembled as he exclaimed: 'What have they brought us to?' and when he threatened that the French should eat horseflesh."

It was in fact this patriotic feeling, which every Russian felt in a greater or less degree, which had mainly contributed to Koutouzow's appointment as commander-in-chief, in spite of a strong cabal against him; the unanimous voice of the nation had clamorously applauded the choice.

CHAPTER XCIX

AFTER the czar's departure Moscow fell back into its old routine; old habits again ruled life, and the excitement of those few days seemed no more than a dream. In the collapse which succeeded the tumult of that time no one seemed to believe in the reality of the danger that threatened Russia, or to understand that, of all her children, the members of the English Club at Moscow had been the first to declare themselves prepared for any sacrifice. However, one evidence of the general excitement produced by the emperor's visit very soon became conspicuous: the actual levying of the men and demands for money, which, coming as they did in a legalised and official form, had to be complied with.

The approach of the enemy did not make the citizens at all more serious; on the contrary, their levity seemed to increase as their position became more critical, as often happens on the eve of a catastrophe. In fact, at such a juncture, two voices are to be heard: one wisely preaches the necessity for estimating fairly the impending danger, and the means at hand for resisting it; the other, even more wisely, argues that the thought is too painful, since it is not given to man to escape the inevitable, and that it is better, therefore, to forget the danger and live merrily till it comes. Solitary men listen to the first, while the masses obey the second; and the citizens of Moscow were an instance in point, for Moscow had never been so gay as it was that year.

Parodies of Rostopchine's proclamations were read and discussed just as V. L. Pouschkine's couplets were. The heading of these broadsheets represented a tavern kept by a certain Karpouschak Tchiguirine, an old soldier and a citizen of the town, who, it was said, when he heard that Napoleon was marching on Moscow, had planted himself wrathfully in the doorway of his shop, and made a speech to the crowd, full of abuse of the French. In this harangue, which was admired by some and criticised by others at the English Club, he declared, among other things, that the cabbages on which the French would have to live would blow them out like balloons, that they would burst on porridge and choke on broth; that they were all dwarfs, and that a woman with a pitchfork could toss three of them in the air at once.

At the club it was reported, too, that Rostopchine had driven all foreigners out of Moscow on the pretext that there were among them spies and agents of Napoleon; a witticism of the governor's, addressed to the outcasts, was in everybody's mouth: "Meditate well, get into the boat (or row with the tide), and do not let it be a boat-load for Charon." It was also said that all the courts of justice had been removed outside the city; and this news was capped by Schinchine's last sally, declaring that for this, if for nothing else, the inhabitants owed a debt of gratitude to Napoleon.

Finally it was rumoured that the regiment which Mamonow had undertaken to raise would cost him 800,000 roubles, and that Bésoukhow would spend even more on his, and that what was most of all to his credit in the matter was that he himself was about to don the uniform and lead his men in person, to be admired gratis by all who chose to stare.

"You spare no one!" cried Julia Droubetzkoï, as she gathered up a little heap of lint she had just picked, and squeezed it in her slender fingers blazing with rings. She was giving a farewell soirée, for she was to quit Moscow the next day. "Bésoukhow is too laughable," she added in French; "but he is such a good soul, so good-natured! What pleasure can you find in being so caustic?"

"Fined! Fined!" exclaimed a young man in the militia

uniform, whom Julia styled her knight, and who was to escort her on the morrow to Nijni—for in her set, as in many others, it had been agreed that French should never be spoken, and everyone who broke the pledge was made to pay a fine which was added to the voluntary contributions towards the defences.

"Indeed you must pay double," said a Russian writer, "for you have perpetrated a Gallicism."

"I sinned and I will pay," said Julia, "for using the French words. As to a Gallicism in speaking Russian, I refuse to be answerable. I have neither time nor money to take lessons in my own language, like Prince Galitzine. Ah! here he comes. Speak of the——" she was just going to quote the proverb in French, but checked herself with a laugh, and put it into Russian. "You will not catch me again! We were speaking of you, we were saying that your regiment would be more splendid than Mamonow's," she added to Peter who had just come in, fibbing with the singular facility of a woman of the world.

"For pity's sake do not mention it in my hearing," said Peter. "If you knew how sick I am of it!"

"You will lead it in person, of course," Julia went on, with a malicious glance at the young militiaman. But her "knight" did not respond; Peter's presence and his simple kindliness were always enough to check the impertinence of which he was the butt.

"Dear me, no!" he exclaimed with a hearty laugh, patting his broad chest. "I should be too good a mark for the French; besides, I doubt whether I could hoist myself on to a horse."

Presently their gossip, flying from one subject to another, turned on the Rostow family.

"Do you know," said Julia, "that their affairs are in terrible disorder? The count is an old idiot; the Razoumovskys offered to buy his house and estate near Moscow, and the thing is slipping through his fingers because he asks too much."

"I fancy that the sale will come off though," said someone, "though in these days it is perfect madness to buy houses."

"Why?" asked Julia. "Do you really think that Moscow is in danger?"

"But, if not, why are you going?"

"I?—what a strange question. Well, I am going because everyone else is; and I am neither a Joan of Arc nor an Amazon."

"If Count Rostow knows how to economise," the militiaman put in, "he may clear himself yet. He is a thorough good fellow, but a poor manager. What keeps them here so long? I thought they were going into the country."

"Natacha is quite well again, is she not?" asked Julia, with a spiteful smile, of Peter.

"They are waiting for their youngest boy, who entered the service as a Cossack and was sent to Biélaïa-Tserkow. He is to join my regiment now. The count would have gone notwithstanding, but the countess would not stir till she had seen her son again."

"I met them three days ago, at the Argharows'. Natacha is handsomer than ever and in capital spirits. She sang a song. How soon some people can forget!"

"Forget what?" said Peter, much annoyed. Julia smiled.

"But do you know, count, that such knights as you are only to be met with in the novels of Madame de Souza?"

"What knights? I do not understand," said Peter, colouring.

"Oh, fie! count, do not say that. Why, all Moscow knows the story; I honestly admire you!" she added again in French.

"Fined, fined!" cried the militiaman.

"What next!" cried Julia out of patience. "It is impossible to talk at all nowadays. But you know, count, you know. . . ."

"I know nothing," said Peter, more and more provoked.

"Well, I know that you are Natacha's sworn ally, while I have always liked Vera best. Dear Vera!"

"No, madam," said Peter in the same tone, "I have not assumed the part of champion of Countess Natacha; I have not seen the Rostows for a month past."

"*Qui s'excuse s'accuse*," retorted Julia, with a meaning smile, as she turned the lint in her fingers; but then she changed the subject so as to have the last word: "Whom do you think I met yesterday evening? Poor Maria Bolkonsky. She has lost her father, did you know?"

"No, indeed. Where is she living? I should like to see her."

"All I know is that she is to start to-morrow for their place beyond Moscow, and is taking her nephew with her."

"And how is she?"

"Very sad and broken. But to whom do you think she owes her rescue? It is quite a romance! Nicholas Rostow! She was surrounded and would have been killed, for her servants were already wounded, when he rushed into the fray and got her out of the scrape!"

"Quite a romance, indeed," said the militiaman. "One

might almost fancy that this general stampede had been got up expressly to carry off our old maids! First Catiche, and then Princess Maria."

"Of one thing I am convinced," said Julia, "and that is that she is really a little in love with the young man," she added in French.

"A fine, a fine! Pay at once!" cried the militiaman once more.

"But how on earth was I to say that in Russian? Tell me that."

CHAPTER C

On going home that evening Peter found on his table Rostopchine's two last circular notices. In the first he denied ever having forbidden the inhabitants to leave the town, as he was reported to have done; it is true he advised the ladies of rank and the merchants' wives to remain, for, he said, "the panic is caused by false intelligence, and I stake my life on it that the wretch will never enter Moscow!" This proclamation was the first thing that had brought Peter to the conviction that the French would certainly enter Moscow.

In the second he stated that the Russian headquarters were fixed at Viazma, that Count Wittgenstein had beaten the enemy, and that those who were willing to bear arms would find a large selection of muskets and swords at the arsenal for sale at low prices. This proclamation was quite free from the tone of braggart irony which stamped the speeches attributed to Tchiguirine. Peter told himself plainly that the storm, which he for his part fervently hoped for, was coming on with giant strides:—"What ought I to do?" he asked himself for the hundredth time. "Enter the service and join the army, or wait and watch where I am?" He took up a pack of cards that was lying on the table. "I will play a game of patience; if it works out right that will mean . . . What shall it mean?" He shuffled the cards, looking at the ceiling for a reply.

He had not had time to make up his mind when he heard the eldest of the three princesses—the other two had married and left—just outside the door.

"Come in, cousin, come in," he called out to her. "If the patience comes right I will join the army," he said to himself.

"A thousand apologies for disturbing you at this hour," said the lady; "but we must make up our minds to do something. Everybody is leaving Moscow, the mob is rising, and something fearful is in the wind. . . . Why do we stay here?"

"But, on the contrary, everything seems to me to be going on swimmingly," said Peter in the light tone he always adopted with her, to escape the uncomfortable sense of being her benefactor.

"Swimmingly? What makes you think that, pray? Only this morning Barbara Ivanovna was telling me how our troops had distinguished themselves, it does them the greatest honour; but here, on the other hand, the people are refractory and will listen to no one—my waiting-maid was most insolent! We shall have to fight before long, and if that once begins we shall not be able to get away, and then—what is more serious still, the French are certainly coming. . . . Why should we wait for them? I entreat you, cousin, give orders that I may be taken at once to St. Petersburg; for I could not bear to stay here and submit to Bonaparte."

"But, my dear cousin, what nonsense! Where did you get your information?—On the contrary . . ."

"I tell you I will not bow to your Bonaparte; others may do as they please, and if you do not choose to take any trouble about me . . ."

"Not at all, not at all! I will make every arrangement for your departure."

The princess, provoked at having no one to quarrel with, sat on the very edge of her chair and muttered something to herself.

"Your intelligence is untrustworthy," Peter went on, "the city is quiet, and there is no danger.—Read this," and he handed her the circular. "The count says that the French will not enter Moscow; he stakes his life on it."

"Oh, I dare say, your count!" cried the lady in a rage. "He is a hypocrite, a wretch! It is he who is driving the people to rebellion. Was it not he who, in those senseless proclamations, promised honour and glory to every man who should catch anyone, without exception, and put him into prison? Sheer idiocy! And now we see the result of all this talking: Barbara Ivanovna was within an ace of being killed for speaking French in the street!"

"But is there not some exaggeration in all this? You take things too much to heart, I think," said Peter, laying out his cards.

The patience came out right; but Peter did not join the army. He stayed at Moscow, which was fast being depopulated, awaiting with indecision and a mixed feeling of satisfaction and dread, the tremendous catastrophe that he foresaw. The princess went off on the very next day. His head steward came to explain to him that the money for the equipment of his regiment could only be raised by the sale of one of his estates, and represented that this fancy would lead him on to ruin.

"Sell it," said Peter with a smile. "I cannot take back my word." The worse the position of affairs, especially his own affairs, the better pleased Peter was, for it showed the steady approach of the catastrophe which he expected.

The city was practically deserted. Julia was gone, so was Princess Maria; of all Peter's intimate acquaintances only the Rostows remained; but he never saw them now. He thought that he would amuse himself by making an excursion into the environs to the village of Vorontzovo, to inspect an enormous balloon constructed under Leppich's supervision by his majesty's command, and intended to contribute to the discomfiture of the enemy. Peter knew that the czar had particularly recommended the inventor and the invention to Count Rostopchine, in these terms: "As soon as Leppich is ready send him a company of picked and intelligent men to equip his car, and despatch a special messenger to inform Koutouzow. I have already prepared him. Enjoin Leppich to take particular care as to the spot he descends on the first time, that he may not run into the hands of the enemy. It is indispensable that he should co-operate with the commander-in-chief."

As he was returning from Vorontzovo, Peter saw a great crowd in the public square where executions took place; he stopped his drosky and got out. A French cook, suspected of being a spy, had just been flogged. The executioner untied the man, a big fellow with red whiskers, in blue stockings and a green coat, who was groaning pitiably. His companion in grief, a pale, lean little man, was awaiting his turn; to judge from their physiognomy they were no doubt Frenchmen. Peter, horrified, and pale as they were, forced his way through the throng of market people, shopkeepers, peasants, women, and officials of every grade—all eagerly watching the entertainment thus offered them. His anxious and repeated questions elicited no answers.

The big man straightened himself with a painful effort, raised his shoulders and tried, but in vain, to be stoical as he pulled his coat on; his lips trembled convulsively, and he broke out into sobs, crying with rage at his own want of pluck, as men of sanguine temperament do cry. The crowd, till now silent, began to hoot, as if to smother its own instinct of compassion.

"Cook to a prince!" said one and another.

"I say, 'Moussiou,' Russian sauce is too strong for the French taste,—sets your teeth on edge—heh?" said a chancery clerk, old and wrinkled; and he looked round to see the effect of his pleasantry. Some laughed; some, with their eyes fixed on the executioner, watched him with terror as he stripped the second victim.

Peter sniffed noisily, and knitting his brows he suddenly turned away, muttering unintelligible words. He got into his carriage again, and as he went along could not keep himself from writhing and starting spasmodically, and giving vent to smothered ejaculations.

"Where are you going?" he suddenly exclaimed to his coachman.

"You said to the governor's?"

"Idiot, gaby!" shouted Peter; "I told you to go home.— I must go, I must be off at once, this very day," he added between his teeth.

This castigation, administered in the presence of a gaping crowd, had made such an impression on him that he made up his mind to quit Moscow immediately. As soon as he got home he desired his coachman to send his saddle-horses at once to Mojaïsk, where the army then was; and to give them a start, he postponed his own journey till the morrow.

On the evening of August 24th, he set out from Moscow. When, a few hours later, he stopped to change horses at Perkhoukow, he was informed that a great battle had been fought; it was even said that the cannon had made the earth tremble there, at Perkhoukow; but no one could tell him which side had been victorious: it was the battle of Schevardin.

He reached Mojaïsk at daybreak. Every house was filled with troops; in the inn-yard he found his groom and his coachman waiting for him, but no rooms were to be had. They were all taken by officers, and troops were still pouring in. On all sides nothing was to be seen but infantry, Cossacks, horsemen, baggage-wagons, caissons, and cannon. Peter hurried forward; the farther he went from Moscow, the more he was lost in this ocean of soldiery, and the more he was conscious of that mixed excitement and self-approval which he had first felt during the czar's visit to Moscow, when the point under consideration was the sacrifice required. He felt at this moment that all which constitutes habitual happiness: the comforts of life, wealth—nay and life itself—were of small account in comparison with the vision he had a glimpse of—so vaguely it is true, that he did not attempt to analyse it. Without asking himself for whom or for what, the mere sense and consciousness of sacrifice filled him with unutterable joy.

This book designed by
William B. Taylor
is a production of
Heron Books, London

Printed on wood free paper
and bound by Hazell Watson & Viney Ltd.
Aylesbury, Bucks

Printed and bound in England

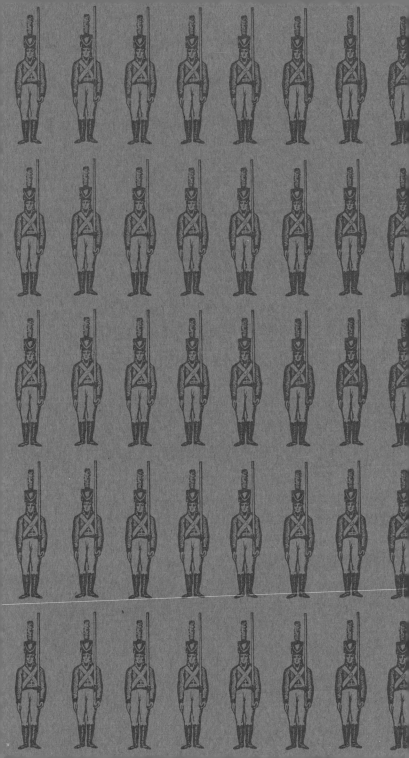